PRAISE FOR N

The Reunion

"Funny, brilliant, and full of swoon. Fans of *The Family Stone* will adore this book. A must read."

—Kendall Ryan, *New York Times* bestselling author

"Are you a fan of the family dynamics in *Schitt's Creek*? Then you will devour this book. Real, raw, and hilarious. Meghan Quinn at her best."

—Rachel Van Dyken, #1 *New York Times* bestselling author

"I was hooked from the very first page; this book has it all. The drama, the romance, the heat, and especially the humor."

—Laurelin Paige, *New York Times* bestselling author

"This laugh-out-loud romantic comedy was also filled with brilliant romance and surprising depth that absolutely enthralled me."

—Corinne Michaels, *New York Times* bestselling author

"Sweet, hilarious, and delightful, *The Reunion* captivated me from page one."

—Melanie Harlow, *USA Today* and #1 Amazon bestselling author

"Laughter and tears with a heavy dose of romance. Highly recommend to any romantic comedy fan."

—Lucy Score, #1 Amazon bestselling author

"An emotional journey of three siblings finding love and family all over again. Meghan Quinn brings both humor and depth in *The Reunion*."

—Skye Warren, *New York Times* bestselling author

"*The Reunion* is a delicate balance of laugh-out-loud moments and thoughtful tones that will leave every reader wanting more."
—Kennedy Ryan, *Wall Street Journal* bestselling author

"Flawless storytelling of six points of view, three love stories, and one big happily ever after."
—BB Easton, *Wall Street Journal* bestselling author

"The way Meghan Quinn was able to carry humor through the emotional aspects of the story was pure brilliance. Another hit."
—Tessa Bailey, *New York Times* bestselling author

"*The Reunion* is positively gripping, with intertwining story lines and six points of view. I wondered with bated breath what was going to happen next in this fun and witty romantic comedy."
—Amy Daws, #1 Amazon bestselling author

"A Meghan Quinn classic! Rich with her signature humor, clever in the storytelling, and brimming with delicious spice!"
—Lauren Blakely, #1 *New York Times* bestselling author

The Wedding Game

"Readers won't have to be reality TV fans to get a kick out of this fun, quirky rom-com."
—*Publishers Weekly*

That Forever Girl

"A terrific read."
—*Once Upon a Book Blog*

"A heart-tugging, slow-burning, second-chance romance . . . This is a couple that I couldn't help but root for."

—*Red Cheeks Reads*

"If you love small-town romances that are rich in scenery and packed with sweetness, heat, and fun and [are] looking for an easy reading escape, look no further."

—*TotallyBookedBlog*

"Filled with emotion, laughter, and loads of sexual tension . . . I dare you to not fall in love with Harper and Rogan!"

—*Nightbird Novels*

"Sweet, sassy, sexy, and sentimental."

—*Harlequin Junkie*

"Second-chance enemies-to-lovers romance at its finest."

—*Bookishly Nerdy*

"I'm a sucker for second-chance romances, and add in the small town and I'm hooked. And who better to give me all the feels with a little humor and a mix of sexiness than Meghan Quinn."

—*Embrace the Romance*

That Second Chance

"With each book I read by Meghan Quinn, I become more in awe of her writing talent. She truly has a gift! *That Second Chance* was simply perfect!"

—*Wrapped Up in Reading*

"A sweet, sexy, swoon-worthy, MUST-READ romance from Meghan Quinn, and I would HIGHLY recommend it! I fell head over heels in love with the quaint and charming small town of Port Snow, Maine, and all of its residents."

—The Romance Bibliophile

"I'm basking in the HEA goodness of *That Second Chance*, which gets five stars."

—Dog-Eared Daydreams

"I adored the small town of Port Snow and the fabulous tight [bond] the Knightly family have not only with each other but their community as a whole."

—Book Angel Booktopia

ALSO BY MEGHAN QUINN

All her books can be read on Kindle Unlimited

GETTING LUCKY SERIES

That Second Chance

That Forever Girl

That Secret Crush

That Swoony Feeling

BRENTWOOD BASEBALL BOYS

The Locker Room

The Dugout

The Lineup

The Trade

The Change Up

The Setup

The Strike Out

The Perfect Catch

THE BROMANCE CLUB

The Secret to Dating Your Best Friend's Sister

Diary of a Bad Boy

Boss Man Bridegroom

THE DATING BY NUMBERS SERIES

Three Blind Dates

Two Wedding Crashers

One Baby Daddy

Back in the Game (novella)

THE BLUE LINE DUET

The Upside of Falling

The Downside of Love

THE PERFECT DUET

The Left Side of Perfect

The Right Side of Forever

THE BINGHAMTON BOYS SERIES

Co-Wrecker

My Best Friend's Ex

Twisted Twosome

The Other Brother

Stand-Alone Titles

The Modern Gentleman

See Me After Class

The Romantic Pact

Dear Life

The Virgin Romance Novelist Chronicles

Newly Exposed

The Mother Road

The Reunion

The Highland Fling

The Wedding Game

Runaway Groomsman

Box Set Series

The Bourbon series

Love and Sports series

Hot-Lanta series

VACATION WARS

MEGHAN QUINN

Montlake

Published by Montlake, Seattle

www.apub.com

Amazon, the Amazon logo, and Montlake are trademarks of Amazon.com, Inc., or its affiliates.

ISBN-13: 9781662506338 (paperback)
ISBN-13: 9781662506345 (digital)

Cover design by Caroline Teagle Johnson
Cover image: © vectorchef / Shutterstock; © Vector_Up / Shutterstock; © Evgenia Zhilyakova / Shutterstock; © Abramova Alena / Shutterstock; © Petro Bevz / Getty

Printed in the United States of America

PROLOGUE

Hey.

I have a story to tell you.

A story of untapped love.

I know this might be an unconventional way of beginning an epic love affair, but sometimes we storytellers must break up our formulaic narratives. Don't worry, though; you'll get up close and personal with the main characters quickly.

But as the author, I need to lay the groundwork first because this story is different.

Ever heard of the Greek gods Zeus and Hera? Some might say theirs was a legendary love affair, and sure, if they weren't siblings who married, maybe I would agree. But this love story I'm about to get into is greater than Zeus and Hera.

Greater than Hades and Persephone because it didn't involve a kidnapping against a woman's will, then dragging her to the fiery underworld, where she was forced to live with her pitiless husband and the souls of the dead.

And dare I say . . . greater than Poseidon and Amphitrite? Shapeshifting into a dolphin to convince the love of his life to spend eternity with him, not needed—although man-dolphin does have an odd appeal to it.

This couple were like Penelope and Odysseus. They didn't need the fancy things like a sibling connection or a slippery porpoise to convince them they were meant to be. Yup, I said it.

Eternal love.

Long-distance romance.

Obstacles in their way.

Unwanted suitors knocking at Penelope's door.

A bitch named Helen who is trying to ruin it all—technically the bitch isn't named Helen in this book, but you get the idea.

This story clocks all the way back to 1999. Whoa, I know, ancient times, am I right? Word on the street is people suffered through dial-up internet back then. How they survived we'll never know. But this is when our main characters, Tessa and Myles, saw each other for the very first time.

You see, Tessa lives in America: New York City, to be exact. She's your run-of-the-mill wallflower with a heart for all things numbers—can you say data nerd? She has a relentless penchant for reading—fantasy lover, this one—and has spent her entire life supporting her twin sister's endeavors, which includes assisting in the following: a run for class president (won), Little Miss Darling of New York (won), and multiple tries at holding the Guinness world record for bouncing on a pogo stick (never, ever beat the record, not even close).

And then there's our hero, Myles. A Greek citizen, but quite the traveler, bouncing between America and Greece. A single child who's been homeschooled his whole life, he's full of worldly knowledge, has a deep desire for hummus, and has been improperly known as "the Bulge" by our heroine and her sister. His family owns Anissa's Palace Beach Resort in Santorini, the same resort where Tessa's family vacations every year.

Can you see where I'm going with this?

They've crossed paths more than once. Let me give you a quick-and-dirty breakdown.

In 1999, they were six, and this was the first sighting. Tessa was playing tag with her sister on the beach. Myles was collecting seashells for the mosaic coffee table project he was helping his mom with. Their eyes connected, the wind whipped around them, waves crashed, and . . . nothing happened. They moved on with their lives.

Then the summer of 2004 came along. Hormones started revving up, and even though they'd seen each other every summer, they'd never really thought about one another—until Tessa stepped out on the beach in a hot-pink one-piece bathing suit. Myles noticed her. Tessa noticed Myles. Hearts floated from their eyes and into the air. It was a sight to behold. And that, my friends, is when the crushes developed.

Summer of 2006, they had their first real interaction. Now, this is not to say they hadn't been watching each other from a distance, but this was the first time they'd spoken to each other. It was a blustery day on the island of Santorini. An avid kite flier, Tessa was attempting to get her frog kite in the air, the very kite she brought with her every summer. As she was winding the kite string back up, a gust of wind knocked her straw hat off her head. Nimble, with catlike reflexes, Myles snatched the hat from the air before it could take off into the Aegean Sea. He held it out to her and said, "Your hat." She blinked. She snatched. She ran.

Fast-forward to 2008, the year Tessa had food poisoning. Fresh from the plane, the family stopped by a quaint food truck on the side of the road on the way to the resort. Tessa settled for the chicken gyro, but the gyro didn't settle well with Tessa. Bound to her room for half the trip, she ordered room service while her family was out enjoying the pool. A living zombie in a holey shirt—the only thing that offered her comfort—she answered the door to a bright-eyed Myles and a wheely cart. Our hero had started a new job, but little did he know, the woman of his dreams would be on the other side of the door, looking like she'd just survived a postapocalyptic attack. Naturally, Tessa was horrified, while Myles wheeled in her room service cart. "Nice day," he said.

"I . . . I . . . I have to stay close to the toilet," she replied. He smiled. She considered stuffing her head in a pillow.

And, of course, I would be remiss if I didn't mention the day Tessa discovered . . . the bulge. It was the summer of 2013. A fresh twenty-one-year-old on the prowl for her next mixed cocktail, she was buzzed and gearing up for a dreamy day of reading, drinking, and enjoying the sea breeze. And then, Myles approached. Golden tan skin, muscles for days, in tight red swim trunks, he was a sight to behold. Tessa's heart pittered. Tessa's heart pattered. Tessa's libido shot straight to the crystal-blue sky. And like she'd seen in many a movie, she was the woman on the lounger, lowering her sunglasses while the object of her affection walked in front of her. In that moment, Mother Nature chose to blow her biggest breath right at Myles's crotch. Now, reader, I don't want to sound crude, but it needs to be said . . . that gust of wind, the one aimed directly at Myles's nether regions? It not only made his swim trunks conform to his crotch but *defined* his crotch. Length, girth, mass . . . some have said the earth shook that day. And when Myles turned to see Tessa, staring right at him, hunger in those twenty-one-year-old eyes, all he could do was say, "Hi."

She replied with a lick of her lips and a drawn-out "Helllll-o to you."

It went on like that for a few years—minor interactions, but no significant moments to further the monotonous, humdrum continuation of nothingness. Well, not until the kiss of 2015.

Yup . . . a kiss, but I'm not at liberty to tell you how it went down. I'm going to leave that up to Tessa and Myles.

Like I said, I'm just here to lay down the foundation, to let you know this journey between them has been going on for years. Their mutual crushes have been master classes in patience. And the moment they finally, and I mean *finally*, let each other know their feelings—well, reader, it's one for the ages.

Are you ready? Are you comfortable? Are you mentally prepared for a whirlwind of embarrassment? Good.

Let's start this off with present day . . .

CHAPTER ONE
TESSA

"Get down, get down, he might see us," I whisper-shout as I shoulder-check my twin sister into the cooling sand.

"What the actual hell, Tessa," Roxane says as she adjusts her skirt that has flipped up toward her belly button, giving a free show to the elderly couple enjoying the setting sun a few feet away.

I drop to the ground as well, curl my arm around Roxane's waist, and army crawl through the sand, dragging her with me a few feet until we're shielded by an overturned boat.

I heave a heavy breath. "That was close."

Sand clinging to her arms, sunglasses askew, and her dress wrinkled up her thighs, Roxane gives me a murderous glare. "Explain yourself, now."

Brushing sand off my legs, I whisper, "It's him."

"Who?"

"You know . . ." I waggle my eyebrows.

"No, I don't know."

"Roxane."

"Tessa."

"Urgh, it's the Greek-god guy, you know, Mr. Red Shorts."

Recognition dawns across Roxane's face as she peeks her head up past the boat, acting like a meerkat staking out its territory. "Where? I don't see him. Are you sure you saw him?"

"Yes, I saw him."

"Could have been someone who looked like him. Did he have the bulge we've talked about?"

"I didn't get a close enough look, not that his bulge is the man's defining characteristic."

"Tessa, that bulge is any man's defining characteristic." She looks around some more, but out of pure fear he might spot her bobbing head, I yank her down by her shoulder. "Hey, stop manhandling me," she protests.

"I don't want him seeing you."

"He doesn't even know us. We could walk right by and he wouldn't know the difference. He'd just think we're two ladies on a girls' trip, headed to the bar, which, you know, is exactly what we're doing. Now get up, I'm not spending my first night in Greece burrowing my body into the sand because the Bulge might see us."

"Don't call him the Bulge!"

"Whatever, come on." She tugs on my hand, but I remain seated. "Tessa, seriously. Come on."

"He's not supposed to be here," I whisper.

"What do you mean?"

"We've been coming to this resort for how many years now? Over twenty? He hasn't been back for seven years, Roxane. *Seven!* And now, all of a sudden, he's back again. What's that about?"

"Uh, maybe he started a new chapter in his life and worked somewhere else for seven years. What does it matter? You've never truly had an interaction with him past one sentence . . ." She pauses; her brow quirks up. "Unless . . . you're not telling me something." I glance away, which of course is a huge mistake when you're attempting to hide a secret. A secret that you've kept from your twin sister for seven years.

Roxane pushes at my shoulder. "Oh my God, Tessa. Did something happen with you two that you never told me about?"

Yes, in fact, something did happen.

Something . . . magical.

To someone else, it might seem small, but to a girl like me, a shy, introverted girl who enjoys reading a good book alone rather than downing a massive margarita at a raucous bar, the "something" that happened feels huge in my head.

Enormous.

Often fantasized about as one of the most heroic and overly romantic moments in my life.

Because . . . well, because I've crushed on "the Bulge" ever since my little romantic heart can remember. When he was a scrappy boy with a mop of curly hair on the top of his head, I would watch him play on the beach during the summers, and as we both grew, my attraction toward him only grew as well. I watched him transform every year, from a playful boy to a steaming heartthrob that canvassed the resort, offering assistance to whoever needed it.

When we would pack for our annual trip to Greece, I always thought . . . *What would I look best in?* in case I ran into him. What would I say? What would I do? Would this be the year that we said more than one word to each other? Would this be the year that he held my hand? Would this be the year that somehow, he noticed me?

Well, it happened, seven years ago. He noticed me, and it was . . . *sigh* it was magic.

"Tell me." She shakes my hand.

Do I want to tell Roxane about my magical moment? Not really, because Roxane has a way of bringing my romantic notions back down to reality with a snarky, yet realistic comment. She's never wrong—she's just stating facts—but it still stings. And this occasion will sting even more, not just because I've liked this guy for quite some time, but because these minor "stings" have been building up over the last few months. Tensions are high with the wedding around the corner, and ever since I overheard a fight between her and Philip, her fiancé, the tension has skyrocketed, which means being her sister, I get the brunt of that tension. But, unfortunately, knowing Roxane and her need to focus on anything other than what's giving her anxiety—*cough* the wedding—I know she won't drop it, so unfortunately . . . as Rafiki from *The Lion King* would say, "It is time."

"It was . . ." I take a deep breath, and the words pour out. "It was stupid and nothing really. He probably doesn't even remember. I'm not very memorable, and it was seven years ago, so I don't know why I'm freaking out, but you know, after the 'something' happened, he never came back to the resort, and I always looked for him, but he was never here, so I thought that I might have scared him away, which very much could have happened, since I'm not the most outgoing person, extremely awkward actually, and—"

"Oh my God, Tess, just say it."

"He kissed me on the cheek." I wince as heat travels up my legs.

That's right, he pecked me, dead on the cheek. No hesitation, just a light, feather-like smack-a-roo on my face. I can remember the exact moment his lips pressed against my skin. The hairs on the back of my neck stood up, my stomach felt like it endured a twenty-rotation flip on a trampoline, and the light-headedness I withstood rivaled even the greatest g-force any pilot has ever experienced.

The boy I first saw that fateful summer when I was in the second grade had turned into a toned and tanned man in red shorts. He kissed me on the cheek, and if I had a motor attached to my bum, that motor would have been revving, ready to run.

"He . . . wait, what?" Roxane blinks a few times. "He kissed you on the cheek? That's the 'something' that happened? The grand thing that you are worried about? A kiss on the cheek? I thought you were going to say you hooked up in a closet or something."

My cheeks burn with embarrassment. Hook up in a closet? Good God, could you imagine?

"Do I look like someone who hooks up with a random stranger in a closet? For heaven's sake, I still can't part with some of my granny panties from college. I'm not the type of philandering woman who endures arduous sex in public spaces."

"But you made it seem like it was off brand for you. A kiss on the cheek, that's nothing."

See, I told you she'd knock me down a few pegs.

A peck on the cheek truly does mean nothing to her. You see, Roxane is the outgoing twin who has no problem leading a flash mob into a Beyoncé-themed dance—she'd own the lead role, flip her hair with pizzazz, and do that knee-breaking squat move that Beyoncé is known for.

I, on the other hand, would be the girl fumbling with her phone, attempting to record it so my sister could post it later, on her thriving social media. See the dynamic?

She's the wild free spirit who throws caution to the wind.

And I'm the one on the sidelines, calculating the probability of her actions ending in pregnancy, jail, or death.

"It wasn't just nothing," I mutter. "He was . . ." I dreamily look up toward the sky. "He was an unexpected but much-needed savior. I was trapped by a sleaze at the restaurant bar, and Red Shorts just got off work from lifeguarding the pool, saw that I was cornered, and pretended to be my boyfriend. The timing was impeccable. His kiss was . . . well, it was more than memorable." I think about it every so often, but I'll just keep that to myself. "After he apologized for being so brazen, I mumbled something about his lips being soft, or maybe I said luxurious—"

"No, you didn't."

I tap my chin, trying to look casual. "I'm pretty sure I said luxurious—actually, I'm positive I said that because he looked confused.

I guess it's not every day someone says your lips are luxurious. In the moment, I thought it was the ultimate compliment, but I think it scared him away because he awkwardly thanked me with a pinch to his brow and then took off without looking back. Ever since my compliment, I hadn't seen him around the resort. Seven years, Roxane. I'm the reason he didn't work here for seven years, because the crazy lady called his lips luxurious. So, excuse me while I—"

"*Yassas*," a deep, rich voice says, greeting us in Greek before switching into perfect, unaccented English. "Is there something I can help you with?"

That voice.

I know that voice.

Roxane's eyes go wide like saucers, buffoonery twitching on her lips as she glances over my head at the man behind me. It's obvious whose shadow is cast over me—from her reaction alone, I know it's *gulp* the Bulge—I mean . . . no, I'm not calling him that, he's Mr. Red Shorts.

Mr. Luxurious Lips.

Do you feel the secondhand embarrassment for me?

"Uh, hi," Roxane says, waving her fingers at him while I stay seated in the sand, stiff as a board. If I don't move, maybe he won't notice me. "We're just, uh, searching for an earring."

Oh, good one. I never have the panache to think that quickly on my feet. Roxane does, though; she always has. I just freeze in place, like I currently am.

"An earring? Well, let me help you. What does it look like?" he asks.

Help is not needed, sir. What is needed is for you to walk away. Keeping my eyes directed at only Roxane, I stare daggers at her while using our twin telepathy to make her aware of my visible discomfort and to divert the Bulge—I mean the man—divert the man away from us.

Thankfully, she hears me loud and clear and says, "Oh, you know what, I found it." She jabs her hand into the sand, picks up a pebble, and flashes it at him. "All good, thanks, though."

"Well, let me help you up, at least."

No one asked for a gentleman in these parts. Move along, man.

But it's too late; his chivalry is already on display as he lends his hand out to Roxane. Naturally, she takes it, and he helps her to her feet. So much for sending him away. When it's my turn, I hide behind my shoulder-length brown hair as his hand floats in front of me. It's been seven years—will he even recognize me? We shared a fleeting interaction, a reaction so small, I'm sure it doesn't even register in his memory. He's probably come to the rescue of many damsels in distress while working at Anissa's. I'm just a blip in the sea of women he runs into day in, day out, vying for his brown-eyed attention. Who's to say I made an impression?

Trust me, I didn't.

As Harold Flaketon said in fifth-period algebra back in high school, I'm the less interesting twin. Even though I'm a semithriving thirty-year-old now, that kind of comment still hovers over me like a dark cloud.

So, it's doubtful Red Shorts remembers me, but even still, the temptation to swat his hand away and yell at him to "begone" is quite appealing, on the off chance he might remember.

But thanks to the rules of society, such brazen rudeness on my end isn't well received by the masses, so I slip my fingers against his. And oooh, boy, mistake, ladies. Big mistake. I hate to sound like a lovesick stripling whose beloved just glanced their way, but the warmth of his palm feels like a perfect sunny spring day. The type of day where the birds are crooning a resplendent aria while the sun's rays fill your day up with hope and meaning.

There's no other way to describe the feel of his palm other than . . .

"Sun-kissed," I mutter as I stand.

"What was that?" he asks as he leans forward to look me in the eyes.

My gaze floats up to his, and *oh God*, he's too close. Way too close. I can smell him.

I can see the dark hair on his tanned chest—every trimmed strand.

And those lips . . . *gulp* they're mere inches from my view, a grandiose display of luxury.

What kind of ChapStick is this man using?

Out of sheer panic that he'll recognize me as the girl who called his lips luxurious, I snap away from him, my hair floating in front of my reddened cheeks, blocking my vision as I attempt to stomp away toward the bar, as fast as I can retreat.

Unfortunately for me, I've forgotten one important detail.

I'm still holding the Bulge's hand.

Like a yo-yo being dangled by a five-year-old, I'm pulled toward him. Between the unstable sand and my threadbare espadrilles, I stand no chance as I lose my footing and fall on my ass with a flop.

From the sheer momentum of my fall, my shoulders are propelled into the sand, followed by the back of my head, my freshly blown-out hair tangling in the soft grains. When my gaze shoots straight up to the sky, it's eclipsed by a pair of red shorts.

Oh, dear heavens . . . the bulge. Right there, in broad daylight—well, technically in broad night . . . light? Is that a thing? Either way, there it is, all bulgy and round and . . . wow, I want to touch it.

Don't, Tessa!

Do not reach out to touch it. That would make this moment way worse.

His eyes intent on mine, he squats down. "Whoa, are you okay?"

It's a noble question, and I hate to be so snarky, but does it look like I'm okay?

I'm a freaking bumbling mess who is infatuated with a man who has barely spoken to her. This is me, the girl who says men's lips are luxurious—the least interesting, butterfingered buffoon of a woman.

And then there he is. Deep-brown irises, so dark they fade into his pupils, leaving no hint where they start and where they end. His hair is clipped short on the sides, with a pile of waves on top, all perfect in that messy sort of way. And that jawline, chiseled from stone, a line so sharp that I wouldn't be surprised if the restaurant shaves gyro meat on it.

He's so handsome that just looking at him makes me feel not only like I'm staring at the sun—his sexiness practically blinding me—but also like if I stare too long, I'll be hypnotized into some sort of Santorini vortex where olives are constantly swirling around us as the winds whip open his white linen shirt, revealing what I can only imagine would be an expertly carved physique. Women would appear at his feet, presenting mounds of baklava on sterling-silver plates, grappling for his attention as he props one leg up on a marble stone, the bulge on full display—

"Miss, are you okay?" he repeats, knocking me out of my haze.

"Uh, she's fine," Roxane says, now bending at the waist and helping me up. "She had champagne on the flight. Little tipsy, this one."

"I'm not tipsy," I whisper as I stand up.

Returning the whisper, but through a clenched smile, Roxane says, "Would you rather him think you were knocked over by your inability to be a mature adult around handsome men?"

"Good point." Act tipsy; that will dispel any sort of awkward opinion he might have of me. Smart, Roxane. She might be honest, but she's always there for me. Putting on a show, I spin around and wave my hand in the air. "To the tops of my toes and to the bottom of my head," I slur out, "I've had too much to drink, so take me to bed."

His brow crinkles as I realize what I said.

God, maybe I *am* drunk.

"Uh, I mean, not you take me to bed, not like . . . you know, like that." His brow intensifies even more. "Uh, like . . . sex. I wasn't offering sex. I was just, you know . . ." I swallow. "Wow, ha, this is weird, huh?" I swipe my hand over my forehead. "You see, the thing is, well . . . boy, it's hot here, isn't it hot?"

"It's lukewarm," Roxane says, making me want to jab her in the ribs.

"Do you need some water?" Red Shorts asks, his voice so smooth, yet devoid of any accent. "I'd be more than happy to grab you some."

"No!" I shout. "I mean . . . no," I say more calmly. "I don't need water . . . although all humans need water." Roxane tugs on my arm, encouraging me to just drop it, but Red Shorts looks so confused that I feel the need to clear the air. "I know this is weird, and you probably don't come across people like me who don't know how to stop talking, but you know what, I'm just going to be honest with you." I lean forward as if we're sharing a secret. "I was pretending I was drunk because I fell on my butt in front of you, and let's face it, that's embarrassing. But if I told you I fell because I just happened to be clumsy, that makes me look all . . . *ahhh!*" I make a crazy face and shake my hands at him. When a horrified expression crosses his face, I realize I'm losing him, and quickly, so I try to giggle it off. "Um, so, yeah, I'm not drunk, just insane, apparently. So, thanks for helping us find our pebble, I mean earring. Thanks for finding the earring, and the hand hold—I mean, the holding, of hands, hand holding for help, I mean . . . God." I point my finger at him. "You have soft hands."

"What my sister is trying to say," Roxane interrupts, "is that we're headed to the bar, where I'm sure she's going to get for-real tipsy now because there's no doubt in my mind she'll replay this interaction over and over again until she passes out, only to relive the embarrassment tomorrow morning at breakfast."

I pat my sister on the hand. "Yes, that is accurate. So, please excuse us."

I offer him a curtsy because it's one of *those* days and turn on my heel. Hand in hand with Roxane, I pull her toward the bar as utter humiliation beats up my spine.

"Well, that went well," Roxane says.

Sarcasm at its finest, am I right?

"Let's just hope today is his last day at the resort, or this is going to be a very long three-week vacation."

14

"I don't know, feels incredibly entertaining to me." Roxane shoots me a mischievous grin. "I don't think I could have picked a more charming way to start my wedding extravaganza."

I could, and it doesn't involve babbling in front of the Bulge.

———

"Roxane, remember what we talked about."

With an eye roll for the ages, Roxane says, "I know, I know. We're not discussing the Bulge, what just happened with the Bulge, or any feelings you might have toward the Bulge being back after seven years."

"Promise?" I beg her as our friends approach the outdoor pool bar.

"Promise." She squeezes my hand tightly, letting me know she means it and putting me at ease. We decided to start our evening outside to enjoy not only the sea breeze but the ever-beautiful Santorini sunset.

"Are we ready to get this night started?" Clea says as she places her clutch on the outdoor bar top and gives us each a hug.

"I've had three drinks already," Lois, our other best friend, announces before blowing kisses in our direction. "Mommy is kid-free, and she will be drinking very heavily."

"Good, because we ordered drinks for everyone," Roxane says just as the bartender brings over four pink drinks. He hands them out, offers a wink, and then turns to help another customer.

I take my drink in hand—a drink I'm hoping helps me forget what happened ten minutes ago—and hold it up. "Here's to a fun week with my best friends."

"To the girls who have been there for me through thick and thin and stressful wedding planning," Roxane says.

"To the bond that will never break," Clea adds.

"And to the sisterhood that will last forever," Lois finishes off.

We tap our glasses together and then take a sip.

"This reminds me of the time we went to that lake house up in the Adirondacks," says Clea. "Remember how the owner greeted us?"

"He offered us massages," Lois says. "Personal massages by him."

"And we were so freaked out that we secured all the doors with chairs under them and slept in the one tiny bedroom we were convinced didn't have cameras watching us," Roxane says. "How does this remind you of that?"

Clea laughs. "Because we're together."

"We were together at Katz's just last week, didn't get lake-house vibes there," I say.

"No, but I sure did get the meat sweats." Clea brushes her hand over her forehead, causing us all to laugh. "Okay, maybe not lake-house vibes, but how about the time we rented that cabin in the Hamptons."

"That was the smallest piece of real estate I had ever seen. The bunk beds were clever, though," Roxane says.

I take a sip of my drink and add, "Too bad they offered a view of the single toilet in the space."

"That's when I demonstrated how my vagina expanded during birth," Lois says with a lopsided grin.

"Please . . . please tell me we won't be reminiscing on that again," Roxane asks.

"Depends on how drunk I get." Lois winks and takes a sip.

"Just not too drunk, like the night before Bethany's wedding, where we had to roll you down the hallway after the rehearsal dinner. That was unpleasant," I say. "Your boob kept falling out of your dress."

"That's what happens when you give birth, the knockers no longer belong to you." Lois gestures to the expansive night sky. "They belong to the world."

"Do they belong to the world tonight?" Clea asks and then nods at Lois's low-cut shirt.

"Perhaps. Only time will tell."

I chuckle. "Well, here's to creating new memories and to Roxane's wedding extravaganza." I turn to my sister, my heart full. "I know there are times where we butt heads, where we don't agree, or we completely misunderstand each other, but I couldn't imagine a day without you in it. I love you, Roxane, more than anything. You're my best friend, my partner in crime—very limited crime because you know I would never survive in jail—"

"She doesn't have street cred," Roxane says.

"And you are my confidante. Thank you for always being there for me, for pushing me out of my comfort zone—"

"If it were up to Tessa, we all know she'd never go for the things she wants in life. She would never leave her apartment and spend countless hours coming up with number puns."

"Guilty." I raise my hand. "So, to that, thank you for never letting me settle. I love you."

Roxane reaches over and pulls me into a hug. "Love you too, sis. Now, let's get drunk!"

CHAPTER TWO

TESSA

"Wake up. Time to get our tan on," Roxane says, jumping on my bed and shaking the mattress just enough to churn my stomach.

"Stop . . . moving," I groan, holding my hand out. "Might . . . puke."

"You had two freaking drinks last night, you can't tell me you're hungover."

I am.

Horribly.

Still reeling from my mortifying interaction with Red Shorts, I found solace in my friends . . . and my favorite cocktail, a raspberry ouzo slush, which tastes just like an Icee. Although from the knife stabbing the back of my right eye, I want to believe the bartender inserted half a bottle of ouzo in each drink.

And now I'm feeling the effects of his heavy hand.

How is Roxane looking so pristine right now? She had the same drinks. Before we left New York, she mentioned needing more "pizzazz" in her life. Maybe that pizzazz could include not putting on makeup for once.

"The girls are already down at the pool—they grabbed us loungers, come on." Roxane tugs on my hand.

"Just go without me," I say into my drool-soaked pillow. When drunk, I always sleep with my mouth open, which results in an ungodly amount of mouth breathing during the night.

"I'm not going without you. You're my maid of honor, my best friend, my sister . . . my everything, Tessa. And my wedding is in less than three weeks, and families arrive in six days." A look of anxiety crosses her face at the mention of her wedding, but before I can say anything, she quickly wipes it away. "I only have so much time left before it gets crazy, before festivities start, and I won't have that much alone time with you anymore. Now come spend time with me down at the freaking pool like the good sister that you are."

"Ughhh, fine," I groan as I sit up, unable to resist Roxane and her impassioned speech. I push my hair out of my face, only to catch my sister recoiling, hand to her chest.

"Good God, you didn't remove your makeup last night?"

"I honestly don't even know if I'm wearing clothes right now. Makeup is the least of my concerns." I let out a heavy sigh. "Am I naked?"

"No, but you don't smell great."

I push a few more strands from my eyes. "Not everyone can smell like a rose when they wake up." I glance at my sister, taking in her outfit, and if I didn't have a massive headache, I'd be shaking my head at how pristine she looks. Hair in waves under a white sun hat with accompanying black ribbon, she's sporting a black two-piece bathing suit, a white sarong around her waist, and a glossy lip.

Beautiful, like always.

"Come on, let's get you cleaned up." Roxane pulls me out of bed but backs away quickly.

"What?" I ask.

"You aren't wearing bottoms—I can see everything."

I glance down, and lo and behold, my private parts. I sigh once again and move past her toward the bathroom. "Give me five minutes," I call over my shoulder.

"Please brush your teeth, I don't want you curdling the milk with that breath."

"Derogatory comments not needed."

"Stating the facts, sis."

"Oh, Clea and Lois are right over there. Cute, they got us a cabana." Roxane bounces next to me as I attempt to walk straight and not tip to my right, directly into the crystal-clear pool.

After a tedious amount of combing, I was able to pull my hair into a side braid, give my face a solid scrub before applying a heavy dose of sunscreen—got to keep the wrinkles away—brush the stench out of my mouth, and slip on my light-blue one-piece bathing suit and white cotton cover-up, which reveals nothing, just the way I like it.

I might not feel like a human yet, but Roxane deemed me worthy to be seen in public.

We all flew to Santorini together yesterday, met at the bar, and "cheersed" to our first night in Greece. We reminisced, we talked about boys—like always—drank, a lot, and then ended up dancing until the early morning. I'd assume I'm not the only one looking absolutely wrecked.

But boy am I wrong. As I walk up to our friends, all I can notice is how un-zombie-like they look.

They actually look fresh and ready for vacation in their cute bathing suits, sarongs, and hats.

I look like death waiting to ruin their good time.

"Look who's here," Clea coos from her lounger, holding a Bloody Mary.

Clea Clooney—no relation to George, as she likes to say whenever she introduces herself—aficionado of all things male, and a filthy-rich podcaster with the number two podcast in the world, where she talks about sex and everything that goes with it. Once popularly known in high school for her "tongue action," she is now a well-respected businesswoman with celebrities clamoring at her door, begging for any tips of the trade. A sassy Leo who'll have sex wherever, whenever with her longtime lover, Beast—that's what we call her, because, well . . . you'll see—she never misses a chance to encourage fun, drinks, and shopping, often tag teaming with Roxane.

Clea stirs the red liquid in her glass, her eyes blocked by large, catlike sunglasses. "Did you brush your teeth?"

"Oh my God, Roxane." I turn toward my sister, who has a guilty look on her face.

"What?" She shrugs. "It was really bad, and I had time to waste while I was waiting for you, so I might have texted the girls."

"Yup, she texted us," Lois says from where she rests on the lounger.

Lois Feathers, the only married member of our group and the only one with gremlins, a.k.a. children. Once a DJ/bartender in her early twenties, she spent one wild night with a sports agent—and one broken condom later found out she was pregnant. Now married to Ed Feathers, the aforementioned sports agent, who reps the top five golfers in the country, they live on the Upper East Side in a four-bedroom penthouse where Lois spends her days—as she puts it—wiping tiny butts and folding and refolding blankets because despite the landfill of toys in their playroom, the only thing her kids like to play with are decorative blankets. She'll complain about her children and the life they have stolen from her until she has no breath left, but the minute she's away from them, she turns into a nutcase worrying every second about where they are, what they've eaten, and if they went to the bathroom and washed their hands.

"Let's just hope she didn't have stank breath when she told the Bulge how luxurious his lips were," Lois says as she reaches to the food platter in the middle of the cabana and snags a large piece of melon. She sniffs it and sadly adds, "My kids love melon."

Nostrils flared, ready to make everyone suffer as much as I am, I swivel toward Roxane, but she holds her hand up before I can say anything. "Listen, we've all been friends since freshman year in high school, we've all seen each other naked at some point, so I think the luxurious-lips thing is something we all should know."

"Why is that something anyone needs to know?" I ask as I drop down on a lounger next to Clea, who hands me a drink. I take it without even asking what the contents are. I thought I established last night that we wouldn't be talking about the Bulge.

And sure, Roxane held up her end of the bargain, but I wasn't aware of the twelve-hour time limit on the agreement.

Rookie mistake on my end.

"Because your interest in men is piqued, which means we have work to do." Roxane sits next to Lois.

Piqued? What does she mean by that?

"Uh, excuse me? What kind of work?" I ask. Clea lifts my hand that's holding my drink, encouraging me to take a sip. "What is happening?"

Calmly, Roxane rests her hands on her lap. "Lois, the contract."

"What contract?" I ask as Lois reaches into her purse and pulls out a file. "What is all of this?" Clea once again encourages me to drink by pinching the straw between her fingers and directing it toward my mouth.

"Is this some sort of intervention? Is it because I said luxurious lips? It was a weak moment, you guys know I'm awkward, it just slipped. I don't think it calls for an elaborate intervention."

Roxane flips open the folder as Clea offers me a plate of roasted potatoes. When I glance at her, she rubs her belly. "To soak up the goodness you drank last night. It's best to be in top form today."

"Why?" Nervous now, I meet my twin's eyes. "What do you have planned?"

She takes a deep breath. "Tessa, are you aware of this?"

From the folder, she pulls out a dingy, wrinkled, lined piece of notebook paper. Spiral shards dangle off the right-hand margin, and the telltale scribble of smeared gel pens is etched along the back.

Oh God.

The contract.

How could I forget about the *freaking* contract?

Confused? Let me help you understand where this is coming from. You see, there are four of us—me, Roxane, Clea, and Lois. Roxane and I have been best friends with these two gals since our freshman year in high school. And on that first day in Mrs. Hemp's English class, we were grouped together, going over sentence structures, when all hell broke loose. The sentence in question was about a sturdy set of cow's udders. Being the mature fourteen-year-olds that we were, we kept calling them cow nips, which of course left us in a fit of uncontrollable giggles. Mrs. Hemp—the kind of teacher who rocked the same feathered mullet as Freddie Mercury and on the daily smeared her red lipstick across her cheek—was not dealing with our cow-nip pandemonium and sent us to detention on day one.

From our obsession with *High School Musical* and Zac Efron's famous hair flip to our matching pink knockoff Juicy Couture velour jumpsuits and our late-night sessions where we spent countless hours adhering diamond stickers to our phones, we formed the kind of bond that could only be described as unbreakable.

From there, we spent every waking hour with each other. We rotated whose house we stayed the night at, we all joined cross-country together and cheated every chance we could, and we all ended up going to college together at NYU.

But there was one fateful night the summer before our senior year in high school. We were unsure if we would all be going to college together and afraid we'd drift apart, so we made a sacred pact. At Clea's parents' house in the Hamptons, out on the screened-in porch, we hovered around an old, tattered notebook where we kept track of everything in our lives—favorite outfits, school crushes, celebrity crushes, and our cross-country cheat routes. With pizza Pringles canisters spilled over, the *High School Musical* soundtrack playing in the background, and a gallon of fruit punch that we drank straight from the bottle next to us, we wrote a list of rules. Rules we've never broken.

Taking in three sets of eyes, I find myself back in the present, on a gorgeous Greek island, unable to fathom this fresh hell. "You can't be serious."

Lois scoots closer and lowers her sunglasses. "Oh, we're serious." She reaches into her bag and pulls out a familiar round pink bottle and sets it on the table. I can practically feel the earth quake at the meaning of that bottle, the wind whipping around like an omen is about to be revealed, rather than a symbol of friendship between four girls.

I gulp as I stare down at it.

Some of the pink has been scratched off the bottle, the bulb-y cap was lost back in college when Clea took the bottle to a "sleepover," and from where I'm sitting, I see that it's now only about half-full of liquid.

What kind of liquid, you're wondering?

None other than Britney Spears Fantasy perfume.

Do you believe in magic? Because we do. The magic of Britney Spears Fantasy perfume.

Let me explain.

We were hanging out at the mall after a riveting cross-country race where we were all disqualified for hanging out under a tree for an hour, only to cut across to the finish line. At every race, there was a fifty-fifty chance that we'd be caught cheating—this time, we were caught. We were sharing a plate of loaded fries from the Fry Depot when a woman came up to us and asked us to hold her shopping bag for her while she ran to the bathroom. Being the naive kids we were, we said sure. Two hours later, she had never returned for her bag. We asked around to see if anyone had seen the lady, but we came up short. Dubious, we took the bag back home, where the four of us locked ourselves in my room and opened it together. We were curious, after all.

The items located were a half-eaten bar of plain white chocolate, the discarded package of a Yankee Candle car freshener, a bottle opener in the shape of a maraca, and the perfume. Unsure of what to do with it all, we eventually tossed the packaging and white chocolate bar, gave the bottle opener to my dad for his birthday, and then shared the perfume, but on one condition: it could only be used for a very special occasion.

Clea was the first to use it, at homecoming, where eleven boys asked her to dance.

Lois was next; she wore it to winter formal and wound up making out with her crush behind the snack stand.

Roxane came in third, with a date to the movies—it was the first time a boy touched her boob.

The perfume power was strong at this point. A boob touch—that was the apex of all of our lives.

And me . . . well, let's just say I got my first kiss ever wearing that stuff.

We quickly came to realize that it wasn't just Britney Spears wrapped up in a bottle that smelled like candy—it was magic potion.

It's the reason Clea has a longtime lover, why Lois is married with two kids, and why Roxane is about to be married in less than three weeks.

Every member of the group was wearing the perfume when they met their soulmate, everyone . . . but me.

"This is absurd," I say. "We are thirty-year-old women—"

"Precisely, thirty," Clea says as she leans over and points at the contract.

My eyes fall to the five rules that are right above our adolescent signatures.

Rule number one: *No matter what happens in life, we will never live more than ten miles away from each other.*

Rule number two: *We will defend Zac Efron until our dying day.*

Rule number three: *We don't run for fun. We cheat to save our feet.*

Rule number four: *The magical perfume is only used for special occasions where love interests are involved.*

Rule number five: *If by the time we're thirty we're not attached, it means we haven't been using the perfume correctly, and we therefore forfeit our right to control our love life to our fellow sisters.*

It's the last rule that's shooting off warning signals at me.

I lower the contract, which of course was notarized by Clea's mom, who is a travel notary. Although young, we were still effective contract developers.

And that effectiveness is coming back to bite me in the ass.

"Listen, we wrote this over ten years ago—we're adults now."

"Are you saying this contract is null and void?" Lois asks. "Because I cursed out a teenager at the Bagel Emporium the other day when she said Zac was sporting a dad bod. I was so intense that I made her cry, and I've been asked to not come to the Emporium again." Her eyes grow serious. "Do you realize how hard it is to find a decent bagel place that doesn't judge my uproarious children?"

"Given the thousands of bagel places around the city vying for customers' money, I'd say pretty easy," I say with a smile.

The smile is not well received.

"Not many places bother making pumpernickel anymore, Tessa. You know that."

I do, unfortunately. It's a struggle we're met with daily.

"The contract stands," Roxane butts in. "These rules have been followed since the day we signed. We all live near each other, some of us within walking distance. Zac is our main man. Clea turned down half a million dollars to be sponsored by New Balance in a marathon challenge, and we have only ever used the perfume when we needed it the most. Therefore, rule five must be followed as well."

Rule five is an abomination.

"That's easy for you to say since you all have a significant other," I protest weakly.

"Because *we* used the perfume properly," Lois says. "Maybe you wouldn't have been in this situation if you'd worn the perfume to my wedding like I told you to. The reception was packed with single men waiting to pluck someone up."

"I had my period—I wasn't exactly in the mood to find my future husband."

"Or at the Rock and Roll Christmas bash three years ago," Clea says. "You knew Horace Randall was on the market. He could have been your husband."

"Horace preferred to have a conversation with my breasts rather than my face," I say.

"It's how the best relationships start," Clea says before taking a sip of her Bloody Mary.

"What about the housewarming party Philip and I held last year?" Roxane lifts her brow. "His best friend, Travis, was there, and if you were wearing the perfume, you probably wouldn't have spilled that cabernet on his cashmere sweater."

Doubtful. I'm prone to spills.

"That spill was not my fault, and you know it. Philip's drunk uncle fell into my legs and knocked me over. And how about not blaming the woman here—Travis could have been a little more understanding. It's not like I spilled the drink on him on purpose."

"No, but then you told him to wring his sweater into your glass so no wine was left behind," Roxane says.

I toss my hands up in the air. "It was a joke. Where's the man's sense of humor?"

Roxane reaches out and presses her hand to my thigh. "Tessa, we've all spoken, and we decided this is the right course of action."

"What is?" I ask, though dread washes over me—I know what's coming.

"Taking over your love life, of course," Clea says casually. "We gave you three extra months to see if you could figure your life out. When you were talking to a dog walker online, we thought maybe there was a chance, but that didn't pan out."

"That's not on me. He was talking to me because he thought I'd be a great fit for his and his wife's 'bedroom adventures.'" I roll my eyes as I make air quotes.

"You're attracting the wrong men and going after the idiots. It's time we fix that," Roxane says.

"Why now? Finding a man in Greece seems counterproductive to rule number one. Correct me if I'm wrong, but last time I checked, Greece is more than ten miles away from where you all live."

"Yes, but . . . there are plenty of men coming from New York to this wedding, and we have confidence that the perfume will work its magic," Roxane says. "We can prep you, train you, get you ripe and ready for next week. And why now? Because we don't leave a girl behind, and with our lives becoming busier and busier, there won't be another time where we can really pull together and make this work."

"This is the perfect time to do it," Lois says. "No distractions. No children nagging me for a snack or lovers pawing at clothes in public." Lois eyes Clea.

"Not my fault my breasts are heavenly." Clea moves her arms inward, making her cleavage pop. She does have great boobs. The best of the bunch easily. Large and perky, exactly how she was built.

"So." Roxane claps her hands. "Who should we start with?" She looks around the pool area. "Oooh, should we see if the Bulge is working today? He may not live in New York, and he doesn't seem like the type to settle down, but he could be a good warm-up. A baseline for us, if you will."

"No!" I shout. "I mean . . . no," I whisper, glancing around to make sure he's not working around the pool. The Bulge is not a warm-up, he's a . . . well, he's a fantasy—a fantasy I don't want to even consider for fear that he'd break my heart. "You'll be wasting your time on him. Wait, what am I saying? I'm not doing this." I set the contract in Roxane's hands and move over to the lounger farthest from my glaring sister. "There's no way in hell I'm going to let you guys handle my love life. Sorry. Not happening. Find something more productive to do on vacation. Like relax, or hey, how about a boat tour? Sunset on the sea, sounds magnificent." I lean back on my lounger and turn away from them, snuggling under a towel.

Forfeit my love life?

They must be out of their minds.

There is no way I would ever let that happen. Contract or not.

They need to start thinking of another form of entertainment, because I'm not it.

CHAPTER THREE
MYLES

My foot bounces up and down as I clasp my hands in my lap. Across from me, a waterfall wall trickles over a cursive logo: *Anissa's Palace Beach Resort* in neon blue, reflecting off the liquid waves.

I remember when the sign was installed. It was a suggestion from my uncle Taki. He claimed the office's reception area needed something flashy and went neon instead of papering the walls with a realistic mural of the Parthenon. Several years later and even though it's still working, its luster has dulled, the tubing now clouded from years of taking a beating from the waterfall.

"Myles?" Jasmine, the receptionist, says as she hangs up her phone. "He'll see you now."

Standing from the uncomfortable white bench, I offer her a grateful smile despite the fifteen-minute wait for an appointment.

Typical.

I move past the reception desk, down the narrow cream halls of the office, the worn ceramic tiles beneath my feet a subtle reminder that renovations are made for the guests, not for the staff. Turning toward the right, I move past a few office doors, placard names at eye level, and head straight toward the end of the hallway to a double-doored office.

I rap my knuckle on the wood and wait. After a few beats, a low-timbred voice bellows, "Come in."

With my nerves frayed, I open the door and step into my father's office.

Wraparound windows filter in the sun that brightly reflects off the Aegean Sea stretched out below. The carpet beneath my feet, plush and new, is a stark contrast to the chipped tile in the hallway. In the center of the office rests a sizable marble-top desk with thick wrought iron legs—the type of desk that a powerful, rich man would purchase for himself.

And at the helm of that desk sits my father in his ergonomic leather chair, hands steepled together, his bushy eyebrows perking up as I shut the door behind me.

I stuff my hands in my shorts pockets and muster up enough courage to sound like I'm not coming back to him, tail tucked between my legs. "Hey, Baba."

"Myles, you've returned."

I nod. "Yeah, I was hoping to see you when I first got here, but I was told you've had a busy schedule. Thanks for making the time to meet with me." Not something a son usually has to say to his father, but then again, our relationship is rocky at best.

"Quite busy," he says, slipping effortlessly into Greek as he crosses one leg over the other and leans back in his chair. "Why don't you take a seat. Tell me how life has been in New York."

Did you catch the bitterness in his voice? It's heavy, weighted, like a giant pink elephant hanging over the both of us by threadbare rope, ready to drop any second.

Keeping my calm composure—I'm prepared for his surly attitude—I take a seat across from him and sit up straight. "New York was great," I say, switching into Greek as well. "The winters were hard to adjust to, but after a few years, I got used to it."

"I see, and your mother? I presume she's well."

I nod. "Very well. She, uh . . . she is very happy with Darren."

"Yes, well, I'd assume anyone would be better than me, right?"

Bitterness. So much bitterness.

"Baba, I don't want to get in the middle of you two. It's been over ten years now. I reserve the right to not have to listen to your bickering anymore. I think we all suffered enough when you were married."

His brow raises as his penetrating eyes examine me so closely, I feel like he's pressing me up against a microscope. "Those are awfully big words for someone who abandoned their father."

"I didn't abandon you," I say as calmly as I can. "I was accepted into a hospitality management program, the top program in the world. I worked damned hard at getting into it—the opportunity of a lifetime."

"Yes, and what exactly could they teach you that I've not taught you here?" He waves his hand around his office.

A lot, actually, but I'm not about to sweep away any remnants of a relationship with a pithy comeback.

"I wanted outside experience, Baba. We talked about this."

"We spoke briefly of your plans, but you never truly told me why. It's hard not to take your distance personally, especially since you went to live with your mom." He glances away as he drags his hand over his gray goatee.

I knew coming back was going to be hard, but seeing such hurt in his eyes, hearing it in his words . . . well, I didn't think it was going to be this bad. It isn't as if I didn't speak to him for seven years. We've stayed in touch, mostly thanks to my efforts. Then again, as he expressed one evening over the phone, it's easier for me to reach out since I'm not the one bleeding.

I don't want to sound like a total ass here, but there are two types of people in my family: the ones with the ostentatious flare for dramatics . . . and all the rest. Can you guess which side I'm on and which side my baba is on?

"I didn't stay with Mom because I was taking her side—I told you, I've taken no one's side with the divorce. The program I was in required

I work for a local hotel in order to graduate. I was fulfilling my duties, and living with Mom made the most sense. But now I'm here. Back with you, ready to learn more, ready to help with the resort."

He looks toward the window, his eyes avoiding mine, and I can't be sure if it's because he is mad or he can't stomach the sight of me. Possibly a bit of both.

He heaves a deep sigh. "I can't have you waltzing in here, thinking that you can just . . . run the resort with your new fancy degree. This is Santorini, not New York City. We do things differently here."

"I know, Baba. And I don't have any expectations by coming back."

"Then why did you?" he asks, resting his hands on his desk now as he leans forward. "Why did you come back if you were comfortable with where you were, with your job, with your mother?"

Because I worry about you.

Because Aretha, your assistant, told me about your depression.

Because there is no one here to watch over you the way I can.

With a shallow swallow, I tuck the truth away for the sake of his pride. "Because this is my home; this is where I'm supposed to be."

After a few beats of uneasy breath, his weathered eyes connect with mine. It's like looking in a mirror, a mirror that ages me a good thirty years. The wrinkles in the corners of his eyes extend down his cheeks, to his smile lines, accentuating that dazzling grin Baba is known for around the resort. Infectious, appealing, always making the customers feel like they're staying not just at a resort but rather at a family compound right on one of Santorini's few beaches.

"This is your home?" he asks me.

"Yes, it always has been."

"Well." He smooths his hand over the marble top of his desk. "We will see about that." He shifts a few papers around on his desk, taking on the appearance that he's busy—in reality, I know he spends most of his time up here in his office, staring over the ocean . . . missing my mom. "Report to Garfield. He's been instructed to assign you responsibilities. You will act as a rover."

"A rover?" I ask. "What do you mean by that?"

"It means that wherever you're needed, we will assign you the responsibility. Might be lifeguard one day, since you are one of few staff trained to be a lifeguard, or it might be server, registration, bellhop, wherever we need extra hands."

I know why he's doing this; it's his way of punishing me. He knows I came to speak to him about a management role, but from the stern set in his shoulders, I can see opening that conversation with him right now will do me no good.

So, with a smile on my face and determination in the back of my mind, I nod. "Sounds good. I'll connect with Garfield right away." Hands on the armrests, I push up to my feet. When I pivot toward the door, Baba clears his throat, which gives me pause.

"Myles," he says, gaze trained on his computer screen, "I'll expect you to show up to Sunday-night dinner."

I stuff my hands in my pockets. "I wouldn't think of missing it."

Instead of a response, he offers me a curt nod, and I take that as my dismissal.

While I head out of his office to find Garfield, who is most likely in the kitchen, I mentally prepare myself for the long road ahead. I want nothing more than to work hand in hand with my father, to run Anissa's Palace as his partner—and possibly even expand to another property at some point—but the first thing I need to do is repair our broken relationship.

Once I've done that, I'll be able to actually tell him about my experience in New York and perhaps apply some of the valuable management techniques I've acquired.

But first things first . . . I'll prove to my baba that I'm here for the right reasons.

CHAPTER FOUR

TESSA

"And where exactly do you live?"

"Vermont. Burlington, to be exact," the stranger, who we met a minute ago in the pool, says.

"Oh, I love Vermont," Roxane says, clutching my arm, making it impossible for me to swim away. "My sister here, who is very single, I might add, loves Vermont. She was just telling me the other day how much Vermont just tickles her fancy."

"I did not say that," I cut in. "I would never say 'tickle my fancy.'"

Roxane laughs and squeezes my cheeks together with one hand. "Isn't she so funny?"

The man slowly inches away. To the naked eye, it might look like the mellow current of the pool could be causing him to drift, but one glance under the water and I know you'd see his toes working overtime to get as far away from me as possible.

"Very," the man says and then jabs a thumb toward the bar. "I'm actually going to go get another beer. I'll, uh, I'll see you guys around." He offers us a quick wave and doesn't give us a chance to respond before he's out of the pool and walking toward the bar—you know, the kind of speed you use in order to catch an almost-closed elevator. Dude is power walking those hips straight to a bottle of booze. After the conversation he just endured, I don't blame him.

"We should find him at the bar later, see if we can get him to buy you a drink," Roxane says.

"Uh, did you fail to see how much he didn't want to be talking to us?"

Roxane dismissively waves her hand. "That's just nerves. He was caught off guard by your beauty."

"Or he was blinded by the glare off my alabaster body. He wasn't wearing sunglasses."

"I told you to self-tan before we came here. God, you never listen to me. I brought some with me. We'll get you hooked up tonight. I'm going to rub it all over you, even your private bits."

"The hell you are," I say. "I'm not letting you see anything."

"How many times do I have to tell you, we're mirror images of each other—what you have, I have. I stare at your boobs every morning in the mirror because they're the same as mine."

I float backward until I hit the edge of the pool. I use the wall for support as I tip back my chin and sigh. "Clearly not mirror image in the personality department."

"That's obvious," she huffs with a roll of her eyes.

"And can you please not lie to people? I did not say Vermont tickles my fancy."

"You said you had a pint of Ben & Jerry's the other day."

"Uh, yeah, ice cream, not Vermont."

"Hello! Ben & Jerry's is made in Vermont, which means . . . Vermont tickles your fancy. I know how much you love ice cream."

"You've had too much to drink today." I've had enough with the water, the sun, and the company, so I make my way toward the stairs leading out of the pool.

"Where are you going?"

"Back to my room for a nap—you've exhausted me."

"Oh, good idea." Roxane follows behind. "Rest up, because tonight . . . oh boy, are we going to have fun."

"Fun at my expense, I'm guessing."

I step out of the pool and rush toward my towel, but Roxane catches up, stopping me from grabbing my cover-up. "Hey, why do I detect sarcasm in your voice?"

"I don't know, Roxane, maybe because I thought we were going to have a fun girls' trip and instead, over the three hours we've been down here, you've tried to introduce me to five men, three of whom were married."

"It's not my fault they floated near us."

"One of them was tying his shoe by our cabana," I say, leveling with her.

"For all I know, he was faking it, trying to get our attention. He was fair game."

"Roxane, this is ridiculous," I mutter. "This trip isn't supposed to be about me finding a man and some silly contract from over ten years ago."

"There's nothing silly about that contract—it was notarized."

"Either way, I don't want to spend this vacation attempting to knock away every man you see breathing within a twenty-foot radius. So please, just . . . just let it be."

She shakes her head. "No can do, sister. Unfortunately for you, I'm a big believer in tradition and rule following. And as you've forfeited your rights, I will spend my entire vacation trying to find you someone to at least talk to."

"Why? Why is this so important to you?"

"Because you've spent way too much time sulking about after your previous relationship with Lionel. He broke up with you over eight months ago, and you're still not yourself."

"That's what happens when you find out someone's been cheating on you the whole time," I say softly.

Yup, boyfriend of two years cheating on me: it leaves a mark, especially since my boyfriend in college cheated on me as well. It's not a pattern you get over quickly.

Roxane takes my hand in hers and squeezes it softly. "You know I love you, Tessa. And until my dying day, I will always seek revenge on the men who've wronged you, but I will also make it my mission to ensure my sister doesn't give up on love. Meaning it's time you get some action in your life." Action is exactly what terrifies me. "Plus, a deal's a deal. If it was anyone else in the group, you'd be enforcing the rules as well."

"No, I wouldn't—"

"Two summers ago, Café Richard," Roxane says. "Do you recall what happened?"

"No," I reply, even though I very much know what she's talking about.

"Let me refresh your memory. I was trying to impress this cute boy by the name of Philip who'd just started working with me. He found out I ran cross-country in high school and asked me to join his running club. That busybody Sharon 'Big Melons' McGirk overheard us and said she'd join, so I said I would too, because everyone knows Sharon was after one thing . . . Philip's penis. And the image of her bouncing around in a sports bra would drive any woman to drastic measures."

"Good God," I mutter.

Roxane pokes me in the shoulder. "And guess who found me with a brand-new pair of running shoes, spandex, and a sports bra at Café Richard thirty minutes before I was supposed to meet up with Philip . . . and Sharon."

I swallow hard. "I did."

"Uh-huh, and who pointed out that I was in fact wearing an outfit that looked an awfully lot like a run-for-fun outfit?"

"I did," I answer.

"That's right. And who called our friends, right there in the middle of the bustling café, to shame me, to tear down my dreams of getting closer to Philip, and force me to think of another way to share time with him, another way that didn't include running for fun since it was against our—as you put it—'code of conduct'?"

I wet my lips, seeing exactly where this is going. "I did—but," I add quickly, "that's what we do, we push each other to do better, and it all worked out, because guess who's marrying him in a few short weeks? You are!"

"Because I practically threw myself at him," she says. "I had to outdo Sharon Big Melons—do you know how hard that was?" She takes a step closer. "It got to the point where every time I was near Philip, I came up with some sort of creative way my breast could brush up against him. You've seen our boobs—you know we don't have a lot to work with." Very true. They are okay but nothing to bounce around town with. "And sure, you pushed me to do better, to try harder, but I think it's time we return the favor." She smiles, but despite her reasoning, it's not an evil smile. More of an excited grin. "So, dearest sister, I'm sorry to bring this to your attention, but out of all four of us, you're the one who has been the rule follower since the beginning. You're the one who's been enforcing the contract."

Unfortunately, she's right.

She makes a very valid point.

I did keep Roxane from joining Philip's running club—mind you, with good intentions.

And if I recall correctly, Lois and Ed wanted to move to a brownstone in Brooklyn that was completely refurbished, any New Yorker's dream. Only issue? It was out of the radius the contract allowed, so they couldn't make an offer—but this was after we'd just gone through a bout of not seeing each other as much. Clea was upset about it; I was helping preserve the group. And don't feel bad for Lois: she lives in a penthouse on the Upper East Side; she's doing just fine—hell, better than fine.

And Clea, well . . . when she was headed to Coachella for the weekend, five summers ago, she asked to bring the perfume in case she met someone. I wouldn't allow it because I said there was no way she'd use it properly. I was right; she ended up sleeping with two men and a woman that weekend, and none of them were keepers—and I held her to the contract. This was after Clea accidentally spilled the perfume on her last "trip." Once again, preservation, good intentions for the group.

So, there's no doubt in my mind what exactly my three best friends are doing.

Preservation—with perhaps a dash of retribution.

And I'm sure they're all loving it.

"You know I'm right." Roxane smirks playfully.

"You're annoying, that's what you are," I say and push past her.

I don't have to look over my shoulder to know she's wearing a smarmy "I've won" expression, a smile so large it's practically eating her nose. Because she knows damn well she has me. They all do. I'm paying my penance, and there is no way they're going to let me off the hook.

I reach the cabana where Clea is speaking with Beast on the phone. Her cheeks are rosy—which only means one thing: they're talking about things I don't want to know about—and Lois is passed out on her lounger, legs spread, arms hanging off the side, and her mouth gaping open, projecting a not-so-subtle snore. A towel is draped over her chest with the hashtag "mom life" embroidered across the center.

I slip my cover-up over my head and am gathering my tote just as Roxane walks up behind me and leans in. "Enjoy your nap," she whispers. "You're going to need it for what we have planned for you tonight."

Head held high, chin up, I spin on my heel and face my sister. "You know, retribution doesn't look good on you."

"It's not retribution, sis, just upholding the contract like you've done in the past," she says with a mischievous grin and then whispers, "I promise we'll make it fun, okay? I only have your best interest at heart. Time to forget the shit men in your life and have some fun, Tessa."

Fun . . . with men? Not sure the two go hand in hand.

I don't bother to respond because there really is nothing to say. I know she's not doing this to be evil and that she's well intentioned. All of them are. My breakups haven't been easy on the group. They've had to pull me out of my circling depression several times, so I can see how they want to make the most of this "fun" situation.

Although their idea of fun seems like torture to me.

Meeting new guys?

Going out on dates set up by them?

That smells more like a disaster than anything. Funny thing about retribution: it can turn into petty behavior quickly. And even though we're at the early stages of the contract being enforced on my love life, I can't help but think that between Roxane's stress about the wedding, my friends' need to have fun, and my single life, they very well might not understand at this point, since they've been in relationships for a while now: this could turn ugly.

I move past her, my slippery feet sliding around in my wet sandals as I make my way toward the hotel. The best decision I made about coming on this trip was not sharing a room with my sister, or either of the other girls, for that matter. I step inside the hotel's cool refuge and take a deep breath. Having a moment to myself is exactly what I'm going to need right now if I'm going to plot out my plan of attack.

One thing you need to know about my group of friends is that we're fighters. And not in the sense that you might be thinking. We don't fight internally with each other—well, I mean, we have our fights, but that's not what I mean. We don't take anything lying down; we come back swinging. There's give-and-take—we're always pushing each other, teasing, joking, trying to best one another whenever we can.

And this is the perfect example. In good humor, they think they have me beat with this technicality in the contract. Well, little do they know, I'm not about to just make it easy for them. Ohhhh no.

I'll let them have their fun and games while they "honor" the contract and get their retribution, but like I said, retribution can turn petty, which can turn ugly. Therefore, like Demeter's daughter Persephone, I need to be ready for when the pettiness sprouts.

Because it will happen.

Yup, a plan for a counterattack.

That's right. Did you really think I was going to lie down and let them dictate my love life? Hell no. I might be demure—maybe not as outspoken or outgoing as my sister, or as sexually charged as Clea, or as downright scary as Lois—but I do have smarts, and that's exactly what I'm going to use. I'm going to use my vast amount of intelligence to counterattack what are now my enemies.

Well, I still love them all. They're not *really* enemies, but sometimes it's fun to be dramatic, right?

Welcome to vacation wars. Buckle up, because it's going to be a bumpy—

"Ooof," I say as I turn the corner of the hotel hallway and slam into a solid wall. I bounce backward and slip on my wet sandal, and as I attempt to catch my balance, my tote bag falls to the ground. I trip over it and fall backward. My body curves over my stuffed tote—for some reason, I always like to carry at least three towels when I'm near water—and I end up lying on the floor, pelvis up, feet in the air, spread-eagled. And the worst of it all, my sandal slips off my foot and clonks me in the head.

"Oh shit," I hear before a very familiar face comes into view.

A face so handsome, it was booped on the nose by a line of Greek gods.

Chiseled.

Tan.

Graced with just enough scruff to make every inner thigh within a twenty-mile radius weep with joy.

The Bulge.

Isn't that just freaking poetic?

"I'm so sorry," the Bulge says. "I should have been paying attention to where I was going. Are you okay?"

Yes.

No.

Does a bruised ego count as not doing okay?

What about a dent in one's lustful urges?

"Fine," I grumble as I rock to the side so my legs aren't dangling in the air anymore. "I, uh, I wasn't paying attention either. Lost in my thoughts. You know, vacation wars and everything, can be kind of time consuming—more like mind consuming, am I right?" I add awkwardly because I think he saw my crotch—covered, but a crotch nonetheless—and I think almost 99 percent of the population would agree that showing off one's covered crotch is not ideal.

Any unwarranted crotch action is unpleasant.

But he doesn't seem to be in the same "crotch covered" frame of mind, because he tilts his head to the side. "Vacation wars?"

That's what he fixated on? Well, got to give the man credit.

"Umm, yeah, with my sister, the pebble finder." He still looks confused, so I say, "I swear I'm not drunk this time—well, I wasn't last night either, but I'm not now—although I would probably make more sense if I was drunk. Right?"

"Uh, let's just get you up."

Yeah, best so he can retreat as quickly as his manners allow him.

I don't have to be a mind reader to know he'd prefer attempting a high-stakes swirly on his own head than be here, with me, mumbling about God knows what. I can feel it. He wants nothing more than to excuse himself from this collision. "That would probably be best." He probably wishes his English weren't perfect so he'd have the blessing of not understanding me.

He lends out his hand, and once again, I slip my fingers against his—oh dear Lord above, his hand is all burly and large—and he pulls me to my feet with ease, then retrieves my sandal and bends down to help me slip it on. Although he doesn't want to be here, that doesn't negate the fact that he is, of course, a gentleman. See? Manners.

His right hand grips my ankle while the other maneuvers my sandal past my toes.

I would like it to be known that this Cinderella moment is probably the most awkward instant of my entire thirty years of living.

Three things that come to the forefront of my mind immediately:

Did I miss any spots around my ankle while shaving?

Is my skin slimy from the mixture of sunscreen and pool water?

And good God, I hope I don't smell weird in any way.

"Oh, that's not necessary." I let out a horrendous horselike laugh, as if my bowels are being tickled up to the base of my throat. But he doesn't listen; instead, he continues to slide my footwear back on. "Don't mind my big toe down there," I say nervously. "It's crooked because I broke it once during a cross-country meet. I, uh, I lost my toenail. I ended up painting my skin the same color as my other toes out of pure shame until it grew back. Have you ever seen a toenail grow back? Kind of some freaky stuff. Have you ever lost a toenail? I bet you haven't. You seem like someone who keeps their toenails in place."

Good God, Tess, stop talking.

The Bulge looks up at me. "No, ma'am, I've never lost my toenail before."

Errr, what was that?

Ma'am?

Did he just call me ma'am?

Well, that's a surefire way to make my lustful labia shrivel up and die.

"Ew, God, don't call me that. That . . . that makes me want to die a slow death."

The corner of his mouth twitches up as he stands, towering over me again. "A 'slow death'? Well, we wouldn't want that either, would we?"

Well, I still kind of do, after all the toenail talk.

"Guess not," I say as he bends down and picks up my tote and hands it to me. "Thank you," I mutter.

"You're welcome. I need to just double-check, though, are you okay? Should I take you to our medical office to get you checked out?"

"Checked out, ha, no one's checked me out in eons, ages . . . way back in the day," I lamely joke and then add a drum sound effect at the end. "Ba da dum-chsh."

"Did you . . . did you hit your head?"

If only.

"I wish that were the case," I say, self-loathing consuming me. "Just, you know, embarrassing myself is all. *Anywho*, I'll be on my way. Thanks for knocking me to the ground—and I mean that in a nice way, not a sarcastic way. Nothing like a good old dose of humiliation to remind oneself of who they truly are. Good day."

I've taken one step toward the elevators when he moves in front of me. "It shouldn't be humiliating when I'm the one who knocked you over."

Why is he torturing himself? Man, I gave you an out. Take it.

"I can see where you might be coming from with that angle, but unfortunately for me, I'm the one who talked about painting my nailless big toe, so . . . there's humiliation."

He gently nods. "Would it help if I offered a humiliating story about myself to call it even?"

I'd still think you're perfect, and good God, it hits me that this is the most I've ever said to him. My fifteen-year-old self would be lapping up every word. My thirty-year-old self wishes to crawl into one of the dresser drawers in my hotel room and wait for Narnia to gobble me up.

"You don't have to—I think you'd be wasting your breath. You see, I've already embarrassed myself last night, so this moment only adds onto that. I'm piling up, and then there's the fact that you don't even remember who I am, which of course makes me—"

"What do you mean, remember who you are?" he asks.

Oh, now you've done it, Tessa. Dredging up the past when it should have just rested there. In the past.

"Uh . . . what now?" I ask. If Roxane has taught me anything, it's to act dumb when in stressful situations. Not sure how this tactic is effective, but hey, we're flying by the seat of our bathing suit crotch at this point, so let's go with it.

"You said I don't remember who you are."

Yes, Tessa, of course he was listening. What now? I guess . . . continue to play dumb.

"Is that what you thought I said?"

"Yes, because that's what you said."

Looks like our bulgy friend is some sort of human recorder. Great . . . although if he were a human recorder, don't you think he would have remembered me? Ha! Got you on that, buddy.

I let out a boisterous laugh and press my hand against the wall for support. "So funny that you would think that's what I said." I wave my hand in front of my face as I catch my breath. "That's not what I said at all. Actually, I said something more serious."

"Oh, what was it?"

God freaking darn it, Tessa.

Really just digging a ditch now, aren't I?

Why would I say something serious? The only thing serious in this moment is the amount of sweat collecting under my breasts. We're one jumping jack away from flooding the hotel floors.

If Roxane was here, she'd have removed me from the interaction when I mentioned losing my big toenail.

"What was the serious thing?" I ask, and he nods, encouraging me to answer him. Well, huh . . . something serious . . . something serious . . . "Uh, I said you, uh, you don't even remember . . . *hooo-man*. Yeah, you don't even remember human, and if that's not serious, I don't know what is."

His pinched brow grows even deeper. "You know, I think we should take you to see the medical staff, just in case you have a concussion."

Great, you've acted crazy enough that he thinks you had a concussion. Way to go.

"Oh no, I don't have a concussion."

"How do you know?"

Yeah, how do you know?

Hmm . . . *mentally taps chin*

Ah, I know.

I tilt my head to the side. "I've always been able to taste a concussion."

"Taste it?"

Here we go, strap in for the ride of your life, folks . . .

"Yup. Tastes sort of coppery." I smack my lips together. "That's science for you. Copper equals concussion. Fortunately for all of us, the only thing I taste is the Bloody Mary Clea forced me to drink because of my hangover. I'll be burping that up for hours—" My eyes go wide. Oh God, did I just say that? "Wait, I mean, no, I don't burp. I'm a lady, a lady with manners. I don't do the burping thing—I don't know why I said that. Do you know why I said that?" I wave my hand at him. "Don't answer that. Anywho, I really think I've overstayed my welcome in this conversation. I can tell from the way your nose is curling up that you'd rather be pretending you have olives for eyes in front of a gaggle of children than listen to me ramble on about burping . . . well, not burping. So"—I clap my hands together—"this was pleasantly horrible. I'm going to leave now. Have a good day, and if you need anything, please let the staff know. Wait . . . I mean, no, you work here. But I guess if you need help, you could still let the staff know. Friends help friends at work, right?" God, end my misery. I take a step away from the crime scene I created. The homicide of my dignity, chalked out, right there on the floor.

"I'll be sure to lean on any staff if needed." He smirks, and that tiny, itty-bitty lift of his mouth makes my entire body heat up in absolute euphoria. That coy look creates a vortex of yearning, and before I know what's happening, I run dead into the wall, smacking my head against it.

"Ooof," I say, gripping my forehead. "That's, wow . . . that's a hard wall."

"Jesus, are you okay?" he asks, coming up next to me again, this time with his hand to my shoulder.

Like a laser beam, my eyes fall to his hand, then to him . . . then to his hand . . . then to his eyes again.

And before I can stop myself, I say, "Good God, man, you have soft hands. Luxurious."

No!

My hand clamps over my mouth. Eyes wide. And lo and behold, I have that coppery taste in my mouth, but it's not from a concussion; it's from the way my teeth are chomping down on my tongue, punishing its mutiny.

"Luxurious . . ."

It happens in slow motion.

His brow slowly unfolds, his eyes narrowing in. His lips are wetted by the tip of his tongue, and then just like that, he smiles.

"And here I thought you forgot about our interaction at the bar."

Oh.

Dear.

Heavens.

Luxurious. That's all it took, one word, for him to relive our interaction seven years ago. *Great!*

"That's why you commented about me not remembering you, right?" He snaps his finger at me as if he's solved the case. And frankly, I'm impressed with him, given our wild-goose chase of a conversation. The man deserves an award.

"Ha," I guffaw, loud enough for the horrendous sound to echo through the hallways. "That's, wow . . . that's, uh . . . something I don't want to talk about, so if you'll excuse me, I am just going to go bury my head between my pillow and pillowcase. Good day, sir."

"Myles."

"Huh?" I ask.

"My name is Myles."

"Oh, well, isn't that nice for you." I offer him a wave and turn on my heel—avoiding the wall this time—and begin walking away.

"What's your name?" he calls out.

And from over my shoulder, I say, "Humiliated. Nice to meet you, Myles. Have a nice day."

CHAPTER FIVE

MYLES

"Can you unload the cups from the drying racks?" Toby asks.

"Sure," I answer as I finish tying my apron around my waist.

This evening, I'm on bar duty with Toby. It's one of my favorite jobs at the resort, not just because bartending under the dim lights of the attached dinner restaurant while chatting with the guests is enjoyable but because it beats standing outside acting as lifeguard, or worse, serving guests at the beach. Easily the worst job out of all of them. But also, Toby is my best friend. Neighbors since we were born, we've been through everything together, including my parents' divorce, his parents' divorce, the cataclysmic tornado that was Calliope Cantos—the girl who tried to date us both at the same time; it didn't end well for her— and life after we finished school, which was spent at Anissa's, working odd jobs wherever we're needed. We've traveled back and forth to the States visiting family, and now that I'm back in Greece, we're making up for lost time.

While Toby enjoys working the bar, hooking up with guests when the time is right—and no one is watching—and spending his off time out on a boat fishing, I've always wanted a little more. It's why I went to New York City. Unlike my baba, though, Toby didn't stop talking to me. We spoke almost every single day, and when it was time for me to come back, he warned me it wasn't going to be easy. He was right. The staff were less than happy to see me, Baba is hurt and bitter over my return, and I'm being run around more than ever.

"I'm grateful you're here tonight," Toby says. "The bar has been crazy lately. And now that Garfield hired some summer help with the beach and lifeguarding, I heard that he might stick you here with me more often since you're the only other person who knows how to bartend."

"That would be preferred," I say. "Although I'll do pretty much anything at this point."

"Taking it the conversation with your baba didn't go as well as you hoped."

"It was . . . awkward," I answer. But not as awkward as the interaction I had with the girl I knocked over today—Tessa. Tessa Doukas, although that's not how she introduced herself. What did she say her name was again? "Humiliated," right? I smile just thinking about it. Not sure I've ever come across someone as uncomfortable in her own skin as she is, but I found it truly fascinating. I always have. Throughout the years of seeing each other at Anissa's, she's always been awkward, always shy, always trying to hide behind her hair. But I noticed her from the very beginning. "But don't worry, he said it was a requirement for me to make an appearance at Sunday-night dinner."

"Really?" Toby is restocking the garnishes, currently elbow deep in the cherry container. "That seems weird. Maybe he's trying to make amends, and the only way he knows how to is to invite you to family dinner."

"He could just talk to me. That works too. I'm not sure I have the energy for a Sunday-night dinner."

"Well, you have a whole week to prepare for it," he says just before he nods toward the entrance of the restaurant. "Looks like we have company."

I glance toward the archway of the restaurant, near the hostess stand, and spot Humiliated—I mean Tessa—with three other women.

The other women are dressed in skintight dresses, cleavage on full display, their hair styled in waves around their shoulders with a few pieces pinned out of their faces. Their legs look infinitely long in strappy open-toed heels, and their makeup looks heavier than what I'm sure they normally wear.

And then there's Humiliated.

Drowning in what looks to be a pink silk robe, her hair is tied up in a knot on the top of her head. She wears bright-red lipstick and nothing else, no other signs of makeup. It's almost as if she played Russian roulette with what she used to get ready.

"Hey, do you happen to recognize the one in the robe?" I ask Toby, motioning to Tessa as I put away my last glass.

"Yeah. The Doukas party," he says. "Roxane Doukas is the bride-to-be—she's getting married in a few weeks, the biggest wedding this resort has ever had. And then the one in the pink bunny suit—"

"I think that's a robe."

"Either way, not the best article of clothing. That's Roxane's twin sister, Tessa. And the other two, they're friends. Not sure on their names, but I do know they're both taken. Tessa is the only single one. Why do you ask? Did you happen to forget who they are? It's been seven years, but with the way you spent our childhood staring at her, I wouldn't have thought you'd forget."

"I'd never forget Tessa," I answer, the nervous lurch of my stomach letting me know how true that is.

"Then why ask, if you know?"

"Kind of had some interesting interactions with Tessa," I say. "I wanted to make sure you remembered her, since I'm not sure how to handle it."

"Describe interesting."

"Just . . . interesting," I say, watching them head toward the bar, "in an awkward kind of way." When Tessa's eyes focus on the bar in front of her and she spots me, she pauses, midstride, causing Roxane to bump into her back.

"What are you doing?" Roxane asks, completely oblivious to the fear in her sister's eyes. "The bar is that way." And then she nudges Tessa.

One of the friends drops her purse on the bar and lets out a deep sigh before making eye contact with Toby. "I have five minutes to down two drinks before my children call me and I have to sing to them 'Twinkle, Twinkle, Little Star' as the cast of *Sesame Street*. It is your job to fuel me with alcohol before that—are you up to the task, sailor?"

Toby steps right up and puffs his chest. "I'm on it. What can I get you?"

"Anything that will warm me up in seconds."

Toby grabs the ouzo and pours her a hefty shot. "Drink up."

"I'll take one of those as well," one of the women says. She looks familiar, like I've seen her face on a billboard in New York. "I just got in an argument with my longtime lover, and I need something to take the edge off."

The mom leans forward after downing her shot. "The Beast was not excited about Clea's outfit."

"The Beast?" Toby asks.

The mom nods. "Oh yeah, this woman is unlike anything you've ever seen. A fitness goddess, sexy, and protective."

"I'm allowed to show skin," Clea says as she downs a shot from Toby.

Roxane joins them and sets her phone on the bar top. "I'll take one as well, if I'm going to get through the evening with the pink blob back there. You know she's wearing that on purpose."

I glance over at Tessa, who is edging around the bar, one tiny step at a time, her hands clutched in front of her. There she is, bashful, trying to crawl into her own skin again . . . just really adorable. I don't know, there's just something about her that has always intrigued me. She's always marched to the beat of her own drum, and unapologetically, this robe instance being one of many.

"Of course she wore that on purpose," Clea says. "She's not dumb. She knows what we're going to try to do to her tonight, so she attempted to make herself look ridiculous. But we can see right through her."

The mom takes another shot and winces before setting her glass down. "Don't do anything without me. I need to sing to these kids—"

"It's not even nighttime there. Why are you singing to them now?" Clea asks.

"Because their grandmother is incompetent." The mom takes off toward the corner, where I watch her lift her phone up to her face and put on a loving smile.

I glance at Tessa again, who is now at least a foot closer, her eyes trained on me. I take that moment to call out to her. "Can I get you something to drink?"

Her eyes widen as they meet mine. I can see the indecision on her face immediately—she's wavering between sticking her head through the tiles on the floor like some freaky ostrich and fleeing altogether.

"She'll take a Shirley Temple," Roxane says. "She's sworn to no drinking tonight."

I glance over at Tessa. "That so? Can't imagine why. Possibly from the concussion?" I wink at her, and she halts in place, still a few paces from the bar. Our very own pink-robed statue in the middle of the restaurant. I'm not even sure she blinks as she stands there, motionless.

"For heaven's sake," Roxane says as she walks up to her sister and loops her arm through hers before dragging her toward the bar and forcing her to take a stool right in front of me. "You sit here and don't move until we come up with a game plan on how to deal with you."

Then Roxane takes Clea to the other side of the bar, where they wait for the mom to end her call. Still staring into the phone, she's doing some sort of dance with her hands, her facial expressions overly exaggerated as she sings in the corner.

Turning back to Tessa, I clock the way her hands are pressed on the top of the bar, her palms flat against the surface. Her back is ramrod straight, not a slouch in sight, and her teeth are worrying over the corner of her lip as she sits there, speechless.

I stop making her Shirley Temple and tilt my head to the side. "Care to talk about what's going on?"

"I think it would be in my best interest if we don't converse."

"That's fair." I set a glass of ice in front of her. "But if we don't converse, I'm going to be convinced that you think robes are the new big thing in fashion, and I'm all about people expressing themselves, but I'm not sure bath-time wear is the way to go."

"Like I said, I think it's best we don't converse."

"Uh-huh." I pour an ounce of grenadine over the ice in her cup. "You know, *Humiliated*, it's okay to talk to me—I don't think there's much more you could say that would change my opinion on you."

"Your opinion?" she asks, her body betraying her as she leans in. "You have an opinion on me? Oh God, I can only imagine what it is. Is it nutcase? Because that would be tame. What's your opinion? Wait . . . don't answer that, we're not conversing."

"Intriguing and funny," I answer, finishing up with the ginger ale in her glass. "Especially now that I've seen you in your finest dinner dress."

"You don't think I'm funny."

"I don't?" I ask. "Huh, weird, because that's what my brain is telling me. Is my brain telling you something else?"

She leans forward. "I know what you're doing."

"You do?" I ask.

She nods. "Oh yeah, I can see what's happening here."

I top her drink off with three maraschino cherries and pass it to her. "And what exactly is happening here?"

She pulls the drink closer, but she doesn't take a sip, just leaves her hand poised at the base of the glass. "You're trying to be nice to the girl in the robe because she walked in with three women who are way better put together, and after the unfortunate interactions we've had over the last twenty-four hours, you're now certain that I'm the loser of the group—"

"I don't think that at all," I say, cutting her off before she can be more self-deprecating. The loser of the group would be the furthest thing from my mind. The most interesting, the prettiest by far, and still . . . the funniest, at least from what I can tell. "Besides the choice of gown tonight, I find you very intriguing, kind of like a puzzle I can't seem to solve."

"Well, don't bother trying to solve it—there are some missing pieces, and you'll only get frustrated in the long run."

"Uh-huh, and what pieces would be missing?"

She holds her finger up, counting. "Well, dignity for one. Sanity went missing the moment I saw you—uh, I mean the moment I saw ewe, as in sheep."

Ewe, ha.

See, she's funny.

Now, I lean my elbows on the bar and smile at her. "Because you assumed I didn't remember you right away, right?"

She lifts her glass to her lips. "This is why I wanted to refrain from conversing with you."

Chuckling, I lend my hand out. "Myles, it's really nice to meet you, Tessa."

"You, uh, know my name?"

"Of course I know your name." I wiggle my hand at her, indicating I'm looking for a shake, but because she's this awkward, beat-of-her-own-drum kind of girl, she grips my index finger and gives it a quick jolt before returning to her drink. Okay, guess that will have to do.

"You know of me." She nods her head slowly. "From what you know, are you wondering what this getup is all about? Possibly curious to see if I was an escapee from some far-off island, an island that has sequestered me from any human contact for years, and perhaps now that I'm out in society, my captors are looking to retrieve me and bring me back to the island where I can live remotely, among the palms and sand?"

"Yes, that's exactly what I was thinking." I shake my head, not quite believing how charmed I am.

"I knew it," she whispers, looking away.

Even with her self-deprecating attitude, she has this undeniable charisma that draws me toward her. I can't quite put my finger on it—might be a combination of those beautiful blue eyes that do nothing to filter her thoughts, or her stark candidness—but for the first time since I've laid eyes on this girl, she's really talking to me, and I'm going to talk to her for as long as she'll allow it.

Wanting to get down to the reason she's on this side of the bar all by herself, I clear my throat, drawing her gaze again. "So, what's really going on? It's obvious you're trying to make some sort of impression with your getup, and from what your sister said, there's something happening between you all . . ." I pause. "Wait, does this have something to do with what you said earlier? What was it . . . 'vacation wars'?"

"God, you really are a human recorder, aren't you?"

"Huh?"

"Uh, never mind." She picks a cherry from her drink and pops it in her mouth. "But to answer your question . . . yes."

"Interesting—care to entertain me with the backstory?"

"Haven't I entertained you enough?"

"Nah, could always use some more," I say, taking the rag from below the bar and acting like I'm cleaning so it seems like I'm not just chatting up a guest . . . a guest in an unflattering robe.

She heaves a heavy sigh and leans forward on the bar, which causes her robe to part an inch. "Honestly, what do I have to lose at this point?"

"You're already missing dignity and sanity, so not much."

That makes her smile before she stares down at her glass. "Guess so." When her eyes rise to meet mine, now free of the panic I've almost grown accustomed to, I notice just how blue they are. The same color blue of the sea that stretches just beyond the white sandy beaches. A crystal-clear hue you don't see very often unless you're walking along the shoreline. "Since you don't know all of the horrifying details, I'll give you the quick and dirty."

"Sometimes I like it quick and dirty," I answer, and her cheeks redden to nearly the shade of her lipstick, which is now smeared in the corner of her lip.

"Well, um . . . you see, I've been in an overbearing relationship with my friends and sister since high school. We're a dangerous shade of unhealthy when it comes to boundaries, like massively involved in each other's lives to the point that we can't buy underwear unless we get the approval of someone else in our group."

"Naturally, underwear is a very serious matter. There must be at least one source of approval before purchase."

She wets her lips, but I don't get a chuckle from her. Unfortunate. "When we were in high school, we came up with this stupid contract, listing out rules—which I won't get into, because I barely know you and this contract is sacred."

I hold my hands up. "I wouldn't dream of asking."

"But in this contract—which we signed and got notarized; we were efficient high schoolers—there's a rule that if we were single at thirty, we'd forfeit our love life to our friends to make the decisions."

I push my hand through my hair. "Oh man, I'm going to guess you're thirty."

"A ripe thirty. They gave me three extra months before jumping on this contract, but now their mission is to hook me up with someone while we're here."

"Ah, and from the tone in your voice and the droop in your shoulders, my guess is, you don't want that—hence the robe."

She nods. "Yup, exactly."

"And that's why you've declared vacation wars, correct?"

"Well, secretly declared. They don't know I've turned this into something more, but . . ." She glances at her group, their heads bent toward each other in the corner. "From the way they're conspiring over there, I think they're onto me. I'm not one to wear a robe out in public, they know that, and they're calling my bluff—I can feel it."

"Yeah, you should have been more subtle when fending off suitors that they toss in your direction."

"What do you mean?"

I lean in close again, propping my hands up on the bar. "Have you ever heard of Penelope and Odysseus?"

"Have I?" she nearly shouts. Her voice is loud enough that it causes a ripple in all the alcoholic drinks around her. Quietly, she adds, "I sometimes think that I'm Penelope. You know, Helen being the pretty one, getting all of the attention, that's Roxane. And now . . . with all these men they keep throwing at me, it's like the search for Penelope's suitor all over again."

"It is." I smile. "But what you have to remember is just how cunning Penelope was about fending off the rows of men."

"Was I not clever with the robe?" she asks.

I shake my head. "You went all out on day one, so now they know you've declared war. Instead, you should have done something secret that created havoc, like . . . sticking a fish in your bra."

"What?" Now she chuckles. "A fish in my bra? Ew."

I laugh as well. "Yes, gross, but fish are smelly, pungent, not an ideal smell for a date. The fish in the bra would have deterred any sort of plan they had for you tonight—they might have even sent you back to your room, where you could have hung out in your private Jacuzzi, drunk some wine, and stargazed while they were down here, trying to figure out how to hook you up with someone."

Her face falls as she thinks about it. "Huh . . . you know, that actually is really smart."

I tap the side of my head. "Not my first battle of wills."

Now she's truly giving it some thought. "You know, if I did the fish-bra shtick, I would have been immediately asked to leave since Clea has a very sensitive nose. I would have acted like I didn't smell anything. Totally gross, but . . . I would have been sent back to my room, and right about now, instead of wearing a robe in public, I'd be reading a book, my feet against a Jacuzzi jet."

"Precisely."

She smacks the bar top. "Urgh, why didn't I think of that? It seems so simple."

"Probably because you're not really thinking about what you can stick in your bra that smells."

"True." She nods, and her eyes snap to mine. "Wait, you said you've been through a battle of wills before?"

"Oh yeah, like my whole life."

"With whom?"

"My father," I answer casually, though it's not a casual answer at all, stemming from too much history to even sort out at the moment. "He has a strong personality, as well as all these ambitions and plans for his son, and . . . well." I shrug and pick up my rag, dragging it over the bar top. "I have my own plans."

Big plans.

"I see. I'm assuming we're not going to go into the fact that you've been at odds with your father."

"Not so much." I smirk at her.

"That's fair . . ." She drums her fingers on the bar. "But you know things, though."

I chuckle. "I do."

"Does that mean you are willing to offer some advice?"

I glance over at her friends, who are all still huddled together, and then back at Tessa. "Are you asking to be in cahoots with me?"

"Well, you know . . . I'm assuming you can tell just how horrible I am at all of this." She gestures to her robe. "And we seem to keep running into each other, so I just figured you might feel like you want to take a poor, lonely soldier under your wing. Because I'm going to be frank with you: I love these girls, but they operate on another level, and it's about to get brutal. I threw down the gauntlet, and now they're picking it up. They're going to throw it back tenfold, and I need help."

"But I thought you didn't want to converse with me?"

"Only because I say stupid things in front of you, and excuse me for not wanting to continue down that path." I chuckle at just how cute she is, and she straightens her back. "But it seems like saying stupid things in front of you is inevitable, so I should call a spade a spade . . ."

"Uh-huh, and what's the spade?"

"You appear to be of value to me."

I can't help it—I bark out a booming laugh. "Oh, please say more."

She lowers her voice, glancing furtively around the bar. "Trickery clearly comes easy to you, so I need *you* to help me in that department. When I said I was at war, I meant it. Things are about to get brutal, and I need a right-hand man. I'd prefer it not to be you, given our humiliating history, but it seems as though I don't have a choice. So, are you in?"

My lips turn up, the smile on my face inevitable. She truly is the most fascinating human I've ever met . . . ever.

"Let me ask you this . . . What do I get out of this arrangement?"

"Great question, and I'm glad you asked. I'd be concerned if you were doing this out of the kindness of your own heart. No one attaches themselves to an unhinged, concussion-prone robe wearer like myself without some sort of reward. So, there are three things I'm able to offer you in return—you are allowed to pick one."

"I do love options." I rub my hands together. "Lay it on me."

"Your first choice is money. I can pay you by the hour. Although it might get tricky with the exchange rate, but it's something we could sort out." She taps the napkin in front of her and slides it across the bar toward me. "You can write a number on there, and then negotiations can begin."

"I don't want your money."

"Fair, fair. I had a feeling that was going to be the case, which is why I offered it first to get it out of the way." She takes her napkin back and sets her drink on it. "Option number two would be my sewing skills. I've become quite good at darning socks. It's an outdated talent but still very beneficial. After growing tired of constantly having to buy new socks, I learned how to fix them. Now, might my socks be a mismatched blend of fabrics and patches? Perhaps, but they are hole-free, just the way I like it."

"Tempting. Hit me up with the third option before I make a decision."

"A proper response. Sock darning seems like the winner, but I'll give you option three, which is my financial services. I happen to love numbers. They're my favorite thing in the world, well, besides a fresh bowl of *samsades*, but that's beside the point. I'm actually a freelance financial consultant. I work with small businesses around New York City, helping them not only manage their books, but also helping them invest properly. I'm not sure you'll need consulting on anything, but if you want someone to play with your numbers, I'm your girl."

"'Play with my numbers'—you make it sound so dirty."

Her face goes stark white. "Not like that! Not like play with your number nine."

"Number nine?" I ask.

"Yes, you know . . . play with your number nine until it turns into a number six." Fist curled together, her index finger hangs low before she perks it up so it's pointing toward the sky.

Ah . . . a nine . . . to a six. Yup, that makes sense, which of course makes me laugh. "Never heard someone describe it that way."

"That's because you haven't met anyone as fascinated with numbers as me. Stick around, there's a lot more where that came from. Anyway, I know you're probably not in need of a lady who can wow you with her Excel skills, so shall I break out my sewing kit?"

"The sock darning is really appealing, especially since I know for a fact that I put a sock on this morning that has a hole in the heel, but I believe I'm going to take you up on the financial consulting."

Frankly, the fact that she's a financial consultant couldn't be more perfect. If I plan on presenting my baba with the plans I've been developing over the past few years to take Anissa's to the next level, solid numbers will go far toward helping me make my case.

"You want the consulting?" Her nose, which slopes gently up, crinkles at the bridge. "But isn't that boring to you?"

"Beneficial, actually."

"Oh, well, okay." She glances away, a smile playing on her lips.

"What?" I ask her.

"It's just . . . you know, whenever I get to talk numbers, it's always with businesses. It's enjoyable for me, but they're more interested in the bottom line, you know? I've never worked with someone individually. Does that mean you appreciate numbers just as much as me?"

"I think I can get there."

"Well, then, it's a—"

"Are you Tessa?" a man asks as he steps up next to her. He wears a blue linen shirt, the top three buttons undone so his thicket of chest hair pops out the top, long enough to tickle his chin. He twirls his mustache as he wets his lip, giving Tessa a once-over.

When I glance over at her friends, they're all watching the interaction with humor in their eyes. I don't need to know much about Tessa to understand the man standing next to her is by no means her type. Not even close. Tessa was right—this is war.

"Uh, that would be me," Tessa answers with a gulp. There is a nervous tremble in her hand—I know this is where I step in.

"Ma'am, I told you, if you're going to show up at the bar, you're going to have to take a shower first," I say.

Her horrified eyes flash to mine.

"Excuse me?" the mustached man asks.

"I'm so sorry, sir, for the smell," I say. "But I've told this woman several times to please go back to her room to shower—she spent all afternoon swimming with the fish, and well, it's nauseating the other guests."

It takes her a second to wipe off the insult and realize what I'm attempting to do. When she does, she jumps right on board with the lie.

Tessa slowly turns toward the man. "Can you smell me?"

Luckily, the man's mustache is large enough that it must act as a homeopathic filter, deterring any smell from reaching his actual nose. He sniffs uncertainly. "Uh, I . . . I don't think so."

Tessa, playing the part well, lifts her arm. "What about now?"

The man takes a giant step back. "You know, I was told that you were looking for someone to buy you a drink, but I don't know . . ."

"My apologies, sir," I say to him. "Let me get you a drink on the house for your troubles. You know, at Anissa's we are proud of our service and cleanliness. I will be sure to ask security to remove this woman at once."

"Well . . . okay." The poor man's eyes dart around, confused.

"Wait down at the end of the bar and tell Toby I said anything on the house. I'll take care of this robed woman and her ungodly fish scent."

"Tha-thank you," he says and then turns toward the end of the bar.

I meet Tessa's eyes. "Don't smile, don't laugh," I say through clenched teeth so her friends can't tell what's going on. "I'm going to act like I'm telling you to leave so your friends believe something happened. But I need you to pay for your drink first and write your phone number down on the receipt so we can communicate about our agreement. Got it?"

"Understood."

"And ignore what I'm about to say as you hand me your card."

"Got it." She reaches for her card and hands it to me.

I raise my voice, pitching it toward her gaggle of friends. "Ma'am, I appreciate your lecture on the importance of numbers, but like I've said five times already, you can't come in here smelling like fish and expect the other customers to not be offended."

I run her card quickly and hand her the receipt with a pen.

"I didn't think I smelled," Tessa says.

"Sometimes, it's hard to smell ourselves. I'll have the spa send up some complimentary soaps and a loofah."

"Is it that bad?" she asks.

"Yes," I say as she hands me the receipt and I spot her number. She hops off the stool, and with her head hanging low, she takes off.

I glance toward her friends, who are now looking thoroughly confused, and I walk over to the housephone, where I put in a quick call to the kitchen and the spa.

Once I'm done, I spend the next twenty minutes serving guests on my end while Toby takes care of Tessa's friends, who are now hovering around a napkin they've been writing on, most likely coming up with their next plan of attack.

When I get a free moment, I duck away from the bar and plug Tessa's number into my phone so I can shoot her a text. *In cahoots* with Tessa . . . I'm not sure how it unfolded tonight, especially since I've seen this girl year after year, pined after her as a teen, and never once held an actual conversation with her, but I'll take what I can get. If that means telling her she smells like fish to help her escape, then that's what I'm going to do.

Myles: Hey, it's Myles. I would have texted sooner, but we got pretty busy. I sent some bubble bath and candles to your room so you can relax and get that "stench" off you. I also had the kitchen bring up some samsades. Enjoy. As for your friends, they're conspiring. We must be prepared—I believe they'll be coming in hot. Man your stations, the battle has just begun.

CHAPTER SIX

TESSA

"Good morning." I smile up at Clea and Roxane as they take a seat at the table I saved for us at the restaurant.

At Anissa's there are two places to eat—technically four, if you include pool or beachside and room service—but when it comes to restaurants, there are two. There's the Olive Tree, which is open for breakfast, lunch, and dinner. It's more laid back, perhaps family focused, with its orange clay tiles, white walls, and bright-blue painted chairs that rest under white oak tables. With a breakfast buffet that rivals even the best in Las Vegas and a beautiful view of the ocean, it's picturesque and everything you would expect when enjoying a meal in Santorini.

Then there's Calypso, where we were last night. A stark contrast to the Olive Tree, it's open for late lunch, dinner, and drinks far into the night. It's painted in a navy blue so deep it almost looks black. The furniture matches the motif, and the only pops of color are glimmers of gold in the chair legs and the bar. Roxane is in love with Calypso, whereas I like to spend my money at the Olive Tree.

Not surprising.

Plopping themselves in their chairs, they mumble a good morning.

"I take it the ouzo got to you last night?" I ask, feeling fresher than ever.

Not that I smelled like fish last night, but the spa amenities Myles sent up to my room were dreamy. They smelled like heaven, with a heavy dose of lavender, and the samsades . . . let's just say the flaky honey-and-nut pastries had me waking up this morning completely refreshed and ready to take on the day.

I'm sure you might be thinking, Are you sure it's not because the totally hot Greek guy with an impressive bulge asked for your number and is now in cahoots with you? Well, that's a great assumption, and I'm sure it might contain a sliver of truth, but that is *not* why I have an extra pep in my step.

Nope, not at all.

It's the soaps.

The loofah.

The yumminess of phyllo dough perfectly crisped and now resting in the pits of my digestive system. Samsades just keep on giving, even after consumption.

And sure, did I gleefully smile when he texted me last night?

Of course, but that was just from the stunt we were able to pull. You should have seen Roxane's texts. Man oh man was she going off.

You smell like FISH?

I don't remember smelling anything.

Then again, Clea doused herself in Dolce and Gabbana last night, I think she singed my nostrils.

God, if you really smelled like fish, that's so embarrassing.

Maybe it's that new deodorant you're wearing. If you need to use mine, just let me know, I brought two sticks.

It was . . . poetic. She fell right for it.

So of course, to inform my cohort, I sent him a screenshot of Roxane's texts this morning. And in response, he sent a GIF of Mr. Burns from *The Simpsons* twiddling his hands together while "Excellent" read out on the bottom.

And I couldn't agree more. It was excellent.

So . . . there you have it. I'm happy, not because of him and the way his brow quirks up when he finds me amusing, or how he tends to smirk before he actually smiles, or the way my stomach flipped when he laughed. No, it has everything to do with the trickery.

"Lovely morning, don't you think?" I ask when Clea and Roxane both slouch in their seats. "They have the sugar-pearly waffles out for the taking. I know how much you guys love them. Want me to grab you a plate?"

Roxane shakes her head as she lifts her coffee cup. "Just liquid. Give me my nectar."

Smiling joyfully, I fill her cup up, as well as Clea's, just as Lois approaches.

"Oh, Moon, that's beautiful. Look at that, you gave Mommy five arms." She's on FaceTime once again. That's how it always is with Lois. She can't wait to get away from her kids, but the minute she is, she's checking on them every two seconds. I guess mom brain never stops, even on vacation. "And Bear, you painted Mommy's teeth green. That's . . . that's not unpleasant at all."

Through the speaker, Bear's little voice says, "It's because they're so yellow, they're green." He laughs, and I swear I can feel Lois's face starting to split in half. Lucky for Lois's mom, the kids have been waking up at three in the morning because they can't wait to FaceTime. Lois has already complained about having to get her kids back on a schedule when she returns. She makes motherhood seem so . . . pleasurable.

"They were yellow that one time because Grandma thought it would be necessary to stick a whole bottle of yellow dye in one cupcake. But that's neither here nor there. I'm at breakfast now, so I should probably—"

FaceTime ends before Lois can finish talking. Lately, it's a race to see who can press the red button first to finish the call. Seems as though Bear won.

"Little shits," Lois mumbles as she tosses her phone on the table. "God, I love them, and I hate them. It's a toxic relationship."

"You paint such a beautiful picture of motherhood," Clea says as she holds her cup of coffee close to her chest, acting like it's a lifeline.

"It's not for the faint at heart, that's for sure. Did you know Moon convinced my mom that she didn't have to go to bed at eight because it gave her wrinkles? She's freaking five, and my mom is sitting there thinking, 'Oh, dear heavens, a five-year-old can't have wrinkles, let her stay up until nine.' Does becoming a grandparent make you lose all sense of reality?"

"It's why I plan on never having children," Clea says. "There's no room in my household for a master manipulator."

Roxane lets out a loud yawn and then sits a little taller. "Are we headed to the beach today?"

"I reserved us four loungers," I say in a cheery voice. "We're expected to arrive at eleven."

"Why so early?" Roxane asks.

"Uh, excuse me, but when I was hurting yesterday from a hangover, you showed no remorse."

"That's different," Roxane says.

"How?" I respond while cutting my fork into one of the sausage links on my plate.

"Because I'm the one who's hurting now, not you." She sips her coffee. "Anyway, we need to talk about something."

"What's that?" I ask her.

"What were you doing yesterday that made you smell like fish?" Clea asks.

"And how come you weren't humiliated that the Bulge was calling you smelly?" Roxane asks.

"First of all, he has a name, and it's Myles—he told me when I ran into him in the hallway yesterday, showed him my crotch, and then proceeded to call his hands luxurious."

"Nooo," Roxane says, sounding more alive now. "You called his hands and lips luxurious? What's wrong with you?"

"Can't be sure," I answer, "but yes, I've declared both lips and hands luxurious, so why wasn't I humiliated to be smelling like a fish around him?" Great question, why wasn't I? God, I should have prepared myself better. Here I was, walking on cloud nine when I forgot I had to face my sister and friends today with questions. Hmm . . . think. Something believable . . . "Because I'm already at rock bottom in his eyes. Just tack it onto the endless embarrassment. Not to mention, I truly thought I offended him with my stank."

"Please." Clea holds up her hand, her nose turning toward the sky in disgust. "Don't ever claim to have 'stank.' It's positively repulsive. We need to add that to the contract, an addendum. None of us have stank." She then points her finger at me. "And do we need to go over hygiene? Do you want me to show you how to properly scrub?"

"No," I answer. "I know how to scrub, I, uh . . . actually, when I went to the bathroom before we walked into Calypso, I assisted someone from the kitchen staff who was carrying in some fish, so the fish juice must have sloshed on me." Oooh, see, that's the clever kind of lying Roxane is able to get away with. Maybe she's rubbing off on me.

"Can we also not mutter the words 'fish juice'?" Clea presses her hand to her stomach. "It doesn't settle well with me."

"Either way, it has nothing to do with my hygiene and everything to do with my good-natured soul, helping someone out."

"Well, you ruined our first pick for you with your penchant for helping people," Lois grumbles. "Carlisle seemed like the perfect fit."

I give her a "get real" look. "How on earth did he seem like my type?"

"You like chest hair." Lois shrugs and picks up a piece of croissant off my plate.

"No, I don't. Well, I mean, I don't mind it. I can go either way, but not when the man has a bird's nest under his chin. Did you see the spinach that was caught up in it? There was actual spinach in his chest hair, green spinach."

"Nothing wrong with saving a snack for later," Clea says.

Roxane claps her hand over her mouth and shakes her head. "Please, let's move past the spinach snack in the chest hair."

I shouldn't garner this much joy from being so deceptive to the people who matter the most to me, but . . . I'd be lying if I said it didn't feel good. I'm always considered the naive one in the group, the shy one, the one who has her nose stuck in a book and never does anything out of her comfort zone. Well, after just one night talking to the Bulge, look at me now!

That's what hydration and a good night's sleep can do for you—you can be on top of your game. "I need to make an announcement."

"Here we go." Lois rolls her eyes.

"Are you going to require us to take notes like you usually do?" Clea asks.

"No," I answer. It's time to go in for the kill. "But I do want to apologize for last night—clearly, I was trying to come in hot with a look that I thought would deter any man you threw at me."

"Yeah, you made that obvious with your choice of lipstick. Frankly, you looked like a deranged clown," Clea says with a shiver. "I had nightmares last night."

"Descriptions not necessary. I think we all are aware of what I looked like last night."

"You made a lasting impression," Clea says while Roxane slouches in her seat, a napkin over her head. "I heard two women in the bathroom at Calypso talking about you. They said you scared some people away from the bar."

I didn't look that bad, did I? Sheesh.

"Like Angelica's doll from *Rugrats*," Clea says.

"Yes!" Lois says. "God, I couldn't think of it, but you're right, that's exactly who she looked like."

"Either way," I interrupt them, "I'm sorry. I think I acted out from the shock of it all. Of the contract rules and whatnot, but I understand I held you all to the rules, so it only makes sense that you would do the same to me." I set my napkin down on my plate. "So, whatever you decide to do from here on out, I will go along with."

The table falls silent. Roxane slowly drags her napkin over her face so one of her eyes is glaring out at me. Clea sets down her coffee, wearing an expression of disbelief, and Lois scratches the side of her head, almost as if she's trying to solve a math problem.

Hold it together, Tessa. Do not let them know that you're continuing last night's trickery. You see, if they believe I'll be going along with their insane plan, when I do something like, let's say, create a smelly fish bra, they'll just think I'm an incompetent dater. They won't realize I'm secretly taking their mission down, one day at a time.

Myles was so right: if I do this in a way that isn't obvious, I can get exactly what I want . . . freedom from this contract.

"I don't understand," Roxane says. "You don't say things like that. You don't just give in. What . . . what's the catch?"

"There is no catch," I say. "Maybe it is time I settle down, and what better people to make that happen than my sister and best friends."

More silence.

And then Clea says, "I don't trust what she's saying."

"Me neither," Lois agrees. "She's up to something. This is exactly how Moon acts when she's attempting to manipulate me."

"And out of the three of us," Clea says, motioning to me, Roxane, and herself, "Tessa is the one who spends the most time near Moon, which means she's been learning from the master."

"Stop, I'm not manipulating anything. I just . . . I felt sad that I couldn't hang with you guys last night, and it's true, this is our last week together before all the craziness starts. We should really spend it together, and if you want to do it by trying to find me the love of my life, then so be it."

"I still don't trust her." Lois eyes me suspiciously.

"Neither do I," Clea says.

"Well, I'll just prove it to you." I stand from the table. "I need to go run some errands before we meet up at the beach. I'll see you three down there." And before they can say another word, I pick up my phone and key card and head out of the restaurant, where I turn the corner and lean against the wall.

I shoot a quick text to Myles.

Tessa: Just got done with breakfast, do you have time to meet up?

Luckily, he texts me right away.

Myles: Yup, been waiting for you. Head toward the main lobby, take a right at the pillars, there is a secret lookout tucked in the corner that no one really knows about. I'll wait outside it so you can find me.

Tessa: Be right there.

***

Myles is standing next to a white wall just outside the lobby. He's not wearing his typical uniform, but instead he's in a pair of light-blue shorts and a white T-shirt. Sporting boat shoes and floppy, messy hair, he looks like he's enjoying some time off from the normal hustle and bustle of his job.

"Morning," he says, smiling brightly, hands in his pockets. *Sigh* He's so handsome, I can't believe I'm actually talking to him.

"Morning," I say, suddenly aware of my white, ankle-length dress flowing in the breeze.

Smirking, he says, "Nice dress, although I miss the robe."

"I think you might be the only one. I was chastised at breakfast this morning about last night's getup."

"After you left, I overheard quite a few conversations about you and your choice of outfit."

"I have massive regrets now. That's why I'm here, so I don't have to wear a robe to fend off the advances of unwanted men."

"I have some great ideas." He gestures toward the alcove. "Shall we?"

I maneuver past the pillar and into a private nook containing two love seats placed across from each other. Made from teakwood, they're lined with plush blue cushions, the same blue as the panoramic ocean in front of us. Directly above, instead of the blistering sun, a gnarled tree twists, providing shade, while votive candles hang from its limbs. The whole scene must be breathtaking at night.

"How does no one know about this little place?"

"Really only employees do, so you need to keep it on the down-low."

"Your secret spot is safe with me."

He flashes me a grateful smile as we take a seat beside each other. "So did you apologize to them?"

"Yup, and of course they didn't buy it, but I told you that was going to happen. That tactic was way out of my personality range, so they were skeptical."

"That's okay—you made the apology, and that's really all that matters. And you're headed down to the beach today?" I nod. "Good. I reserved you the loungers right in front of the beach volleyball game, which is full of a bunch of gym bros."

"Really?" I ask. "It's going to be easy pickings for them."

He shakes his head. "No, Tessa, it's going to be easy pickings for *you*."

"Huh?"

He smirks. "Let me explain."

***

Armed with an arsenal of trickery thanks to Myles, I drape my cover-up over the back of my lounger and adjust the straps to my one-piece bathing suit. It seems to have shrunk since the last time I wore it—I'm showing off a large amount of cleavage. But I'll embrace it this time—I don't have that many bathing suits, and I might get some male attention, which would only play into my plans.

There isn't a cloud in the sky, so the umbrellas shadowing our loungers are much needed from the blistering sun today. Only the lightest of breezes kicks up off the Aegean Sea, but it's just enough to offer respite from the sun. The beach is one of very few on the rocky, craggy island, tucked into a cove and offering only twenty white-cushioned loungers to resort guests. Off to the right is a beach volleyball court, which is surprisingly popular given people come here to relax, not engage in sand sports. And just to the left is the beach hut, a white plaster building with a large "takeout" window where all your beach needs are kept, like towels, snorkels, drinks, and sunscreen. This is the same hut where I've watched Myles work for countless summers.

"Look who came prepared," Clea says, taking in my bathing suit while she walks up to her lounger. "Tessa, look at that suit. It's so hot."

I glance down and then back up at her. "It's nothing special."

"It's not a cover-up, and that's new for you." She smooths her hand over my waist. "You really should wear more formfitting clothes. You look good, girl."

"Oh, well, thank you," I respond, not quite sure how to take the compliment. Out of all my friends, I dress the most conservatively, but conservative is a far stretch. I just tend to lean toward more comfortable clothes—like loose-fitting T-shirts and comfortable joggers.

Roxane shifts on her lounger and looks up at me. "That suit really does look great on you."

Huh . . . I don't normally receive compliments from Roxane. Maybe that apology really did work this morning.

"It's the perfect bathing suit to help us attract some men over here," Roxane adds, letting me know her intentions behind the compliment. "Now, question is, who do we want to pick out first?"

"Oooh, I saw this guy who was grabbing towels over by the pool— he was wearing lime-green swim trunks and had a thick beard," Lois says. "I could totally see you loving a beard."

Ehhh, not really. I like scruff.

"And I saw someone carrying four beers in one hand," Clea says. "A guy with a shirt that said 'Check Out My Chest Hair.' He looked like a winner."

"He sounds like a winner," Roxane says. "The shirt is a great conversational piece for Tessa since she struggles with small talk."

Doesn't everybody?

"I say we go with beer-chest-hair man, and then neon shorts. I think we have more potential with someone who's been drinking heavily," Lois says.

"Wow, thanks," I say as I hold my arms.

"Hello, ladies." I hear Myles's voice from behind. "Can I offer you a drink, something to eat?" He told me he was working the beach today, which he wasn't happy about—he said it's the worst job at the resort, but because he's training a few people, he's stuck here. He did make sure to put us in these particular loungers, so there's a plus side for me.

I turn around and catch his eyes glancing down my body and then back up. He offers a very subtle wink, but I catch it, just a signal between us that he approves. During our conversation, he said I needed to show up today ready to mingle. That I needed to look overeager, which meant not showing up in a robe and partially smeared lipstick.

After all the rumors about me being the deranged resident who wandered into the bar, I'm ready to make a better impression. I showed up with my hair in two French braids, some tinted sunscreen, and a light coating of mascara, which you can't even see behind my sunglasses, but whatever, I know it's there.

I'm glad he approves—I feel lighter, brighter beneath his gaze.

"I think some ice water with lemon and lime would be great for all of us, right, ladies?"

Clea and Roxane both agree, while Lois gives us a thumbs-up from where she's sitting on the edge of the lounger, recording a video for Bear about the importance of washing his hands after going to the bathroom. She's been stocking up on videos that her mom shows the kids throughout the day.

"Anything to eat?" Myles asks.

"How about a simple fruit-and-cheese plate?" I ask.

"Right away, Miss Doukas." He takes off toward the kitchen, walking unsteadily through the sand, which he told me was the reason he hates beach duty so much.

"Interesting how you can talk to him normally without stuttering," Roxane says.

"What do you mean?" I ask, realizing she's right. Ever since we made our agreement, I've been more relaxed around him.

"I'm just saying, you went from bumbling fool to being able to casually order food and drinks? Seems suspicious."

Oh crap.

Think of a reply, something good.

"Well, the sweat on my palms tells a different story, want to feel it?" I hold out my hand, which she quickly swats away.

"Ew, I don't want your sweaty palm near me."

That did the trick.

Taking a seat on the lounger, I get comfortable and prepare for my plan of attack.

I clear my throat. "Wow, looks like there might be some entertainment for us here."

"What kind of entertainment?" Clea asks just as a dozen men walk over to the volleyball net, all shirtless, all fine specimens. Clea lowers her sunglasses. "Well, would you look at that. If I were into men and muscles, I'd think there was a smorgasbord right in front of me, ripe for the picking. Lois, look at all the shirtless men."

"Ugh, I have to redo that video—you can't say 'shirtless men,'" Lois complains.

"You've recorded twelve videos this morning. I think the kids will survive, so sit back and enjoy the view."

"I have a nice view back at home," she says. "Ed is plenty of man for me." Which is true; Ed is on another level. One of those guys who goes to the gym every day, he can do one hundred push-ups in one sitting, and he's generous enough to wipe down the equipment when he's done. A real catch.

"Doesn't mean you can't look. I have the Beast, and I'm still checking out the pecs on some of these men."

The Beast and Ed work out together. I failed to mention that. Gym partners, they are quite the pair.

"Well, I'm sure eating up the view," I say, drawing the three pairs of eyes next to me. "Just look at those, uh, those nipples. Wow, makes your mouth water, doesn't it?" What the hell am I saying? Doesn't matter, I'm still going with it. "And the, uh . . . the happy trails. Guide me to the promised land, am I right, ladies? Nothing beats a line of hair that basically whispers *come hither* while you're nuzzling their belly."

"Nuzzling bellies?" Clea asks. "What the hell are you doing behind closed doors?"

"Uh, you know." I clear my throat. "Just casual . . . sentimental things."

"Nuzzling a belly is sentimental?" Lois asks now, sitting up so she can see me over Clea and Roxane, who both have confused looks on their faces.

"Yes," I answer, absolutely hating myself. This is why I don't lie—I'm awful at it and wind up saying something that really shouldn't be said at all. Like nuzzling bellies. "You can really tell the essence of a man by nuzzling his belly. Doesn't work on women, though, sorry, Clea."

"Don't apologize, nuzzling stomachs really isn't my brand."

"It shouldn't be anyone's," Roxane says.

"Well, you guys are missing out, because it's one of the best things you can do to a man. They love it. It's . . . uh, it's better than touching their private area."

I realize that was a mistake the minute it leaves my mouth. As a society, I think we can all agree that there is nothing more pleasing to a man than having his private parts touched by a lover. That takes the cake, every time. Private parts play is where it's at, mainly the penis. Balls are second. But the penis wins, hands down, no questions asked.

But I'm running with the belly because I'm already committed.

"When was the last time you had sex?" Clea asks me. "Because even I know the penis is better than the belly, and I haven't had sex with a man in several years."

"That's not relevant." I wave my hand at her just as Myles walks up, tray of drinks and food in hand.

His presence doesn't deter my friends, though.

"So, you're saying that I can make a man more turned on by nuzzling his stomach than touching his penis?" Roxane asks.

Why on earth did Myles have to choose this moment to show up? He has the worst timing I've ever seen.

"Um, well, depends on the man," I say quietly.

Myles sets the tray down on the end table near my lounger, and I catch a glimmer of mischief in his dark eyes. "Talking about belly nuzzling? I had a girl do that to me once, and I've never been more turned on in my life." He offers Lois a drink, the confused look on her face making me almost burst out in laughter.

"Hold on," Clea says, reaching her hand out, which Myles uses as a reason to give her a glass. "You're telling me you've done this face-nuzzling stuff?"

"Of course. Haven't you?" he asks, as if she's the one who's weird.

"Well, no, I'm with a woman."

"Ahh." He nods. "That makes sense."

Roxane sits taller. "Well, I haven't done it."

"Missing out," Myles says once he's done handing out drinks. He sets the fruit and cheese in a more centrally located position and then sticks the empty tray under his arm and holds his hands in front of him. "Anything else I can get you ladies?"

They all shake their heads, looking like their minds have exploded, and all I can think about is how I can't wait to talk to Myles about this.

When he takes off, I see Roxane on her phone, texting away.

"Are you asking Philip?" I ask her.

"Yes, I want to know if any other woman has nuzzled his stomach."

I smile to myself. This wasn't the plan, to throw them off with some obscure sexual act, but to my surprise, it's working. My awkward lie has actually distracted them from trying to hook me up with a random man.

Lois is on her phone as well. "I don't think I've ever nuzzled Ed, but now that I think about it, there was this one time I kissed him down his stomach and he was really hard when I reached his penis. Do you think . . . do you think that was a clue that I should have nuzzled?"

"Totally," I say, making everything up on the fly and actually enjoying it. "But of course, avoid the belly button, that's a no-fly zone. Too sensitive. Might . . . deflate them, if you know what I mean."

"Really?" Lois asks. "Wow, you learn something new every day."

"Oh my God," Roxane says as she looks up at us. "Philip said he had a girl kiss around his stomach once and he got really turned on." She folds her arms and scowls. "I can't believe it."

"Well, maybe it's something you do when he gets here," I suggest, using every ounce of self-control not to burst out in laughter at the frown on my sister's face.

"Oh, you can bet your abundance of cleavage that I plan on doing just that." She settles into her lounger, her lips turned down, her mood completely shifted.

And that, my friends, is how it's done.

Just like Myles said, deflect and redirect.

I was going to get them talking about something from the old memory bank, something to distract them, but this worked even better.

Smiling to myself, I pick up my phone and text him.

Tessa: Oh my God, you totally saved me back there. Now they really think the nuzzling thing is real, Roxane even got a weird confirmation from her man that he liked being kissed there.

He texts back immediately.

Myles: Do I even want to know why you were talking about that?

Tessa: You don't, just another rambling moment for me, you know . . . like "I used to paint my nail-less big toe" moment.

Myles: Say no more. Have they backed off?

Tessa: Totally. They're all texting about it. I think we're safe for now.

Myles: Good. And you can still meet me around three today?

Tessa: Our secret hiding spot?

Myles: Yup.

Tessa: Perfect. See you there.

I set my phone down, pick up a piece of pineapple, and chomp down on it. Here I thought vacation wasn't going to be that much fun, but it seems as though I'm the one having the most fun out of the four of us.

Now I just need to think of other ways to keep them off my back.

CHAPTER SEVEN
MYLES

"Dude, wait up, where are you going?" Toby calls out as he jogs up to me in the main lobby.

"Uh, just have a meeting I need to get to," I say.

"What kind of meeting?"

Not wanting to say it too loud in case any unwanted ears are in the vicinity, I pull him off to the side, behind a jungle of bushes we maintain as part of our indoor gardens. Anissa's doesn't really believe in doors. Back when my mom was here, she'd insist we needed to be just like Hawaiian resorts and bring the island inside.

When I think the coast is clear, I say, "So you know how I told you about those plans I have for Anissa's? The ones where you'd help me . . . expand?"

"Yeah."

"I found someone who can help me figure out the numbers of it all and come up with a report I can present to my baba."

"Oh shit, really? Who?"

"Uh, Tessa Doukas?" I answer, gripping the back of my neck.

"As in the girl who showed up in a robe to the bar last night, the same girl everyone says smells like trout?" he sarcastically asks.

"There was no specific fish mentioned, but yes, that's her. And she didn't smell like fish—I just made that up to get her out of a tight situation."

"And the same girl that you helped years ago as well, when some man was trying to talk to her at the bar?"

"Yes," I say, exasperated. That was . . . well, that was a bold move on my end. I told myself I was helping her out, but hell, the moment I saw her check in that summer, I was a fucking goner. She was . . . she was devastatingly beautiful, and when I saw some guy trying to invade her space, I lost it and acted in a way I probably shouldn't have. But that kiss to her cheek—for a millisecond, it actually felt like she was mine, crazy as that sounds.

"And isn't Tessa the same girl you'd leer at whenever she lounged by the pool reading a book?"

"Leer seems to be a strong word." But also, accurate.

I would leer.

"I remember it as leering. Also, sweating, drooling . . . remember the time you drooled while eating a sandwich when she walked by once?" Yup. I remember. I remember everything. A whirlwind of memories blows through me.

Her on the beach with a magnifying glass, checking out different grains of sand.

Her traipsing through the hotel lobby with a plateful of baklava that she'd baked herself during a workshop with the chef.

Her getting her flip-flop stuck in the elevator doors because she was trying to stop them from shutting so Roxane could hop in.

Every summer, a new core memory formed, and it always involved Tessa.

Always.

"Yes, I remember, and we don't need to go into the details," I say as he smirks, knowing exactly what he's doing—pulling my leg. "I remember everything about Tessa Doukas. Let's leave it at that."

85

"I would be shocked if you did forget. You've always thought she was really freaking cute. You crushed on her every summer."

"Yeah, I know. And now . . . hell." I pull on the back of my neck. "Now she looks different." More beautiful than before.

"It's called growing up. It's been seven years since you've seen her—a lot can happen."

A lot did happen. Her face thinned out. Her hair is no longer frizzy but rather sleek and silky looking. And, well, she filled out in places—we'll just leave it at that.

"Yeah, a lot can happen." I shift uncomfortably. "But you know, not that her appearance changes anything."

"Oh, it changes something." Toby smirks.

"What is that supposed to mean?"

"It means that you and I both know you've crushed on this girl every summer, and she just happens to be helping you now? Seems to me like something's going to happen." Toby wiggles his brows, and I roll my eyes in response.

"Nothing is going to happen. We have an arrangement."

"What kind of arrangement?"

"Well, she's in the midst of vacation wars with her sister and friends—long story—but I'm helping her win the battle of wills, and in return, she's helping me with the finance stuff."

"Uh-huh, and who offered to help who first?"

"I did, but not because of some secret crush or anything." At least that's what I'm telling myself. "It's not like that, dude. She looked sad, I felt bad, and I thought I'd offer my help. She was the one who offered to help in return." I don't mention the three choices, because I'm second-guessing the whole sock thing—my big toe is flirting with a hole at the moment.

"Uh-huh, well . . . we'll see. Crushes like the one you had don't just die—they live within you. Spending this much time with her is just going to awaken it."

It's funny how delusional Toby is. Sure, is spending time with Tessa a positive thing? Of course. She's gorgeous, and funny, and interesting, which adds a spark to my life, but that doesn't mean anything other than just that . . . a spark.

"Okay," I deadpan.

When I start to walk away, he calls out, "Still on for pool time down at Nu Nu's?"

"Yup. See you then," I say before taking off toward the "secret hiding spot"—Tessa's words, not mine.

Tessa freaking Doukas. When I saw her in the sand behind the boat the first night she was here, I felt this connection to her, like we were kindred spirits. But the truth burns like the Santorini sun—I saw her every single summer growing up. Lusted after her. Not her sister, who was always well put together, but Tessa. Because Tessa was the one who enjoyed looking at spiders. She was the one who always tried to feed the stray cats on the property. She was the one who brought a kite with her every summer and flew it while the other girls her age would try to impress boys. She was always different, always unique.

Always just . . . Tessa.

When I turn the corner into the secret nook, Tessa is already sitting there, but instead of staring at her phone or tapping her toe because I'm a touch late, she's folding a spare napkin from her drink into an origami swan.

"Hey," I say. "That's pretty neat."

She holds it up just as she finishes. "I taught myself through YouTube one summer while I was here. I had nothing better to do. Our hotel room was filled with napkin swans. I'm pretty impressed that I remembered how to do it."

I take a seat on the same couch as her but move toward the opposite side, giving her space. "Do you only know how to fold swans?"

"Yup, I couldn't bother learning anything else. I like to master one thing and then move on to the next."

"What have you mastered lately?"

"I'm in the midst of learning how to make the perfect sourdough starter. I'll be honest, I haven't been successful so far, but I'm getting there."

"I could show you."

"Really?" she asks.

Laughing, I shake my head. "No. I haven't baked a day in my life."

"Oh." Her brows draw down as she chuckles. "For a moment there, I truly thought you were a jack-of-all-trades."

"Not quite, although I know how to do a lot of repairs around the resort. Learned a lot about plumbing, and spackle, and painting, all the handyman things you can think of. My baba, or dad, thought it was vital I learned how to do our own repairs, never rely on someone else. It was smart, because now if something needs to be fixed, I can quickly get it done instead of calling someone."

"Wait . . . your dad? As in . . ."

"As in Hermes Cirillo, the owner of Anissa's Palace."

"Hold on." She blinks a few times. "You're the owner's son?"

"Correct."

"But . . . but you don't seem like the owner's son."

I chuckle. "You can just say it. You wouldn't expect the owner's son to be doing the kind of jobs I do, right?"

"Well, not to support nepotism, but you were just complaining about having to be on beach duty—I'd assume you wouldn't have to do something you didn't want to do."

"Yeah, it's complicated."

"Complicated how?" she asks. Her tone is curious, concerned.

"Long story."

She crosses one leg over the other and turns toward me. "Well, I have time. Roxane and the girls are all getting massages, and you're off work. Go ahead. Lay out the complications. Maybe understanding your backstory will help me get you on track to your financial goals."

I don't normally talk to anyone about this—only Toby, actually—but she might have a point. If she knows where my financial aspirations stem from, she might be more likely to assist me.

"Well, my parents are divorced. They've been divorced for a while. My mom is from Manhattan—"

"Really?" Tessa asks. "Me too. Where about?"

"Upper West Side, around Eighty-First Street."

"Seriously? Holy crap, I live around Ninetieth and Columbus. Same neighborhood."

"That's odd. You live there now?" She nods. "I just moved back here from living with my mom for a while. Never ran into you."

"That's so crazy. Sorry, I interrupted you, but small world."

"Yeah," I say, smoothing my hand on my jaw. "Very small world." Not sure what I would have done if I ran into her in New York. Probably gawked. Stumbled. Asked her out on a date, because that . . . that would have been fate. "Well, they got divorced, and when my mom moved back to the States, I'd split time, going back and forth. I was homeschooled, so I didn't have to worry about missing any school, but I would always spend the summers here, in Greece, because Baba needed the help."

"That's why I always saw you here."

I nod. "Yeah, and I always saw you."

She shakes her head. "You didn't remember me."

"Yes, I did," I answer honestly. "You're a hard one not to remember, Tessa."

"Oh yeah . . ." She smirks. "Prove it."

Easy.

I just need to hold back so I don't look too insane recounting all the times I've watched her over the years.

"Well, when you were younger, you'd fly a kite out on the beach, every summer. Sometimes it was a frog kite, other times it was a regular diamond kite, but you were always out there, doing your own thing.

And I remember a time I saw you scouring the beach with a magnifying glass. I wasn't sure what you were looking for, but you were looking hard. And another summer you brought a stack of books with you. You sat by the pool with the stack, and I watched you read a different book every thirty minutes. I thought it was so freaking odd."

"It's called a book mash-up." Her cheeks are bright red, as though I caught her doing something shameful. "Song mash-ups were huge, so I thought it would be interesting to try it with books. I picked three that were similar in style and story line, and I took turns reading each one every thirty minutes."

"What was it like?"

"Extremely confusing." We both laugh. "But then, I realized I should do it with a series." She taps her head. "So, I took a fantasy series and started reading the three books in the thirty-minute increments, and guess what?"

"What?" I ask, enjoying the way she gets animated when something truly brings her joy.

"It was like I was reading an entire book in past, present, and future. It was so freaking awesome, seeing how it all came together. Honestly one of the best reading experiences I've ever had."

"Interesting. Have you done it again?"

She shakes her head. "No, I feel like I'd be chasing a high I'll never find again. The series I picked was perfect. It really set the pace for the correct timeline jumping. Everything flowed, it made sense. I just don't think I could ever find a series that worked like that again. And I don't want to try and ruin the original experience."

"That makes complete sense. Anyway—" I let out a sigh. "I remember you—you look so different now."

"It was the robe that threw you off, wasn't it?"

"Something like that," I admit.

And then silence falls between us as our eyes connect.

It's odd because it feels like there is so much history between us, and yet we've barely spoken to each other. How can that be?

And why are we finally talking to each other now?

Whatever reason, I'm glad.

"But back to backstory," I say.

"Yes, backstory. Tell me everything."

"Well, when I was around twenty-two, I heard about this hospitality program in New York City, the best in the world. I really wanted to help my baba around the resort, but I also wanted to help him improve the business, so I thought if I applied to this program, I might get the opportunity to learn and really be an asset. I honestly didn't think I would get in, but when I did, I knew I had to take the opportunity. When I told my baba, he was not thrilled. He claimed I was abandoning him to be with my mom. He couldn't understand the idea that I could possibly learn about the business from someone other than him."

"That Greek pride, it can be damaging sometimes," Tessa says. "My dad holds his in a death grip."

"Exactly. They clutch onto it, never letting go. So, it didn't help that I was in New York City for seven years."

"Wait, seven years?" she asks, her brow pinched together.

"Yes."

"Is that . . . is that why I didn't see you again, after, you know, you rescued me at the bar? You were in New York?"

"Yes, I left after that summer."

"Oh my God, I'm such an idiot." Her hand falls to her forehead in shame.

"What do you mean?" I ask.

"Nothing. It's stupid. Back to the story—"

"No, tell me why you think you're an idiot."

She shakes her head and leans her shoulder into the back of the couch. "God, this is so humiliating, but you know, I think we've already crossed that line." She takes a deep breath. "After I called your lips luxurious—"

"Oh hell, I remember that." I let out a low laugh. I'd never been praised like that before, and I fucking liked it.

"Oh lovely, so glad you remember," she says, her voice full of sarcasm.

"It was a great compliment."

"Glad you see it that way—I, on the other hand, turned a shade of green after I said it."

"Hmm." I tap my chin. "I don't recall you turning green, but I do remember the compliment."

"Either way"—she waves me off—"I thought that I freaked you out and that's why you never returned to Anissa's the summers following."

"Keeping track of me?"

Her cheeks flush. "No, I mean . . . not really, no. I wasn't looking for you or anything, just, you know, was, uh . . . was trying to say thank you, and then I never saw you and thought, well, I must have scared him off." I don't buy it, but I let her off the hook. "After the fourth summer of not seeing you, I decided that I in fact did startle you with my compliment, so much that you didn't think you could come back here. Little did I know you were the owner's son and that you were gone for a hospitality program."

"Uh-huh. You know, you babble when you're embarrassed."

"I'm well aware of my defense mechanisms. Let's move on."

I chuckle. "Well, once the program and my internship were up, I wanted to come back here so I could help my dad with everything I learned. Let's just say it was a less-than-stellar welcome. I had to schedule an appointment to actually talk to him."

"Oh, that's sad. But you were able to speak with him?"

"Yes, but he was defensive. He doesn't believe I left for the right reasons, and it doesn't help that he's an old man set in his ways and full of regrets. He's not open to anything new, but I thought if I got you to help me, we could put together a financial plan that could help him see the benefit of my ideas."

"And what are your ideas?"

"I want to open another resort. It wouldn't be beachside, but it would be in the heart of Oia, cliffside, with a private pool. There's a property that's up for renovations, and with the right amount put into it, it could be a destination hot spot."

Her face brightens. "I love Oia. Crowded, and probably the most touristy part of Greece because of how iconic the landscape is—those whitewashed buildings and blue-domed roofs crowded on a cliffside—but oh man, the sunsets are so gorgeous."

"Nothing is better than a Santorini sunset."

"Could not agree more," she says. "Okay, so . . . you want to impress him, you want to get him to expand."

"Yes."

She nods. "Can I offer you some advice? And please tell me if I'm overstepping."

"I'm all ears," I say as I rest my arm on the back of the couch, my body turned completely toward her now.

"Well, I think if we work out the numbers and everything seems right, you could impress him with a new idea that will expand his legacy."

"That's what I think—"

"Hold on." She brushes a stray piece of hair behind her ear. "But it might be a waste of your time if he's not receptive toward you right now. Which means you need to build back that relationship first, and then when he trusts you again, that's when you can approach him with the idea."

"But I didn't do anything wrong."

"Well, sure, you were trying to help the resort, but from what you've said, he definitely doesn't see it that way. You ran away in his eyes, and he's not past that yet."

I pause, her words clicking in my head. He does believe I ran away, ran away to my mom, and thanks to his stubborn pride, he can't see it any other way. If I brought him a new idea that stemmed from when I "ran away," there is no way he'd be receptive. He'd just stamp it with his disapproval before I could get a sentence out.

I need to build back my relationship with him first.

Groaning, I drag my hand over my face. "I think you're right."

"I know I am. My dad is the same. Heavy on trust, stubborn as a mule, but full of love. Not on purpose or because you wanted to, but in his eyes, you broke that trust, and as you know, trust is big in Greek families, especially close ones, so you need to earn that back."

"Well, how do I go about earning his trust?"

"Great question, glad you're receptive." She smiles proudly.

"Didn't get the stubborn pride from my baba."

"Good thing. As for earning your baba's trust back? You need to think about what's important to him. The resort and family, right? So, working hard like you do already will help, and then making the attempt to spend time with him."

"Easier said than done, given that he makes me schedule time with his assistant in order to talk to him . . . but I'll see him at family dinner on Sunday."

"What about tonight?"

"What about it?" I ask.

"You're clearly off work. Maybe ask him to do something."

That won't be awkward at all. We've barely spoken to each other, and I'm just going to ask him to hang out? He most likely is going to say no, and then what do I do with that kind of response?

"I don't know. I'm supposed to play pool with Toby tonight."

"That's perfect," Tessa says. "You can invite him to go along."

I press my hand down on my thigh and shift. "Pool really isn't his type of activity."

"Maybe not, but at least you're giving him the opportunity to say no. And what's the worst that can happen?" She shrugs. "He doesn't go? At least give him the chance. Then you can know where he truly is, and we can assess from there."

"Why does it feel like you're doing more for me now than I am for you?"

She dismisses me with a hand wave. "I'm sure it'll all even out in the long run. Just ask him."

"Okay, I'll text. That will be the easiest way to get in touch." Silence falls between us as she looks at me expectantly. I finally ask, "What?"

"Did you think I was just going to leave and believe you texted him? No, I want evidence."

Rolling my eyes, I take my phone out of my pocket, and I shoot him a text, knowing very well he's going to say no.

Myles: Hey Baba. Headed to Nu Nu's with Toby tonight to play some pool, wanted to send you an open invite in case you wanted to hang out.

"There, sent. Are you happy?"

"I am." She smiles just as my phone dings.

No fucking way did he text back that quickly. I glance down at my phone and see *Baba* appearing across it.

Shocked, I open up the text to read it.

Baba: What time? I'll be there.

"What?" I say in complete disbelief.

"What's going on? What did he say?" Tessa leans toward me, trying to grab a look at my screen.

I look up at Tessa. "He said yes."

"Ha!" She claps her hands. "We're off to a great start."

Chapter Eight

TESSA

"The restaurant is over there." I point to the Olive Tree as my friends and sister head out toward the lobby entrance.

"We're not going to the Olive Tree tonight," Roxane says.

"Oh. Where are we going?" I ask as I catch up to them.

"You'll see." She winks.

I should have known something was up the minute I saw them in the lobby. They aren't dressed for a casual dinner at the Olive Tree—they're dressed like they're about to get into some trouble. And when I say trouble, I mean trouble with me.

All three of them are wearing shorts, Roxane in a white lace pair, Clea and Lois both sporting denim. Wearing a variety of slinky tops that show off more skin than I'm comfortable with, their makeup is heavy, and they jangle with every step from the number of accessories they've piled on. They all communicated before I came down here, and I was not part of that memo. Because I'm wearing a simple yellow sundress with ruffled sleeves. My footwear doesn't have a spike at the heel like my friends'. There's no heel at all—I'm wearing Birkenstocks.

"Well, you could have warned me about the dress code," I say, following them outside.

"Would you have worn this?" Roxane asks, gesturing to her tube top, which is showing off pretty much everything—I can even see the outline of her nipple . . . and nipple piercing.

I remember the day she got her nipple pierced. Just one, because after the first one, there was no way she was getting a second. It was part of her rebellious phase. We'd just turned eighteen, and she, according to her, was a free woman who could do anything she wanted. Well, she did something all right, and I had to sit there and watch it happen. Naturally I passed out when I saw the needle go through her nipple. I woke up to Roxane explaining to me how one nipple piercing is way better than two, but we all know she was too traumatized from the first one to get the second. I'm just glad I didn't have to sit through another.

"I could have put on my Bermuda shorts," I say. "We could have been the shorts girls."

"I like the sundress better than the Bermudas," Clea says. "Those shorts don't hit you right. You need something shorter."

I glance at Clea's shorts, which rest an inch below the juncture of her thighs. Don't think I'll be taking shorts advice from her.

A black SUV pulls up under the awning of the hotel, and the doorman opens the door for us. We all file in, Lois taking the front seat so she can tell the driver if he needs to take curves slower, which is odd, because I've been in the car with her. She owns a minivan—as an Upper East Side mother—and I don't think I've ever been more fearful than when she's behind the wheel. She's more of a threat on the road than some of New York City's craziest taxi drivers. She whips in and out of lanes, honks mercilessly at pedestrians when it's not their right of way, and when she's dropping you off somewhere, she never fully stops.

"Can you give me a clue where we're going?" I ask, buckling my seat belt.

"Somewhere local," Roxane says. "You distracted us this morning with the whole stomach-nuzzling thing, so we have some time to make up tonight on finding you someone."

Great.

Here I thought I did a good job distracting them. Seems like they're doubling down tonight.

"Oh, fun," I say, putting on a smile.

But I must not be convincing enough because Roxane eyes me suspiciously as Clea sits uncomfortably between us. I continue to smile but slowly open my purse and unlock my phone, typing a text out to Myles.

Tessa: Red alert! They're taking me somewhere local to meet some guys. What should I do? They just sprung this on me.

Thankfully Myles texts back right away.

Myles: Somewhere local? I think they're onto you. If they take you to a second location, it's harder for you to retreat to your room. They're playing hardball.

Tessa: They are. Roxane just looked at me as if she knows exactly what I did this morning. We're dealing with some serious vengeance experts. What should I do?

Myles: Do you know where you're going?

Tessa: No idea.

"Who are you texting?" Roxane says as I startle in my seat.

"What? Who saw a duck?" I ask, glancing out the window, attempting to change the subject in the blink of an eye.

"No one saw a duck," Clea says. "Your sister asked who you were texting."

"Oh." I laugh . . . obnoxiously, so loudly that Clea puts her hand over her ear. "What a misunderstanding. Am I right?" I elbow Clea in the side.

"What is wrong with you?" Clea asks.

"Me?" I point to myself. "Nothing. Why, does it seem like something's wrong? Because nothing is wrong. Everything is great. Perfect. Wonderful. Splendid. Just, you know . . . all around a great time."

"She's babbling," Lois says from the front seat right before she leans over to the driver and looks at the speedometer. "Two miles over the speed limit? Sir, what are we, in a hurry? Slow it down."

"You only babble when you're uncomfortable or hiding something." Roxane leans forward in her seat to get a good look at me. I smile, but I feel my lips twitch. I can practically see them flap under my nose.

"Just enjoying the evening," I choke out, casually closing my purse. "Shall I expect you three to get drunk tonight? Do I need to be the designated hotel finder?"

Designated hotel finder is an important job. This person is to direct all transportation to our lodgings, and then it's their responsibility to make sure everyone in the party is escorted safely to their assigned room. This person is allotted no more than two drinks—it's pretty much my dream job.

"No, Lois has already claimed the title," Roxane says.

"Mama needs a break from the booze for the night. Got to pace myself," Lois says from up front. "Very good," she adds, talking to the driver. "That was a perfect stop at a stop sign."

There is no way this man will be picking us up, no matter how much Clea is probably paying him.

Thankfully, Lois takes over the conversation, droning on about the drinks that make her the most hungover now that she's a thirty-year-old mother of two, and I take that moment to sink into my seat. I feel the buzz of my phone, letting me know Myles texted me back, but I don't dare check it—I know Roxane will call me out, so I keep quiet as we make our way to our destination. The more I can disappear and be quiet, the less the scrutiny is on me.

So that's exactly what I'm going to do.

"Attention, everyone," Roxane says from her barstool while holding up a Messina—local beer. "We have a single friend here looking for a good time. Fun, witty, and looks beautiful in yellow. All inquiries of potential suitors must go through us first, but just being up front with you all—we're easy to impress. Stop by if you're interested."

My cheeks are flaming with embarrassment.

My hands are pools of sweat.

And for the first time in my life, I feel like if I punched my sister right in the boob, she'd actually deserve it.

Up until this point, our war has been tame. Slight embarrassment here, forcing conversations there, but nothing that has turned my face an ugly shade of red. Well, guess what, retribution meet pettiness, because we've crossed the line.

We finally arrived at our destination, to a place called Nu Nu's, which of course Lois says is the sound her kids used to make when she breastfed them and how fitting that the "local watering hole" is named after the sound effect. When I tell you that's all I can hear now . . . nu nu nu nu . . . I mean it. I can't get the image of Lois breastfeeding out of my head. *Shudders*

From the moment we walked through the doors of the dive bar—which looks just like that, a dive bar, with its plain wood floors that creak with every step, dark plastered walls, and neon beer signs—Roxane has made it known that I'm single and ready to mingle. She even stopped a few guys who walked by us to tell them I'd be game for a dance later. Being that we're in a less touristy part of Santorini, messing with the locals and their night free of outsiders, you can tell none of them are in the mood to tamper with the "single one on the prowl."

"Are you insane?" I whisper to her, clutching tightly onto my pear hard cider. "That was humiliating."

"Was it? Because look, there's a wave of men walking toward us."

Wait, where? There can't be. No one was interested.

Then I catch a few men approaching, hunger in their eyes.

Oh . . . *those* kind of men.

"Yeah, who think I'm an easy lay."

"I didn't mention anything about sex, just that we were easy to impress—well, hello, gentlemen, can I assist you?" Roxane asks as she beams over my shoulder.

"I heard you're looking for someone to take your friend off your hands," a man's voice says behind me.

"Sister," Roxane says. "Twin sister, actually. And she's looking for a good time—what can you offer her?"

I'm calling it: this has officially gotten out of hand.

Multiple men . . . looking for a good time.

Nope.

Not only is this way out of any comfort zone that is remotely near me, but this is frankly irresponsible. We know nothing about these random men in a skeezy bar. How do we know they're not predators on the prowl? "I don't want anything offered to me," I whisper to her, keeping my back toward the men.

"I can offer her conversation," I hear one guy say. Doubtful, that's a ploy.

"I can tell her how wine is made," another declares. Already know, thanks for inquiring, move on.

And one more guy says, "Does she want to go to the bathroom with me?" That would be a resounding *Jesus Christ, no!*

"Oh my God," I mouth at Roxane. "This is borderline dangerous."

She gives me a reassuring look. "Bathroom guy, you're out. Gross, no one wants to hook up next to a dive-bar toilet." She shoos him away with her hand. "Begone." She then looks at me. "Conversation or wine. Entirely up to you."

"Oh, is it?" I ask. "That's shocking. How about neither. Unless you can do a quick background check."

This is a bamboozlement. I wasn't prepared to be thrust into the sweaty palms of local men when I was getting ready. I expected a calm night at the Olive Tree, delighting in some falafel.

Not this.

This is . . . this is Roxane switching the "fun" into something not fun at all.

"Does that mean you want me to pick for you?"

"No, I don't want anyone to pick. I just want to have a nice evening with my friends and sister. Come on, we've barely spoken about the wedding. How about this: we find a peaceful corner, see if they have any food to order, and just chat, joke around. Doesn't that sound nice?"

"No," she says flatly. "We are finding you a man. I'm thinking wine guy."

"I'm thinking you've lost it," I reply just as I spot a very familiar man walking toward the bar, his eyes trained on me. Unwavering. Laser focused.

I've seen that face before.

Those structurally sound shoulders.

That devilish smirk . . .

How do I know him?

He holds up a hand. "Can I offer a round of pool?"

Pool . . . wasn't Myles playing pool tonight?

And then it hits me. This is Toby, the bartender, Myles's best friend. Wait, are they here?

Oh God, did they hear Roxane's announcement? They must have if he's here, which means Myles must be here too.

Myles is here!

Praise the heavens above.

"I take the man offering pool," I shout, as if I'm volunteering for tribute. "He wins!" With that, I ignore Roxane and push past the other two gentleman to Toby, who drapes his arm over my shoulder. "Please tell me you were saving me," I whisper.

"I don't only serve drinks—I can be a white knight like Myles." Oh, thank freaking goodness. He guides me toward the back of the bar, where there are three pool tables lined up under light-blue pendant lighting. The pool tables are scuffed, all lined with blue felt, and occupied by locals who are keeping their distance from the bar, quietly chatting among themselves. Off to the right, leaning against the plaster wall with a beer in one hand and a pool stick in the other, is Myles.

He looks . . . well, let's just call a spade a spade. He looks hot. He's wearing a pair of black jeans and a heather-gray T-shirt that fits tightly around his chest but is loose where his hips narrow. His five-o'clock shadow has come in, outlining the strength of his jaw. Away from the resort, this is a different side of him. Face scruffy, hair messy, casually dressed: this is Myles when he's comfortable. It's very, very hot.

"Look who I found," Toby says as he drops his hand from my shoulder.

Myles pushes off the wall, a smirk on his face. "I assumed you were going to come here when you said you were on your way to somewhere local. Germaine at concierge told me he suggested Nu Nu's to some girls earlier. And of course, when Roxane made the announcement for everyone to come offer their greatest dowry to talk to you, I knew I had the perfect way to get you out of it."

Why is he just so freaking perfect in every way?

Maybe it's my crush talking, but isn't he perfect?

"Thank you," I say as Myles pulls up a barstool for me. I take a seat while he reaches past me to set his beer down.

When he pulls away, he pauses for a moment and glances down at my dress. "You look nice, by the way."

"Oh, thank you, I, uh . . . I got this dress on sale. It was a last-minute find before we came here. I wasn't sure if I could pull the yellow off, but it seems to work. I would have dressed in something different if I knew we were headed to the bar, but, you know, I didn't know where we were going. I just put this on thinking we were going to the Olive Tree, but yeah . . . got it on sale."

He smirks again, dark eyes full of laughter. "Good to know."

He heads toward the pool table where Toby has racked up the balls.

Why do I do that? Whenever someone says they like what I'm wearing, I can't just say thank you and leave it at that—nope, I have to shout to the rooftops that I got it on sale. No one cares!

While my mind churns with self-loathing, I watch Myles bend over the pool table and rest his stick on his finger, and then with one powerful punch, he shoots the cue ball into the triangle of balls, shattering them across the blue surface.

My oh my, would you look at that.

So strong. So masculine. Who knew pool was so hot?

When he stands, he picks up the chalk and rubs it over the top of his stick. "Have you played, Tessa?"

"Uh, you know, here and there, but I'm no shark. You wouldn't want me on your team, if that's what you're asking. Wait, are their pool teams? I don't think there are, but if there were, you wouldn't want me. My hands get really sweaty in tense moments, and I'm afraid I'd do more harm than good."

"You can't be that bad," Toby says, coming up next to me as Myles assesses his attack on the striped balls. "Now my sister, she's bad. Myles tried teaching her, but she was more interested in cuddling up next to him."

Oh.

Cuddled up next to him. I mean, who wouldn't want to cuddle up next to Myles? From just his adorably cute grin, he has "cuddle me" written all over him. But, you know, inquiring minds would like to know . . . Are they . . . are they a thing? As in Myles and Toby's sister? It would be a fair assumption, given that Toby and Myles are best friends.

"Oh yeah?" I let out a horrendous snort and quickly cover up my mouth and nose with my hand. "Wow, that was . . . that was not something I do often."

"Snort loud enough to shake the change in my pants?" Toby asks with a smile. But that smile does nothing to stop me from wanting to crawl under the table and hide until the bar closes. Sensing my anguish, he nudges me with his shoulder. "Lighten up, I'm only kidding. I like a good snorter."

"He does," Myles says. "You should have seen this girl he dated when we were sixteen." Myles shoots another ball into a hole, and I'm impressed. That's three in a row now. "Melinda—she snorted so loud that you could hear her from two resorts away."

"You could," Toby concurs. "But she had the best lips I've ever kissed."

"Some might call them . . . luxurious," Myles says, looking up and winking.

My stomach curdles in embarrassment, but I feel myself warmed by the teasing as well. Sensations are flying all over the place, and I'm not sure what to do with myself, but something lingers in my mind.

"So . . . do you still, uh, teach pool to Toby's sister?"

Myles shakes his head just as he barely misses getting the ten ball in the corner pocket. Wincing from his miss, he switches places with Toby. Myles leans on the nearby high top while Toby takes in the pool table, assessing what his next move is going to be.

"Athena isn't much of a pool player anymore. She was just doing it to get close."

"Oh." I smile awkwardly. "I'm assuming it worked out well for her."

"I mean, it is what it is."

That's evasive.

What does that even mean?

It is what it is?

Well . . . what is it?

Are you single or not?

Not that it matters or that I really care, but you know, it's just nice to know things.

But I just nod wisely. "Oh yeah, I totally understand it is what it is, because that's life, right? Is it or is it not? Well, guess what, it is what it is, and the faster we understand that it is what it is, the better we can just understand everything."

Did that even make sense?

From the look of confusion on Myles's face, I'm going to guess no.

I let out a forced laugh. "So . . . do you like pistachios in baklava?"

He lifts his bottle of beer to his lips, his eyes staying on mine. "I do."

"Oh wow, look at that, we have something in common—what a relief. For a second there, I thought maybe our agreement was the only thing pulling us together, but you love pistachios too. If that isn't a foundation to build a friendship on, I don't know what is."

Sweat trickles down my spine. The level of uncomfortable awkwardness I'm feeling is at blackout status.

He chuckles. "You're something else, Tessa."

Not sure if that's a compliment or not.

Toby misses his next shot and squeezes his stick in disappointment as he trades places with Myles. "Myles gave me a brief rundown of what's going on with your sister and friends. You're at war?"

I let out the deep breath I was holding just now with Myles so close. *Come on, Tessa, relax.*

Ease up.

"Yes, sort of. Battle of wills. If it weren't for you and Myles, I'd probably be listening to some random stranger tell me about how wine is made, so I'm grateful."

"So, shots were fired when you came here, right?" Toby asks as Myles sinks another ball, now only leaving one more before he gets to the eight ball.

"Our battle was mild before this, but yeah, you're right, shots were fired when we walked into this bar."

"What are you going to do to retaliate?"

"You think I should retaliate? I thought I was retaliating."

"How?" Toby asks.

"Well, you know, their plan failed because I'm here, with you two, people I know, rather than with a stranger in the corner trying to escape small talk."

"But they don't know that. For all they know, they won," Toby says. "Plus, that announcement was pretty humiliating."

"Very humiliating," Myles says.

So humiliating.

More humiliating than the time I walked out of the girls' bathroom in high school with a panty liner stuck to my shoe.

"Therefore, it's your turn to shoot back at them."

Well, when they put it like that. "Huh, I guess so. What should I do?"

Toby's eyes gleam with devilish possibilities. "Send them some Santorini Sauce."

"What's that? Like a barbeque sauce? I'm not sure what they would do with that, other than just pack it up and bring it back to New York. That doesn't seem very vengeful to me."

"No." Toby shakes his head and laughs. "Santorini Sauce is a drink they serve at Nu Nu's. No one knows what's in it, but it's a surefire way to get your friends drunk and passed out. They won't know what happened to them."

Drunk and passed out. Hmm, that feels a touch extreme.

"Is it safe? Like they won't get sick or anything—they won't end up in the hospital?"

"No," Myles cuts in. "It's completely safe."

Well, they did humiliate me, and I did claim this was vacation wars. Maybe it wouldn't be such a bad idea, right? Roxane was onto me in the car. I think that's why she made the announcement in the bar. She's not holding back, so why should I?

But Santorini Sauce?

"Oh, that feels very diabolical. I'm not sure if I have that in me."

"Eight ball, corner pocket," Myles says before he shoots his pool stick forward and scores, ending the game. Toby lets out a deep groan and collects the balls.

Myles walks up to me, still holding his cue. "The Santorini Sauce is a good idea. It won't hurt them, but it will teach them a lesson about announcing your singledom in a local bar. Maybe show them they need to back down because you're not one to mess with."

"I don't know." I twist my hands together. "Maybe it's best if we just end it now. Call a truce."

"Do you think they're going to call a truce?" Myles asks.

I glance over at Roxane at the bar, laughing and drinking her cocktail. She's my twin. I know her inside and out, and when she has her mind set on something, she's going to see it through.

Even if I call a truce tonight, that doesn't mean she's going to respect it and stop this "finding me a man" nonsense.

Therefore, Myles very well might be right.

"I don't think they will call a truce," I say.

"Then I think it's time you listen up." Myles leans in close. "It might be time that you get a little tougher with your sister, because dressing up in a robe to deter her plans isn't going to cut it. You said this is vacation wars, so . . . act like it."

I mull it over, my teeth pulling on my bottom lip. He's right; Roxane would never hold back if the shoe was on the other foot. She would make it her mission to win this undeclared battle. Maybe it's my time to be the bolder one, the braver one. They want me stepping out of my comfort zone? Well, here's my chance. "You're right. I should teach them a lesson. Let's order the sauce . . . and . . . and set six-in-the-morning wake-up calls for them with the front desk."

"Oh shit," Toby says. "That's brutal. Looks like you unlocked that diabolical side of yours."

"About time," Myles says with a wink.

From across the bar, Roxane holds up her drink, thanking me from a distance. With Toby's arm draped over my shoulder, we wave and then turn away, the smirks on our faces too telling.

"They're in for a rude awakening tomorrow morning," Toby says as he nudges his shoulder against mine.

Just as tall as Myles and with the same build—I can only imagine if they're workout partners—Toby has fairer features with longer blond hair that he ties in a topknot and light-green eyes. He's very handsome, but not in the way that has me flustered and stumbling over my words.

Not the kind of handsome that Myles embodies, the kind that hits me like a ton of bricks directly in the sternum.

"I feel like hell will rain down upon me tomorrow." I drag my finger over the tabletop, doubt seeping in.

"Yeah, but we'll be prepared," Toby says just as Myles walks up to us from having gone to the bathroom.

"What are we going to be prepared for?"

Toby steps away from me. "When the girls find out what Tessa did to them."

"Oh, yeah." Myles's eyes flutter over toward the door again, for at least the twentieth time since their last pool game ended. I know he's looking for his dad; it's written all over his face. He said he'd be here, but it's been at least forty-five minutes since I got here, and he's still a no-show. I can practically see the anxiety circling through Myles's head.

"Has he texted you?" I ask quietly.

Myles shakes his head. "No. He's probably not going to come. It's fine, I'll just have to come up with something else to do."

"But you're disappointed," I say.

"Of course I am. I thought . . . hell, I don't know what I thought." He leans against the wall next to me. "Doesn't matter. One night wouldn't have changed anything anyway."

"But it could have been the first step. Why don't you text him?"

Myles runs his hand over the scruff of his jaw. "No, by not showing up, he's telling me exactly where I stand. No need to text him."

"Are you sure?" I ask.

"Positive." He lets out a sigh. "Do you want me to grab you another drink? Something to eat?"

"I'm good, and you don't have to serve me, Myles. We're not at the resort."

"It's called being a friend," he says with a lackluster smile and then heads toward the bar.

Toby finishes up racking the balls and then walks over to me. "It's a complicated relationship between him and his dad. He's right when he says one night isn't going to change things."

"Well, it could have been a step in the right direction."

"Agreed, but Hermes is an interesting man. Very proud—it's going to take a lot to get him to change." He turns toward me. "So, why don't you want your friends to hook you up? Are you pining after someone, perhaps?"

"What? No, of course not," I say, attempting to play it cool, but I know I'm more gawky than anything. "I just don't think it's necessary for my sister and friends to try to find me a random person. I can do this love thing on my own."

"Uh-huh, and have you? Done the love thing? Like actually been in love?"

"Yeah, in college. And about eight months ago."

"What happened?"

"Um, well, in college he got drunk one night, cheated on me, and wound up getting the girl pregnant. And the other guy, well, he cheated on me too." I used to be embarrassed, sharing that two men have cheated on me—two men that I loved, no less—but after some time and help from Roxane, I've realized I'm not the one who should be ashamed. It doesn't lessen the sting of it all, but at least I'm not blaming myself.

"Oh shit, really?"

"Yeah. College Guy is married and going through a divorce now. Clea keeps me updated. And the guy from eight months ago, I believe, is dating someone else. Since then, I've just . . . dated here and there, but I haven't found anyone I want to commit to, and not because I'm jaded or anything like that. I just want to be sure, you know?"

"Yeah, that makes sense."

"What about you?"

"Eh, hard to really fall for someone when the people you meet are in and out of your life all the time. Dating in a tourist destination is hard."

"Myles doesn't have a sister you could date? You know, like . . . he's dating your sister."

There, I said it, put it out there.

Toby chuckles. "Digging for information?"

"What? No!" I squeak. "Why would I do that?"

"You tell me." Toby leans on the bar-height table, his eyes questioning, looking for answers, but thankfully Myles walks up at that moment with a new round of drinks for everyone.

111

"A hummus plate is on its way as well."

Seems like even though he's off the clock, his instinct is to help those around him. I can tell Myles feels most valued when he's helping others, and that's a very admirable quality . . . you know, just in general.

"Thanks, man," Toby says.

"What were you two talking about?"

Toby lifts his fresh drink to his lips. "Tessa was wondering if you're dating my sister."

"What?" I feel myself go bright red. "No, I'm not. I didn't say that." I look at Myles. "I didn't say that. We were just, you know, chatting about love, and I asked if you had a sister that Toby could date, like you're dating his sister. I wasn't inquiring, there were no inquiries." I glare at Toby. "Why would you say that?"

He chuckles and moves toward the pool table.

God, talk about being flustered in a matter of seconds.

"Interested in my dating life, Tessa?" Myles raises a brow.

"No." I shake my head. "Nope, that is your own personal business, not mine. I thought I was just helping Toby solve a problem— you know, the whole dating-at-a-tourism-destination problem—but it seems as though he took it the wrong way. Maybe I should go check on my sister."

Myles rests his hand on my shoulder. "You're not going anywhere. And don't let Toby get to you like that—he's an instigator."

Well, he's good at it.

But also . . . can we talk about how Myles avoided the question again?

What's the big deal? If he's dating her, then that's fine, good for him, but why so secretive?

Toby misses his first shot and lets out a loud "Fuck" before he joins me by the table.

Apparently unfazed by calling me out, Toby asks, "So, if you had to choose between eliminating one of these from your diet forever, which would you choose? Samsades or baklava?"

So that's how it's going to be? We're just going to roll on to the next question? Figures. That's how guys are. I feel like they're never easily offended. He can move on from a comment while I'm still reeling over here. But for the sake of the conversation, I play along.

"Impossible, I would rather get rid of both. That way I have no guilt over eliminating one over the other."

"You know food doesn't have feelings, right?"

"I know, but I'd still know in my heart what I did, and I don't think I could forgive myself for choosing."

Toby chuckles and then taps his beer against mine. "I'd do the same, Tessa. Looks like we have something in common."

"Looks like it." I smile back at him before I take a sip of my drink.

"So you're telling me, you both lived in New York City, within a few blocks of each other, and didn't bump into one another?" Toby asks right before taking a sip of his beer.

The boys let two guys take over the table for one game and one game only as we snack on the food Myles ordered. The bar might be less than picturesque, but the food is amazing. The hummus plate is to die for, full of pita, this amazing pesto hummus, brined feta, and a selection of olives and roasted tomatoes as well as grape leaves all drizzled in a delicate oil. Freaking spectacular.

"Never bumped into each other," I say as Myles stands off to the side, one hand in his pocket, his drink in the other.

Toby has taken the main stage in the conversation, moving in so he's sitting across from me and leaning on the table, while Myles has sort of taken the back seat.

"You *never* saw her?" Toby asks Myles as if he doesn't believe it.

Tight jaw, eyes narrowed, Myles says, "No, never saw her." And then some weird secret conversation passes between them. It's the kind of covert telepathic conversation I have with Roxane.

"Shocking." Toby picks up the last green olive and pops it in his mouth. "You'd think somehow, someway, you would."

I shrug. "Maybe we did, just didn't realize it." Noticing how uncomfortable Myles is, I decide to switch the conversation to focus on Toby. "Have you ever been to New York?"

"Plenty of times," Toby answers. "My mom is best friends with Myles's mom, and they both live in the city now. So, we've been back and forth several times."

"Oh wow, really? That's unique."

"That's us." Toby grips Myles's shoulder. "Totally unique. Right, man?"

"Yeah. Unique."

Releasing Myles, Toby turns his attention back to me and leans in even closer. "Tell me, Tessa, what do you do for a job?"

Sensing the tension, but with no idea why, I decide to keep it light and breezy and answer his question. "I'm a financial consultant. I do my own contract work with multiple small businesses in the city. I basically look through their books and see how they can improve, how they can invest their money, and what changes they can make to help them be more profitable. I actually started my career with a major law firm, but the hours were brutal, and I wasn't really enjoying it even though I loved numbers, so I decided to go out on my own."

"How did you find clients?"

"Word of mouth. My friend Clea helped me out at first. She's a marketing wizard and helped me create a website, a brand, and an easy way for companies to understand my business model. It's been steady work ever since. And I get to make my own hours, work where

I want to work, and I get to work in other sectors of the business world."

"Are you telling me you're a bit of a data nerd?"

My cheeks blush as I twist my almost empty drink on the tabletop. "A bit, yeah."

"That's hot," Toby says. "Isn't that hot, Myles?"

We both turn toward Myles, who looks like a deer in headlights, unable to move.

"Uh"—he clears his throat—"yeah, that's, uh . . . that's hot."

Cue the inferno.

I'm gobbled up into a tsunami of bashful flames.

"So hot." Toby smiles, leans back, and finishes off his drink. Totally pleased with himself.

"I'm sorry if Toby is making you feel uncomfortable," Myles says while Toby is in the bathroom. "He can be pretty up front."

"Oh, he's fine. I'm not great with small talk—or entertaining, for that matter—so it's nice to have someone carry the conversation." Myles's eyes drop, and I realize the backhanded insult I might have just delivered. "Not that you haven't been able to carry the conversation. You do a great job carrying it, actually. Quite the conversationalist. You should be proud of yourself."

He lightly chuckles. "You don't need to compliment me."

"Oh, but you know, I deliver compliments when they're deserved. So, A-plus on the conversation."

He shakes his head and lets out a deep breath. "So, are you a fan of Nu Nu's now that you've been here for a bit?"

"See, great at conversation," I point out, which only causes him to roll his eyes.

"Just answer the question."

115

"Right . . . uh, yeah, it's pretty cool here. The bar area seems too much for me, very noisy and lots of people. I like being back here, secluded, where there aren't a bunch of bodies touching other bodies."

"Are you a germophobe?"

"No, not really, but I don't really care for other people's bodily fluids on me. Sweat is just, eh, not my thing."

"Understandable. Not sure anyone enjoys other people's sweat."

"I do," Toby says, coming out of nowhere. "Only in bed, though. If I can feel a girl's sweat, I know I'm doing all the right things, especially if she's sliding against my chest."

My eyes widen.

Myles's eyes narrow.

And now, all I can picture is Toby with a girl on top of him, riding him like a Slip 'n Slide. I'm not sure I've ever had sex carnal enough to be slipping around everywhere.

What does that say about me?

"From the look on your face, Tessa, I'm going to guess you've never experienced a sweaty night."

"Uh . . ."

"You don't need to answer that," Myles says.

"Myles has had plenty," Toby says with a smirk. "Dude knows how to make a sweaty night happen."

"Jesus," Myles mutters as he pushes off the wall, grabs Toby, and directs him away from me and toward the pool table, leaving me with many questions.

How many sweaty nights, perchance?

Were any of those with Athena?

And what exactly is performed during these sweaty nights to make them so . . . sweaty?

"No way." I shake my head while Toby grips the barstool.

"Twenty euros, Killer. Come on."

Killer: that's Toby's new name for me after I beat him in pool, under Myles's direction, of course. Did he cuddle up next to me like he apparently did to Athena? That would be a no, but Toby had his fun as he tried to distract me by twerking against the table, making moaning sounds—that was a treat for everyone—and then, of course, accidentally bumping into me. His tactics proved useless as I sank the eight ball. So he dubbed me Killer and has been trying to get me back ever since.

Currently he's betting me twenty euros that he can balance the barstool on his chin.

"It feels dangerous."

"Danger is my middle name." He wiggles his brows. "Come on, Tessa."

I sigh. "Fine."

Smirking, he holds his hand out to me, and I take it. He helps me off my stool, and I adjust my skirt.

"Get ready to pay him the money," Myles says beside me.

"You couldn't have warned me?"

He just shrugs. "Best you learn by making your own mistakes. But I would clear out of the way since he's had a few drinks." With that, Myles wraps his hand around my waist and pulls me toward him so I can feel his chest against my back.

I'm transported back to the moment he kissed me on the cheek. To the time I held his hand, when it felt like birds were singing upbeat melodies in my ears. To the moment I called his lips, his hands, luxurious.

Would it be too much if I described his chest the same way?

Granted, my scapulae are reaping all the benefits of our connection right now, but still, from the reports from my scapulae, I can conclude that his chest is luxurious as well. But out of self-preservation, I'll keep that thought to myself.

Toby lifts the chair up to his chin and balances one of the legs on his face, and then, to my astonishment, he lets go.

Well, would you look at that.

He's balancing a chair on his chin. You don't see that every day.

After a few seconds, he grabs the chair off his face, sets it back down, and then takes my hand in his and spins me around in a circle before picking me up and depositing me back on the chair.

He leans on the table, and the look in his eyes tells me he's fishing for compliments. Who am I to deny him such pleasure?

"Wow, that was . . . that was something else."

"Impressed?" He wiggles his eyebrows, which makes me chuckle.

"Very. I guess I owe you twenty euros."

I pick up my purse from the table and reach for my wallet just as I hear, "Oh God, look, Clea, she's giving him her number." Oh goodness, I completely forgot they were still here. What kind of sister does that make me?

I glance up at that moment to see my very drunk sister and two very drunk friends approaching. So much for Lois being the sober one of the group.

"I told you they looked like a cute couple," Clea says as she wobbles toward me, one of her fake eyelashes barely hanging on to her lid.

What the heck was in that Santorini Sauce? I almost feel bad about the alarms we set up for them for tomorrow morning.

"Almost" being the key word.

"Is she giving you her number?" Roxane asks, closing the space between us.

With a heart-melting smile, Toby says, "Hell yeah, she is." He wiggles his fingers at me. "Give it up, Killer."

"Killer." Roxane clutches her chest. "Oh God, you already have a nickname for her. This is . . . this is great. Oh my God, girls, she needs the perfume."

Oh no.

This is so not a perfume moment. Not even close.

Perfume-worthy would be like going on a third date with the knowledge in the back of your mind, this could be it. This person was meant for you.

Pool in a dirty bar . . . that's not the moment.

"Uh, you know what, we should probably get you back to the hotel." I hop off the stool, but Roxane stops me by placing her hand to my chest.

"You need to give him your number."

Oh right.

I reach into my purse and pull out a business card. "This has my cell phone number on it."

"Ew, why are you handing him a business card?" Roxane asks. "Write your number on a napkin. That's sexier."

"But this is efficient." I hand him the card, which he flips through his fingers and then sticks in the chest pocket of his T-shirt.

With a wink, he says, "I'll call you, Killer."

And honestly, in this moment, after spending a great deal of the night with Toby, I can't decide if he is being serious or not. He was flirty, but was that because he was putting on a show or because that's how he really is? And toward the end of the night, when Myles grew increasingly quiet, clearly disappointed his dad didn't show up, Toby stepped up and kept me entertained.

So now I feel more confused than ever.

"Go ahead," Roxane says, shoving me toward Toby. "Give him a kiss."

"Oh, no, that's not—that's not necessary," I say.

"Scared, Killer?" Toby wets his lips and . . . Uh, what's going on?

I thought he wasn't into the whole tourist-dating thing. Is this really for show? I mean, he's handsome, but I don't feel any real attraction between us.

Toby must sense my confusion because he laughs and pulls me into a hug. I'm buried into his fresh mountain scent, my nose to his chest as I wrap my arms around him as well. And then, unexpectedly, he kisses the top of my head, causing this anxious, fluttery feeling to slip through my stomach.

So caught off guard by the feeling, I quickly push him away, my eyes trained on his. He gives me a wink and lifts his beer to his lips. "See you later, Killer."

"Yeah, see you later," I answer before I glance at Myles . . . Myles, whose jaw is clenched tightly. He's looking at Toby almost as if he's trying to silently communicate with him. If only I could follow their best friend secret language, then I'd have a better understanding of what transpired tonight, how our friendship has shifted, and what they're communicating through their pointed looks.

But I don't have enough time because Roxane is looping her arm through mine and pulling me toward the exit. "What a night!" she shouts. "We found you a boyfriend. Next time you see him, it's perfume time."

Great . . .

CHAPTER NINE
MYLES

I'm mid-bicep-curl when the door to the gym opens and Toby walks in, water bottle and lifting gloves in hand.

"Ah, would you look at that, you've started without me. How come I'm not surprised?"

"I'm trying to get my workout done early so I can catch my baba before he goes to his office this morning," I say, finishing up my reps. I set the forty-five-pound weights back on the rack and reach for my water bottle.

"I see, and this has nothing to do with the fact that you were mad at me last night."

"I was not mad at you," I groan.

Even though . . . yeah, maybe I was slightly irritated. Not that I'm interested in starting anything with someone who's only visiting, but Tessa, well, she's different. On top of my baba not showing up, I had to watch Toby shamelessly flirting with Tessa. I noticed every time he touched her, every time he made her laugh, every fucking time he tucked a piece of hair behind her ear.

It was uncalled for, and I can't tell if he really likes her or if he was just trying to fuck with me.

"Really? You weren't mad? So, after Tessa left, you didn't just storm off without saying goodbye?"

I furrow my brow.

"Or you weren't mad that before she left, she gave me a hug."

I set my water down.

"And you wouldn't be mad if I planned on texting her this morning to see if she wanted to meet up for lunch?"

That triggers me. My head snaps up. "You don't even like brunettes."

"Nah, but she's gorgeous and intriguing. Fun in a weird kind of way. I like what comes out of her mouth—never know what to expect."

I like that about her too.

"But you know . . . if *you* were interested in asking her out, then I would step aside."

"Step aside." Jesus, as if he's doing me a favor. I'm the one who started talking to her. I'm the one who's in cahoots. I'm the one who should have been charming her last night.

"You didn't have to ask for her number," I say before I can stop myself.

Toby lets out a boisterous laugh. "Dude, I can see right fucking through you. It was all over your face last night—your childhood crush is alive and well. Why didn't you just come over and talk to her, kick me away, stake your claim?"

"Because . . . she's not, I'm not . . . we're both not looking for any-thing like that. We're just helping each other out."

"Uh-huh. Well, if that's the case, then I'll call her. Take her out. Maybe drive her around the island on my bike. Girls love that. See if she's interested in one of those sweaty nights we talked about."

My teeth grind together. "Or maybe you just leave her the fuck alone," I say before I can stop myself. "She's here for her sister's wedding."

"Yeah, but if I take her out, date her for a bit while she's here, then her sister will lay off with that whole 'trying to find her someone' situation. Feels like a win-win to me." He grabs a jump rope from a peg on the wall and starts warming his body up.

It's not a win-win for me. Feels like a lose-lose. If I know anything about Toby, it's that girls easily fall for him—he's charming and good looking—but when their time is up, he doesn't put up a fuss. He's a player, and that's okay—it works for him—but Tessa doesn't seem like the kind of girl who can handle a guy like Toby.

"I think you should just leave her alone."

"And why's that?"

"Because it's complicated, okay?"

"Dude, just admit that you like her," Toby says as the jump rope snags on his shoe and he has to start his rotations over again.

"I don't like her . . . like that," I say, even though the words don't feel right. "She just has a lot going on, so leave her be."

"Uh-huh, and you're saying that as an unbiased friend who has nothing but her best interest at heart, not because you've been staring off at this girl from the moment she first came to the resort with her family? Not because she actually intrigues you and you want to keep her to yourself? Right?"

I swallow hard. "Right."

Toby scoffs and shakes his head, but he doesn't say anything else. The rest of the time, we work out in silence.

I check my watch one more time, knowing that any minute Baba is going to walk through the lobby doors, grab his morning paper from the concierge, who'll also have a black coffee waiting for him, and head into his office.

A black sedan with a Greek-flag hood ornament pulls into the circular driveway, and my baba pops out of the driver's seat. He tosses the keys to a valet, buttons his peach linen suit jacket, and walks into the resort, glasses covering his eyes, offering smiles to the guests.

Like a stalker, I eye him as he picks up his coffee and paper. As he draws nearer, I mentally prepare myself for what I can only imagine will be a confrontation that will leave me feeling empty and unwanted inside. Can't wait.

He moves closer and closer, and just as he's ten feet from the front office, I step out from behind the pillar where I was hiding and right into his path, startling him backward.

"Myles," he says, looking shocked. "What on earth are you doing?"

"Wanted to catch you before you headed into the office."

He glances at his watch and then back up at me. "Don't you have service duty at the Olive Tree right now?"

"I have ten minutes to spare, so I decided to come over here and see how you were doing, you know, since you didn't show up for pool last night."

I can't help the bitter tone in my voice. I know it will throw him into defensive mode, but hell, I am bitter. I'm upset. I'm embarrassed. My own father stood me up—it doesn't get more pathetic than that.

"Myles, I'm not in the mood for you to cause a scene."

"I'm not causing a scene. I'm speaking to my father. And I wouldn't have to approach you like this if you actually gave me the time of day and talked to me."

"That is enough. If you'd like to speak with me, set up a time with Jasmine—"

"I'm not setting up a time with Jasmine. I'm your son, which means you make time for me."

He stares at me for a few breaths and then walks past me toward his office, without another word.

I feel like the boy who wants to cower away in a corner and cry over the fact that his father doesn't have time for him, but I know that's not going to do anything for me. So I follow him all the way to his office, where I shut the door behind me.

He frowns at me. "I have work to do."

"Yeah, and you have a son who's wondering why you stood him up last night." I approach his desk as he takes a seat behind it and wakes up his computer. "Do you realize how hard it was for me to ask you to hang out last night? Extremely hard, and not because I didn't want to, but out of fear of rejection." Not looking at me, he takes a sip of his coffee as I continue. "And then, to go to Nu Nu's excited that maybe, maybe, our relationship isn't dying, that there's a chance to save it, only for you to not show up so I feel that rejection all over again. Fuck, Baba, it hurt."

He removes his glasses and rubs his forehead with the back of his hand. "I don't have the luxury of being able to take time off, Myles." His eyes finally connect with mine, and I notice how bloodshot they are, how weary and weathered they look. "You have no idea the kind of impact you had on this place when you left. You were training for management. I was priming you to take over. You took responsibilities off my plate, and then you left. Guess the only one who could take over your neglected duties was me. It's been seven years, but I'm still recuperating from it."

"You could have hired someone else."

"I didn't want to hire anyone else," he booms. "You are my son. You're the one who's supposed to help me. You're the one who's supposed to be by my side, not some random person who fits the qualifications. You, Myles. You!"

Shocked by his anger, I take a step back. "How am I supposed to help you when you won't even make time to see me?"

"You were supposed to never leave."

"Jesus Christ, Baba," I say with a large eye roll. "You can't keep bringing that up. I went there so I could *learn*—are you going to hold that against me forever? Because tell me right now." I jab my finger into his desk. "Tell me that's how this relationship is going to go, because I'm not sticking around if that's the case."

He leans back in his chair, his mustache twitching as he studies me, and when he doesn't answer, I toss my hands up in defeat.

He's so fucking stubborn. So stubborn. There's no winning with him, so why am I trying?

Giving up, I turn around and stalk toward the door.

"I'll see you Sunday," he calls.

"No, you won't," I say from over my shoulder.

"Myles," his voice booms again, and when I turn around, he's standing, both hands on his desk. "You will come to Sunday dinner."

"No, Baba, I won't. What's the point? You clearly don't want a relationship with me, but you just want to pretend like we have one for the benefit of your family. I'm not your fucking pony to prance around. If you want me to show up to your Sunday dinners, then show me that you actually want to repair our relationship, not destroy it."

"I suggest you rethink what you're saying."

"Why?" I ask. "Or else I won't be able to work here anymore? Well, the only shame in that is that I wouldn't be able to work in the place I grew up, but with my credentials, with the degree I earned, I could work at some of the finest hotels in Oia and make more money there. I came back here to be close to you, to help you, but you can't seem to understand that." I shake my head. "It was one simple request: come hang with me. That's all you had to do."

"I told you, I had business to tend to."

"If that's the actual truth, then a text would have been sufficient, and it would have been better than silence. I hope you realize that if this threadbare relationship we have ever falls apart, it's not my fault—that rests entirely on you."

And with that, I walk out of his office and into the Olive Tree, where I put on a happy face and serve our customers.

CHAPTER TEN
TESSA

"What is wrong with you?" Roxane says, her hair sticking up in all directions, her sunglasses askew. She has on a pair of sweatpants that she wouldn't be caught dead wearing in public, but it seems as though her six-in-the-morning wake-up call has washed away any fashion concerns.

Honestly, I felt a little guilty this morning when I knew Lois, Clea, and Roxane were all called by the front desk, letting them know it was their courtesy wake-up call. Getting disturbed after a rough night of drinking is never easy. And from the wrath in Roxane's voice, I think I'm going to regret it.

Then again, she was the one who announced to the whole bar that I was single and ripe for the picking, so maybe she deserved it. Maybe the guys had a point.

I fold my napkin on my lap at the breakfast table I reserved for us. "What do you mean?"

She lifts her tortoiseshell sunglasses, showing off her intensely bloodshot eyes. *Oh, dear God!* "You know exactly what you did."

I swallow hard. "Um, I don't think I'm aware of what you're talking about."

"Oh really? Have a touch of memory loss, do ya? Do you remember sending us those drinks as a thank-you for meeting that guy last night?"

I nod and take a sip of my water, hoping she doesn't see the light tremble in my hand. "I do recall that. I heard those were the best drinks in the bar."

"And what about when you called the hotel and set up three separate wake-up calls?"

"Huh, now, that doesn't seem like something I'd do."

"You are such a liar," she hisses just as Myles comes up to our table with a pot of coffee.

"Would you like some coffee to start your morning?" he asks, his voice sounding distant.

When I glance up at him, he doesn't bother looking at me. Did I do something wrong last night, other than calling in for those wake-up calls? Although despite the guilt, watching Roxane melt into her chair is entertaining.

"Coffee, and keep it coming." Roxane holds up her cup to Myles.

"Oh coffee, praise Jesus," Clea says as she stumbles into her chair, finally joining us. "I feel like all I can taste is that bar. I need something strong to wash it away." She smacks her lips together. "Why does it feel like I sucked on a toe last night?"

"Because you licked the bar top," Lois says as she takes a seat as well, not looking nearly as destroyed as the other two. "I told you not to lick up that cashew, but you did anyway, and look what happens: you have toe-tongue now. I hope you're pleased with yourself."

Quietly, Myles pours us all a cup of coffee and then asks, "Will you be doing the buffet this morning?"

"Yes," I answer while Roxane groans, Clea plants her face in her cup of coffee, and Lois lifts from her chair, declaring the bacon will be her bitch this morning. "Uh, thank you," I say to him before he walks away.

"I just have one question," Roxane says, holding up her finger. "Why? Why would you do something so horrific to us? What did we ever do to you?"

Not truly paying attention, I watch Myles tend to some other tables. The droop in his shoulders is concerning. I haven't known him very long, but I've observed him for almost two decades, and I don't think I've ever seen him like this, so . . . disheartened. And then it hits me—his dad didn't show up last night. It has to be that.

"Hello, I asked you a question," Roxane says.

"Uh-huh. I like pineapple." I just shoot off an answer, not caring as I stand to go talk to Myles.

"That's not what I asked," Roxane says, but I keep walking, past the buffet and around the corner where I've seen the waitstaff walk in and out. At the end of the short hallway, there are two swinging doors that I assume lead to the kitchen, so that's where I wait—he has to come this way at some point.

And thankfully, after a few minutes, he does just that. When he spots me, he stumbles backward. "Tessa, is something wrong?"

Now, I could do this one of two ways. I could ask him if he's okay and if he wants to talk about it, which I know will be greeted with a "I'm fine" and a general pass on the conversation. Or I can ask him for help, get him secluded and away from the situation, and then draw it out that way.

Plan B has more potential, even though it's slightly out of my comfort zone.

"Uh, do you work later?" I ask, my hands twisting in front of me.

"I work the bar later tonight, but I have the whole afternoon off. Why?"

"Well, I was wondering if you wanted to go to Oia with me?" I improvise. "Roxane seems a bit angry about the whole wake-up call—well, all three of them seem angry, and I doubt they'd want to help me. I'm looking for a bracelet to buy, and I don't know, I just thought, since you know the area so well, that you might have some advice as to where to go. But if you're busy, that's totally okay. Just thought I'd ask, you know?"

His frown lifts, and his face softens. "Of course. How about I meet you on the west entrance of the resort—I can drive us. Meet at eleven?"

Holy cow, he said yes. My entire body perks up. "That would be amazing. Thank you."

"Of course. You could have texted me."

"I know, I just . . . well, I wanted to ask you before you made other plans. Wasn't sure how often you check your phone while working."

"I'd check for you." He smirks. "Everything good with breakfast?"

"Yes, it's great. Thanks." I rock on my heels. "Well, I better get back to the table."

"Okay, let me know if you need rescuing."

"I will."

I stand there awkwardly, unmoving, as he shifts past me, chuckling. "Okay, see you at eleven."

"Yup. Bye." I wave, even though his back is turned toward me, and head back toward the table.

Oia with Myles. This is . . . unexpected, yet exciting. Look at me, taking charge!

"Where the hell did you go?" Roxane asks, still clutching onto her seat like she might melt right onto the ground.

"Just had to check on something," I answer as I unfold my napkin and rest it on my lap again.

"Well, we've been talking while you were gone." That doesn't seem good on my end. "And we've come to the conclusion that you purposefully got us drunk and then rudely woke us up this morning."

"What?" I attempt to act shocked. "I'd never do that, not after you so classily announced my single status to the bar and thrust me into the grabby hands of a bunch of single men."

"Oh please, as if you didn't have a good time with the bartender last night," Roxane says.

"She had a very good time," Clea adds while stirring her coffee. "I saw her laughing."

"I saw her flirting with the Bulge," Lois adds.

"No, I wasn't," I say quickly, not sure why.

"Don't bother with him," Roxane says, tossing her hand in the air. "That's just some far-fetched fantasy that won't work out the way you want it to."

Why does she have to be such a dream crusher? Sure, she might not know the extent of the fun I've been having with Myles, but that doesn't mean she should just write him off, especially after everything she knows about him and how I feel.

"I'm not bothering with him," I lie.

"Good, because waste of time," Roxane says.

He's not a waste of time.

He's been fun.

Exciting.

Protective in a way.

And also, he's made me realize that perhaps I'm not the pushover everyone thinks I am.

"He's hot, but yeah, you can't make fantasies become a reality," Lois says before biting into a piece of bacon.

"Bartender seems like he has more potential," Clea adds.

"Well, it doesn't matter," I say, wanting to just clear the air, "because I think we all need to press the reset button. Not that I'm saying I got you drunk and made those wake-up calls, but you know, I think we're all even at this point. Why don't we just take a moment to gather ourselves and then move on with our vacation as planned." I offer smiles around the table, ready for a friendship truce, but I'm alarmed when I'm met with scowls.

"The wake-up call made me throw up," Roxane says.

"I nearly ripped my breast off as I attempted to reach for the phone to shut off the ringing," Clea says. "I caught it on the edge of the dresser, and you know I sleep naked."

Yes, she does. I can't imagine that felt good.

"It was brutal, but just the kind of shock to the system I needed," Lois adds. "But doesn't mean you weren't wrong."

"Well . . . you guys embarrassed me at the bar, which I think means we're all even. So, let's just press that reset button. Shall we?"

Roxane sinks deeper into her chair and mumbles, "Sure, Tessa. We'll just press that reset button." She lifts her coffee to her lips, and as I watch her take a sip, I know for certain she doesn't mean it.

This is not a truce.

We're about to embark on the next battle.

It's moving from petty to downright ugly.

***

I'd like to say I didn't worry about what I was going to wear to Oia, or how my hair was styled, or if I should put on more mascara, but that would be lying. Because I cared a lot. I cared more than I should have, since this was not a date.

After breakfast and receiving the silent treatment from Clea and Roxane—Lois was more impressed than anything—I retreated to my room, where I read while soaking in the private in-ground Jacuzzi. It was peaceful, just what I needed to relax because my nerves had been bouncing.

The thought that fantasies never become reality kept pulsing through my mind, over and over again. I'd put Myles up on such an unreachable pedestal that it was making me an absolute wreck while getting ready. The only thing propelling me forward was that I knew he was having a rough morning, and asking him to Oia was my way of trying to brighten his day.

I quickly washed off, braided my hair into two French braids, and changed my outfit six times. I settled for a pair of yellow shorts—not Bermuda, because now I felt self-conscious about those—and a white blousy tank top. I threw on my Birks again and called it a day. A casual outfit, nothing that said "I'm going on a date with a man who doesn't think we're going on a date," but in the back of my mind, I sort of wished it was a date.

I live a complicated life.

Today was supposed to be a pool day, but thanks to the wake-up calls and Santorini Sauce, all plans have been canceled until tonight. Worked out for me. Still feeling guilty, still sort of not sorry.

With my crossbody clutch slung over my shoulder, I head toward the west entrance, where I immediately spot Myles leaning against the wall, waiting for me.

I'm so freaking glad I went with my outfit, because he's wearing a pair of gray chino shorts and a dark-blue T-shirt. Super casual. As I approach, he looks up from his phone, and when he spots me, he smiles and slides it into his pocket.

"Hey, hope I didn't keep you waiting," I say.

"Nah, I just got out of the shower after work and headed over here." His hair must dry quickly, because it's not drenched, just a little wet at the roots.

"Well, good. Are you ready?"

"Yup. This way." He nods toward the exit, and I follow him.

"How was, uh . . . the rest of work."

"Same old, same old," he says, holding the door open for me. I have to brush past him as I step outside, and I catch a whiff of his fresh soapy scent. Like dew on a single blade of mountain grass, that's what he smells like, all earthy and masculine. Like he belongs in an Old Spice commercial, riding a white horse, spreading the word about how he smells like a quintessential Bath & Body Works candle, the type of candle that guests always compliment you on—*ooh, I love the smell of your candle*—thank you, it smells like euphoria and man all bundled into a jar of wax. "Uh, I hope you don't mind riding on a scooter. I grabbed the last rental." *Huh, oh yes, you're not alone. Focus, Tessa.*

"Not at all. We took scooters to Oia last year. Easier to park and totally fun."

"Glad you said that, because I was worried about parking." He directs me toward a green scooter parked off to the left. "Do you care if I drive?"

"No," I answer. "That works."

That means I get to hold on to him and smell him some more. That realization shouldn't make me smile, but it does. I can't tell you the number of times I've pictured this scenario in my head. When I was a teenager, getting whisked away on a scooter was all I could think about when I saw him. All I hoped for was that maybe he'd notice me. That one day when I was reading one of my books down by the beach he would interrupt me, tell me how much he likes my bathing suit, and ask if I want to hang. We'd then take a ride on a red scooter all around the island, the wind whipping my linen shirt back so it flapped away like a flag of exuberant joy. Only took how many years for this to happen?

And it's not even a date.

But that doesn't mean it's *not* fulfilling a childhood fantasy.

Oh God . . . fantasies don't become reality. This is exactly what Roxane and the girls were talking about. I need to take deep breaths before I start to get carried away. Myles hops on first and then takes my hand, helping me get on the back. Once situated, he says, "Okay, wrap your arms around my waist. Let me see if you have a good enough squeeze—I can't have you bumping off the back."

Chuckling, I loop my arms around his narrow, muscular waist and hold on tight.

"Whoa, okay, we have a clinger."

"I hope that's a good thing."

He starts the scooter. "A very good thing." He pulls out of the space, and with our feet kicked up on the footrest, we zoom down the resort driveway and out to the main road. By vehicle, Oia is about ten minutes away, not far enough, and it offers the perfect view of the deep-blue coast as we travel along, the sea to our right. To the left are the grassy plains that house a thriving donkey farm, their dark forms dotting the landscape. Sometimes, early in the morning, you can hear them braying in the distance.

Because the wind is whipping by us, there isn't much room for chatter, so instead, I just soak up the moment. The bright sun beating down upon us, the sea breeze keeping us cool, and the gorgeous views of the Greek isles in front of us.

I've been coming here every summer for as long as I can remember, and for the life of me, I can't imagine a more beautiful place in the world. This island, this view: it holds so many great memories in my mind. If it wasn't for the contract, I might have even moved here after college, that's how much I love it.

The culture.

The people.

The towns.

The whitewashed buildings that carry so much history.

I cherish every moment here, and now, with my arms wrapped around Myles, it feels like . . . well, it feels like I've been missing something my whole life—something that's been right in front of me.

When we reach Oia, Myles squeezes the scooter into a parking spot and hops off, lending out his hand and helping me off as well.

"Good thing you braided your hair, or else that ride might have been a different experience for you."

I chuckle. "You probably would have thought a pack of birds made a nest on the top of my head."

"Kind of sad I missed out on that." He pats his stomach. "Think we can grab something to eat first? I'm starving."

"Of course. Yeah, I could definitely eat."

"Good. I know this gyro stand that's not too far. It's tucked away, so it's not busy with tourists, only with locals."

"Sounds good."

He leads the way, and we walk side by side, our steps falling in line with each other. Oia is a very popular destination on the island because it's what is photographed the most, drawing tourists with picturesque views of whitewashed buildings, stacked up on the cliff, with blue-domed roofs, pebbled sidewalks, and blossoming pink flowers in just about every window box. Walking around the quaint streets reminds me why this is such a beautiful place to visit. If anything, the friendly and beautiful atmosphere sells the trip.

"So, from what I saw at breakfast, it looks like the wake-up calls were not appreciated."

"They were not. Roxane was practically murderous. I fear what she has in store for me later tonight. I tried claiming a truce, but from the evil eye she was tossing my way, I'm guessing she'd already vetoed it in her head. Clea and Lois weren't as mad as Roxane, but Roxane is the alpha in the group, and whatever she decides, they will follow—though Lois said the wake-up call was invigorating."

"So, you have Lois on your side."

"Eh, I think she's middle ground. Not sure she'd stop Roxane and Clea retaliating big time."

"So, you're watching your back."

"Basically." I dodge a couple who are holding hands and examining a pile of art prints outside a shop.

"Do you regret it?" he asks.

"You know, I was feeling sort of guilty last night and this morning, but then, I saw that there was no remorse in Roxane's eyes over what she did at the bar, so, not really. I think they got what they deserved, but I do fear that I set the bar higher."

"Oh, you did for sure." He bumps his shoulder with mine. "But don't worry, I've got your back."

We move around a line outside a bakery that smells absolutely divine. "Thank you. At least I have that going for me."

"Do you really think they would come back with a vengeance?" His hand falls to my lower back as we squeeze past another line to a more open walkway.

I nod. "Oh yeah. I'm not sure you quite understand our relationship. We're best friends—we would do anything for each other, and if anyone messes with us, we are the first to step up and fight back—but we're not afraid to push each other's buttons. We get in fights, and there are times when we've said some pretty mean things to each other, but that's what being soul sisters is all about."

"Have you ever gotten into a battle like this before?"

I smile and nod. "Yeah. It was our sophomore year in college. We were celebrating the New Year out in the Hamptons at Clea's parents' house, and we were playing a brutal game of Scattergories. Have you heard of it?"

"That's the game where you have categories and have to write things down based off a letter rolled?" He guides me to a tight staircase that squeezes between two plaster buildings, one yellow, one white. And this is why I love Oia so much—all these secret corridors.

"Yes. It's our go-to game. A favorite, and we're savages when it comes to accepting answers. Well, the score was really close, meaning separated by two points, and the judging started to get very questionable. Roxane ended up winning, and Clea came in second. She wasn't happy. So that night, when Roxane was passed out on the couch, Clea pulled a Ross Geller and drew a mustache on Roxane's face with permanent marker, knowing full well she had a date the next day. That led to Roxane shredding Clea's favorite purse."

"Jesus."

"Yeah, and it just escalated from there. Somehow, Lois and I got involved, and by the time we went back to school, we weren't talking—that was until Roxane found Lois crying in the library one night. Lois's boyfriend had broken up with her. Of course, all was forgotten—we rallied around her and made the ex-boyfriend's life a living nightmare."

He chuckles. "Would hate to be that guy."

"After Clea was done with him, you would."

"I'm too scared to ask."

"Best you leave it that way. But yes, we are sort of like a dysfunctional family. We don't hold back with each other, but if someone messes with us, we come together and take them down."

"You don't seem like the vengeful kind of person, though. Your ideas have been rather tame. I think last night was your most brutal, and that wasn't even your idea. I can't imagine you taking down an ex-boyfriend."

"Well, I go about it in a different way, a more subtle approach. Mind games, things like that, while Clea, Roxane, and Lois go for the throat."

He rubs his hand over the base of his neck. "You, uh, you didn't mention that I encouraged you last night, did you?"

I laugh and shake my head. "No, I took full responsibility."

"Good, I think I'll sleep better at night." We pass a few clothing stores that I've shopped at before, Roxane at the helm, showing me what would look good on me. I feel a twinge in my chest, a small part of me wishing things were calm with her, that we could go shopping together. Some of my best memories in Oia were spent with her holding dresses up and asking which would complement her eyes.

We turn down a pathway that transforms into a set of at least thirty steps. One of the best things about Oia is that it feels like a giant puzzle of pathways scaling the side of a cliff, almost like you're constantly defying gravity. I love it.

"Last night was fun," I say to keep the conversation moving. "I have to admit, though, I didn't expect you to be that good at pool. It seemed like you were giving Toby a run for his money."

"I started playing when I was young. Always a hobby, but a hobby I obsessed over. While I was in New York, I joined a pool club and would play every Tuesday. Not sure Toby played much when I was gone because it was kind of our thing."

"He's probably glad you're back."

"He is." He's silent for a second. "Seemed like you two got along well yesterday." We turn down another set of stairs, where I spot a shack of a store with a carryout window only and a decently sized line.

Once we fall into line, I shoot him a quizzical look, unsure what he's implying. "Yeah, he was a nice guy. I was grateful for the save. Not sure how I would have done with the wine man."

"Probably wouldn't have had as much fun." He shoves his hands in his pockets. "Has, uh, has Toby texted you?"

I shake my head. "No, that was all for show. He wouldn't text me."

"Wouldn't be too sure about that," he mutters while he toes the ground.

"Oh . . . why, did he say something to you?"

"Nah, just seemed like there was more there."

"I didn't think so. I thought he was just being kind, you know?"

"Yeah," he says quietly.

"Why does it feel like you're not telling me something." This time I nudge him with my shoulder, and I notice just how easy it feels to talk to him now. I'm still nervous when he's around, but I don't find the need to constantly feed the silence or overexplain myself. I can have an actual conversation without embarrassing myself. It's probably because he's seen me at my worst—robe girl—so what more could I possibly do at this point? Also, he's just easy to talk to. He has a kind soul and a helping heart, and he's someone who isn't as intimidating as I first thought. He's actually really approachable, and he seems to care about what I have to say.

"I mean . . ." He lets out a deep breath. "You know Toby's my best friend, and I would do anything for the guy, and I mean anything, but he's also . . . well, he's a player. He's never had a girlfriend for longer than three months. He's more about having fun. And maybe that's what you're looking for, I don't know, but I just thought I'd warn you."

What I'm looking for is you to look at me like Toby looked at me last night.

With hunger.

With interest.

With the urge to be the man who texts me the next morning.

"Oh . . . well, thanks. I kind of got that vibe from him. And let's be real, he's a guy with a topknot. It's hard not to stereotype him as a ladies' man."

"He didn't always have long hair. When we were teenagers, his head was buzzed."

"Seriously? I can't picture that."

"Oh yeah, and then one summer, he decided to grow it out, and he hasn't gone back."

"Have you ever grown out your hair?"

"This mop?" he asks as he sifts his fingers through his adorable hair. "No. I think if I grew it out, the curls would get too crazy. It's too long right now as it is."

"I think it looks good," I say before I can stop myself.

"Yeah?" he smirks. "You like the curls, Tessa?"

I wet my lips and look away, unable to say this while staring into his dark eyes. "Always thought curly hair is cute on a guy."

"Oooh, tell me more," he jokes, but I can feel the flame of my cheeks.

And thankfully, we're next in line, so I focus on the menu. "What's good here? What do you usually get?"

"The peppers-and-steak gyro with hummus. Really freaking good."

"Sounds delicious. I think I'll get the same." I reach for my wallet, but he stops me, placing his hand on mine.

"I got it."

"Oh no, you don't have to do that. I'm the one who asked you to help me."

"And I'm the one who asked you to eat with me, so I'm paying."

I know arguing with him won't do me any good, so I just drop it. He orders a gyro and a water for each of us and pays because he's a nice guy, and then we step off to the side, where we wait for our order.

"There's a stone wall just down the way that looks out over the water. I usually sit there whenever I come here. Does that work for you?"

"Sounds great. I'm at your disposal. You know the way, so I'll follow you."

"Given the number of times you've been to Santorini, I'd think it would be a second home to you by now—you could probably show me around."

"I wish. Mom and Dad really liked staying around the resort. We'd only venture out maybe once or twice during a vacation, and when we did, we normally went to the same places that they loved. I'd shop around with Roxane too, but she always led the way, so this is a new experience for me, walking the streets with a local."

"Get ready to have your mind blown. I know all the shortcuts and all the good stores, but there will be walking involved and hills, lots and lots of hills."

"I'm up for the challenge."

Once we get our food—which smells so freaking good; my mouth is watering just looking at the thick wrap in my hand—we find a spot on a chipped stone wall that offers a view of the pristine Aegean as well as a plethora of blue-domed roofs, winding staircases that lead down to the port, and two windmills in the far distance.

"I'm not sure I'll ever get over this view. It's breathtaking. Pictures don't do it justice."

"They don't. And granted, I loved living in New York City—it's fun and so fast paced—but when I came back to Greece, I felt my soul actually take a second to rest. I love it here, very much."

"I'm jealous you get to live here." I take a bite of the gyro, the meat melting in my mouth along with the seasoned peppers and hummus. A moan escapes me before I can stop it. "Oh my God," I say with a mouthful. "This is so good."

"Best on the island." His eyes gleam with laughter. "Now you know for when you come back. But don't go telling everyone. I don't need my secret spot being blown up by all the thirsty tourists."

"Your secret is safe with me."

"Okay, what kind of bracelet are you looking for?" Myles asks.

We tossed our trash and washed our hands with my hand sanitizer, and now we're walking around together, casually strolling and taking in the scene around us.

The streets are narrow, made of stone, a natural mosaic beneath your feet. Fresh potted plants are on every store corner, while signs and shutters add charm to each business. And if the shutters or roofs aren't blue, then they're a pastel color, so precisely picked to flow with the color explosion against the whitewashed buildings. There's no way to describe Oia other than tranquil.

"Well, I was put in charge of Roxane's 'something old' and 'something blue' for her wedding. I was going to get her something old when we were in New York, but I just felt like it would be more special if I got it here. I was thinking maybe an antique bracelet or a charm."

"I have just the place for you." He places his hand at my lower back and maneuvers me around a crowd. It's the second time he's done this, and just like the first, butterflies flutter in my stomach from his touch. "This way, we can cut through an alley and avoid this pileup."

"Okay." He takes me behind a tan building—one of few in town—and then leads us through a gated area full of trash cans.

"Uh, are you sure this is okay?" I glance around nervously.

"Yes, it's not private or anything—it's just a spot to avoid having the trash cans out in the open. Don't worry, I wouldn't get you in trouble."

And I believe him. I don't think he would. I think he'd protect me at all costs, and it's why I follow. Once we cut out through the back and end up on a main thoroughfare again, he nods toward the right.

"This way."

"Wow, I'm so lost. There's no way I would be able to find the scooter."

"Good thing you're with me, then."

"Good thing."

After a few moments of silence, he says, "Do you think it's kind of weird that we've been in the same place at the same time for almost all of our lives and never really talked until now?"

"I do," I answer. "But then again, I've never been super outgoing, so I can't imagine myself saying hi or anything like that."

"I remember there was this one summer when I saw you in the pool. You had goggles on, wearing flippers and a scuba mask. You were flopping around, pretending you were scuba diving, and I thought it was the most interesting thing I'd seen all summer. I couldn't stop watching you. You didn't have a worry or care that you were getting guests wet with your splashing or that you were deterring others from getting in the pool. You were in your own little world, and I thought that was pretty fucking cool."

He remembers that?

I remember it like it was yesterday. I was so determined to practice.

"That was the year my dad wanted to go scuba diving, and I told him I was going to go too, but he claimed I wasn't a strong swimmer.

Mind you, he was right, but I wanted to see the fish, so I showed him how good I was."

"Did he believe you?"

I chuckle and shake my head. "Not even a little, hence the flopping around, but he knew how much it meant to me, so he slapped a life vest on the both of us, tethered us together, and then he swam while I just bobbed around, looking at the fish."

"Wow, sounds like you have a pretty awesome dad."

"Yeah." I smile, thinking of my goofy, adventurous dad. "He's great." And just like that, I can feel the mood shift entirely as we continue down the hill. This might be the perfect opening I was looking for after seeing him so down this morning. "I don't want to overstep here, but since I am helping you out with some things, I noticed you were kind of upset this morning. Was it because of your baba?"

"Partially, yeah."

"Partially?" I ask.

"Well, I was sort of irritated that Toby grabbed your number."

"Oh, because of the whole player thing?"

"Yeah . . . ," he says but trails off, almost like he wanted to say more. "And then I got in a serious fight with my baba. He didn't have a reason for not showing up, beyond his work responsibilities. We exchanged words. I told him I wasn't going to Sunday dinner to pretend for his family how everything is fine when it's not. And then he threatened my job, and I told him I'd just go work somewhere else and probably make more money." He rubs the back of his neck. "It wasn't pretty, and it put me in a shit mood. That was, until I spotted you in the hall. You had perfect timing."

That puts a smile on my face. "I think you might be the only one who thinks that, but thank you."

"Seriously, I needed this little outing. It's clearing my head."

"Well, do you want to talk about it? Maybe I can help."

"Not much to talk about, unless you know how to change the mind of a stubborn man." He points toward a turnoff on the right. "I know I shouldn't have lost my cool on him this morning, because that didn't help, but I feel like I'm trying. I called while I was in New York, so many times, and he never picked up the phone to call me. I invited him to play pool, and we know how that worked out, and if I want to talk to him, he tells me to schedule time. I know he's doing this on purpose because he's hurt, but I don't know how to get through to him that I wasn't hurting him on purpose—I was trying to help."

"Maybe . . ." And then it hits me. "Maybe you *do* walk away."

"What do you mean?"

I pause and turn toward him. "Hear me out—sometimes we don't know what we're missing until we don't have it anymore, so maybe he needs to see that."

"I already left—that's what got me in this mess."

"Not the island this time, but maybe . . . maybe a new job."

"I don't want a new job, though. I . . . fuck, Tessa, I . . . hell, can I show you something?"

Confused by his jump in conversation, I just go with it. "Of course."

"It won't take long, I promise, and then we can go to the jewelry store."

"I have all the time. Show me."

With a boyish grin, he takes my hand in his and pulls me in the direction opposite where we were headed. His pace is somewhat taxing as we wind through the sun-drenched streets, and the silence nearly eats me alive, but the fact that he's holding my hand, it . . . it awakens something within me, something I thought was dead when I found out my last boyfriend cheated on me.

But there it is, blooming in my chest, this unconscious, euphoric feeling of connecting with another human being. Not just any other human being, but with Myles, the boy—now man—I looked forward to seeing every summer. I dreamed of moments like this with him.

Our fingers still twined together, he weaves me through tourists, up a few flights of steps, down another alley, and then around a corner until we are standing in front of a boarded-up building. With curving outdoor staircases straight out of a Dr. Seuss book, archways for doors, and long, nearly floor-to-ceiling rectangular windows, it rests just on the edge of the cliff, with not one building obstructing its view. The white paint is chipping, and there is a great deal of roadwork that needs to be done, given the potholes near the entryway, but it's quaint and cute.

"What's this?" I ask.

"A hotel," Myles says with such joy in his voice that it actually broadens my smile. "Well, at least I'd want it to be a hotel. Right now, it's kind of dead to the public. I . . . I want to buy it, remodel, and name it Cirillo's Nest. It could only have about ten rooms, but each one has its own private pool that looks out over the Aegean. We would have sunset happy hours, in-room breakfast, and personal concierge for each suite. It will be a boutique feel, a quaint space for couples only. Very romantic, quiet, a sanctuary. And you can't see it from here because of the arches, but there is a large olive tree in the courtyard that I'd hang votives from, like in our nook."

Our nook . . .

I don't miss that little slipup—I revel in it.

"And the doors inside are original, carved, and just need a light sanding. It's a big undertaking, but fuck, Tessa, I want it so bad."

I approach the boarded-up blue doors and take it all in—the possibility and romance of this place—and I see it. And I see him here, happy, doing what he does best, making other people happy.

I turn toward him. "It's so beautiful, Myles."

"Yeah?" he asks, hope in his eyes.

"Yes. And creating a boutique atmosphere is so smart, especially if you gear it toward couples only. I bet you could get a very good price per night."

"I think so too."

"So, let's make it happen."

He pauses and turns toward me. "What do you mean?"

"Let's run the numbers—like we were planning for earlier, but you shifted to trying to patch things up with your baba. Unless . . . do you need your baba's help to make this happen?"

"Uh . . . no." He shakes his head, looking almost confused that it's as easy as doing the numbers. "I have a decent amount of money that my grandpa—my mom's dad—left me when he passed. I've been hanging on to it for something like this."

"Then let's figure it out. You said you weren't really happy with what you were doing at Anissa's, so do something here. Make your dream come true."

"But . . . do you think I could?" The insecurity in his voice is adorable.

"The only thing that would hold you back is the capital, but it seems like you have that, so now, we just have to work out the numbers, and you know me, I love numbers. And you said it yourself: you know how to fix things, and you know . . . spackle." He laughs, and I poke his side. "Seriously, Myles, if this is what you want, then let's see if we can make it happen."

"You're serious."

"Very serious. That's what the plan was all along, right? To run numbers."

"Yeah, but it was always to get my baba on board. I don't think I ever thought about doing this myself."

"That's why you have me." I smile up at him. "So I can help you realize that this is attainable."

He looks behind at the hotel and takes a step back, letting my words soak in. "Holy shit," he whispers.

And I'm smiling all over again.

CHAPTER ELEVEN
TESSA

Myles parks the scooter back at Anissa's and then hops down before helping me off. When I'm standing, he smiles down at me. "Thanks for asking me to go with you. I had a lot of fun."

"Me too." I hold up my bag. "I think Roxane will love this bracelet. At least I hope she does."

"She will," he says.

After we left his dream hotel, we strolled back down to the antique store, where we perused the many bracelets until I found a sterling-silver cuff with aquamarine diamonds. It's beautiful, and I'm almost jealous that Roxane gets to wear it—plus, it was a steal at about one hundred American dollars.

With bracelet in hand, we headed back up the hill, but I pulled us into a paper shop, where I found a blue leather-bound notebook. The color caught my attention first, but I bought it for what it meant, and when I handed it to Myles after purchase, his confused look will forever live in my mind. I told him it was for his dreams and plans, the first step toward making it all come true.

His face softened, and he thanked me several times before buying me some gelato that we ate together at a table, down by the coastline. And I don't know how long we sat there, but long enough for me to drip ice cream all over my shirt, for us to talk about every boat we saw and speculate over how many fish the fishermen catch every day.

Before I knew it, the sun started to dip toward the horizon, and I realized we had been gone for over six hours.

"Do you want me to walk you to your room?" he asks, pulling me back to the present.

I wave him off. "No, that's okay. I'm sure you don't want to be seen with the gelato girl much longer." I point to the giant stain on my white shirt.

He chuckles. "The pointing from tourists was a little much."

"People pointed?"

"No." His lips tip up in mirth. "But I did hear someone say that the gelato on your shirt looked good."

"Shut up," I say, laughing and pushing at his stomach.

He laughs as well and then sighs. He holds his notebook close to his side. "Thank you again, for all of this. Are you going to be out later tonight?"

"Yeah, the girls want to meet at the bar—I'm sure they want to make my life a living hell. Let Toby know to look out for me. I might need him to save me once again."

"Or you can just hang out on my side of the bar the whole time and talk to me."

I guffaw loud enough to insult him, and his brow furrows "Why is that funny? You nearly spent the whole day with me."

"Yeah, but that's different."

"How is that different?" he asks.

"Because we were alone. I'll be with my girls tonight."

"Oh." He presses his lips together. "You're ashamed or something?"

"What?" I nearly shout. "No." I close the space between us and press my hand to his forearm. "I'm not ashamed, it's just . . . well, Roxane wouldn't believe it."

"Believe what?"

"That I'd be able to just . . . talk to you."

"Why?"

God, why is he making this so hard?

"Um, because, you know . . . I've kind of had a crush on you for a long time, and given our interactions, she knows that I probably wouldn't be able to just talk to you like normal."

He smooths his hand over his jaw, amusement playing in his eyes. "You crushed on me, Tessa?"

"No need to make a big deal about it," I say with a roll of my eyes. "But yes, she'd be suspicious, and that's the last thing I want right now. If she saw us talking, she'd just—ugh, she would make a big deal about it. Like . . . a really big deal."

"Because of your crush." He playfully tugs on my shirt.

"Can you not rub it in? God, I can feel my cheeks heating up."

"Oh yeah, they're red."

"Wow, okay, well, I'm going to just go lock myself in my room now." I turn to walk away, and he grabs my wrist, tugging me back.

When our eyes meet, he says, "For the record, I crushed too, so you weren't alone."

"No . . ." My mind goes blank with disbelief. "No, you didn't. You're just saying that to be nice."

"I'm not. You can ask Toby—he knows all about it."

He . . . errr . . . he what? He knows all about it? The crush?

I don't know what to say other than . . . OH MY GOD!

Clutches chest

Does mental happy dance

Internally screams

Myles Cirillo crushed on me.

ME! Tessa Doukas. He had a crush on me.

Bend me over backward and slap me on the ass because I'm in disbelief.

Lord, please don't let this be a joke.

"Oh. Well, that's, uh, that's information," I answer because I honestly don't know how to process this.

Chuckling softly, he pulls me into a hug. "I'll see you later tonight."

"Yeah, okay, see you." I hug him back, and when we part, he offers me a wave before taking off.

Myles crushed on me? The girl with the kite? The girl who practiced snorkeling in the resort pool? The girl who would spend her vacation days with a magnifying glass in hand? That girl. I'm not sure I believe him, because I'm not sure anyone could crush on that girl. But then again, he remembered all those details, so maybe . . . maybe there's validity to what he said.

Either way, I have pep in my step. *Myles noticed me, maybe even crushed on me.* I can't help but smile at the thought.

On my way back to my room, my phone buzzes in my purse, and I pull it out.

Myles: Stick your shirt in a bag when you change, and I'll be sure to have a staff member pick it up so they can treat the stain.

Tessa: Really? That would be amazing. Thank you.

Myles: Of course. And thanks again, for today, for believing in me. I have a lot of fun with you.

I can't hold back my smile. I'm freaking beaming from ear to ear.

Tessa: I had a lot of fun, too.

Myles: See you tonight, Tessa.

Tessa: See you tonight.

God, he's so freaking cute. Isn't he? I've dated a few guys before—a personal trainer who thought I should hit up the gym with him: no, thank you. Next was a data nerd like myself. We had so much in common that it started to get weird and monotonous, and neither one of us was pushing the other for more. And then there was the political hopeful who said all he wanted in life was to have a government job with a "killer" pension but did absolutely nothing to get that job. I truly believed he thought he could manifest an offer without even applying. And, of course, the two men who cheated on me without even looking back. They all had their quirks, their negatives, and their positives, but none of them compares to Myles. He's so unguarded, protective, goal oriented. He has passion in his eyes and truly cares about the people in his orbit. I had fun today because of him, because he makes me smile and laugh . . . and forget about everything else around me.

With a wide grin, I remove my key card from my purse, and when I reach my door, I unlock it and walk in, only to find a pile of clothes stacked on my bed.

What on earth?

I walk over to the clothes and sift through them—they're Roxane's dresses, her revealing dresses. Why would she put these here? Maybe to get dry-cleaned?

Maybe to do laundry?

Either way, I leave them on the bed and go to my dresser to pull out another shirt. When I open the drawer, it's completely empty. That's weird. Did she move my clothes around? I open up another drawer, and another . . . and the closet, but I come up short there too. The only thing hanging in the closet is a bikini I've never seen before.

Am I in the right room?

I go into the bathroom, where I see all my neatly laid out cosmetics, creams, and face wash. Then I return to the main room, where my book is resting on my nightstand.

So, what the hell is going on with my clothes?

Confused, I shoot a text to Roxane.

Tessa: Did you do something with my clothes?

She immediately replies, as if she's been waiting this entire afternoon for a response.

Roxane: Yes, I took them. That's what happens when you mess
with the queen, you get burned.

Oh.
Dear.
God.

Tessa: What did you do with my clothes? I need those. I have to
change—I spilled something on my shirt.

Roxane: You have plenty of clothes at your disposal, they're all
on your bed.

I glance at the piles of dresses. Strappy, thin fabric, some cheaply
made, all of them bearing high hemlines. She can't be serious. These are
articles of clothing I would never wear. Ever. They're far too revealing.

Tessa: Roxane, I'm not wearing those. Bring me my clothes.

Roxane: Hmm . . . let me think on that . . .

Roxane: Gave it some thought and I'm going to go with no. You
can get them back tomorrow.

Tessa: Fine, I'll see you tomorrow morning.

Roxane: I thought you'd say that. The only way you will be getting them back is if you wear one of my dresses out. TONIGHT. So, you can either stay in your room until the end of time, or you can pick a dress and meet us at the bar.

This is the problem with having a twin—they know your weaknesses, your soft spots, sometimes better than you know them yourself. And then they have zero shame in taking advantage of those weak points.

Tessa: I hate you.

Roxane: You're the one who started this. Don't start something you can't finish. Kisses. Oh, and go with the blue, it barely covers my butt.

Urgh.

I growl out in frustration and toss my phone on the bed.

I should have known she wasn't going to take the whole drink-and-wake-up-call thing well or the truce to heart. But to steal my clothes, to push me out of my comfort zone: she truly knows how to hit me where it hurts . . . just like I messed with her sleep cycle. Guilty as charged.

Take notes: never declare war with a sibling. These are the results.

I sift through the dresses, more horrified with every single one I pick up. Barely there hemlines, cutouts all over the bodices, so much skin showing that I won't know what to do with myself. And no built-in bras: the absolute horror.

And I have to go to the bar tonight . . .

Where Myles will be working. He's going to see me in one of these. What will he think?

Probably that I've lost my absolute mind. I went from clumsy girl with a gelato stain on my shirt to rabid streetwalker in an hour.

Needing some help with my current predicament, I send another text to Myles.

Tessa: Roxane has countered her attack. Stole all my clothes and left me with slutty dresses. I can't have my clothes back until I wear one. What do I do?

I lean back on my bed and wait for him to text back. I don't think he's started his shift yet, because he texts me back right away.

Myles: How slutty?

Tessa: Could possibly pass as a swimsuit . . . dare I say, modest lingerie.

Myles: Modest lingerie, feels like an oxymoron.

Tessa: LOL. Myles, what do I do?

Myles: Just a wild guess, but I think Roxane is looking to humiliate you, right? To make you uncomfortable, to give you some sort of discomfort like you gave her, so the best thing you can do is pick out a dress you think you can wear for the night, show up at the bar and own it. Show off your confidence because that will drive her even more nuts.

Tessa: I don't know if I have enough confidence to pull any of these dresses off.

Myles: You don't need to pull it off, you just need to wear it and pretend like you're pulling it off. Don't let her win this. Walk into the bar tonight and show her exactly who she's messing with.

These dresses are not going to take you down. This is child's play.

Tessa: You think so?

Myles: Yes. You got this, Tessa.

Tessa: Yeah, you're right, I can do this.

I can't freaking do this.

I feel naked.

I feel like everyone is looking at me.

I feel like my boobs are about to pop out of this dress.

I spent the last hour sifting through the dresses, trying them on, laughing into the mirror at the absurdity. I finally settled on a purple sweetheart strapless dress that hits me midthigh, barely long enough to cover my back end. I will say this: if I drop anything, consider it gone forever. The sheen of the fabric is flashy, something I would never wear, and the neckline is nonexistent. The bodice features a few cutouts as well, but they're tasteful compared to the hatchet job on the other dresses.

I did feel a flash of brilliance as I squeezed myself into the afore-mentioned dress. So, Roxane wanted me to wear one of her dresses? Fine. I'd become an exact replica of her. I pulled my hair up into a high bun like she would, painted my face with a thick layer of makeup like sister dearest, and slipped on some strappy heels that were made specifically to torture women's feet. We're talking Tower of London, torture-dungeon kind of heels.

But the pleasure of besting my sister outweighs the love I have for my feet.

Before I left my hotel room, I took a long, hard look at myself in the mirror, and all I could think was how much I look like my sister. It's startling because I've always considered us two separate people, even if we look identical. Our style has been the one thing that differentiates us to the masses. A low-cut tank top for her, a sweet peasant blouse for me. Thigh-high heeled boots for Roxane, ergonomic and sensible boots for me. That's how it's always been, but now that I've stepped into one of her outfits, I can truly understand why she has so much confidence.

Something I wish I could muster in this moment, with the pitiful amount of confidence I did gather before I left my room fading with every step.

With every time I have to tug the skirt down.

With every wobble on these heels.

And with every time I feel a light breeze on my boobs—that stab of terror that I've been walking around with a boob out and didn't notice.

For the record, the boobs haven't fallen out, but man oh man do they feel like it.

When I round the corner into the lobby, I spot my enemies—I mean friends—and attempt to hold my head high and put on a show, because if Myles was right about anything, I'm not going to give Roxane the satisfaction of besting me. If I own this, it will only drive her crazy.

"Oh my God, I didn't think you would do it," Clea says as I approach.

My eyes shoot over to Roxane, who turns around and lifts her head from her phone. It's the briefest of frowns, but I catch it, and despite my discomfort, my aching feet, and my waning confidence, man, does that frown make everything worth it.

"Well, look at you," Roxane says with a smile.

Yes, look at me.

I hope it's burning a hole inside of you that I'm actually dressed like this.

Myles was right: taking away the purpose of her revenge has never felt more . . . poetic.

"Dare I say her boobs look better in this dress than yours," Lois says, and Roxane's eyes narrow. I hold back my chuckle, because even though this is giving me great joy, I also know not to poke the bear—the bear being my sister.

With pursed lips, Roxane moves in front of me, her critical eye slowly taking me in. I don't flinch; I don't move; I'm not sure I even breathe as her gaze lands on the purple eyeliner I used in the outer corner of my eyes, like she does.

After a thorough, borderline evasive examination—just missing a cavity search—she folds her arms over her chest, a classic defensive position. "Let's see how long she stays in public. She might have worn it down here, but for all we know, she's going to sprint back up to her room." Her smile grows mischievous as she adds, "And that would be a shame, because that hot bartender is working again."

Of course he is.

There's one thing you need to know about my sister—she always has a reason, a motive for what she's doing. So yes, she took my clothes out of a direct response to my drink-and-wake-up-call prank. But she isn't just taking my clothes; she's forcing me to put myself out there, in front of a man she deems worthy.

"The bartender's name is Toby, and don't you think getting his attention would be a bad idea?" I ask.

"How so?" Roxane says. "He's hot. He seems to like you. What more could we ask for?"

Uh . . . how about heart, intelligence, compassion, composure—to name a few, but who am I to lecture on what we should look for in a significant other? I'm the only one without one.

But I still need to make a point. "He lives here, in Santorini. Aren't you forgetting a small detail like . . . we can't live ten miles away from each other? This seems like a very bad idea in general, trying to hook me up with someone who has a life in another country."

Then again, Myles is in the same boat—lives here, has plans to stay here—but you know . . . I'm just not going to think about that right now. And it doesn't even matter because we're just friends, right? Friends who had crushes on each other. That's all.

Roxane chuckles and grips my shoulders before meeting my eyes. "Maybe he lives here, but he could always move."

"How do you know he doesn't want to live and die here?"

She smiles as if she knows something I don't. "Oh, Tessa, you silly, silly girl. Don't you remember, we have the perfume, and if we've learned anything from the perfume, when used properly, it works its magic."

Oh, crap. The perfume.

Why do I feel like the perfume thing is carrying less and less validity as time goes on?

Maybe because we convinced ourselves it was magical back in high school, when we all still had braces?

"You know, maybe we should take a moment tonight, together, and reconvene about the whole contract thing," I say and then quickly hold up my hand to stop all protests. "Not because I'm trying to get out of anything, but because, you know . . . we're all entering new chapters in our lives, and it will be hard to adhere to all of the rules."

Roxane fixes me with a somber stare. "I will live and die with that contract close to my heart. Now, let's get you a man."

"Don't you think this has gone on long enough?" I ask.

"You tell me. Do you have a man in your life?"

"Roxane, seriously."

"Seriously, Tessa," she says, looking me in the eyes. "This is what's happening tonight. Now get over it."

And that's the end to the conversation. She loops her arm through mine and pulls me toward Calypso. There's no discussing. There's no reasoning. It's Roxane's way or the highway, and I know this is her special week, but it's starting to wear thin.

The sun has set over the horizon, leaving the lightest of glows in the sky. Inside the restaurant, the atmosphere is moody, with dim lighting, sensual music, and intimate table settings that consist of flickering mini votive candles and small circular tables, barely offering enough room for two plates. The tables themselves are placed throughout the open space, some high top, some bistro sets, while a scattering of room dividers are ideally propped up to offer guests the illusion of intimacy.

And at the back of the restaurant, which features a line of windows showcasing the resort's spectacular seaside views, a large bar spans the length of the room. Barstools with shimmering gold legs are tucked under the bar top, while lights from above offer a subtle ambiance, reflecting off the glitter in the chairs.

Although the Olive Tree is my favorite, I have to admit, Calypso does have its charm.

"Oooh, there he is," Roxane says gleefully. My eyes flash to Toby, who is tapping away at the register on the back of the bar with his key card, his hand flying fast over the touch screen. And with his back toward us, I notice the perkiness of his behind and how his waist is narrow just like Myles's. Even though both of them have toned bodies, I would say Toby might be a bit broader. And yet despite his handsome features and devilish grin, he doesn't do much for me, not like Myles.

We pull up to the bar just as Toby turns around. His eyes scan our group. "What can I . . . ," he says before he trails off. "Wait, Killer, is that you?"

My cheeks flame as I place my hands on the bar top. This was exactly what I was dreading: the reaction of anyone who might know me. I'm just grateful our families and friends aren't here for the wedding yet. "Hey, Toby."

Grinning from ear to ear, he leans across the bar top, so close that I feel like there's only a foot between us—a classic move of a hopeless flirt. To my right and to my left, my friends are glued to the interaction, their mouths salivating over the fact that there is a man near me, as if their entire lives have led to this one moment. It takes everything in me not to wilt beneath their conspiratorial gazes.

His eyes slowly—and I mean . . . turtle-like, snail-in-the-middle-of-the-road, stubborn-cow-won't-move slowly—trail up and down my torso. It's so painfully slow that it feels like the air between us becomes stagnant, and a collective breath from our girl group awaits his response. Finally, with a lick of his lips and a smirk in his eyes, he says, "Nice dress, Killer."

My hand trembles in my lap.

A droplet of sweat forms at the base of my neck.

And it takes every fiber of my being not to deflate my shoulders, pretend he said nothing, and crawl under the bar until this godforsaken moment is over.

Instead, my brain tells my lips to smile, and I just hope my face is following directions.

"Doesn't she look great?" Roxane asks, butting in.

"She does." Toby raises his gaze and looks me in the eyes. "But she looked great last night as well."

"You should ask her out on a date," Roxane says, nudging the conversation along.

Good God, Roxane, keep it in your pants. Let me warm up before we start handing over the milk . . . is that how that saying goes? Either way, warm the man up before you start asking for dates.

"Roxane, I think we should give Toby a second to breathe before you start bombarding him with demands. Look, he's busy. We should just let him do his thing and serve us alcohol."

Clearly amused, Toby asks, "You want me to ask you out, Killer?"

No.

My sister does, whereas I have no desire to go out on a date with you. I want Myles to ask me out.

Speaking of Myles, where is he? He said he'd be at the bar tonight, but he's nowhere in sight to save me from this dreadful conversation.

"He asked you a question," Clea says, nudging me with her elbow.

Deflect. That's my only choice. I want to save face with Roxane, show her that I'm unfazed by her attempts to hook me up with someone, but I also don't want to flirt with a man who I can't get a read on. He's best friends with Myles and yet is *shameless* when it comes to perusing the goods.

The goods being me.

"Oh, uh, sorry for the holdup. I'll take a Rum Runner, thanks."

Smirking, Toby pushes off the bar. "Coming right up."

Roxane makes an irritated sound next to me. "Make that four Rum Runners, and excuse us for a moment." She hops off her stool and drags me with her, Clea and Lois following closely behind.

"Hey, don't tug on me so quickly. I don't want my boob popping out. This dress is not very secure."

"I once crowd-surfed in that dress at a Billie Eilish concert and didn't have one flash of the boobs. Trust me, your chest is concealed."

They don't feel concealed; they feel like disobedient teens, itching to escape curfew.

Roxane moves us over to a dark corner and then holds her hand out to Clea. "Desperate times call for desperate measures."

"What are you . . . ?"

I can't finish my sentence because I'm knocked mute by the scene before me. In horror, I watch Clea dip into her purse with a grin so mischievous that I fear for Beast's life and then pull out a bottle, only to lift it to the sky, like it's Simba on Pride Rock for the first time.

What bottle, you ask?

The bottle.

The magical bottle.

The bottle that seems to control our love lives.

"What are you doing with that?" I ask.

No answer.

Not a single response as they all step back at the same time—in unison. Did they rehearse this? Lois and Clea both clasp their hands together, looking on like proud grandmothers as Roxane slowly raises her arm, the bottle aimed right at me, nozzle in my direct line of vision.

Understanding hits me.

Outrage pings me in the chest.

Desperation attempts to bring this farce to a halt.

I close my eyes and elicit a guttural "Nooooooo" from the very depths of my five-foot-five being.

Unfortunately, there's no reasoning, not with Roxane's one-track mind at the helm, and before I can close my mouth, it's too late.

We have a direct hit.

Three puffs of eerily sweet perfume mark me like a skunk does its prey.

I cough.

I wave my hand in front of my face.

I attempt not to gag on the bitter taste of a decades-old confectionary aroma.

Entirely too pleased with herself, Roxane caps the bottle and hands it back to Clea, who stuffs it in her purse as if hiding the bazooka she just uncapped on an unsuspecting mobster.

With a brush of her hands and a tilt of her chin, Roxane stoically says, "It had to be done."

"It had to be done"? That's her response?

The sacred perfume, the perfume that we've spent years upon years believing to be the key to our love lives, was just used like a pawn in our stupid vacation wars.

"Nothing had to be done," I choke out, my throat dry and bitter from the spray. "There is no love interest of mine within any general vicinity." I jab my finger at Roxane. "That was a direct violation of article A, the only article in our contract. Never to use the perfume without a love interest."

"Not yet, but there's potential, and potential is all we need with the perfume." She brushes off the whole thing as if she didn't just disrespect sacred rules that bind us as a quartet.

But none of them see any problem with the treachery transpiring in this moment. And that seems to always happen, even when we were younger. When Roxane is leading the way, Clea follows suit because she enjoys the ride, and Lois is too nonconfrontational to put up a fuss.

So here we are again, just like the time Roxane wanted to start a girl band, despite none of us having any sort of musical talent. Clea and Lois are following her every move, while I try to be the voice of reason.

Fine. If this is how it's going to be, then I guess that's how it's going to be.

I thought that maybe after I wore the dress and spoke about a truce, we could tone down the battle, possibly put this all to rest, mediated by an unbiased party, but ohhhh no. Not now.

Not after the treason I was just subjected to.

This is going too far. They talk a big game about upholding the rules of the contract but then just neglect the fact that the perfume was designed to be used when we were sure of a love interest, not to flippantly attract a man.

I can barely hang on to these rules at this point, and this . . . this just pushed me over the edge.

Unperturbed, Roxane blithely clasps her hands together. "Now, do we need to go over the fundamentals of flirting?"

She can't be serious?

But then Clea chimes in, "Remember, touching is important."

"And leaning your breasts on the bar top is a total must. Give him a show," Lois adds, poking my braless right boob, making it jiggle. "That's how I got Ed."

"Don't forget to smile." Roxane pulls at the corner of my mouth, lifting my frown into an unwanted grin.

"And compliments are always good." Clea says. "Beast loves it when I tell her how toned her forearms are. And stroke the forearms while you compliment." Clea strokes my arms with her fingernails, eliciting a line of goose bumps.

"And if you get the chance, make sure he catches you staring at his crotch. Men love a good crotch stare," Lois says while using two fingers to motion to her eyes and then down south to my private parts. "Stare hard."

Clea jumps on board. "Oh yes, crotch stare for sure."

"Whenever I crotch stare at Philip, we have the best sex. He becomes a total animal. So, when in doubt, crotch stare," Roxane says.

"Stare so hard that you almost see through his pants," Clea says with a flip of her hair.

How does that even make sense? Does she believe I have the secret powers of Clark Kent and possess x-ray vision?

I stand there, arms loose at my sides, my eyes bouncing back and forth between my sister and friends, listening to them drone on and on about what I need to do and what I don't need to do when talking to Toby: Don't mention numbers. Don't show him your moles and ask if they're cancerous. Don't be too loud. Don't lick your lips too much . . .

For the record, I don't overly lick my lips. Not sure where that demand came from.

No eating smelly things in front of him.

No asking about his 401(k)—which I doubt Toby has, given he lives in Greece and works for a small company.

No rambling about how I believe the Brentwood Boys book series should be made into a made-for-TV drama, preferably streamed on HBO or Netflix for max nudity purposes.

As if I would ever say that to a guy . . . pfft. I save my passion for the fan groups, thank you very much.

Either way, they've gone too far.

Retaliation is imminent.

The only question is, what do I do this time?

Do I burn all their bras?

Do I tie their underwear together in a makeshift kite that I fly out on the beach?

Do I text all their significant others and reveal a secret that I've held on to for many years?

That would be a direct violation of trust, but at this point, I'm not sure I have any reservations.

They broke the trust by taking my clothes, spraying me, and thrusting me toward a man I don't want.

"Now, go back there and flaunt your stuff," Roxane says, spinning me around and slapping me on the ass.

"Hey," I protest, stumbling forward just as my eyes find Myles standing on the other side of the bar, pint glasses in hand, his eyes trained on me.

My breath slows to a dull whisper as I straighten up and pat down my dress, his gaze sending warmth through my veins, heating up the cold jolt of irritation I was just experiencing.

What is he thinking? Does he think I look nice? Does he . . . does he think I look ridiculous?

Insecurity plucks at my thoughts, creating a demure set to my shoulders, curling them inward. There goes my confidence, in a blink of an eye, completely vanished—

That's until I watch his eyes roam over me, just like Toby's. But whereas Toby was overtly acting flirtatious, Myles is more curious . . . for lack of a better term, starstruck.

I'm making such a bold assumption because he hasn't moved since he saw me. He's frozen, except for his eyes, which roam my body until they meet my gaze again. The corners of his lips turn up.

That little smirk: it replenishes me with confidence.

My insides turn all gooey.

My head becomes dizzy.

And my heart flutters in my chest.

With just the slightest upturn of his lips, he eases my burning soul, vanishes the revenge I was plotting in my head, and helps me focus on what's important—exuding confidence in this moment.

Oblivious to what's going on, Roxane pulls me toward the bar. "Come on. Toby's coming back." Her tug on my arm pulls me and Myles out of our staring contest. He goes back to pouring a beer while I am directed back to my bar seat just as Toby turns the corner carrying a full bin of cherries. He plops one in each of our drinks and then slides them across the bar toward us.

My eyes still on Myles, I bring my drink to my lips and take a large sip to calm my racing heart. Was it just me, or was Myles staring longer than he should have? It's been such a fast-paced evening that I can't tell if I'm hallucinating or if it was reality.

But I don't have enough time to ponder it as Toby leans on the bar again right in front of me. Because it's Thursday, the restaurant is pretty tame, since guests often travel to Oia or Fira later in the week, when the crowds aren't so big. So, Toby isn't very busy, and it shows as he spends his time on our side of the bar.

"Gave you an extra cherry, Killer."

"Oh, uh, thank you," I answer, feeling all stumbly with my words again. That smile Myles gave me tilted me on my axis, threw off my equilibrium. "That was, uh, sweet of you."

"Very sweet," Roxane chimes in.

"Just the sweetest," Clea says.

"Couldn't think of anything sweeter," Lois says in a monotone voice, just joining in because she knows it's her responsibility.

"Wow, a resounding sweet accolade from all. Makes me think I should give her one more cherry." Toby grins.

"Or you can take her cherry," Roxane says, making me snort Run Rummer right out my nose.

"Jesus, Roxane," I say as Toby hands me a napkin. The alcohol and juice sting my nostrils, and my eyes water as I clean up the dripping mess on my face.

"I thought Jordan Maxwell took her cherry," Lois says, leaning forward.

"He did," Roxane replies. "But it's been a while, you know."

"Can you not discuss that?" I ask, blotting at my nose.

"I'm just trying to help you."

I shoot my sister a glare. "You're not helping."

Sensing the tension, Toby says, "For what it's worth, I would be very gentle with your cherry."

Dear.

God.

Clea leans in close and whispers, "Flirt, flirt, flirt."

Lois gives me a thumbs-up, and Roxane needles me in the side.

For the love of God, I hate them all.

They want me to flirt? Fine, I will flirt.

I'll flirt the way they asked me not to.

I take a deep breath. "Toby, can I ask you a question?"

"Anything, Killer."

I prop myself up, and then . . . like they told me not to, I overly wet my lips, dragging my tongue all over my mouth, like a windshield wiper, tossing it back and forth, back and forth.

"She's doing the tongue thing," Clea whispers.

"Enough with the tongue." Roxane jabs me.

"I never noticed how long her tongue was," Lois observes.

Another jab from Roxane. "Tongue in your mouth, for the love of God."

"Oh, sorry about that, my mouth just gets so . . . dry. I like to thoroughly wet it." Toby gives me a strange look, so I swipe my tongue over my lips one more time, really going slow.

"Uh, yeah, my mouth gets dry too," he replies, I think out of kindness, because man am I going for it.

"Anywho, my question." With one finger, I boop the tip of his nose. They want touching, I'll give them touching.

He startles from the unexpected boop, so I take that moment to boop him two more times.

Beep.

Boop.

He winces.

He blinks.

He looks so confused that I almost snort.

"Dear God, she's booping him," Clea says.

"Not sure the boop will work," Lois chimes in. "Ed hates the boop."

"No one likes the boop," Roxane whispers behind my back and then leans in so her lips are pressing against my ear. "Enough with the booping."

"Uh . . . is everything okay?" Toby asks as Roxane removes her lips from the inside of my ear.

"Just great." Roxane recovers. "I believe Tessa was going to ask you a question."

"Yes, a question," Toby says, leaning slightly farther away now. "I'm on pins and needles."

Inwardly smiling, I slap my arm on the bar top, startling Toby and the girls. With a flourish, I pluck my biodegradable straw from my drink, suck the liquid off the end, and use it to point at the mole on the inside of my arm near my elbow.

"Are you aware of the degree to which a mole might be melanoma?"

"Mole talk. She knows how to murder a conversation," Lois mutters before sipping half her drink down.

"You see, I've had this mole for a while . . ."

Clea dry heaves next to me. "Why does it have that black hair?"

"And my doctor says I'm all good, but you never can be certain, you know?"

"Don't answer that," Roxane steps in. And as if Toby isn't standing right in front of us, Roxane presses her fingers on my cheek, forcing me to look her in the eyes. Through clenched teeth she says, "I swear on my wedding, if you don't change the subject right now, I'll tug on that dress so hard, your nipple kisses the bar top."

Well . . . that's a threat if I've ever heard one.

For the sake of my shy nipples, I turn back to Toby and flash him my teeth, an attempt at a smile, although it feels more like a horse trying to chomp a carrot than flirtatious *come hither, big boy* vibes.

"But you know, no need to look at a mole when the doctor said it was okay, am I right? Anyway, do you like numbers?"

"No," Roxane says while she clenches my thigh under the bar. "No numbers."

Toby looks between us, confusion wrinkling his nose. Something I didn't think about when going into this dive-bomb of an idea is that there's a very high chance—and I mean extremely high chance—that Toby is going to walk away from this interaction thinking I'm insane. And then possibly communicate that with Myles.

Will he tell Myles I'm a face-licking, nose-booping, mole-with-a-black-hair kind of girl who talks about numbers? I really hope not.

Finally, he says, "Uh, I don't know. Haven't really thought about an affection toward numbers before."

"Doesn't matter." Roxane waves him off and then lifts my drink to my lips. "Drink up, sweetie." She turns to Toby. "Long day in the sun, you know how it is. Sometimes we go a touch cuckoo, but who doesn't?" She gently shakes the glass in front of me. "Drink, drink."

But I don't, because it seems as though Roxane might be at her breaking point—my goal all along. So, despite being fully embarrassed for my behavior, I keep pressing. "Toby, let me ask you this. Why was sixty-nine afraid of seventy? We're talking wiggling-in-his-loops nervous."

Humor crosses over Toby's face as he shrugs.

"Oh, uh . . . because eight was involved? Something like that?" Clea asks.

"Hey!" Roxane slaps at Clea. "Don't encourage her."

"No, that's why six is afraid of seven," Lois says. "Because seven eight nine."

"Oh, that's right," Clea chuckles.

"Ladies, we're derailing. Please, for the love of God, help me," Roxane groans.

"Why was sixty-nine afraid of seventy?" Toby asks. "I don't know."

"Because sixty-nine and seventy once had a fight, and . . ." I brace for Roxane's inevitable grumble. "Well, seventy-one."

It takes him a second, but when the joke sets in, he tips his head back and laughs. In the corner of my eye, Roxane slouches in her chair, absolutely defeated. And now I get to walk away, the winner.

"Here I thought you were going to tell a dirty joke, Killer. Got any more of those?"

"Lots," I say. "Shall I meet you down at the other end of the bar so we're not, you know, disturbed by these witches?" I gesture to the girls, and they all gasp.

"I'd love that."

Smiling, I bump Roxane's shoulder as I hop off my barstool, grab my drink, and walk over to the middle of the bar, where I take a seat, Toby following me. I don't have to look back to know Roxane is glaring at me. Unfortunately, I was trying to deter Toby from wanting to spend more time with me, but I guess I'll switch courses and hang out some more, but only because I know Roxane is dying a slow death inside over the fact that I won him over with a numbers joke. You'd think she'd be happy that I'm alone with Toby, but here's the thing about Roxane—she needs things done her way. And I got Toby alone, my way. She won't be happy about that.

When I take a seat, I'm right in front of Myles, who is making some sort of cocktail. I watch as he shakes the mixing tumbler, his forearms flexing, his curly hair bouncing. His eyes fall to mine, and instead of his usual smile, I'm instead met with a furrowed brow as Toby leans across the countertop.

"So, care to tell me what this getup is all about?" Toby asks, now that we're far enough away from my sister and friends that they can't hear us. But from Toby's body language, the way he's intimately leaning toward me, it looks like we're carrying on the flirtation—or the numbers jokes.

I let out a sigh. "Roxane took all of my clothes and forced me to put on this bathing suit."

"Is it a bathing suit?" he asks, his eyes scanning me again.

"No, but it feels like one."

"I think you look good, Killer," Toby says.

Myles sets the drink down on the bar top, and a waiter walks by, whisking it away to a table. He dries his hands on the towel draped over his shoulder while he glances down at me.

Toby flashes him a grin. "Don't you think she looks good, Myles?"

Myles goes to pick up a receipt from the printer near the register indicating a new order. "She always looks good." And then he's back to mixing a drink, keeping his distance while Toby turns his attention back to me.

"Hear that, he thinks you always look good."

"I heard him," I say, my cheeks blushing.

"You know, you're not fooling anyone," Toby whispers.

"What do you mean?" I ask, though I can guess what he's talking about.

Toby glances over his shoulder at Myles and then looks back at me. With a sly smile, he says, "You like my boy."

It's a statement, not a question, not an inkling, a straight-up statement, like he couldn't be more certain about anything else in his life.

"What?" I say, my acting skills probably D-list level. My shocked facial expression most certainly does not match the words coming out of my mouth.

"You like him."

Well, there it is again, right there, out in the open. I catch Myles glancing in my direction before turning back to the drinks. I can feel him waiting on my answer, but I feel tongue tied.

Why is this so hard? I'm in my thirties; this shouldn't be an issue. I should be able to speak freely about my feelings and not care. But it feels like I'm sixteen all over again, hoping that he just glances my way at some point.

"Ah, you don't have to answer it," Toby whispers. "I can see it all over your face. So, my question is, why are you talking to me when you can be talking to him?"

"Um, well, it's complicated." I smooth my finger over the surface of the bar top.

"I have time. The restaurant isn't busy—why don't you sip your drink and tell me all the reasons why it's complicated."

I look over at my friends, and they all animatedly give me the thumbs-up while Roxane holds up a napkin that says *TOUCH HIM* in red lipstick.

Lois holds up another napkin. *NO BOOP.*

And then Clea. *I'M HUNGRY.*

Could they be any more exhausting?

Wait . . . I take that back. I know they could.

I don't want to tempt the universe with how much more exhausting they can be, because I'm not sure I can freaking take it.

CHAPTER TWELVE
MYLES

Am I jealous that Tessa has been talking to Toby all evening?

No, not in the slightest.

Do I wish that he would back away from her and take some of the restaurant orders?

Nope, I'm fine doing all the goddamn work.

Do I want to gut punch my best friend for driving me nuts all night?

Not even a little.

Nope . . .

Can you sense my sarcasm? Because *fuck*! What the hell is he doing? I'm only getting bits and pieces of their conversation, though it sounds like she's telling him her life story, and correct me if I'm wrong, but it feels like I'm the one she should be telling that to, unless I read her completely wrong this afternoon.

Which I don't think I did.

Hell, I know I didn't.

I felt the way she clutched me, how her palm pressed against my abs as we rode along the coast. I saw the way she'd steal glances at me while we ate our gyros. And I felt the connection zap between us when I held her hand and wove her through the streets of Oia. Not to mention the way she lit up when I showed her the hotel I want to buy.

Then there's her texts.

Her attention.

How her smile grows wider when I walk into a room.

There's no mistaking that.

So why the fuck is Toby talking to her?

Better yet, why is she talking to Toby?

"Okay, well, I'm going to call it a night," I hear her say as I fill up another pint of beer.

Clea, Lois, and Roxane all left about half an hour ago, looking like they'd just accomplished a large feat. All proud of themselves for their apparent matchmaking. But Tessa stuck around.

"Yeah, it's getting pretty slow," Toby says. "The late-night crowd is most likely over at Oia right now."

"Roxane texted me that's where they're headed."

"Are you going to join them?" Toby asks.

Tessa glances at me and then shakes her head. "No, I think . . . I think I might just walk around, enjoy the evening."

"It's a beautiful night. You should take a walk along the beach."

"Maybe," she says and then adds, "There's this place I like to sit, it's quiet. I think I might go there." She hops off her stool and then lays down some cash, but Toby pushes it back to her.

"Roxane already covered it. Tip and all. She also included your phone number in case I lost the business card, an invite to her wedding, and the schedule of events coming up next week that I'm welcome to escort you to."

I roll my eyes and move toward the other end of the bar, wiping it down, not in the mood to hear Toby's voice anymore.

I'm in the middle of scrubbing off some spilled sugary drink when I feel Toby step in next to me. "You seem like you're agitated."

"What gave you that impression?" I snap as I watch Tessa's back retreat out of Calypso.

"I don't know, maybe the constant growling. You're giving off this vibe that says, 'Touch her and die.'"

"Touch who?" I ask.

"Don't be fucking stupid." Toby turns me so I'm facing him. "You want her."

"You've known she was my childhood crush, and I've finally talked to her, but for God knows what reason, you can't seem to leave her alone."

"Dude, it's all an act. Chill."

"Yeah, well, I don't fucking like it." I toss my towel on the bar top.

"I can see that. How about this: I'll finish up here, and you go cut out early. It seemed like she was trying to convey where she was going. Maybe meet up with her." When I don't answer right away, Toby presses his hand to my shoulder. "She's into you, man."

"Yeah, but she also doesn't live here."

"Neither did your mom or my mom, but they moved because they fell in love. They both did long distance for a while. You two are clearly into each other. Why not at least see if there's more there than just infatuation?"

"And what if there is?"

He shrugs. "Then you figure it out. In this day and age, distance should never be a reason to not explore feelings. And dude, I've known you for a long time. We've been back and forth to the States together, we've been through our parents' divorces together, we've even been through our seven-year separation"—I laugh at that—"and I don't think I've ever seen you this protective over a girl before."

I press my hand on the bar top as I let out a sigh. "I don't know, Toby. There's just something different about her. I like how awkward she is, how she rambles on about weird things and doesn't seem to know when to stop."

"Yeah, like moles and dry lips."

Unsure what that's about, I continue, "Not to mention she's gorgeous, but she also seems to have a beautiful heart too. She's unlike anyone I've ever met."

"So, go find her. See where it takes you."

"But don't you think the timing is bad?" I ask. "I can't seem to keep a relationship with my baba, I don't know what I'm going to do with my career, and I'm pretty sure I could be fired any day. My life is messy."

"When is life not messy?" he asks. "There's never a perfect time to get involved with someone else. There will always be something holding you back. But if you don't at least get to know her better, you're going to regret it."

"Yeah." I pull on the back of my neck. "I think you're right."

"Of course I am." Toby smiles, grabs the towel off the bar, and whips it against my leg. "Now get out of here."

Chuckling, I start to leave when I turn around. "Hey, Toby?"

"Yeah?"

When our eyes meet, I say, "Don't fucking flirt with her again, or I'm going to have to take you out."

He lets out a boisterous laugh as he nods. "Got you to notice your feelings, though, but don't worry, I won't go there again."

"Smart man."

After I left the bar, I went back to the staff locker room, where I quickly changed into a pair of jeans and white T-shirt. I checked on my hair, just in case it got out of whack while working, sprayed on some cologne, swiped my deodorant, and then took off toward the nook.

I'm not sure this is where she'll be, but if she's not, I'll text her.

I'd be shocked if she's not here, though.

As I head toward the nook, I hear my name echo through the lobby. I turn just in time to catch my aunt Velma approaching. With long black hair with two gray streaks in the front, she's a tiny package in pearls and a black dress. I've never known her to wear anything else.

"*Agóri mou!* Look at you," she gushes in rapid Greek as she presses her hands to my cheeks and brings me down to her lips so she can kiss me on the forehead. "Myles, my baby boy, how come you haven't come to see me yet?"

"Aunt Velma," I say while I give her a quick hug before pulling away. "I'm sorry, just been busy since I got back."

"Too busy for your aunt?" she asks, hands on her hips.

"Never, but you know, priorities."

"I see, well, don't let it happen again. You need to come over to my house for some lamb."

"Yes, I, uh, I will. Soon."

"You know your cousin Angelo was looking for you the other day, said he's ready to learn his way around Anissa's. Hermes has been too busy to give him a job. So, I told Angelo to talk to you. You will give him a job, right?"

"Yes, of course," I answer, knowing this is the family way. "I'll let Garfield know, and we can get him started."

"Good. Good." She pats my shoulder. "That boy needs to learn responsibility. Just like you."

Unsure of what to say, I point toward the direction I was walking. "Yeah, just have him contact Garfield, but if you'll excuse me, I have to meet up with someone."

"Okay. Sure. I'll see you Sunday for family dinner."

Probably not. But instead of saying that, I smile and just give her a wave before walking off.

I'm kind of shocked this is the first relative I've seen around Anissa's. This truly is a family-owned business. My baba might be in charge, but my aunts and uncle very much have a stake in the resort as well.

They're always walking around, offering suggestions as to what changes can be made.

I'm just glad she didn't catch me with Tessa—I'd never live that down. It would become a two-hour spectacle of her interviewing Tessa. I know Tessa is from a Greek family, but she's not from *my* Greek family.

Nerves jolt through me as I walk down the hallway toward the cove. Not sure why. I spent the whole afternoon with her, so it's not any different. But the stakes loom higher now that I spoke to Toby and admitted my feelings. They feel more real now.

Coming up on the nook, I round the corner and slip into our space, only to see that it's empty.

She's not here. Huh, I for sure thought she would be here. With the votive candles lit up and dangling from the tree above, the soft waves of the sea lapping against the beach, it would be the perfect place to hang out tonight, especially knowing her friends and sister went to Oia.

From my back pocket, I pull out my phone and open our text thread. I start typing out a text when I hear the rustle of a bag. I look up just in time to catch Tessa stepping inside the nook, gift shop bag in hand. Instead of the much-maligned dress she had on earlier, she's in a pair of pink cotton shorts and a white tank top, both branded with the Anissa's logo.

"There you are." I smile at her. "I was just going to text you."

She lifts her bag, and that's when I notice the sandals she purchased as well. "Couldn't take another moment in that outfit. I didn't think you were going to get off work that early."

"Toby covered for me." I stick my hands in my pockets. "I was over the night. Too many drink orders for the restaurant, not enough conversation."

"Oh yes, you like to socialize at the bar, right?"

"Yeah, but it seems as though Toby had that luxury tonight."

"He's really talkative." She sets her bag on the ground next to the couch and takes a seat. I join her but leave at least a foot or so between us. "I was also eager to get out of that dress. How Roxane wears outfits like that every day, I have no idea. I prefer comfort over the fear of a nip slip."

I chuckle. "If I wore that dress, I'd be just as fearful of a nip slip."

"I can only imagine what it would look like on you. Probably barely cover your stomach."

"There would be some fit issues, but I'd make it work, you know, all for the name of fashion." She chuckles, and I take that moment to drape my arm across the back of the couch just close enough that if I wanted to, I could reach out and twirl her hair in my finger. "You looked really good, though. Not sure if that's what you want to hear, because you don't need a dress to make you look good, but you did."

"I didn't look ridiculous?"

I shake my head. "No, Tessa. Not at all. Although you did look a little too much like Roxane."

"That's not a bad thing."

"It is when you're already dizzy from shaking a drink tumbler over and over again."

"Are you trying to tell me you were seeing double at work tonight?"

"Sort of. It was freaking me out. I like your more natural look."

She smirks and looks down. "Thank you."

Now that her hair is out of that bun, I reach out and tug on a strand. "Have fun talking to Toby the whole time? He didn't say anything embarrassing, did he?"

"No, I think I did most of the talking. Roxane, Lois, and Clea were out for blood tonight. Right before I sat at the bar, they gave me an objective for the night: get Toby to like me. They told me all the things not to do, so naturally—thinking the Myles way—I did exactly those things, a little too well."

"Oh yeah?" I chuckle. "Like what?"

"I'm surprised Toby didn't tell you—he looked horrified when I was licking my lips like a camel, or asking him about possible melanoma, or booping him in the nose."

"Licking your lips, huh? Can I get an example of that?"

"Oh, of course. But please note, I only did this to troll my sister. It's not an everyday occurrence."

"Noted." I nod for her to proceed. She sticks her tongue out and swipes it all the way around her mouth, causing me to laugh out loud. "Jesus, what was his reaction?"

She leans in. "I think his ass clenched with fear."

Another laugh escapes me. "I could see that. He once dated a girl who had an obsession with licking his ear, so I'm sure it brought back some memories."

"Oh, so glad to hear that. He totally thinks I'm a freak."

"Didn't seem like it—he looked pretty invested in the story he was telling. I saw you two, looked rather cozy."

She rolls her eyes. "He's quite a flirt, but you know, it was all to appease the viewing party on the other end of the bar."

That makes me feel slightly better. I know Toby would never act on the flirtation, but it's good to hear that she wasn't really into it, that it was all for show.

"Ah, right, the epic battle between twin sisters and her fellow comrades. Since they're not hounding you, they were appeased."

"Oh yeah, they were. They've sent me many lewd texts about kissing Toby and making sure the dress I was wearing hits his bedroom floor. Little do they know, the dress is stuffed in a gift shop bag along with a Derby candy bar."

"A Derby bar, huh? Any plans for that?" I ask, ignoring the first part of what she said—focusing on it will put me in a shitty mood.

"Are you asking if I want to share it?"

"Depends . . . are you willing?"

She laughs and nods. "I think I can manage sharing." She reaches into her bag and pulls it out. Turning so she's completely facing me, she unwraps the candy bar. "I remember the first time I had a Derby bar. We spent the day hiking around Santorini. Dad thought it would be a fun family outing, but of course he chose the hottest day of our vacation, when there wasn't a cloud in the sky. And as you know, there's pretty much no shade between Fira and Oia."

"Not much at all. You must have been cooking."

"I recall saying something along the lines of 'This is what hell feels like.'"

"I think many have said the same thing under those conditions."

"We were exhausted, thirsty, and in the need of some sugar, so we stopped at the first shop we found. Too tired to go inside, Roxane, my mom, and I all sat on a stone wall while Dad went into the store and bought us at least twenty chocolate bars and huge bottles of water. He was also able to locate the bus station, so he knew how to get us back to Anissa's. In the pile of candy bars, there was a Derby. I was so exhausted and hungry, and when I bit into it, I fell in love." She pauses to unwrap the bar of chocolate-and-coconut goodness. "So, whenever I'm here, I always try to have as many as I can, and of course, I might stock up, so I have some when I go home."

"Was this for your stash?" I ask as she hands me half the bar.

"No, I had a feeling I'd be sharing it tonight. Or at least I hoped."

My pulse picks up. I tap my piece against hers and take a bite, keeping my eyes on her the entire time. "Thanks for sharing, Tessa."

"Of course."

I watch her cheeks turn pink, which I think is one of the cutest fucking things, so I can't help myself when I say, "When do you think you'll stop blushing around me?"

She presses her hand against her cheek, her face heating up even more. "Not sure that will ever stop. It just happens. Apparently, I'm a very blush-y type of person."

"Is that the medical term, blush-y?"

"I think so." She smiles.

"Well, I like it."

"Thanks, I guess."

I finish off my half of the candy bar, savoring the taste almost as much as her presence. I rest my hand back down on my thigh, even though I want to reach out to take her hand in mine. "So, any plans on taking Toby to all of the wedding festivities?"

She cringes and shakes her head. "God, no. That would be a disaster. Although I know Roxane will be relentless about seeing him." She groans. "Ugh, why do they have to be so annoying?"

"You know . . . you could always take me."

Her eyes flutter to mine. "Do you realize how obnoxious my family is? If you think Roxane is bad, wait until my mom and dad get here in a few days, or when my aunts and uncles get wind that you're attending—you'll be running for the hills."

"You fail to realize that my family is the same way."

"Yeah, but not like this. It's different."

"How so?"

She gnaws on the corner of her lip and then sighs. "Because, well, they all knew how I felt about the cute boy in the red shorts. So, if you're my date, it's just going to be a whole show."

"Your family knew about your crush?"

"Of course. I told Roxane, who then told my mom, and my mom is the epicenter for all things gossip in the family. She was on the phone with aunts and uncles before I could finish telling Roxane how I like your curly hair."

"I see." With a surge of courage, I reach over and take her hand in mine. I can't wait any longer; I want that connection with her. "So, what would happen if I asked you out on a date?"

"Uh, you . . . you want to do that?"

"What do you think?" I ask her as I entwine our fingers together, enjoying the feel of her skin against mine.

"Is that a hypothetical question? Because if not, I have an answer. Which I'm sure you don't care to hear because it was a hypothetical question, but you know, if I were to sit back and assess the situation, and given the history, and the text messages that have been sent—"

"The answer is yes, Tessa," I say on a laugh. "I want to take you on a date."

"Yes, sure, of course. That was what I was going to conclude."

"And . . . what would you say if I asked you out . . ."

"Oh." She laughs nervously. "I'd say yes, but fair warning, I haven't been on a date in a while—I would most likely be awkward, and you'd probably regret asking me after I rambled on for half an hour about the magic of spreadsheets. I don't perform well under pressure, and with a label like date, oh man, that's a surefire way to get me to panic, to worry, and to second-guess everything and anything I say. Which, I guess it all makes sense as to why I'm so out of practice—because I'm too fidgety and too talkative." She looks up at me and then clamps her hand over her mouth. "See, this is what I'm talking about. I mention the word date and I start twitching with random thoughts in my head."

"But that's who you are. And I like that about you."

"You like the word twitching?"

I nod. "I do. It suits you."

***

Legs curled up on the couch, Tessa has moved in a touch closer to me now that she's settled down and gotten comfortable in our nook. It's funny, watching her, listening to her. If you give her something to talk about, a topic she's confident with, she doesn't give off a whiff of nerves. She speaks with ease, but the moment you bring something up that she's not comfortable with, she starts backtracking on her words, second-guessing, and transforming into a rambling lunatic.

And oddly, I like both sides of her.

"You can't be serious," she says. "Myles, New York pizza is superior."

I shrug. "Sorry, but deep dish is where it's at for me. I like the crust."

"But . . . but you lived in New York City. Not only should there be loyalty, but you've tasted good pizza. You have a baseline of goodness."

"And that baseline changed when I had my first Chicago-style pizza."

She tosses her hand up in frustration. "I don't think I can trust you now."

"Wow, that's all it takes? Wish I would have known the parameters of trust before I answered the basic pizza question."

"I guess you live and learn, right?" She drops her feet to the ground. "Well, it was nice getting to know you, but I think we both know this can't possibly go any further, so I must bid you adieu." She starts to get up, but I grab her wrist and keep her in place, making her laugh.

"Knock it off, you can't get rid of me that easily."

"Really? Seemed easy."

"But wasn't it better that I told you the truth? I could have lied, knowing where you live, but I told you my true feelings. Now that has to count for something."

"Very valid point—really, you're building trust."

"Precisely."

"That's fair. So, if we're building trust, can I ask you a question?"

"Hit me."

"Did you really leave here for seven years because of the hotel program, or was it because I called your lips luxurious? I know you said it was because of the program, but the insecure part of me needs that final confirmation."

How long has she been stewing on that question? Clearly long enough to bring it up.

"All honesty?"

"Please."

I look away. "It was the luxurious thing. I was like, how the hell do I get out of here? This girl is a total freak. And then I found the hotel program."

"Stop it."

I laugh and shake my head. "Honestly, I don't remember much from the 'luxurious lips' night. My baba and I got in a fight, a really rough one. That's what happened right before I saw you at the bar. I didn't think much of it, just sort of acted, and then when I realized I kissed you, I freaked out a bit, scared I overstepped, and yeah . . . sort of blacked out from there. I went to New York because I wanted more than what I was doing here, and I think I needed a break. I didn't expect to be gone seven years, but I had a great internship, I was hanging with my mom. It was good."

"Why did you come back if it was so great?"

"The need to finish what I started. I know Baba wants Anissa's to stay in the family, and that would be me, since I'm an only child. And if I don't take it, then it would go to one of my cousins, and my dad thinks they're all lazy nitwits. Also, my mom and I are solid, but my dad . . . well, he took the divorce hard. I believe he needs me, we both need this relationship, but . . . hell, it's tough. I want to make things right, but it feels impossible."

"Why did your parents divorce? If you don't mind me asking."

"I don't. They were fighting a lot. It was when the economy crashed in 2007. Baba was stressed about finances and tourism, he took it out on my mom, and there was no recovering from there. Mom went back to New York, where she was from, and Baba stayed here. Since most of my life was here, but I split time with my parents as much as I could, I mainly stayed here during the summer to help my baba. I know he still loves her—I can see it in his eyes whenever he talks about her—but she's moved on. She's engaged now, and I doubt she could ever forget the things he said to her back then."

"That's so sad. Business can be tough on a marriage."

"It is. Not sure they could have withstood it anyway because Baba was so obsessed with pleasing the guests that he sort of lost sight of being there for my mom. Even before the economy crashed, it's like he forgot to be a husband first, business owner second. I remember when they were going through the divorce, I swore to myself that when I got married one day, I'd never treat my wife like that. The business is what feeds the family, but without a family, why even care about the business?"

"That's really mature that you're able to recognize that. So, I'm assuming you want a family?"

"I think it's in my DNA to want a family. A big one. Since I don't have any brothers or sisters, I want to make sure that I have at least two kids. I'd prefer four."

"Four? That's a lot. Was there a reason you were an only child? Were you so terrible, your parents decided they were one and done?"

I chuckle. "No. They had a hard time getting pregnant, and Mom had a tough pregnancy, lots of health issues. So, once she had me, Baba got a vasectomy, and that was that. He cared about my mom too much to put her through that again."

"Jeez, it sounds like he really loved her."

"He did," I say softly. "They truly were in love. I can remember all the good times we had as a family. I think everyone was shocked when they divorced, but my parents weren't the only ones. Toby's parents divorced around the same time as well, over the same thing. When you work in tourism and the economy sinks, it's really tough to just hang on, let alone recover."

"Does that worry you when you think about buying your own hotel?"

"There's always risk when you venture into something new, but you just have to decide if that risk outweighs the reward at the end. With me, the thought of developing and owning my own boutique hotel lives deep in my soul. I know that if I let the fear of failure cloud my mind to the point of not accomplishing a dream, I'd regret it for the rest of my life. I'd always wonder what if. I'd rather fail tenfold than live with regret."

She slowly nods, and I can see that she's contemplating something. Maybe her own regret? I have no idea.

But when her eyes flash to mine, I see a renewed sense of confidence take over, and before I can ask her what's going on, she lifts herself up, closes the space between us, and grips me by the back of my neck. With a sharp tug, she brings my mouth right against hers. But from her exertion and my uncertainty about what's going on, instead of our lips connecting, our teeth audibly clank together. In almost perfect unison, we pull away and slap our hands over our mouths with a groan.

What the hell was that?

Was that supposed to be a kiss?

When our eyes connect, all I can see is absolute mortification—I have about a second to recover this moment before she flees.

"Oh God," she starts, "I clanked our teeth together. I'm . . . I'm sorry. I was trying to not regret, you know, from your speech and all, and I haven't really been assertive in the romance department before, so I based that off what I've read recently, and it seemed like just grabbing you by the neck and kissing you seemed so easy, you know?" I lost my second, I realize—she's getting long winded. "It's not like I was trying to perform some sort of reverse-harem position where it's like, I have three holes, pick one—and don't be gentle. It was a simple kiss, but I guess you weren't ready for a kiss. A ninja kiss. Not that I'm a ninja, but it felt like a swooping-in, fly-by-the-seat-of-your-pants kind of kiss. A drive-by kiss. A flyby kiss. God, I almost said 'flyby fruiting,' like in *Mrs. Doubtfire*. Love that movie. Have you seen it? Do they have that movie out here? Maybe you saw it at your mom's, who knows, but I will say this: when Matthew Lawrence walks in on Mrs. Doubtfire peeing, all I could think of as a kid was that Matthew—such a hunk—saw Robin Williams's penis. I wasn't aware of movie magic back then. Did you know Matthew was married to Cheryl Burke from *Dancing with the Stars?*"

Finally, I place my hand on top of Tessa's, hoping to calm her down.

"Are your teeth okay?" I ask gently. She nods, but I can see tears welling up in her eyes. "No need to get upset."

"But . . . I nearly knocked your tooth out with my tooth. That's . . . that's unheard of, and the sound it made, the clunk, it will live in my brain until the day I die."

"I liked the sound."

"No, you didn't. No one likes the sound of two teeth knocking. No one."

"Did you take a poll?" I ask.

"Of course," she lies. "Just now, and ninety-nine percent of people say no to teeth knocking. One percent is crazy Uncle Felix, who thinks it's funny because he has a weird sense of humor that no one quite understands, but we still laugh anyway. That attempt at a kiss was an abomination, and I truly think I might need to go bury my head in my pillow and scream."

"Tessa?"

"Hmm?" she asks, looking up at me.

I don't say anything, I just slip my hand against her cheek and slowly—I mean slowly—move forward, looking out for any sudden jerky movements. When the coast is clear and my lips are centimeters from hers, I whisper, "If you want to kiss me now, you can."

Her eyes flit back and forth before she gulps loudly. "Okay." She wets her lips, leans in so our noses touch, and just as she moves her lips that last few centimeters, a loud howl startles both of us backward. It's followed by even louder cackling.

The moment is lost.

Shit.

"That must be the first shuttle back from Oia," I say.

"Which means—"

"Oh, pardon us," a middle-aged couple says as they stumble into the nook. "We didn't think anyone was in here."

The lady's hand is in the man's pants, actually stuck right down the front, while his hand is up her shirt.

"Beach, babe. Let's do it on the beach," the man says.

"Oh, you naughty man."

They take off around the corner, and that's when Tessa flops back on the sofa, arm draped over her eyes. "I don't think this place will ever be the same again." She looks up at me. "I think it might be time to call it a night."

I don't want to. I really don't. I was so close to tasting her lips, but from the look in her eyes, I know the moment is over—she's probably wondering if her sister and friends came back on the first shuttle. So, I stand from the couch and offer her my hand.

She takes it, and I help her to her feet. Before we leave, she grabs her bag and then leads the way out of the nook. We walk side by side, not hand in hand, unfortunately, as we make our way to the lobby. What bad fucking luck. This close. I was this close to kissing her.

Before we step into the lobby, she turns to me and pushes a stray piece of hair behind her ear. "Well, thanks for the hangout."

I raise a brow at her. "Do you really think I'm not going to walk you back to your room?"

"You don't have to, Myles."

"I want to." I nod toward the elevators. "Come on."

She follows me to the elevators, where we're joined by a couple who smell far too flammable. We all politely smile, and when the elevator doors close, the woman looks me up and down. "Aren't you the hottie behind the bar at Calypso?" she asks.

"I do work the bar, but you might be referring to my friend Toby."

She shakes her head. "No, I'm talking about you. I remember because I couldn't get enough of your hair. Didn't I say that, honey?"

The man nods. "She did. She put you on her list."

"I did, which means . . . when in Greece." She wiggles her eyebrows, and thank God for the elevator—it dings, and the doors open to Tessa's floor.

"Rain check." I wink at the lady, hoping to God tonight is her last night here.

Once we're off the elevator and headed down the hallway toward Tessa's room, she nudges me with her shoulder. "She seemed lovely. Bet she's a total cougar in bed." There's no mistaking the humor in her voice.

"Can we not talk about that?"

"Why not? I couldn't think of something more entertaining than talking about being on Drunkie's list."

"Was that her name? I didn't catch it."

"It was written in the alcohol fumes coming out of her mouth."

"Ah, missed that."

We make it to her room, and she turns toward me, bag in both hands. "Thanks for walking me back. I'm glad you did, because watching you fight off Drunkie's advances was rather entertaining."

"That's what I'm here for: your entertainment." I move in closer and take her hand in mine. "So, about that date. When can I take you out?"

"Not sure. Family comes in soon, so nights are going to get pretty busy." Her fingers entwine with mine while her thumb rubs over my knuckles.

"I'll take lunch or breakfast."

She shyly smiles. "Okay, can I text you tomorrow? And we can talk about the hotel on our date."

I shake my head. "Nah, I don't want to cloud the date with that—we can have a separate meeting."

"Well, I'll have some downtime during the days, probably when you're working. If you text me the details about your projections and cash flow, I can crunch the numbers and then lay it all out for you."

I scratch the side of my jaw, contemplating how to handle this. "I don't know, Tessa. I feel guilty asking you to help, especially with, you know . . . asking you out on a date. I don't want you to think I'm asking you out for any other reason than spending more time with you."

"I don't think that at all."

"Are you sure?"

"Yes, positive."

"Okay." I move in a few more inches, leaving not much space between us. "Then I'll send over the details later, and you can take a look at everything. You really don't mind?"

"Myles, numbers are my specialty. Of course I don't mind. This will be fun for me."

A brisk laugh falls past my lips. "Not sure I've ever heard anyone say that before."

"Well, I'm unique."

"That you are," I say as I glance down at her lips.

I really want to kiss her.

Badly.

But I just feel like this is not the moment, after talking business. Seems wrong. Feels like I'm using her, and that's not the case at all. So, I squeeze her hand, take a step back, and stick my hands in my pockets. I know our moment will come.

"Okay, well, I'll let you get some sleep."

"Okay. Good night, Myles."

"Night, Tessa. I'll text you."

When she's in her room, door shut, I take off down the hall with a spring in my step.

Tessa is really fucking cool. Smart. Funny. Incredibly beautiful. She's the entire package. And not to mention, she believes in me, in my idea. She sees the potential just like I see it. I just wish . . . fuck, I just wish she didn't live so far away.

But like Toby said, there's no excuse to not get to know her. None at all.

CHAPTER THIRTEEN
TESSA

The sun shines through the window, heating up my body, announcing the morning.

But I have no urge to get out of bed. Not after the dreams I had last night.

So many dreams of Myles.

The two of us walking along the beach.

Sitting in our nook, the candles offering the only light in the space.

His hand on my thigh.

My hand on his chest.

Leaning in close . . .

"Why is she puckering her lips like that?" Clea says, startling me right out of my bed.

With a twist and a flop, dragging the blankets with me, I plop down on the floor, landing in a heap. I grip the side of the bed and look up at Clea, Roxane, and Lois all staring down at me.

"What are you doing in here?" I ask, trying to catch my breath.

As one, they fold their arms across their chests, hips jutted out, positioning themselves as an enemy ready to attack.

Three against one. I'm not sure I can handle this.

"Care to explain what happened last night?"

I brush my hair out of my face and slowly rise to my feet. Still in my comfortable gift shop outfit from last night, I gently sit on the bed, poised for what I assume is going to be some sort of argument.

I'm not sure what they saw, who they saw me with, or what they heard, so the trick here is to lead them into telling me what they know without giving anything up. You know, like that I was with Myles last night, and we almost kissed twice. He asked me out, and all I thought about last night was him.

No, that would be detrimental. They've made their feelings about Myles quite clear. If they found out about Myles, they would only try to damage the potential between us rather than foster it.

"What happened last night?" I say, face neutral. "Uh, well, let's see, you accosted me with perfume and forcefully pushed me toward a man. Do any of you recall that?"

Roxane plants a hand on her hip now. "Yeah, we do, and we left the bar pleased with ourselves despite you clearly disobeying our request to not talk about numbers—thankfully you and Toby were really hitting it off."

"We were," I say. Using Toby as a decoy, I think, will work very well. He seems to be on board, and I'm sure if I explain the situation, he could totally vouch for me and Myles. "We had a wonderful time, actually. Once you left, we had a late-night dessert together—some samsades with chocolate dip—and we just sat under the stars, at the beach, talking and enjoying each other's company. You know, I really think that perfume did the trick. So . . . thanks, ladies." I offer them a thumbs-up.

There. Now they can stop trying to set me up with random people.

But their expressions don't change. If anything, their eyes narrow, as if . . . as if they don't believe me.

"Is that right?" Roxane asks. Uh-oh, she's using her challenging voice. "That's what happened last night?"

"Uh, yeah. Give or take a few things. I stopped by the gift shop because I didn't want to get sand all over your pretty dress." I smile. I envision my teeth sparkling in the bright sun, reminding them just how charming I can be.

Doesn't seem to work, though.

"You shared samsades?" Clea asks.

"Yesss," I drawl out. "The last in the restaurant," I add just in case they tried to order some and Calypso was all out. See, covering my bases.

"And you went down to the *beach*?" Lois asks, and I remember the beach is closed after a certain hour.

"Snuck down, actually." I wince. "I know, I know, that's so not like me, but the perfume was making the decisions last night. So yeah, broke the rules, but well worth it."

"Interesting," Roxane says as she starts to pace the room. "Did you hear that, ladies? She was down on the beach with Toby last night, eating samsades."

Clea paces as well, tapping her chin. "I did hear that. Down on the beach, eating samsades, with Toby."

Uh, what's going on here?

"So, the beach, samsades, Toby," Lois asks, clarifying one more time.

"What is this, some sort of dating version of Clue? Yes, it was Toby, down on the beach, with samsades."

"And what time was this approximately?" Roxane says as she lunges toward the bed, her hands digging into the mattress.

I rear back from the unexpected attack. Her eyes bulge as she waits for an answer, and the sneer on her lips makes me think that I'm about to be busted. But on the other hand, this could be an interrogation tactic on their end. Badgering the suspect with multiple questions, using forceful techniques like tapping chins and lunging at beds. That has "gotcha" cross-examination all over it.

No way am I falling for their techniques. They're going to have to try a lot harder than that.

"Time? Well, the answer in my heart is that time flies when you're having fun, but I know that won't satisfy you, so I believe it was around nine thirty. Myles covered the rest of Toby's shift, and we were able to escape. The beach was his idea, the late-night snack was mine."

Lois moves in for the kill by slapping her hand against the wall and propping herself up before shooting me a look I can only describe as mother-on-her-last-nerve. "And what did you have to drink?"

"Uh . . . the whole night? Or just when I was with Toby?"

"When you were Toby," she says.

Not sure how this is relevant, but I say, "Water from a bottle he snagged from the restaurant."

"Uh-huh, I see," Clea says, stepping in now, arms folded, chin held high. "And please tell us, Tessa, who did you see when you were on the beach, eating samsades with Toby?"

I'm starting to think that maybe they know something that I don't. I mean, there's interrogation to make sure I'm telling the truth, and then there's the smarmy looks on their faces, like they're cornering me into the giant lie I'm attempting to feed them.

But I'm in too deep now to change up my story. "No one. Since the beach was closed, we didn't see anyone."

"Ah, well, did you hear that, ladies?" Roxane says. "She was completely and utterly alone with Toby, on the beach, eating samsades and drinking water from a bottle he snagged from the restaurant."

Her tone is triggering.

This doesn't seem like it's going to go well for me. I can sense it. They know something that I don't, and they're just watching me dig myself a hole.

And then it hits me . . . oh God, did they see me with Myles outside my hotel room? We're all on the same floor; could they possibly have come home early from Oia?

"One more question." Roxane holds up her finger. "And then we'll be done with this."

"Sure." I smile mildly, even though my stomach is starting to trip over itself.

"What time did you get back to your hotel room?"

"Uh . . ." I give it some thought, trying to decide on a time that would seem plausible for staying out on the beach eating samsades, but my mind is starting to blank as panic takes over.

I was cool and calm; I had this in the bag; but now, not so sure.

All three of them stare down at me, like hyenas ready to pounce.

"Let's see. We had a lot of fun. We talked about your wedding," I say to Roxane, unsure why I find the need to go into detail. "He wasn't sure he could get the time off for the itinerary, and I told him not to worry about it because that's a lot of pressure to put on someone. He laughed, of course, when we talked about your fear of falling into the sea while you get married. He said not to worry about that." I reach out to her, but she doesn't take my hand. "And, well, we packed up, and when I got back to my room—I'd say maybe around eleven; I can't be sure—pretty much passed out right after he left, and before you ask, no there was no kiss, but I know he wanted to. I kept my lips to myself because I thought it was important to not hand out all the goods at once. But he's hooked, ladies." I offer us all a gentle clap. "He is abso-lutely hooked. Now, who's hungry for breakfast?"

"Not so fast," Roxane says as she holds her hand out to Clea. "Phone, please."

Uh-oh.

A phone is involved in this interrogation?

You know what that means.

They have evidence.

Freaking EVIDENCE.

We are on a sinking ship, ladies! Prepare yourselves.

Freaking rookie mistake! Of course they have evidence. They came in hot with the questions—that should have tipped me off immediately.

Now I need to know, what kind of evidence are we talking about here? Did they . . . oh God, did they capture me and Myles together? Is that why they kept saying the place, person, and . . . well, dessert over and over again?

With a smirk, Roxane taps away on the phone. "Care to explain this?"

She flashes the screen at me, and my eyes zero in on the picture.

It takes a second for my eyes to communicate to my brain what I'm looking at, but when my neurons finally fire up, I'm able to understand the dark, grainy picture.

It's Toby, at a club, with a woman in a red sparkly dress plastered up against his chest. His arm is wrapped around her waist, and with her back to his front, her ass is pinned right into his crotch. If you say the phrase "bump and grind," this would be the epitome. There seems to be a lot of bumping and a lot of grinding.

Good for him. And she's pretty too. Short auburn hair, curled in that cute way that short hair curls, all messy and adorable. And look at those boobs. Wow. I hope he had fun with her last night.

"She's hot," I say, and then realize that is not what I was supposed to say. I was just so relieved they didn't have evidence of me and Myles together that I forgot the lies I'd spun this morning. "I mean, *oh my God!*" I exclaim. "I can't *believe* he'd do that to me. After our intimate outing on the beach? The absolute audacity." I shake my head. "And to think I let him double-dip in the chocolate sauce. Absolutely grotesque. Well, he's off the list." I clasp my hands together. "Anywho, are we ready for breakfast?"

Roxane takes the phone from me and leans closer, the devil in her eyes shining through.

Huh, so we're not done with this interrogation?

"You lied to us."

"What?" I ask, shocked, stunned. maybe a touch insulted. "I didn't lie to you."

"Oh, you didn't, did you?" Clea asks as she reaches into her purse and pulls out a rolled-up piece of paper and hands it to Lois.

What time did they wake up? Good Lord.

Lois unrolls the piece of paper and holds it as if she's the town crier of our girl gang, ready to deliver news from the queen herself—the queen being Roxane, because we all know who's running the show.

"From some internal investigation on our end, we have come to the following conclusion." She clears her throat, and I just pray that they don't bring up Myles.

"Toby arrived at the club around ten, or slightly after. He had one drink halfway gone, in hand, when we first saw him. Assuming you were with him, we followed him around, only to watch him shamelessly flirt with another woman."

Roxane holds up the phone with the picture of the hot girl dancing on Toby. "Exhibit A."

"And of course, once we saw the treason, we decided to catch a car back to Anissa's." Oh God, please don't let there be an exhibit B of me and Myles. "Once at the resort, we went straight to your room."

Crap, here it comes. They saw me.

"Which brings us to exhibit B."

I wince.

I clench.

I hold my breath as exhibit B is held in front of me. Half expecting to see me knocking Myles's tooth with my tooth, I squint open an eye, but I'm pleasantly surprised to see a picture of my empty room.

"Please note the time stamp. It was ten thirty, and you weren't inside, and Toby was in Oia with another woman. So . . . care to explain to us exactly where you were?"

Good news: they don't have evidence of me and Myles.

Bad news: they're going to be looking for answers.

Well, either I can keep lying, or I can tell them the truth.

Lies will get tangled and messy and complicated.

Whereas the truth might be annoying, thanks to their constant badgering, but it might set me free.

But it might spoil the delicious secret that is Myles.

Hmmm . . .

You know what? After the hell I've been through ever since arriving, this is an easy decision where they are concerned.

Lies it is.

"Fine," I grumble. "No, I wasn't with Toby, okay? I think I was too weird for him. We chatted, but we went our separate ways. I think it was all the numbers talk."

"We freaking told you," Roxane says, tossing her hands in the air.

"And the lip licking." Clea points at me. "That was some freaky-ass shit, and if I was him, I'd be running for the hills. No one likes red-rimmed lips, and you were two swipes away from guaranteeing a bloody ring."

"Not to mention, she probably asked about the mole when we weren't in earshot." Lois lowers her "scroll." "Did you ask about the mole?"

I look between my friends and then slowly nod.

In unison, they all toss their arms up in the air, grumble out their displeasure, and start pacing the room.

The scroll is on the bed, the phone was tossed on the floor, and I'm not sure if I should be happy about the outcome of this interaction or horrified.

Either way, they don't know about Myles, and that's all that matters.

Myles: Morning, Tessa. Wanted to see what your schedule was like today.

Tessa: Headed to the pool now where I'm sure I'll get a two-hour lecture from my sister and friends about how I'm ruining their lives with my inability to date properly. But free after that.

Myles: Two-hour lecture, huh? Seems brutal. What has spurred this on?

Tessa: They saw Toby last night at a club. Toby was with another woman, which elicited outrage.

Myles: Oh shit. I should have told him not to go.

Tessa: God no. I don't want him altering his plans because my girl gang has absolutely lost their minds. I'm just glad they didn't catch you and me together. If they did, they'd be scouring the resort, looking for you. It wouldn't be good.

Myles: Oooh, am I your dirty little secret?

Tessa: More like . . . handsome, tall secret.

Myles: LOL. Well, if you feel like taking a risk, have lunch with me today?

Tessa: I would love to. Where? When?

Myles: I'll send you the details in a bit. As for now, should I warn Toby about three irritated women looking for him?

Tessa: I don't think it would hurt.

Myles: He's well versed in pissing women off, so maybe we just let them spring it on him. Would be more fun that way.

Tessa: Oooh, evil.

Myles: Stick with me, Tessa. You'll learn quickly.

☀

"We told you not to talk about the mole," Roxane says from her lounger.

"You know, we can talk about something else," I reply, growing irritated from the constant nagging I've received ever since I had unexpected visitors this morning.

Eventually, they all settled down enough to let me take a shower. They thankfully brought back my clothes—they might be vicious, but they're also fair, and a deal was a deal—and I got dressed and met them down by the pool for a late breakfast.

They were humming about my blunders from last night while I gleefully scarfed down a spinach frittata topped with feta. *Chef's kiss* While I was making my way through my fruit salad, they discussed possibly finding an earpiece they could use to feed me lines.

After I finished my first mimosa, I had to listen to them groan on about how I never should have let Toby slip through my fingers.

And now, as I flip my floppy hat down, protecting my face from the sun, I am once again lectured about proper date conversations while a family splashes around in the pool only a few feet away from us.

I swear, I'm not this bad when it comes to dating.

Sure, I might have asked a dermatologist I went out with about a mole or two. That's just common sense. Free medical advice? Who's not going to jump on that?

And perhaps when I dated a guy whose sister was in the chorus line of *Chicago*, I asked if he could score any extra tickets—before we even had a sip of our first drinks. But you know, I thought I was showing interest in his family.

Then there was the time I was at a Mets game with a date who was a die-hard fan. I thought it was cute. He loved baseball, I loved numbers; I would shoot him statistics, and he liked it. But all I knew about baseball was the number presented in front of me. Nothing else, so when I got out of my seat to go to the bathroom during a perfect game, my date nearly leaped out of his seat to yank me back down on the uncomfortable, plastic fold-out chair. When I scowled at him for getting nacho cheese sauce on my arm and bending me in an uncomfortable position—completely oblivious—the other team hit a home run. Not only ending the perfect game, but the no-hitter and the shutout. These were all things I learned as he broke up with me, right then and there. Who knew baseball fans were so superstitious?

But overall, I'm a good date. Just ask . . . uh . . . well, just ask . . . huh, there has to be someone we can ask. Mentally going through my boyfriend Rolodex, I start to wonder, *Wait . . . am I a bad date?*

"I think we need to move on from Toby," Clea says, the disappointment obvious in her voice. "As much as I loved him, he clearly won't be coming back to Tessa."

"Are people really so picky that numbers talk is a deal breaker?" I ask, feeling perplexed.

"Yes," they all say at the same time.

"The only other person who'd like numbers as much as you would be a financial analyst," Roxane says. "And since that's what you do, it would be a horrible match. You need someone to push you out of your comfort zone. That's why Toby was so great."

"You barely knew Toby," I say, even though I know she's right. I do need someone to push me out of my comfort zone—that's why I love these wenches and keep them around, despite the aggravation they put me through.

"I knew enough about Toby." Roxane sits up and lifts her sunglasses, staring me down. "Do you know what makes me the maddest?"

"What?" I ask. Can't wait to hear this. Not like I haven't already endured two hours of nonstop chatter about my inability to date; just pile it on.

"We sprayed you last night. That was perfume wasted. And you . . . you sabotaged that date on purpose by bringing up numbers and licking your lips and talking about the mole. You knew exactly what you were doing."

"First of all, you put those thoughts in my head. I would have been fine, but you are the ones who brought up numbers and moles. And also, I didn't ask you to spray me—you did that on your own—and maybe, I don't know, it's time that we think about the perfume as coincidental rather than magical," I say.

And oh boy, was that the wrong thing to say because like zombies rising from the grave, Lois and Clea lift from their loungers and stare me down, along with Roxane.

"Excuse me?" Clea asks, her fingers pinched together. "What did you just say?"

"I believe she stated that the perfume we all have worn when meeting the loves of our lives is just nonsense," Lois says. "Did I get that right?"

"You did," Roxane adds.

Once again, they all fold their arms, and I'm struck with the feeling that no matter what I do or say, they're always, and I mean *always*, going to be convinced that the perfume creates soulmates. If I'm going to save myself another two hours of lectures, I need to backtrack.

"I'm sorry," I say, sitting up as well. "It's just been . . . well, it's been embarrassing, okay?" Not really, but hey, anything to gain some sympathy from these three clucking hens.

"What's been embarrassing?" Roxane asks, her voice softening.

Huh, maybe this is the correct approach. Get them to show me some sympathy, and then they'll get off my back.

"You know, being the only single one when clearly the perfume has worked for you three—maybe there's something wrong with me?"

"Yes, there is. You talk about moles on dates," Lois chimes in, but Roxane quiets her down.

"Tessa, there is nothing wrong with you. You just need to . . . be more open."

"What do you mean, 'be more open'?"

"She's telling you in a nice way that you're being a curmudgeon," Clea says before sipping her mimosa.

"A curmudgeon. How am I being a curmudgeon?" I ask.

Roxane sighs. "From the moment we got here, you've been unsusceptible to finding love."

"Uh, maybe because we're in a foreign country for your wedding extravaganza, and the last thing on my mind is trying to find the love of my life."

"The wedding stuff doesn't start until next week." Roxane waves her hand at me. "And nothing would please me more than knowing my sister is going to settle down."

"Do you see how this doesn't make sense, though?"

"Not at all." Roxane smiles. "Which brings me to our next suitor."

"Excuse me?" I ask, my stomach plummeting.

"Oh, Jeremiah, over here!" Roxane waves to someone across the pool. No freaking way.

This seriously can't be happening. I thought we were done with the dates after the Toby fiasco. How on earth does Roxane already have someone lined up?

"Jeremiah? Who the hell is Jeremiah?"

"Philip's cousin. He arrived early," Roxane says. "And guess what, he lives in New York as well. Works with a real estate mogul and dabbles in some off-off-Broadway plays. He's sort of nerdy, a touch awkward, and nicks himself all the time shaving, so you might see a piece of toilet paper stuck to his skin. But a real sweetheart, and sure, he might be five years younger than you, but I bet he's a true stallion in bed."

"You don't know if he's a stallion," I shout-whisper.

"The awkward ones always are," Lois cuts in. "They try harder, so you come harder." She gives me a thumbs-up and then leans back on the lounger.

"Now," Roxane starts with an evil grin. She knows exactly what she's doing. This isn't about the contract anymore; this is about torturing me. "I'd say this is a perfume moment—"

"For the love of God, don't spray me," I say.

She shakes her head. "No, I'm not going to. I think we learned our lesson last night. We need to have a little bit more of a connection under our belt before we spray you." She glances over my shoulder. "He's coming. Remember, no moles. Smile, be nice, and tell him how much you love Shakespeare in the Park."

"But I don't."

"Oh really? I told him you did. Either way, just fake it. Oh, and he's taking you out to lunch."

"But I have plans for lunch," I blurt out.

"Plans?" Roxane asks. "What plans?"

Yeah, Tessa. What plans?

"Err, with myself," I say. "And I always swore I would never cancel plans with myself."

"Nice try." Roxane smiles brightly just as a shadow falls upon me.

Urghhh, just when I thought this was all over. So much for gaining sympathy.

"Jeremiah, it's so great to see you," Roxane chirps. "I take it you traveled well?"

"Okay," he answers in a monotone voice. "The flight attendant spilled ginger ale on my pants, so my penis was wet for a decent amount of time."

I snort, unable to control the outburst. But come on, who says it like that. Could have just said he was damp for the better part of the trip . . . but his penis was wet? That's just . . . too much.

"Tessa." Roxane jabs me. "Our poor friend Jeremiah had some rough travels—don't you have anything to say to that?"

I turn to look up at him, and I'm met with a tall, lanky man wearing round glasses. The mop on his head is disheveled, but not on purpose—more like he has never heard of the term "pomade" before. And his clothes consist of short shorts and a long shirt. The combination makes him look . . . odd, like he couldn't remember if he was tall or short when he got dressed.

So not my type, not even close.

"Do I have anything to say?" I ask. "Of course." Smiling up at Jeremiah, I say, "I'm sorry your penis was wet."

"Tessa." Roxane smacks me on the arm.

"What?" I chuckle. "It's true, a wet penis is a sad penis."

"Not the way I see it," Lois says. "A wet penis in our household is a happy penis."

"Can we not be grotesque in front of our guest?" Roxane chastises. "Honestly, he's going to regret ever talking to us."

"I don't mind," Jeremiah says. "Penis talk has never scared me away."

Good to know.

"Well, thank you for being so understanding," Roxane says. "Sometimes when we're out in public, we fail to utilize our filters. But I'm glad you're so easygoing, which is why I think you and Tessa would really hit it off."

Jeremiah glances down at me and pushes his glasses back on his nose. "You're Tessa?"

Nope, don't know a Tessa, maybe try the loungers to the left.

"That would be me," I admit grudgingly.

He nods. "Then come on." He gestures me to follow him, but when I don't get up, Roxane rises from the lounger and tugs at my arm to stand.

I don't.

"Tessa, get up and follow him."

"I don't want to follow him. He's not my type."

Through clenched teeth, she says, "You don't even know him. How can you make that assessment?" She tugs again.

"My gut instinct."

"Your gut instinct told you to buy a pair of neon-orange gaucho pants and wear them to Aunt Franny's wedding."

"I remember those pants. Woof," Clea says right before opening a gossip magazine.

"Everyone thought you were a construction cone," Roxane continues, "so excuse me for not . . ." She tugs on me. "Trusting . . ." Another tug; this time I'm lifted off the lounger. "Your gut." I careen forward, only for her to push me toward Jeremiah.

Off balance with a slightly wobbly leg from sitting, I pitch right into Jeremiah's atrophied back.

Because the man is a waif, he falls forward, straight into the pool, with a resounding splash.

"Oh no," I say, my hand clasping over my mouth as Jeremiah flaps his impressive wingspan around the pool, surrounding himself with a tornado of water.

"Oh God," Roxane says as she crouches at the side of the pool. "Can you swim, Jeremiah? From his flipping and flopping, I'm going to guess no. I don't think he can swim. Help! Help! He's drowning."

"He just needs to stand up," I say and then shout, "Jeremiah, use your legs, stand up." I make the universal sign to stand up with my hands.

"Looks like his penis is really wet now," Lois chimes in from her lounger, not helping one bit.

"Jeremiah, *stand up!*" Roxane shouts just as a flash of red bursts out of nowhere and splashes into the water.

In seconds, Jeremiah is scooped up and pulled to our edge of the pool, where two other lifeguards appear and help him, flopping him on the deck.

Jeremiah lies there like a dead fish—though breathing—arms spread, toes pointed up, and an open-mouthed-carp look on his face.

Good God, what a scene.

Yes, Roxane, this is the type of man I want to go out with. He seems like a real winner. Not only can he apparently not follow directions when it comes to basic human survival, but he has the density of a stick being tossed around in the wind.

Even though I have zero interest in the man, I still politely bend over with Roxane. "You okay there, champ?" I mutter.

He just blinks, sucking in sharp breaths of air.

Checks out. He'll be just fine.

Satisfied that Philip's wafer-thin cousin is all right, I lift up at the waist, just in time to come face to face with Myles.

A shirtless, wet, very bronze Myles.

When our eyes meet, a devilish grin spreads across his face right before he presses his hands to the edge of the pool and begins the process of lifting his body up and out.

Yes, I said "process" because that's exactly what it is. This isn't a simple lift and he's out. Ohhh, no. This is a spectacle. There are stages; there is fanfare; somewhere in the distance Ginuwine is singing about jumping on his pony.

Time stands still as his forearms are the opening act, like tiny jolts of electricity firing off in anticipation of the main affair. Up next, the biceps-and-triceps combo, a pair unmatched, pushing and pulling together to create a symphony of eroticism not suitable for work.

And then there's the main event. Ladies, gird your loins, take a seat, and have your oxygen masks on hand, because you are bound to hyperventilate. If this man's body was described on a marquee on Broadway, all it would say, in bold, was **PECS**.

PECS!

Mound-like pecs.

The kind of pecs that most definitely have been named by many women in the past. Names like Arnold and Schwarzenegger. Mount My Rushmore. Pectual Attraction. And let's not fail to mention the very juvenile but most accurate, Tonka Tits.

Water dribbles down his carved chest, past his perfectly proportioned nipples—which of course are hardened to a point, because a floppy nipple isn't as sexy as a pointed one—and down his stomach, which defies all normalized standards for the male form.

You guessed it: six-pack . . . wait, no, eight-pack!

An eight-pack, an actual modern-day marvel of the gym.

Stacked, one right on top of the other, like a brick road leading you to the promised land.

The finale.

The encore no one was expecting—no one but me.

Because he wasn't named the Bulge for nothing.

Nope.

Red, wet bathing suit fabric clings to his every contour, defining him in a way that makes me imagine him on a stage while I sit below him, a wad of ones in hand ready to slip into the waistband of his—

"So, shall we go to lunch now?" Jeremiah says, shaking me right out of the male spectacle in front of me and back to reality.

Somehow, I manage to pull my eyes off Myles and back to Jeremiah where he's sitting up now, his hair plastered to his pickle-shaped head.

"What now?" I ask, blinking a few times as I feel Myles next to me, completely emerged from the water. *Thanks a lot, Jeremiah.* I didn't get to read the credits—the credits being Myles's final emergence out of the water.

"Lunch." He pushes his glasses on his nose and sniffs. "Are you ready to escort me to a meal?"

Me . . . escort him?

"She is," Roxane says, moving me closer. "More than ready."

"What? No, I'm not." I pull away from Roxane. "Are we just going to negate the fact that Jeremiah here wasn't smart enough to lift himself out of the four-foot section of the pool?"

"Tessa, where is your decency?"

"Back in my room," I say to her, my teeth grinding together. "I told you, I have plans." I say it loud enough for Myles to hear me—as he stands next to me, drying off.

"Plans with yourself are not plans. Now, I've reserved a private table for the both of you over in the veranda. A Mediterranean affair will be served."

"But . . . he's still wet." I gesture toward Jeremiah.

"I'll dry."

"Oh, so you can stand to be soaking, but when you feel like your penis is a little wet, that's a problem?"

Clea takes that moment to lean forward, holding up her bag, which we all know contains the perfume. "Do we need to spray her?"

I hold my finger up. "There will be no spraying."

"Spraying?" Jeremiah asks.

"Stay out of it," I snap at him. Poor Jeremiah, just a victim in all of this. He has no idea that my plans are really with the insanely hot man currently patting his chest with a towel. A man I've lusted after for God knows how long. Nope, Jeremiah just thinks I like to be alone with myself.

"Tessa, a word," Roxane says through clenched teeth.

"Yeah, I can cover your lunch shift," Myles says loud enough for me to hear.

"What?" the lifeguard next to him says.

Myles pats him on the shoulder. "Don't worry, I got you." Then he turns to us. "Is everyone good here?"

No.

Everyone is not good.

I'm not good.

I know exactly what Myles is doing—he's telling me to go have lunch with Jeremiah, but that's the last thing I want. I can't imagine sitting through a meal with him.

"I believe we are." Roxane smiles. "Now, Tessa, if you will just come with me for a second."

Not in the mood for another lecture, I walk back over to my lounge chair, grab my beach bag, and sling it over my shoulder. I look over at Jeremiah, who looks like a drowned rat, and say, "Come on."

Oblivious to my mood and reluctance, he stands from where he was sitting on the pool deck and joins me as we make our way toward the veranda.

Won't this be a special time?

☀

"Your eyes are too far apart," Jeremiah says before taking a sip of his water.

"Oh . . . why, thank you for the disparaging observation." If Roxane hadn't already set up a lunch order for us, I'd be focusing on the sides right now, trying to find the smallest item on the menu that would get me out of here fast enough.

Is the table nice? Of course. It's picturesque, actually, with an unmatched view of the Aegean Sea. Potted plants with overgrown trees surround us, offering shade, and to my dismay, lit candles softly illuminate the space, despite it being noon.

Is the weather perfectly delightful? Annoyingly, yes. So perfect that it's driving me nuts that I could be enjoying this afternoon with Myles instead.

Is the company atrocious? Naturally. Need I say more about Jeremiah, or do you have a general understanding of what I'm dealing with?

I think you get it.

"So . . ." He drums his fingers on the table. "What brings you to Greece?"

Is he kidding me?

"Uh . . . Philip and Roxane's wedding. I'm her sister and the maid of honor."

"Ah, right. I thought you bore a resemblance to Roxane."

"Bore a resemblance?" I ask, dumbfounded. "We're identical twins."

"Identical?" he asks, adjusting his glasses again. Dude, if you have to push them up every minute, on the minute, they might not fit you well. "That's a bit of a stretch."

"It's not a stretch, it's scientifically proven."

"By whom?"

Roxane is going to pay for this . . . absolutely pay.

"The doctors," I answer just as our waiter comes up to our table. Thank Jesus. The quicker we can eat, the faster I can get out of here.

Attempting a smile, I glance up at our waiter and feel all the breath leave my body.

Standing there, in a white polo and black shorts, is Myles, hands behind his back, grinning.

When I said I wanted to spend lunch with Myles, this was not what I had in mind. Not even close. The last thing I want is for Myles to wait on me and the man who thinks my eyes are too far apart on my head.

"Miss Doukas?"

"Yes?" I ask, confused.

"I was just told your sister is trying to get in touch with you. Seems urgent. She said your phone was dead. You can use the housephone." He gestures his hand toward the resort. "If you'll follow me, I'll show you the quickest way."

"My phone's not—" Myles winks at me. "Errr, my phone's not on me, actually." And then, feigning worry, I clutch my chest. "Wait, she said it's urgent? Oh, dear me, what could it be? We were just with her."

"I'm not sure, but let me get you to the nearest phone."

I stand from my chair, nearly knocking it over out of excitement, and pick up my bag, knowing full well what Myles is doing. He's my escape plan.

Not wanting to be entirely too rude despite the way my "date" has acted, I offer Jeremiah a sympathetic smile. "Do excuse me. I need to tend to my sister."

"Yeah, sure," he says. "When is the food coming out?"

"Just a moment, sir," Myles says and then takes me by the elbow. Together, we silently head into the air-conditioned building, down a hall, and into an office. Myles shuts the door behind us, and when I turn to face him, he lets out a large laugh.

"Why are you laughing?" I poke his side.

He grips his stomach. "Your date, oh man . . . what was your sister thinking?"

"She's not thinking, she's just acting on pure evil instinct now." I set my bag down and lean against the wall. "God, he was . . . he was what we call a 'last resort.' Like there's no one else on earth, and Jeremiah is the only man who can help repopulate the world. That's the scenario in which you go on a date with him."

"End-of-the-world date? Nah, he wasn't that bad."

"He said my eyes were too far apart." Myles pauses and studies my face.

"Well . . ."

I playfully shove at him. "They are not."

He chuckles. "No, they're not. Your eyes are quite perfect, actually." Taking my hand in his, he entwines our fingers. "I'd never leave you out there, alone with him. Not when I was supposed to be your date this afternoon."

"So, is that what we're doing? We're going on a date . . . in an office?"

His smile is contagious as he shakes his head. "No, unfortunately, I can't go on a date right now. I picked up someone's shift here to get you out of the disaster back there."

"Oh." My hopes fall.

"But we can go out tonight."

"I have plans with the wenches," I say as I sag in disappointment.

"I was thinking about that. How thrilled are you with them right now?"

"Not thrilled at all. Why, what are you thinking?"

"What are your thoughts on . . . aiding with their sleep tonight?"

I give him a smirk. "I'm listening."

CHAPTER FOURTEEN
MYLES

Hurrying to the register, I swipe my key card and clock out. I have half an hour before I'm supposed to meet Tessa. The plan was to only work the afternoon shift, but Toby called in, asking if I could cover him at the bar because he had to bring his dad to a doctor's appointment. Once again, I changed out of my server uniform and into my bartending outfit. He showed up thirty minutes ago, but because we had the five-o'clock rush, I helped him out until things calmed down. Now, I'm running behind.

"Thanks again, man," Toby says as he fills up a pint glass from the other end of the bar.

"No problem," I call out as I head out of Calypso.

The staff have two choices when it comes to where they want to live—off resort or on. If you live off, you're looking at some higher-priced living and a drive, since Anissa's is outside the major towns, Oia and Fira. But if you choose to live on the resort, like myself and Toby, you stay in one of the modest apartments my baba had built about ten years ago.

They're in the back of the property, masquerading as villas. There's a fence stopping any tourists from entering and signs that say **No**

TRESPASSING. Baba wanted to make it quite clear that the staff quarters were off limits.

Head down, not wanting to run into anyone else, I quickly walk through the employee halls, through a tunnel that connects the apartments to the resort underground, and then through the gate that leads to the apartment hallway—where I stop dead in my tracks as I come face to face with my baba.

"Myles," he says, hands in his pockets.

"Baba," I say, slightly breathless from how fast I was walking. "What, uh . . . what are you doing here?"

"I came to see you."

Color me shocked, because I don't believe he's ever come to visit me here . . . ever.

"Oh, uh, well," I stammer, knowing I'm on a time crunch. "I have to meet up with someone in, like, twenty minutes, so I can't really talk."

"I'll join you while you get ready."

"Baba, I—"

"I said, I'll join you."

Knowing there's no arguing with him, I capitulate and lead him to my third-story apartment. My work key card doubles as my apartment key card, so I give my door a quick swipe, open it, and then switch on a light, leading my father in.

The apartment is small, with one bedroom, a quaint living room–dining room combination, and a galley kitchen that opens up to the living room. The entire apartment is completely white, from the walls to the tile to the kitchen to the appliances. It's stark, the only character being the blue rug I added and the curtains I hung because I couldn't stand how sterile it felt.

Not bothering to offer him a drink or a place to sit, I head straight to my bedroom and connected bathroom. I switch on the shower, strip down, and leave the door open as I call out, "What's up, Baba?" I hop in the shower and make quick work of my soap.

"I want to talk to you about Sunday."

Of course he does.

"I'm not going," I answer before he can get into it.

"That's not an option."

"It is for me," I say, rinsing my body off as I pick up my shampoo.

"Myles, the whole family will be there."

"I'm well aware, but I'm not about to pretend like everything is okay between us when it's not."

I dip my head under the water and push my hands through my hair, attempting to wash out the shampoo as quickly as possible.

He's silent, and I wonder if he's left. I wouldn't put it past him. I would leave too. The whole conversation is exhausting. All we do is go around and around in circles. He's got to be sick of it as well. I finish up, not bothering to shave because there's not enough time. I turn off the water, grab my towel, and wrap it around my waist, only to step out of the shower and see Baba leaning against the bathroom doorframe.

"Jesus." I startle back. "I thought you left."

He slowly lifts his head, and when his eyes connect with mine, he lets out a quiet sigh. "I need you there, Myles."

"Baba, I told you—"

"I'm selling Anissa's, and I have to tell them Sunday before they see it go on the market. It's a family affair; you are family; therefore, you're required to be there."

"You . . . you what?" I ask as my heart stutters in my chest.

Sell . . . sell Anissa's? Why would he do that? He's always said from the very beginning that Anissa's is for the family, that it will forever be in the family, and now he's going to sell?

"No need to get into details, but your presence is required."

"Wait, what do you mean, 'no need to get into details'?" I grip my towel at my waist. "Baba, you can't just drop some bomb like this on me and not offer me any explanation. Why are you selling?"

"Why do you think I'm selling?" he asks. "The expenses are out-weighing the income."

"How?" I ask. "You are sold out through the end of the year. How is that even possible?"

"I'm surprised you don't know, since you went to your special college and all."

My eyes narrow. I can feel my irritation spike in a matter of seconds with one simple comment.

"Are you really going to start a fight with me right now? You know how much Anissa's means to me, how much I fucking care about continuing your legacy. That's why I went to New York, despite what you might think—I wanted to earn the right to take over one day, so if you don't mind, I'd like to know how it's possible to be so in the red, to the point of needing to sell?"

He takes a step away from the doorway. He's distancing himself, shutting down, closing off. I can see it in his expression, the tense wrinkle in his forehead. No matter how much I try to convince him that leaving Santorini had nothing to do with him and everything to do with my aspirations.

Finally, he says, "That's none of your concern. Just be at family dinner on Sunday."

"It is my fucking concern." I follow him to my front door. "Let me help you, let me figure out why this is happening."

"I don't need your help," he snaps at me, the venom in his voice stinging. "You had your chance, and you left."

I pull on my wet hair, drowning in frustration. "Jesus Christ, you're stubborn. Fuck." I wave my hand at him. "Fine, fucking sell the place. Do whatever you want. But I'm telling you right now, if you actually open your eyes, you're going to see that the solution to your problems is standing right in front of you—but because you're too stubborn to realize it, you're going to lose your resort *and* your son . . . for good."

"How on earth were you able to reserve this table?" Tessa asks as we take a seat at Fiora, one of my favorite restaurants in Oia.

Settled right on the edge of a cliff, it offers one-eighty views of the coast and the colorful sunsets of Santorini. But besides the sunsets, the food, and the peacefulness of the dimly lit outdoor restaurant, what I love about Fiora is the live music that plays every night—and we're not talking an obnoxiously loud live band in the corner, drowning out any conversation. Fiora books local artists who specialize in acoustic covers.

It truly sets the mood. Before my mom left for New York, she took me here, just the two of us. And all I could think about was how one day, I'd take a date here, someone special.

Tessa is special.

"How was I able to reserve this table?" I ask. "I know people." I try to be lighthearted despite the rage pulsing through me, and I think it's working because Tessa hasn't seemed to notice.

Once my baba left, I didn't have time to sit and simmer on the news he'd so casually dropped upon me. Instead, I quickly threw on clothes, did something with my hair, and headed out the door with my fists clenched at my side.

"Well, I'm grateful you know people because this is the prettiest view I've ever seen."

I could say the same about the woman in front of me.

After we talked about how we were going to get the "wenches" off her back for the night, Tessa didn't think a "sleeping potion" was safe, so . . . she found some laxatives and gave them each a cupcake as an apology for her behavior earlier with Jeremiah and any embarrassment she might have caused them. They all hugged her, ate their cupcakes, and then, just like clockwork, they were sequestered in their rooms, giving Tessa the freedom she wanted.

When we met at the west wing again, let me fucking tell you, even though I was simmering with the need to charge toward my baba's office, when she walked up to me, it felt like she unloaded some of the weight I was carrying. Just like that, in seconds.

She chose a simple light-green dress that flows all the way to her ankles and cinches her tightly in at her waist. She styled her hair half-up, half-down, and really coated her eyes with mascara to make her stunning irises pop.

Breathtaking.

It's the only thing I could think as she leaned in and gave me a hug.

Instead of using a scooter, we drove to Oia because I knew I was going to have a reserved parking spot at Fiora thanks to my childhood friend Ralph. I held her hand the entire drive over here, which felt like a much-needed lifeline as I was internally drowning.

Lifting my glass of water to my lips—we ordered ahead of time, because Tessa was starving by the time the poop-capades started, so I called ahead and put in an order for two oven-roasted lamb entrées served on a bed of orzo and mixed summer veggies—I say, "Are you nervous about what might happen tomorrow?" Small talk to keep my mind off this crumbling, consuming feeling I have inside.

"Maybe a little." She winces. "I received a few text messages—they were all saying how they can't leave the bathroom. And like a dumbass, I said I was fine."

"Ooooh, Tessa, that's a rookie mistake."

"I know. I know." She shakes her head. "I think they pieced it together. They stopped texting, which means they're most likely texting each other on another thread, plotting out my demise."

"Brutal. You should have told them you weren't feeling well either."

"I know, but I was fresh out of the shower, and I really wanted to look nice for you—I just responded without thinking. I'm regretting it now."

"Well, for what it's worth, you look really nice . . . well, more than nice. Beautiful."

Those telling cheeks of hers flame up. "Do you want to hear something sort of stalkerish?"

I chuckle. "Always."

"Please don't judge me when I say this, but every year when we came to Anissa's, I always looked forward to it so much. Of course, it was a great family vacation in the most beautiful place on earth, but part of that excitement came from knowing I was going to see you. And sure, I had no idea what your name was or who you actually were, but I always looked forward to seeing you. And in my adolescent mind, I always thought that maybe, one day, you'd look at me and say those exact words—that you thought I was beautiful."

And I always thought of saying them to her. All those summers, watching from afar. I never thought I'd get a chance because she was a guest who lived far away. But now, I have my chance.

"You're hearing them now. You're beautiful, Tessa."

"Thank you."

Our eyes stay connected as I reach across the table and take her hand in mine, the sun just starting to set against the horizon, creating a bright-orange glare that slowly eclipses the blue sky.

"And . . . you look beautiful too, Myles," I say, eyebrows raised in encouragement.

She laughs with a genuine, humorous eye roll. "Oh, sorry. You look beautiful too, Myles."

"Really? Wow, I mean . . . this shirt is, like, five years old, but you know, can't throw away a goodie."

"Is this your playful side?"

"It is. Do you like? It usually comes out when I'm more relaxed." Which is shocking because I feel anything but relaxed.

"Should I take that as a compliment?"

"You should."

"Well, I do. And I do like this side of you. I also like the conniving side and the protective side. And the part of you that has big hopes and aspirations."

Aspirations.

One word is all it takes: one word to collapse the happy facade I was barely hanging on to, because all I've ever wanted was to help Baba with Anissa's, to expand the brand, to take on a project like the boutique—something I could call my own.

And now that Baba is selling, it feels like everything I've worked toward for the past seven years feels pointless.

"Are you okay?" Tessa asks.

"Oh, yeah . . . sorry," I answer, leaning back in my chair and looking out toward the sunset.

I can't believe he's fucking selling, without even talking to me. He just made a decision like that. Sure, he's a stubborn man—he's been stubborn his whole life—but this is *Anissa's*, his pride and joy. Why won't he just at least talk to me about it?

"Hey." Tessa tugs on my hand. "Where did you go? Did I say something wrong?"

"What? Oh . . . fuck . . . no." I blow out a heavy breath. "I'm sorry, my baba just gave me some shitty news before I met up with you for dinner, and I seem to be drifting off to that. I'm really sorry." I take a deep breath and look her in the eyes. "So, you never came to Fiora before?"

She shakes her head. "Oh no, we're not going to just sweep your feelings under the rug. Clearly whatever he said to you is really bothering you. Talk to me about it."

"I don't want to talk about that on our date."

"But you're not going to be able to enjoy yourself until you do. And I didn't give my sister and friends laxatives so your mind can be halfway in this date. I want all of it."

I lightly chuckle. "Really coming at me with the laxative guilt?"

"I hold back nothing." She smirks and then tugs on my hand. "Come on, Myles."

"Okay." I wet my lips. "When I was headed to my apartment to get ready for our date, I ran into my baba. He's not one to hang out in the staff apartments, so I was caught off guard. He said he wanted to chat, but I told him I had plans. He ignored that and followed me, and while I was taking a shower, he told me he wanted me at Sunday dinner."

"Again?" she asks. "I thought you already told him you weren't going."

"I did, but there are two things you need to know about my baba. For one, he's relentless, and secondly, he's stubborn. I may have said I wasn't going, but that doesn't mean it was going to stop him from asking . . . but come to find out, there was a reason he was demanding my attendance."

"Why?" she asks, her expression soft, concerned, and I realize how much I need this right now. A listening ear, someone to talk to, who's going to understand me. I feel comforted knowing I can talk to Tessa without judgment.

"Because he is selling Anissa's."

"What?" she says, her reaction mirroring mine.

"That's what I said, I think in the same tone as well."

"But why? I thought . . . I don't know. I thought this was a family business."

"So did I, but he's been operating in the red, and I'm not sure why. We're booked out for the year. How could a company be operating in the red when it's booked nonstop?"

"There has to be something he doesn't see in the books. Someone is taking advantage of him, or payments aren't going through . . . something."

"He said it costs money to run a resort, which, yes, we all know that's the case, but to be in the red to the point that he has to sell? I don't fucking get it." I push my hand through my hair as Tessa leans back in her chair.

"Can you help him?"

"Believe me, I tried offering my help, but he wants nothing to do with it. That's where the stubbornness kicks in. He'd rather sell than ask for help."

"That's just stupid pride."

"Tell me about it."

"So, what are you going to do?" she asks softly.

"I don't know." I shake my head. "A part of me wants to sneak into his office, go through his books, and figure out why this is happening. But the other side of me, the spiteful side, wants to just wash my hands of it all and move on."

"But that's not you, is it?"

"No." I push my fork around my plate, needing something to keep my restless hands busy. "But I'm also not very good with numbers either. Probably marginally better than my baba."

"So then let me help."

"No, that's not what I'm saying."

"I know it's not, but Anissa's means a lot to me as well, and I can't imagine it being under someone else's management."

"Me neither, but I don't want this to take away from our date, so let's just . . . forget about it for now."

"Will *you* be able to forget about it, though?" she asks.

"Yes," I lie. Baba's announcement is going to live in the back of my head until I can figure out more information.

When I glance up at her face, I know she doesn't believe me.

"How about this? We take a rain check on dinner, go back to my hotel room, and try to figure things out?"

"No." I shake my head. "I want to have a fun evening. Just . . . just help me forget it for a night because I know it's all I'm going to worry about moving forward."

"Are you sure?" she asks.

"Positive."

"Okay, so then . . . what should we talk about?"

And this is why I like her so much—because she's not going to push me on this topic. She can read me better than I can read myself, or at least it feels that way. She knows I'm looking for a lifeline, and she doesn't skip a beat in helping me.

"How about the first time you ever thought to yourself, *This man . . . he's the sexiest man I've ever seen in my life.*"

She dramatically rolls her eyes. "So, you're telling me that if I rain praises down upon you, that will magically help you forget your baba?"

"Yes." I give her my best grin.

"Seems like a cheap way to garner compliments, but hey, I'm here to please." She taps her chin. "First time I thought you were sexy?"

"Sexiest man you've ever seen in your life," I correct her.

"Well, who's to say that's true? That I believe that statement?"

I feign shock. "Are you telling me you don't?"

"I haven't seen all the men in the world. I can't be so bold like that." I give an exaggerated scowl, which only makes her laugh. "Okay, fine, the moment I realized that you were possibly the sexiest man I've ever seen in the world? That would be when I was twenty."

"Twenty? I thought we were talking a longtime crush here."

She nods slowly. "Crush, of course, but sexy? That's different. You were on the beach, lifeguarding. I heard you speaking to a guest about Santorini and how they should visit the other islands but they won't find anything that matches the views here. You were animated and sweet, and the way you used your hands . . . well, it felt like I had a spiritual awakening just watching you. I told Roxane how hot I thought you were and how I wished you'd look my way. Never did."

"Not true. I didn't look your way when you were looking at me. I was coy about it. I stole glimpses here and there, when you were engrossed with your family, or reading a book by the pool, or attempting to find treasure in the sand with a metal detector."

She laughs. "Hey, I found some jewelry that I kept and pawned when I got home."

"Did you really?" I ask, intrigued.

She nods. "Yup."

"What did you do with the money?"

"Donated it."

"Donated it? What? So, you came to Greece, found jewelry, went to the trouble to pawn it, and then just donated the money?"

"Well, you see, this weird thing happened to me after the trip. With money in hand, I was attempting to figure out what I wanted to do with it. Over one thousand dollars. Our first night back, I stashed it away in my pillowcase, but when I went downstairs for dinner, well, I tripped over my pajama pants and went tumbling down the stairs and broke my arm."

"Jesus," I say. "That's brutal."

"It was, but out of all the years I wore those pajamas and walked down those stairs, I never tripped, ever. So, I took it as a sign. The universe was mad at me, and karma was coming to collect. I should have turned the jewelry in to the lost and found at Anissa's, but I'd just kept it for my own benefit, and I was paying the price."

"Wow, you're right . . . you were." I laugh at the absurdity of it all. "So, who did you donate to?"

"My school's library." She winces. "I didn't want to attract my parents' suspicion, and I was worried I couldn't mail money, so when we had our book drive at my school, I just slipped it into the donation fund one day. The principal nearly had a heart attack, and because of the donation, the school could buy some new computers."

"So, in the long run, it did benefit you."

"Well, not just me, but everyone's education, and if we're not focused on advancing children's education, then what are we really doing with our lives, Myles?"

"Wasting them, obviously."

"Obviously." She smirks.

☀

"Are you trying to make it impossible for me to ever date again?" Tessa asks as she dreamily stares at the sunset.

Yes. Not too keen on the thought of her going out with someone else.

Our food was delivered about five minutes ago, and we've already demolished half of our plates. But the sun started melting into the horizon, and it was hard not to take our eyes off the descending light.

"What do you mean?" I ask.

She turns back to me. "This food, this view . . . your ability to make me blush every other minute—you're truly setting a standard here."

"Good," I say. "I intend to continue setting the standard."

Why? Tonight is a prime example. I entered this date feeling agitated, hurt, like I don't truly matter in my baba's eyes, and somehow, Tessa has made me feel worthy again. She's helped me forget, and she's quickly turned this night around so I'm no longer feeling worthless but rather . . . worthy.

So yeah, I'll continue to set the standard for this woman.

"I see, and how do you plan on continuing that?"

"First of all, this is just the beginning of this night, so, buckle up—there's more to come."

"'Buckle up.'" She chuckles.

"And secondly, I don't plan on this being our only date, and before you remind me that you live in New York and I live here, we have time to sort that all out."

"Do we now?"

I nod. "Yup. Plenty of time. Little over two weeks, right?"

"Yes, that would be correct."

"All I need is one week to truly get you hooked—I'm halfway there."

"I see." She turns to me fully, her expression full of humor as she picks up her fork and dives into her plate again. "And what happens after you hook me?"

"What happens? Do you not know how romance works?"

"I'm a bit rusty. Why don't you remind me?"

"Looks like I'm going to have to do all the heavy lifting on this date." She chuckles some more as I pretend to crack my knuckles. "You see, romance works like this. You meet someone that you find attractive, inside and out. Then, you start seeing each other more and more. Communication increases, minds are consumed, and before you know it, you're head over heels in love with another human being."

"Uh-huh. And according to your proclamation, this will happen in a week."

"Give or take." I wiggle my hand. "If someone's sister gets in the way, that will make it a touch harder."

"That's fair." She smirks.

"But once the love happens, the commitment happens, and once the commitment happens, that's when you sign all the papers saying you're soulmates until death." I hold my hand out for emphasis. "Did you hear that, Tessa? Death."

"Death . . . now, would that be after a person's last breath?"

"Yes, that kind of death. And once those papers are signed, well, that's when things really ramp up."

"How so?"

I pick up my fork and shove some orzo in my mouth. "Kids. They change everything. They're the real test in life. Kids will tell you if you chose the right person. Kids will either make or break a relationship."

"You are so wise. Please tell me more."

"Now, I'm going to assume you don't have kids."

"I don't, but I've seen them suck the soul out of my friend Lois. I have secondhand experience."

"So you know how much they test you?"

"Definitely. I've heard many a story from Lois." She crosses one leg over the other and settles her elbows on the table, staring back at me.

"Those tests, they're not from the kid itself, but rather the universe."

Her eyes widen playfully as she whispers, "No."

I nod vigorously. "Yup. The universe steps in and says, *We shall see if this couple was truly meant to be.*"

"Wow . . . very fascinating." I love that she's playing along with me. "So, what you're telling me is that you are setting and keeping the standard for every guy I ever date, and within a week, we will be in love, and then we will sign the commitment papers . . . and then be tested by the universe through raising some tiny humans of our own?"

"Correct."

"Now, is that specific to our situation or everyone in the world?"

"Just us."

And I could see that with Tessa. I know it's crazy to think about at this point, but we just seem to click so easily. Like we've known each other for years upon years. And in a way, we have.

"Fascinating. I'm glad to be educated on where this is going. No wondering about what's happening between us, who's going to call who next, whose tennis court the ball is in. Just straight facts. This is what's happening. Deal with it."

"Exactly, much easier that way."

She lifts her glass. "Then I guess cheers to falling in love in a week."

I clink her glass with mine. "Cheers."

"Where are we going now?" Tessa asks as we hold hands and walk down the stone path toward the water. The streets are pretty clear, with most tourists stuffed away in restaurants or clubs, leaving the pathways around the quaint town abandoned, blanketing the dark night with a sense of serenity.

"Dessert. You didn't think I forgot, did you?"

"I just thought you were full."

I shake my head. "Remember, setting the standard. The standard includes dessert."

"Well, I could get used to that," she says. "I'm assuming you have something in mind that will seal the deal on best date ever?"

"Would you classify this as your best date ever? There were some blunders. You know, with my baba ruining the beginning."

"Some vulnerable blunders that only made me appreciate you even more. They helped me see that you aren't just some hot robot, working odd jobs at Anissa's." Good to know she appreciates vulnerability.

"What else did you like about the date?"

"The obvious—the food and the view and the sunset. The handsome man who sat across from me was a real charmer too. I truly enjoyed his story about getting lost on the subway, somehow changing trains completely at Grand Central, and riding all the way upstate."

"Not my finest moment."

"And the story about how you had to give mouth-to-mouth to a man on the beach—until you realized he was just thirsty for your lips."

"It was a solid kiss. I didn't hold it against him."

"And my favorite thing of the night, when you moaned with every bite of lamb. It was the kind of moan that you only hear in dirty films."

"Do you know a thing or two about dirty films?"

"I've seen my fair share." She smirks. "And your food moan, plucked straight from a blow job at the pool lounge."

"What?" I laugh hard. "Tessa, I feel scandalized."

"So do I, after that meal. Who knew lamb could be an aphrodisiac?" She pauses and looks up at me, eyes full of laughter. "Hmm, you know, now that I'm hearing myself talk, I think I might have had one too many glasses of wine. I don't normally talk so boldly."

"I like it," I answer. "Loose Tessa, I feel like I can find out more about her."

"You probably could."

We pass a tourist shop where Greek trinkets, scarves, and clothes are sold, the air-conditioning feeling good on my arm as we move on by.

"Then let me ask you this: if I were to kiss you tonight, would you kiss me back?"

"Oh yeah." She bobs her head. "One hundred percent."

I shouldn't be cocky, but I felt like I knew that answer was coming. Doesn't make it any less impactful, though. Kissing Tessa has felt like a lifelong dream, so knowing it's a locked-in possibility only makes this night that much better.

"And if I said . . . let's make out in the back seat of my car, what would you say to that?"

"Show me the way. I love a good back seat." Again, she pauses and then adds, "For the record, I've never done anything in the back seat of a car, but it holds some appeal."

"You love back seats." I laugh. "Not sure I've ever heard that before."

"Not sure I ever heard a guy ask about kissing me before. They always just do it. Then again, sometimes going in for the sneak attack doesn't work, hence the whole tooth jam we had."

"I want to say that was both our faults, but you came at me with fangs. There was no stopping you. Tooth jam was bound to happen."

"Oh my God, I can't believe you're blaming me."

"Honesty, Tessa. Remember, if we're going to be in love in a week, we need to be open and honest with each other."

"Oh . . ." She leans in close, our shoulders brushing against each other. "Is that what we're going to do? Okay . . . honesty is the best policy."

Her smirk, her tone of voice: I know it's teasing, but it also makes me think I'm in for it.

"Uh, how come I have the feeling this is going to backfire on me?"

***

"Oh . . . God," Tessa moans as her head tilts back, her lips parted.

I shift uncomfortably in my white outdoor chair. "Hey, stop that."

"Stop what?" she asks.

"Stop having a sexual experience with a cake. You're making me jealous of a baked good."

She pops her eyes open. "I know I should probably apologize for my behavior, but I'm not sorry. This is the best *revani* cake I've ever had. The citrus flavor is so . . . so . . ."

"Luxurious?" I tease.

Her eyes narrow. "Don't use my word. That's reserved for your lips and hands only."

"My mistake." I hold my hand up in apology. "Seriously, though. Stop moaning, it's making me horny."

"Horny, huh? Now you know how I felt when you were eating the lamb."

"I was not that loud."

"Loud enough." She licks her fork, and I watch as her tongue spreads over the tines, soaking up every piece of sweetness. *Jesus.* "So, claiming you're getting horny, is that declaration part of the honesty train we're on?"

"It is—complete transparency. At least that's what you have led me to believe."

"Oh yes, so much transparency, because communication and all that fun stuff, right? That's what will create this envelope of love that's supposed to be delivered in a week."

"Right," I say, wondering where she's going with this.

"Then I must say . . . if we're being honest about everything, not holding back. There's something I have to admit." Here we go. "My sister and friends call you the Bulge."

"The what?" I laugh out loud. I wasn't expecting that kind of honesty.

"The Bulge. Because, well . . . for many summers, we've stared at your . . . you know, *bulge* in your swim trunks. Therefore, that has become your nickname."

Stared at my swim trunks, huh? Well, that's, uh . . . that's news to me. Her cheeks redden.

I feel my cheeks redden.

And we sit there, staring at each other until we both crack smiles and laugh together.

"The Bulge? I mean, it's flattering, that's for sure."

Playfully, she taps her chin with her fork. "But is it accurate?"

Man, that wine really has loosened her up, not that I'm complaining. Because I'm not. I love seeing her like this, loose and confident rather than a bundle of nerves.

"Are you asking if I have a large dick?"

"Hey, ho, whoa." She waves her hands at me. "That's coming on a bit strong, don't you think?"

I chuckle. "I *think* white wine makes you goofy."

"I think you might be right about that." She takes another bite of her cake. "I don't feel drunk, though, just relaxed, which is why I probably told you about the Bulge. Then again, I tend to ramble, so I'm sure that it would have come out at some point, and since we're laying it all out on the table, I have a collection of pictures I've taken of you over the years."

"Really?" I ask, fascinated by this new confession. Let's keep them coming. "Where do you keep these pictures?"

"In a box. I printed them all out. Of course, Roxane is in the picture somehow. Her head, her arm, her leg, but you are in the background." Her nose scrunches up. "Is that TMI?"

"I actually think it's cute."

"Aw, look at you developing Stockholm syndrome."

"To have Stockholm syndrome, wouldn't you have to capture me?"

She wiggles her eyebrows. "What do you think tonight is?" She brings another bite of cake up to her mouth and then tilts her head to the side. "You know, if I step back and think about what I just said, it's incredibly creepy, and maybe you should just leave me here and take off."

I laugh. "Considering it, Tessa."

"There has to be something embarrassing you can tell me," Tessa says as we walk back up the hill toward the car.

"There are plenty of things, but do I want to tell you? Not so much."

"Come on." She tugs on my hand. "I told you about my box of pictures. We're being transparent, therefore it's time you tell me something embarrassing."

"Yeah, but my shit is way more embarrassing."

"Oooh, then it has to be good." She turns toward me as we continue up the hill, lit by the local shops and softly glowing bulbs built into the short white walls that line the walking path. "Give me the goods."

"I'd rather not."

"Please, Myles." She squeezes my hands. "We're open books, remember? The only way we can fall in love in one week is if we continue this open line of communication."

"This might scare you away, though. There's communication, and then there's too much communication."

She shakes her head. "No, there's never too much. We're building trust, so tell me your best cringeworthy stuff."

I sigh. "Fine . . . God, this is humiliating."

"It's okay." She pats my hand. "I'm right here to take it all in."

"Yeah, I know, that's the problem." I push my hand through my hair. "Okay, it was when I was . . . I want to say fourteen or fifteen. A very horny teenager."

"I love how this is starting out."

"I'm sure you are. I saw you and Roxane at the beach. You were getting up out of your lounger, and you were wearing a bathing suit, a looser one, and, well, when you got up, I got a peek down the front and saw the edge of your nipple. I got so fucking hard."

"Stop." She laughs. "No, you did not."

"I did. And it was in public, and I had to tell myself to calm the fuck down because I didn't want anyone seeing."

"Did anyone?"

"No, not that I know of, but I did hide behind a tree for a minute or so. Longer than I should have."

"Aww, I gave you a boner."

"You did."

"That's so . . . sweet."

"Is it, though?" I wince.

"In my mind it is." She clutches onto my arm happily and holds me tight as we make our way up the rest of the hill, to my parked car. I bring her to her side of the car and open the door, only for her to face me with a frown. "Is our date over?" she asks.

I shake my head. "Not even close. I want to take you to one more place."

"Okay, good."

I tilt her chin up with my index finger and smile. "Not ready to say good night just yet?"

She shakes her head. "Not even close."

Me either.

I pull the door farther open, and she ducks her head under my arm and sits down. Gripping the top of the car, I lean in. "Don't get too comfortable."

Then I round the car, get in on my side, and start it up. With my hand on the headrest of her seat, I back out of the parking spot and pull onto the road.

"So where are we going? Or is this a secret?"

"A secret," I answer while I navigate Oia's narrow streets.

"Good secret or bad secret?"

"How could it be a bad secret?" I ask as I make a left-hand turn.

"Can't be sure, but I'm buzzing with excitement, and I'll probably fill the silence with nervous chatter, so if I don't make sense, that's why."

"You don't have to fill the silence. Sometimes it's good just to enjoy each other without talking."

"But if we're going to fall in love in a week, then shouldn't we be talking? Getting to know more about each other?"

"Probably." I glance at her smiling face for a moment. "Maybe we do a lightning round, then."

"What's that?" she asks.

"Quick questions. Answer and then ask. Rapid fire."

"Oooh, yes, let's do that."

"Okay. I'll start." I clear my throat as I make a right onto a wider street. "Did you have a pet growing up? If yes, I want a name too."

"Yes, an orange tabby cat, and her name was Yammy, but she also responded to Yam Yam."

"That's a great name."

"Thank you," she says. "Same question."

"No pets. My mom was allergic, and my baba didn't want any dog or cat hair on our clothing because we were always around guests. But at one point I did have a fish. He died after four days. After that, I didn't bother."

"That should concern me that you killed a fish in four days, but eh." She shrugs.

"I appreciate your low standards in that regard. Thanks for not holding that against me. Okay, next question. What's a nickname your parents would call you?"

"Tessa Toot," she answers. "And I swear if you call me that, this mini love affair is over."

"Yikes, okay. Not calling you Tessa Toot, even though it's quite catchy and most likely now etched in my brain forever."

"Great." She chuckles. "Beach or pool?"

"Pool, all day every day. After working the beach for so many years, sand and I have become sworn enemies."

"I believe you've mentioned that before. Trunks or Speedo?"

"Hey, it's my turn to ask a question."

"It's an additional question to mine. Just answer." She bats her eyelashes, and hell, I give her what she wants.

"Both. When I'm working, I have to wear trunks, but I don't mind a Speedo."

"With that bulge? That's just being reckless."

I laugh loud enough for the sound to echo through the car. "Tessa Doukas, who knew you were going to be so funny?"

"It's because I feel comfortable around you. You've seen when I'm uncomfortable—it's an unwanted nightmare for everyone. The babbling, the unnecessary commentary. But relaxed, I can be a good time."

"I'll take you either way." I pull into an empty parking lot. "We're here."

She looks out the window and then back at me, a smile ticking at her lips. "Myles, this is an empty parking lot, looking over a cliff, the lights of the town just to the right of us . . . Are you implying something here?"

"Take it how you want." I put the car in park and turn toward her.

She turns toward me.

Our eyes lock.

Our smiles mirror each other's.

And as time slows down, I know exactly what she's thinking, because it's what I'm thinking as well.

I need her lips.

She needs mine.

And we can't wait any longer.

At the same time, we lunge toward each other, arms reaching, chests heaving, only to be violently stopped by our seat belts and flung back into our seats.

"Oh my God," she says, gripping her chest. "Your car is cockblocking us."

Chuckling, I undo my seat belt, lean over the center console, and grip her cheek. My thumb glides over her soft skin, and as I move in close, I feel her light intake of breath right before her lips meet mine.

Then, it's a sigh of relief. For both of us.

Soft, subtle, delicious. I've wondered for so long what it would feel like to kiss this woman, if her lips tasted as luscious as they look. And they do.

In the midst of our kiss, she unbuckles her seat belt and turns for a better angle, which gives me more room to work with her mouth.

Her hands fall to my shoulders as I dive my fingers into the silk strands of her hair, my body heating up in seconds while her tongue swipes against my lips, wanting me to part.

I do just that, switching from soft, gentle kiss to open-mouthed kiss in seconds.

Her grip on me tightens while our tongues tangle, and my need for her intensifies. I move in even closer, smoothing my hand down her spine, right to her lower back. That's where I hold her tight, not letting her get away. Not after all these years of seeing her from afar, thinking about her during those long summer nights.

She's here, in my arms, kissing me.

This is not a fantasy.

This is real.

After a few more seconds, she pulls away, and our gaze connects. We're both breathing heavily, smiling.

"Want to get in the back seat?" she asks, wiggling her brows, making me laugh.

She's such a freaking goof, it makes being around her that much easier, like I can be myself—I don't have to worry about judgments or trying to impress her.

"What do you think?" I ask.

"I think yes." She lets go of me, hops out of her side of the car, and then goes to the back seat. "What are you waiting for?"

"No idea," I say as I get out of the car as well, only to get back in.

The moment I sit down, she's on me, straddling my lap, her dress hiked up around her thighs.

"This is a first for me," she murmurs. "Making out in the back of a car."

"I'd like to say me too . . . but I'm afraid not."

"Transparency—can't be mad about it. But let me ask you this . . . Am I the first girl you crushed on for years that you've made out with in the back of a car?"

"One thousand percent yes," I answer right before her mouth descends upon mine.

While her hands grip my face, holding me in place so her tongue can explore, I move my fingers to her waist, down to her hips, and then to her thighs, where I bring her in closer. I angle my head back to give her better access to my mouth, and thankfully, she takes charge. From the previous interactions I've had with her—the awkward ones—I never would have suspected this kind of confidence, but then again, there's a lot I wouldn't have suspected from her.

As her tongue dances across mine, her hips rock to rub against my pelvis, the friction feeling so fucking good that I melt into the seat as I savor having her on top of me like this.

"Mmm," she moans into my mouth as she drives her hips harder.

"Shit, Tessa, you're making me hard."

"Good," she whispers as she continues to rotate her hips.

I can't tell you the last time I had a girl in the back seat of my car. It feels so juvenile, and yet . . . so right for us. Like we should have been doing this years ago. Many, many years ago, and now we're making up for lost time.

And because we're making up for lost time, I decide to test the waters and slip my hand up her side, along her ribs, and anchor my palm just under her breast.

Moaning again in my mouth, she reaches down to my hand, and without even giving it a second thought, she guides me to her breast. A hot burst of pleasure shoots through me as I palm her. Her chest isn't very big, but not small, almost the exact right size for my hand.

"Fuck," I groan as I settle deeper into the seat, letting her take charge as I rub my thumb over her hardened nipple.

I'm not sure how long I've wanted this, but this moment is fulfilling so many fantasies I've had over the years.

She tilts my jaw up, giving her better access to my mouth while her hips continue grinding down, creating an endless heat between us that burrows in my stomach and rotates, over and over again.

Our tongues swipe, touch, dance against each other, fighting for control. She wants to take it, and I want to give it to her, but with every stroke, I feel this animalistic side of me wanting to take over, wanting to pin her to the seat and show her just what I want and how I want it.

But this is new, and I don't want to scare her away, so I refrain and let her hold the lead.

A lead that she handles very well as her hands float down to the hem of my shirt, under the fabric, and toy with my blazing skin. Her nails scrape along my abs, up farther and farther, almost to my pecs, only for her to drag them back down.

It feels so fucking good.

So good to be touched by her.

Kissed by her.

Held by her.

And oddly, it feels like she's just returning home, like I've had her before, many times, and this is all just . . . right. Not new, but rather where she's supposed to be. Where I'm supposed to be.

Wanting to add a touch of control, I slide my hands up her thighs and to her hips, where I help guide her over my aching—

BAM BAM BAM.

"Ahhhhh," Tessa screams as we both startle out of our own skin.

I buck up, my chest spasming in fear.

Tessa flies to the side, crashing into the door, her skirt floating up around her waist.

All the while a light flashes brightly through the fogged-up window right at me.

"Open up," he says, in English this time. *BAM BAM BAM.*

Shit.

"Oh my God, Myles. Oh my God, we're going to get arrested." In a state of panic, she twists, attempting to sit upright, but whacks my crotch with her knee instead.

"Mother . . . fucker," I groan. "Tessa, you hit my hard dick."

"Oh God, really?"

"Open up." *BAM BAM BAM.*

"Yeah, one second," I groan as Tessa flails, her head now stuck deep in the bottom of the car where your feet go, her legs mindlessly kicking around.

I cup my crotch. "Watch it, Tessa, you're going to get my dick again."

"Stop saying dick. He can hear you through the door. He's going to know what we were doing."

"He probably already knows what we were doing," I say, my cock still hard, though pain pulses down the center. It's all very confusing.

"Just answer him. It's not polite to keep him waiting."

"Yeah, well, you're upside down with your ass hanging out. You really want me opening the door to that?"

"Well, help me?" she grunts.

"I would if you didn't paralyze me." Breathing heavily through the pulsing agony, I attempt to pull her upright, but she's wedged so far down that I think the only way to save her is to get out of the car and give her a swift pull.

"I'm stuck!" she shouts.

"I know you're stuck."

"Open up. NOW! Hands up," the police officer shouts.

"Jesus Christ," I mumble. "I have to open the door."

"But I can't hold my hands up, only my feet. What is he going to think?"

"Doesn't . . . matter," I groan as I reach for the door handle and push it open. Hunched over, dick still very much in pain, I hold my hands above my head and squint as the light above me flashes. "Hello, Officer."

"Out of the car, now."

"Yup, sure." In a crouched position, arms over my head, I waddle out of the car.

"Stand up." The slight police officer stands with flashlight in one hand, his other hand on his belt.

"Kind of . . . hard," I say. "She, uh, she accidentally kicked me in the crotch with a hard . . . uh . . . a hard penis."

"Were you attacking her?"

"What? No!" I shout. "It was all consensual. Tell him, Tessa."

That's when I glance back at the car. Tessa is now lying flat against the floorboards, legs extended up like she's performing the Superman workout.

"I . . . I can't raise my arms, but I have my legs raised as best as I can, and if I'm going to be honest, I can already feel a cramping sensation in my hamstring. I'm not the most fit person out there, I work out from time to time, but not on the regular, and I surely don't stretch like I should, and boy is that showing because . . . oy, crap, oh God, charley horse. Ahhhh, charley horse. Oh fuck me . . . oh God." She pounds the side of the car with her fist. "Breathe through it. Breathe through it. You're going to be okay. Oh crap, God, what a bitch of a feeling. Have you gotten a charley horse, Officer? Probably in the most inopportune time, right? I heard men get them a lot during sex, is that right? Have you ever gotten one during sex?"

"Miss, please stop talking."

"She does that when she's nervous," I say.

"Miss, I need you to get out of the car."

"You and me both. Just struggling a bit here, sort of stuck. Would you be of assistance, please? Just give my legs a bit of a tug."

The police officer looks between us and then says to me, "Get on your hands and knees on the ground. If you make one move, I will arrest you."

"Yes, sir," I answer and do as I'm told, appreciating the reprieve from having to stand.

When I'm situated, he pulls on Tessa's ankles, giving them a solid tug until she's able to shimmy her way out and up on her feet. The moment she's out of the car, she doesn't bother to brush her dress down or fix her hair. Instead she shoots her arms straight up to the sky, fingers spread . . . legs spread.

And this is our first date, me on all fours, in the dirt, my cock throbbing in pain while Tessa stands next to me, ready to be frisked, her dress tucked up, showing off her pink underwear, and her hair fanning over her face in a mess.

I almost laugh. We are a sight to behold.

CHAPTER FIFTEEN
TESSA

"I had a lot of fun tonight," I say as I walk hand in hand with Myles toward my hotel room.

"I did too." He smirks. And I know what that smirk is from. It's the smirk he gave me all the way home after our little session in the back seat of his car.

Honestly, I have no idea what came over me. Maybe it was the wine, maybe it was the night, maybe it was the feeling of being free, but I relaxed and enjoyed, without another thought in my mind, and it felt really freaking good.

So freaking good.

Until we were busted by the police, let off on a warning, and then told to get back to our resort. We scurried back rather quickly, neither of us one to toy with the law.

"Do you think I can see you again?" Myles asks as we reach my hotel room.

Feeling courageous, I turn toward him. "I was hoping that maybe you'd stay for a bit."

His brow raises in the cutest way before he nods. "Yeah, I'd like that."

Holy crap.

Look at me taking charge, asking for what I want.

I swipe my key card and unlock my door. When we both walk in, I flip on the light and then take my shoes off. "Make yourself comfortable. I'm going to change quickly."

"Yeah, okay," he says, pulling on the back of his neck.

I grab a pair of cotton shorts and a tank top that I sleep in and slip into the bathroom. With the door shut behind me, I look at myself in the mirror for a moment, noticing the beard burn that runs along my jaw and neck. My fingers glide over my kiss-swollen lips as I realize it's been so, so long since I've been kissed the way Myles kissed me tonight. He treated me like I was precious, like I was the most important thing to ever walk into his life. It felt amazing.

This light, careless feeling that's pulsing through me, I wouldn't trade it in for anything. As a matter of fact, I want to hold on to it for as long as I can.

Happy, and for once not second-guessing myself, I change into my shorts and tank top and then quickly wipe away my makeup before pulling my hair loosely up into a scrunchie.

Pleased, I exit the bathroom and find Myles lying on my bed, hands behind his head, ankles crossed, looking casual and comfortable. His eyes fall to my change of clothes as a small smile tugs at the corner of his lips.

"Why are you smiling?" I ask, my hands twisting into the hem of my shirt.

"Because you look adorable."

"Adorable, huh? Not sexy?" I show off my tank top. "These are my finest cotton clothes—shouldn't they spark some sort of arousal?"

He chuckles. "Tessa, it's not the clothes that spark the arousal, it's you."

"Oh." I feel my cheeks heat up. "Well, that's a compliment."

"Don't get awkward on me now." He pats the bed. "Come lie down with me."

"I'm not trying to be awkward," I answer as the reality of the situation starts to dawn on me. "But I think the wine has worn off, and I'm realizing just how much I enjoy your company."

"Well, good. Now come enjoy it next to me." He pats the mattress again.

I hop on the bed and crawl toward him. I sit cross-legged right next to him, but that's apparently not close enough because he loops his arm around my shoulder and pulls me down so my side is pressed against his and my head is resting on his chest. I can't help but notice how well our bodies fit together.

"There, that's better. Are you comfortable?"

"Yes," I answer. "Very. Are you?"

"Probably the most comfortable I've been in a while," he admits, his arm bringing me in tight.

I press my hand to his chest. "Do you think this is kind of weird?"

"What do you mean? I don't think this is weird at all. Rather perfect, actually."

"I mean in the sense that this is sort of our first official date, and yet it feels like we've known each other for much longer?"

"Ah, I see. Are you feeling the same strong connection that I'm feeling?"

"Yes," I answer. "Very much so. Do you think that's weird?"

"Not really," he answers. "I think people go in and out of our lives who make an impact, and we've been in and out of each other's lives for so long that this was bound to happen. At some point, we were supposed to get this close."

"Does it scare you?"

"A little," he answers. "But only because it feels real."

"I agree," I answer.

"I think we just take it one day at a time, okay?"

I nod. "I think that's a good idea."

"I don't want to think about what happens in two weeks. I want to focus on the here and now."

What happens in two weeks . . . yeah, I can't even process that right now. I won't let my analytical mind process it.

"I can do that."

"Good." He pulls me in closer, close enough that I shift to lie on top of his body. Straddling his legs, I sit up and rest my hands on his stomach as he presses his palms to my thighs.

"What do you think you're doing?" I ask with a smile.

"Just wanted to get a good look at you. At your pretty face."

"Uh-huh, that's all? You're not trying to finish what we started in the back seat of your car before we were interrupted?"

"Not at all." He shakes his head. "Wouldn't dream of it. Actually, I really enjoy the feeling of blue balls. Nothing feels more masculine than an unobtained orgasm with a beautiful woman. A true dream."

"Oh yeah?" I ask as I shift myself over his lap.

He bites down on the bottom of his lip as he nods. "Yeah, total dream. I prefer not having orgasms actually. So, don't you even dare think about it."

"Oh, I wouldn't." I hold my hands up but shift myself again, rubbing against his hardening erection. "I wouldn't ever want to make you come when you're clearly not in the business of granting yourself pleasure."

"Precisely, not in the business."

My hands dip under his shirt and travel up his heated skin, over his abs. His stomach hollows from my touch as he shifts beneath me, a whisper of a breath passing his lips.

"So glad, but do you mind if I get comfortable?" I ask, feeling deliciously evil. "I just can't seem to find a comfortable position."

"Please, get comfortable all you want."

"Okay, it might take me a second," I say, smiling as I start to rock my hips over his.

"Take all the time you need." His lazy smile nearly eats me alive as a haze falls over his dark eyes.

"Sure, do you know what might help my comfort level?"

"Hmm?" he asks.

"If you'd sit up, lean against the headboard."

"Oh yeah. I can do that."

I slide off him for a moment as he positions himself, and then I straddle him again.

"And you know, this shirt of yours, it's so clumsy, do you mind if I remove it?"

"Not at all, can't have anything bothering you."

He reaches behind him and pulls his shirt up and over his head, only to toss it to the ground, leaving his chest bare.

"That better?" he asks.

"Much," I answer as my hands smooth over his hairless pecs and then to his shoulders, where I grip onto them and position myself so I can maximize the pleasure between both of us. But it's hard with his jeans. "Think you can remove the jeans too?" I venture.

He raises a brow, but instead of saying anything, he reaches between us and unbuttons his jeans, and then as I get off him, he shucks them. He's wearing nothing but a pair of black boxer briefs, his bulge on full display.

Happy with myself, I sit back down on his lap, and now that there is nothing between us besides two pieces of thin fabric, I can practically feel all of him.

"That better?" he croaks out when I adjust on top of his lap.

"So much better." Hands on his chest now, anchoring myself in place, I rock over him as his fingers fall to my hips, lightly guiding me. "Now that we're comfortable, what should we talk about?" I ask as I glide over his length.

"Uhh . . ." He blinks a few times as he leans his head against the bed frame. "Things," he answers before licking his lips, his eyes falling to my mouth.

"You seem distracted, Myles."

"I am," he answers.

"And what exactly are you distracted by?" I ask, grinding down on him.

A hiss escapes him. "Fuck . . . Tessa. You, you're distracting me."

"Oh," I say innocently, maybe enjoying this a bit too much. "Should I stop what I'm doing?"

"No!" he shouts and then shakes his head. "No, but I think . . . I think I'm going to need to explore your mouth, because, you know . . . science."

"Science? How does that have anything to do with our conversation?"

"It doesn't," he answers before he grips the back of my head and pulls me to his mouth. I chuckle right before he parts my lips with his tongue, and just like that, all the humor is gone as our tongues tangle. The mood shifts from playful to heated in seconds, his desire radiating into the room, letting me know exactly where he stands, though he never takes too much. He goes off my cues, he waits for me to make the move, and when I do, he expands that feeling between us.

Feeling him grow even harder, I lift and let him shift himself until he's angled up, along his stomach, and that's when I take advantage of the way he's positioned himself. I fit my body right in line with him so when I rock, he's rubbing right along my center, hitting me exactly where I need it.

Still kissing me, he tightens his hand against my scalp, his fingers tangling into my hair, heightening the pleasure pulsing through me.

"God, Tessa," he breathes as he rocks his hips up into mine. "You have no idea how long I've wanted this, to be this close to you."

"I have an idea," I say. "Because I felt the same way." I pick up my pace, which causes him to slip his hand off my thigh and then up my shirt.

"Give me your lips," he says. "I want them all over me."

I want that too, so I press a kiss to his mouth. Then I move over to his jaw and up to his ear, where I bring the lobe into my mouth and tug on it with my teeth.

He groans, and his hand moves farther up my shirt.

"Yes," I moan lightly into his ear, letting him know exactly what I want.

And he listens.

As I kiss down his neck, his hand moves farther up my shirt until he's cupping my breasts over my bra.

"You shouldn't be wearing this," he says as he moves his hand to my back and with a flick of his fingers undoes the clasp to my bra. The straps loosen over my shoulders, the cups part from my body, and then he grips it and slips it off, with some help from me. When the garment joins his shirt on the floor, he moves his hand back up my stomach, past my ribs, and just below where I want him. The tip of his thumb teases me, stroking the sensitive flesh, letting me know he's right there, but waiting for the right moment.

So, I grind down on him harder, really moving my hips over him now.

"Fuck," he whispers right before he grips my hips, moves me up the bed, pins me down on the mattress, and then moves on top of me.

My hair loosens from the scrunchie and fans out around me as he hovers above me, one of his hands pinning mine into the mattress while the other plays with the hem of my shirt.

"You know this is far more comfortable." I smile up at him.

"Way more comfortable," he answers as he parts my legs and then presses his erection against my center, our clothes still between us, but now creating this warm, sacred friction that is building faster, burning harder now that he's on top, rocking his hips against mine.

With a good pace that is driving me wild with need, he slips his hand under my shirt again, but this time, he doesn't play, he doesn't tease, he doesn't take his time. Instead, he goes straight for my breasts, gripping them in his palm.

"Yes, Myles," I say while his fingers toy with my nipple.

"Fuck, Tessa," he groans as his hips drive harder into me, hitting me in just the right spot to spark this burning ember into a full-on inferno.

Wanting more, I part my legs even wider, wishing there wasn't fabric between us, but I also know I don't have any protection and I'm not sure he does, so what we're doing will have to suffice.

"Harder," I whisper, right before he pushes my tank top all the way up my chest, exposing me. He dips his head to my breasts and brings his hot, wet mouth to my nipples, where he sucks them in hard. My fingers dive into his curly locks as a low moan falls past my lips.

A brief glance down between us shows me his hardworking abs, undulating his body so his hips rock into mine, the low hang of his boxer briefs giving me a quick glance of the tip of his erection. It's probably the most erotic thing I've ever seen.

His beard scrapes against my sensitive skin as he brings my nipples into his mouth, one at a time, paying a great deal of attention to them right before he presses a kiss between them, then to my ribs, then to my stomach, and then lower . . .

"Myles," I say, my nerves kicking up.

"Yeah?" he asks, moving down my body some more.

"I'm not . . . I'm not sure about that."

He pauses, the lust in his eyes fading for a moment. "Okay, I don't have to."

"I just . . . I've never really done that successfully, so I don't want to disappoint."

A charming, sexy smile passes over his lips. "That might be because you haven't been with the right guy." He moves south some more, kissing along the way. When he reaches my shorts, he pulls on the waistband, exposing my pubic bone, where he presses a kiss.

That one little kiss, right above where I'm throbbing, needy, it feels like a straight shot of vodka through my body, warming me up and relaxing me all at the same time.

"Can I?" he asks, his eyes pleading, and hell, I want him so badly. So, I nod. "Yes."

Smiling now, he lifts up and pulls my shorts until they're completely off, and since I wasn't wearing underwear, I'm fully bare, open to his perusing eyes.

He drags his hand over his smile before he looks up at me, keeping his eyes connected, and lowers his mouth to my center. With two fingers, he gently parts me. I hold my breath as his tongue gently presses against my sensitive nub. And with one simple flick, my muscles all contract at the same time.

"Hell," he whispers. "This is going to be fun."

He positions himself so my legs drape over his shoulders. While one hand parts me, the other moves up to my chest, where he toys with my right nipple, plucking, tugging, twisting—borderline painful but never crossing the line, just toying with it, shooting a new sensation through me, a sensation I didn't know I enjoyed until this very moment. All the while, his tongue is lapping against me, flicking softly and then taking long, slow strokes.

My mind is so overcome with emotion that it doesn't know where to focus other than right in this very moment, on what he's doing with his tongue, matching the strokes with the tugs on my nipple.

Simultaneously, he works me up into a frenzy, a kind of euphoria that I don't think I can ever escape, building and building until I'm gasping for air, my hand digging into his hair, my fingers pressing into his scalp.

"Oh God, Myles," I cry out.

He might sense the pleasure in me heightening, because he picks up his pace, never stopping, never taking a break, only focusing on my pleasure until I'm panting, twisting under him, fighting off an early orgasm, but there is no use, it's right there, tightening every muscle in my body.

I can't stop it.

I can't hold out.

And with one more stroke, I arch my chest into his hand, my legs fall open even wider, and I grip his head, keeping him fully in place as I ride his tongue.

White-hot pleasure rips through me, like a boomerang inside my bones, spinning me dizzy, never to return to earth.

Pulse after pulse, my body takes everything from him as he continues to lick until my hips finally settle back on the bed, leaving me completely spent.

"Oh my God," I say as I open my eyes to find Myles lazily smiling up at me, his hair an absolute mess from my hands and a satisfied look on his face. "That has never happened to me."

"Because you weren't with me," he says right before he makes his way back up my body, pressing kisses the entire time until he pauses at my mouth and kisses me there. That's when I feel his massive erection on my leg,

Not wanting the man to have blue balls twice in one night, I reach between us and cup him in my hand, giving him a good tug.

"Ahhh, fuck, Tessa," he mumbles against my lips. "You don't have to."

"You need relief. I can feel it in how tense you are." I slip my hands back under the waistband of his boxer briefs and run my hand over the tip.

"Shit," he grumbles. "I can, uh, I can go take care of it in the bathroom."

"No," I answer as I push on his chest and force him to the mattress. "I want to take care of you."

I move between his legs, and then with both hands, I pull on the waistband of his briefs, exposing his erection, and oh my God . . . Roxane was right when she called him the Bulge. Wide eyed, I stare down at him until he sighs. "Seriously, Tessa, I can take care of it." But I don't listen.

Instead, I lean forward between his legs, grip the base of him, and then lower my mouth over the tip. I take it one inch at a time, letting my mouth explore as he melts into the mattress.

Long, girthy, delicious, he's unlike any man I've ever been with. Not only physically, but he's also more relaxed, not trying too hard, letting me take charge when I need to. I'm setting the pace.

Both hands behind his head, he stares down at me, wonder in his eyes. "So fucking beautiful," he says.

I pull off his cock for a moment, letting my mouth adjust as I make eye contact with him. Gripping his base, I stroke him lightly, letting my hand run over his soft skin, pulling, tugging, making him bring his teeth over his bottom lip. It's so sexy.

I move my mouth back over his tip and swirl my tongue around the head, noticing how the muscles in his legs twitch whenever I do that, so I swirl again, and again . . . and again.

His stomach muscles bunch.

And again.

His hand falls from the back of his head and to the blankets, where he grips them into his fist.

Another swirl.

"Hell," he whispers.

Another swirl, but this time, I stop at the underside of his head, where I flick my tongue against the sensitive skin.

"Shit, Tessa." He shifts, but I press down on his legs, keeping him in place.

"Don't move," I say as I bring my hand back to the base, where I deliver long, tight strokes and move my mouth to the underside of his head, flicking fast, relentlessly.

I feel him grow even harder, his skin stretching to its max, his arousal in full force now as his chest rises and falls at a rapid rate.

"Tessa . . . fuck, babe . . . I'm getting close."

I move faster. I grip him tighter. I focus mainly on that sensitive skin that I know is driving him crazy until I feel him swell in my hand.

"Fuck, Tessa," he says.

I move my mouth over his tip, suck hard, and he comes, his beautiful groan filling my hotel room.

"Jesus Christ," he says as he takes deep breaths. I lick around his length for a few moments and then pull up, loving the way he is completely sated in the bed, unable to move.

I climb up his body and place a kiss on his chest, then his jaw, and then his cheek. "You okay?" I ask.

"Fuck . . . yes, I'm more than okay." He turns his head to look at me. "I think you just ruined me for every other woman out there."

"Good." I smile. "Just the way I like it." I give him a peck on the cheek and then hop off the bed, but not before picking up his shirt off the ground and putting it on myself.

I quickly take care of business in the bathroom, and when I exit, Myles goes in after me. Unsure what he's thinking about doing for the rest of the night, I sit awkwardly on the bed and wait for him to come back out.

"I hope it's okay I used some of your toothpaste," he says as he appears at the doorframe of the bathroom.

"Totally fine." I try not to nervously twitch as I wait for him to make the next move.

Will he leave? Will he stay?

I'm really hoping he doesn't think this is the end of the night.

"My shirt looks good on you," he says.

I smile. "Do you want it back?"

"Nah, you sleep in it. I'm good in my briefs." And then to my delight, he walks back over to my bed, pulls down the blankets, and slides in under the covers. He flips the sheets over to the other side of the bed. "What are you waiting for? Get in here."

Giddy can't even describe how I feel as I slip into the sheets next to him. He turns toward me, so I position my body away, letting him pull me against him so I become the little spoon. With his hand tucked around my stomach, his head pressing against mine, he quietly sighs into my ear.

"This feels right," he says.

"So . . . no regrets?"

"Are you kidding me?" he asks. "Why would you think I have regrets?"

"Just insecurities coming in hot. I always question myself when it comes to sex."

"Well, don't let them. If I had regrets, I wouldn't be here, in your bed, wanting to spend the night. I'd already be out the door. Trust me, there are zero regrets. I actually wish I did this a lot sooner."

"You were gone for seven years—that put a dent in our potential."

"Very true. So are you going to say this is all my fault?"

"Allude to it, yes."

"At least you're keeping up with that honesty." He lightly chuckles and then kisses my head as I yawn. "Get some sleep. I'm sure tomorrow is going to be brutal, given the cupcakes today."

"Already mentally preparing. Maybe I can just hang out with you, in your pocket all day. Do you have a shrink machine?"

"Yeah, out back."

I chuckle. "Perfect." I let out a large sigh. "Hey, Myles?"

"Yeah?"

"Tonight was perfect. Well, besides the interruption in the back of the car."

"Nah, that just added to it being perfect."

"True, it did."

He squeezes me close, and then, together, we both fall asleep, his arms wrapped tightly around me.

"What do you want for breakfast?" I ask as I take a seat on the edge of the bed, room service menu in hand.

"What time is it?" Myles asks as he rolls toward me, the sheets bunching up at his waist.

"Almost seven thirty."

"Jesus, Tessa, why are you up so early?"

"My mouth felt creepy. I had to brush my teeth. And I was a bit self-conscious, you know. I didn't want my mouth to scare you away."

"If anything, your mouth is a reason to keep me here longer."

"Oh . . . I feel like you're flirting with me, and so early in the morning."

"I'm always going to flirt," he says as he pulls me back on the mattress and curls around me. He kisses my shoulder and then nuzzles into me.

"You're so warm."

"Exactly, so stop trying to order food and lie here with me." His hand slides up my shirt and rests on my stomach.

"Uh, sir, your hand seems to have slipped under my shirt."

"Yeah, so?"

"That's presumptuous, don't you think?"

"No," he says as he reaches up and palms one of my breasts. "This would be presumptuous." He toys with one of my nipples. "And this would be presumptuous." He twists it, and I feel my body gear up for more. "But this"—he slides his hand back to my stomach—"this is just wanting you close to me."

"Uh-huh . . . and what's presumptuous again?"

He chuckles and brings his hand back to my nipple, pinching it. "This."

I hold back my moan. "And, uh, and what else?"

He glides his hand down my stomach, under my shorts, and between my legs. I easily part for him as he flips two fingers over my clit. "And this . . . ah, fuck, Tessa. You're wet."

"Oh no, looks like you're going to have to do something about that."

He chuckles some more, lazily kisses down my body, and slides his large frame between my legs, taking my shorts with him. With both hands, he presses down on my thighs, getting all the access he needs, and then glides his tongue over my arousal.

I take a deep breath and then sigh as I melt into the mattress, his tongue doing the work.

"God, Myles. You're so good at this."

"Can't hear that enough," he says as he slips two fingers inside me, the whole time keeping his tongue stroking right where I want him, right where I need him.

He truly is good at this. Even half-awake, he's good at this. Like it's programmed into him, how to make me come within minutes, because that's exactly what's happening as he curls his fingers upward inside me.

"Oh fuck, what . . . what was that?" I ask as this unsuspecting pleasure shoots through me.

He just chuckles and keeps doing the same upward stroke, over and over again—along with his tongue. The combination sends me into a frenzy.

My muscles begin to bunch, my stomach starts to hollow, my legs and arms immediately go numb, and before I can even tell him I'm about to come, my orgasm rips through me so hard that I scream out and jolt my upper half off the bed in shock. He holds me down by my pelvis and continues the pleasure until there is nothing left inside me.

Panting and out of breath, I lie there on the mattress, staring up at the ceiling in disbelief as he works his way back up my body, curls around me again, and nuzzles into my side. His erection is evident, but he's not asking for relief.

"Myles."

"Hmm?" he asks, his legs twining with mine and his large, beefy arm anchoring my waist.

"Are you really going to act like you didn't just give me an explosive orgasm?"

"I didn't know you wanted me to participate in fanfare after the orgasm."

"I don't need fanfare, but oh my God, Myles."

He chuckles. "You just tell me whenever you need me to do that. I'm at your disposal."

Uh, how about every chance I can get, because wow, what a freaking feeling.

"What about you?"

"What about me?" he asks.

"I can feel your erection."

"Then we have something else in common. I can feel it too."

I laugh and shove him. "Let me do something about it."

"Nah, I just want to lie here with you and sleep some more."

"But I'm not tired."

"You should be after all the convulsing you just did."

"Ew, don't say I convulsed."

"That's what you were doing, babe. Sorry to say, but you were shivering all the way down to your toes. It's okay, it's a side effect of being with me. Involuntary convulsing while orgasming. Just wait until I'm inside you, all of you. It will be a whole new experience."

"Okay, we're being a little cocky, don't you think?"

He lightly thrusts his pelvis at my leg. "Very cocky."

"Oh my—"

The door to my suite beeps and then opens. Without a knock, without a warning, Roxane charges into the room, red eyed, hair a mess, looking ready to kill.

"Roxane?" I say, sitting up from the bed, Myles still clutched around me, his back to Roxane.

Her eyes narrow in on the scene in front of her and then back up at me. "Who the hell is that?" She points at Myles. He goes to turn, but I keep him in place.

"Uh . . . no one," I say.

"What do you mean, no one? I can clearly see there is a man in your bed—naked, I presume."

"Not naked, he's wearing boxer briefs . . . errr . . . I mean, there's no man here. You're hallucinating."

Roxane charges over, and I hold my hand out. "Stop right there. If you get any closer, he bites. I'm just trying to save you."

Myles chuckles, shaking the bed.

Still not buying it, Roxane comes closer.

"Wait," I call out in panic. "It's, uh . . . oh God, this is so embarrassing. He's a blow-up doll, okay, very lifelike, I know. I didn't want to tell you, but, yup. I brought a blow-up doll with me, so if you could just give me some privacy, I think I'm going to break things off with him. Give him a solid pop. I can't stand the humiliation anymore."

"You're an idiot," Roxane says as she closes the rest of the space and pulls on Myles's shoulder so he's lying flat on the bed. She clutches her chest and gasps loud enough for the entire resort to hear. "The Bulge."

God . . . why?

Why is this happening?

And why did I let her keep a key to my room after the whole clothes swapping?

He sticks his hand out politely. "Myles, actually, but nice to officially meet you, Roxane."

Roxane doesn't take his hand but rather swats it away and glares at me. "What the hell do you think you're doing?"

"Uh . . . enjoying myself?" I ask, unsure of what she wants me to say.

"Enjoying yourself? You're supposed to be entertaining Jeremiah."

She can't be freaking serious.

"Jeremiah was a cretin."

"Jeremiah is eccentric, like you. I thought you two would be perfect together, but instead, I find you in bed with the Bulge? Honestly, Tessa."

"His name is Myles, and what's wrong with this? I thought you'd be happy—you know, I'm getting out there, seeing a guy."

"A guy you've been crushing on for years? We all know it's just a fantasy, and temporary. You need something that's going to last."

"You thought going out with Toby was going to last."

"Yes, because of the perfume."

I roll my eyes as Myles says, "What perfume?"

"Don't freaking ask," I mumble.

"Wait . . ." Roxane holds her hands out as if everything is starting to make sense. "Is this why . . . is this why you gave us those laxative cupcakes last night? I knew the icing tasted off."

"Laxative cupcakes?" I clutch my chest. "What on earth are you talking about? Those were genuine 'I'm sorry' cupcakes." *More like you've pushed me too far with Jeremiah, and action needed to be taken.*

Furiously, Roxane points her finger at me. "You know they were poop cupcakes. Don't lie to me."

Yeah . . . they were. And sure, I second-guessed my decision for a mere second, but you can only push a girl too far, and taking away my lunch date with Myles to make me share it with some gangly guy who can't swim was pushing me too far.

"Well," I say, trying to find the bright side, "a good cleaning out before the wedding is always smart, you know, for the dress."

"You think this is funny, don't you?"

"No, Roxane," I sigh and then turn to Myles. "Maybe . . . maybe we should have this conversation in private."

"Oh no." Roxane folds her arms across her chest. "I think your little friend here needs to hear just how manipulative you are."

"I'm not manipulative. You're the one who's been trying to put me through this crazy dating show while we're supposed to be on vacation, enjoying each other. I didn't ask for any of this. Is your life really so boring that you have to find something within mine to pick on?"

"Excuse me?" Her face clouds with anger. "My life is not boring."

"Come on, you were just saying before you left how you wish there was more pizzazz in your life. Your words, not mine. How things have become monotonous with Philip, and you were worried that you'd lost the spark. That's why you really wanted this trip before the wedding."

"My life with Philip is perfectly fine."

"Is it? Because how many times have you called him since you've been here?"

Her jaw falls open. "I've been busy trying to find you someone to love. You can't be a loser spinster forever."

"I'm not a loser spinster," I say as I feel Myles grip my thigh for reassurance. "I'm just not going to fall for the first person who gives me an ounce of attention, or the person you think I should use the perfume on."

"No, you just pine for the same guy year after year, hoping he looks at you once. Well, congrats on your one-night stand. I'm sure he's going to regret his decision."

"Hey," Myles says as he sits up, but I press my hand to his chest, guiding him back down.

"I can handle this," I say to him softly before taking his hand in mine. "Roxane, I suggest you leave before you say anything too damaging."

"You know she has a box of pictures of you, and she'd look at them before we left for Greece, every trip?"

"Roxane." I feel my anger rising, my cheeks heating up.

"And that she actually wrote a *Twilight* fanfic, but it starred you and her as the main couple so she could pathetically make you two kiss?"

"Roxane, stop." I sit taller.

"And that every time we arrive at Anissa's, the first thing she'd do was go look for you, but she never . . . ever talked to you? And that one time, she caught you hosing off down by the beach and took a picture of your wet crotch—"

"Enough," I say as I charge out of bed and right at my sister. I push her toward the door. "You need to leave."

"I'm just telling the truth."

"You're trying to ruin this for me—I have no clue why." I keep moving her toward the door. "Maybe it's because you're having cold feet and second-guessing marrying Philip, but don't project your situation onto me."

"I'm not, I'm just looking out for you."

"How is what you're doing looking out for me?" I yell at her.

"Because, Tessa, are you so desperate for this man's attention that you're just going to fall in bed with him? He disappeared for seven years, and he never once went up to you before that. He's clearly just using you for sex, and your heart is going to get broken."

"He is not," I say, even as insecurity wraps me in a choke hold.

"How do you know that?"

"Because we . . . we've talked."

"Oh, great, you've talked. Perfect. Yup, because you *talked*, that's all that matters. Talking will get you nothing." She says it with such venom in her voice that I have to wonder—are things really okay with her and Philip?

"Roxane, what's going on? Did something happen with Philip?"

"No. Nothing happened with Philip. Stop trying to make my life look as shitty as yours. Face it, Tessa, the only reason you're with that man right now is because you feel left out, because you're the one left behind, with not a prospect in sight. You're so freaking pathetic that you will do anything to look like you're just as put together as me. Try all you want, but it will never happen."

And with that, she charges out of my room, slamming the door behind her.

I just stand there, silent and shocked.

I don't know . . . I don't know what happened.

But I am mortified.

So mortified that I don't want to turn around and face Myles. He was not meant to hear that, any of that, but he had a front-row seat to dysfunction.

Knowing I have no other choice but to face him, I turn around, just in time for him to slip on his jeans. He's dressed in everything but the shirt I'm wearing. I don't blame him; I'd want to get out of here as quickly as possible too.

"I'm s-sorry, Myles," I say, tears springing to my eyes. "You shouldn't have heard that. I know you want to leave, so let me just give you your shirt back."

I head toward the bathroom to change, but he grabs me by the hand and pulls me toward the bed, where I land on his lap.

"Myles—"

"Shhh," he says as he strokes my back.

"But—"

"I said, quiet, Tessa." I shut my mouth, but it doesn't stop the tears from falling. They cascade over my cheeks and onto his shirt, dampening the fabric. He lowers my head to his shoulder and quietly holds me, letting me cry for several minutes until there's nothing else left.

"That wasn't fair," he murmurs once I've calmed down. "What she just did to you. It doesn't seem like what she's been doing this whole trip has been fair. I want you to know that, okay?" I nod. "And I'm sure one of the reasons you're crying is because you're embarrassed from what she said, right?" I nod again. "That's what I thought, but just know I did some crazy shit too, when I saw you. That's what people do when they have a crush on someone else: they daydream and sometimes act on those daydreams. That's okay."

"But it's humiliating."

"No, it's not. Just makes for a fun story. Hell, Tessa, I remember one summer, when I was nineteen, I think, I saw you in this pink floral dress, and it looked so fucking good on you that I wrote a goddamn novel to Toby, describing the dress and how beautiful you were. Ask him. You weren't the only one doing crazy things."

The pain in my chest eases, slightly.

"And you know why I left for seven years, and you know this isn't a one-time thing. You know I want to get to know you more, I want to take you out more, I want to spend as much time as possible with you."

"In love in a week," I whisper.

He chuckles. "Exactly. We have plans, Tessa. Don't let anyone take those plans away from us, okay?"

"Okay." I wet my lips. "But it's still embarrassing you had to see that. My family must seem so dysfunctional."

"First of all, what family isn't dysfunctional? There's no such thing as a perfect family. And if they say they're perfect, they're lying and hiding from the truth. Secondly, that fight was mild compared to the fights I've had with my baba. I don't want you thinking what happened just now changed the way I feel about you, because it doesn't. I still want to get to know you, I still want to hang out, I still want to see where this takes us."

"Are you sure?" I ask, in disbelief that a man would want to still hang around after that crazy show.

"Yes. I do. We're good, Tessa. Okay?" I nod. "Now, I have to get out of here because even though I want to stay and hang, I checked my phone while you were talking to Roxane by the door, and I've been summoned to the Olive Tree to serve breakfast. But I want to see you later, even if it's just for a moment. I know you must have some conversations with your sister ahead of you, so whenever you're free."

I nod. "Okay."

He lifts my chin with his finger and forces me to look at him. "You good about us?"

"Yes," I say with a sigh of relief.

"Good." He leans in and presses a sweet kiss to my lips, his mouth parting ever so slightly, only to kiss me again . . . and again, his hand sliding up to the back of my head.

The kiss intensifies, and before I know it, I'm lying on the bed as he hovers over me, his body lined up with mine and his fingers tangled in my hair. I wrap my leg around him, keeping him in place as he open-mouth kisses me, our tongues swiping.

"Fuck," he mumbles against my lips. "Tessa, I have to go."

"I know." I ease up on my hold.

"I wish I didn't have to."

"It's okay. I get it. I should probably take a shower and go find Roxane." He cups my cheek. "Text me after you talk to her. Okay?"

I nod. "Okay."

He presses one more kiss to my lips and then reaches for his shirt and pulls it up and over my head, leaving me bare.

"Christ," he says as he moves the covers of the bed over me and bends down for one more kiss.

On his way out, he slips the shirt on and then looks over his shoulder with a smoldering smile, a smile that gives me enough courage to get ready for the day and face my sister.

"I really don't think you should go see her," Lois says as she plops a grape in her mouth from the bowl resting on her stomach.

When I went looking for Roxane, I spotted Lois and Clea lounging by the pool, both wearing large straw hats, with mixed drinks in hand and bowls of grapes on their stomachs. They look like they don't have a care in the world, which I'm sure they don't.

"Why, did you talk to her?"

"Ohhhh yeah," Clea says from her lounger, where she sips her Bloody Mary. "She nearly plowed through my hotel door. She was huffing and puffing . . . I was nervous she was turning into the big bad wolf, and I was just a little piggy in her way."

"Can you not refer to yourself as a piggy?" I say.

"It's a great analogy. I wish my house was made of bricks, but she blew me over like a pile of sticks." She pulls out her celery stick and takes a bite. "She told us that you had a sleepover with the Bulge. Didn't know you had it in you."

"Or to lace cupcakes with Ex-Lax," Lois says. "That's more on brand for me, not for you."

I twist my hands in my lap. "And I'm sorry, it was immature to do that rather than talking to you. This whole vacation has gotten really carried away, and none of us have been at our best. I just . . . I really wanted to spend time with Myles, and you guys kept throwing other men at me. I didn't know what else to do."

"Ah, I can see how you were put in such a tight situation, given how hard communication is," Clea says sarcastically.

"I tried telling you guys I didn't want you setting me up, but you didn't listen. So why would you all care about Myles when you were already knee deep into hooking me up?"

"She has a point," Lois says, and I feel a flash of gratefulness. "After the perfume debacle, we were dead set on righting a wrong. We never would have agreed to her seeing Myles."

Clea taps her chin. "Hmm, possibly. Still, would have been nice to know."

"Agreed, although it was nice having a night to myself," Lois says. "With the kids, it's rare I get a moment to myself. Last night was that. It honestly put me in a better mood. I think that's why I'm so receptive to your apology—you did me a favor."

"You're welcome?" I ask, unsure how to respond.

"Granted, the night had its downfalls, but all in all, some solid alone time." She pops in another grape. "But anyway, Roxane is in a state and in no way ready to even see you."

"But you realize I really didn't do anything wrong, right? I went out with a guy that I liked. Why should I get in trouble for that?"

"You know Roxane," Clea says. "She wants control over everything, including you. She's always been able to turn your head in whatever way she wants, this vacation included. And for once you're sticking up for yourself. Do you really think she's going to just let you do that without repercussions?" Clea shakes her head. "No way."

"Not to mention, you voiced what all of us have been thinking about her and Philip," Lois adds. "She told me yesterday that she hasn't talked to him once since being out here. Don't you think that's a huge red flag? I think it is. She was also saying she thinks the perfume is cursed, was trying to convince us last night. Twenty bucks says the wedding is called off and she blames the perfume and throws it in the garbage."

"Ooooh, good call," Clea says. "I could see that happening. Although she's been really stubborn about her situation with Philip, very much in denial."

"Very in denial."

"And why haven't we talked about this?" I ask. "As her sister and best friends, don't you think we should be bringing this up to her?"

"And get blasted like you did this morning?" Lois shakes her head. "No freaking thank you. I get enough passive-aggressive attitude from my five-year-old. I don't need it from Roxane as well."

"Do you hear yourself?" I ask. "This is not how we act with each other. We are open, honest. We help each other."

"Is that right?" Clea asks. "So where were you when my dad was in the hospital, getting surgery on his heart?"

I blink a few times. "You said . . . you said you didn't want me there."

"I said you didn't need to come," Clea says. "That doesn't mean I didn't want you there. Lois showed up every day, found a babysitter, sat by me, and held my hand."

Guilt swarms me. "I'm . . . I'm sorry. I didn't know."

"And what about when I had that breast-cancer scare?" Lois says. "You and Roxane didn't even check up on me, didn't show up to the appointment."

"I had a big meeting," I say, realizing I'm coming up with excuses when I should probably be saying sorry.

Because . . . they're right. If I truly think about it, if I'm honest with myself, over the past year or so, we've slowly been separating. Our lives growing busier and busier, our dates growing fewer and further apart. I think I've been in denial about it, not wanting to focus on the three most important relationships in my life disintegrating, not after another failed romantic relationship.

But putting it in perspective now, listening to them point out my flaws . . . it . . . well, it hurts. It hurts because it's true.

"This wasn't Roxane's idea," Lois says. "This trip before the wedding. It was mine and Clea's because we saw where our quartet was heading. We wanted to try to bring us all together."

"It was my idea to bring along the contract and perfume," Clea chimes in. "I thought they could help us reminisce, but when Roxane saw, she was dead set on trying to find you someone."

"Why did you go along with it?"

Lois shrugs. "Seemed like a good idea at the time, like it could be fun and bring us together again, you know? Didn't know it was going to blow up like it did."

"Man, did it blow up," Clea says. "And no offense, Tessa, but we didn't think you were actually going to go for it with the Bulge."

"His name is Myles."

"Sorry, Myles," Clea corrects herself. "But we didn't think this was going to be a big deal, and . . . yes, we know we got carried away."

"We were borderline offensive," Lois says. "Jeremiah was a bad call."

"Very bad call," Clea agrees. "And I'll be the first to say sorry about that. But Roxane was leading the way at this point, and you know how she is. Relentless."

"And we are grown women," Lois says. "But we were grasping, I think, onto anything that was holding us together, even if it meant acting like teenagers again. We were supposed to be setting you up, but it also felt like old times. All the pranks and the back-and-forth, it felt like we were pulling back together." Lois sets her grape bowl down on the side table. "It did not work."

"It didn't. Maybe we should just all go talk to Roxane together. Work this all out," I say.

Lois shakes her head. "She's too hotheaded right now. There's no reasoning with her. Trust me, she's livid. She needs to simmer down, alone in her room."

Yeah, but I don't like that we're all apart. I don't like that she's alone. I don't like the unsettling feeling I have in the pit of my stomach after the fight we had in my hotel room. I don't like to sit on fights; I like to work through them.

"We can't just let her be angry up there. We need to solve this," I say.

"We will, but give her a moment," Clea says. "I know she's your twin, but we've also seen this play out so many times between you two. You try to fix things too soon, she blows up even more, and then things escalate. Just let her have a moment." Clea pats the lounger next to her. "Take a rest, and then let's come up with a smart way to attack this."

"But . . . that doesn't feel right."

"Of course it doesn't," Lois says, "because you're the fixer, the mediator who tries to make everything okay before it's ready to be okay. You can't force her to be happy, so we'll just take our time with this." Lois crosses her ankles. "Let us handle this one for once. Lie back and soak up the sun."

Sounds so easy—just lie back and let it rest—but that's easier said than done. Roxane and I get into our fair share of fights, and I'm the one who usually brings in the apology, the peacemaking, like Lois said. Roxane is different; it's harder for her. She's more stubborn, more emotional. It's easier for me to just make sure we're okay.

But maybe Lois and Clea are right. Whenever I try to go in too early, she sometimes isn't ready to talk things out.

And sure, she embarrassed me. She said things I didn't care for, but that's why I want to talk to her about it. Were those things she truly believed, or was she saying them in the heat of the moment? And what about Philip? Was I right—are she and Philip really struggling? Not to mention the fissures in our friendship, which Lois and Clea saw so clearly.

I could deny it. I could say that we are just as close as we were all those years ago, but . . . now that I think about it, we *have* started to grow apart. It's hard—Lois has kids; Clea is a celebrity in her own right. Meanwhile, Roxane has been infatuated with Philip and planning her wedding, and I . . . well, I've been living the single life, happily.

"You're thinking too much," Clea says from beneath her hat.

"I know, but . . . do you really think we've been drifting apart?"

"Yes," they say at the same time.

"That makes me feel ill," I reply.

"Then why don't you do something about it and listen to us. Lie down and just be with us. We don't get a lot of time like this . . . so just relax. Maybe tell us a bit about this Myles guy."

"Okay . . . yeah, I can do that."

"Wait, let me get this straight," Lois says, a huge smile across her face as she dips her strawberry into a bowl of melted chocolate.

After we lay in silence for what felt like an hour, Clea woke me up from my sun-induced daze with a clap of her hands and said she was ordering some snacks and drinks. Lois took off for a bathroom break, and once everything arrived and we moved our chairs into a circle, Lois proceeded to ask me for all the details about Myles.

"You two were making out in the back of his car, then a police officer knocked on the window, and you somehow wound up head down, ass up in the back seat?"

I chuckle. "Yes, and I was able to somehow knock Myles in the crotch with my leg. He was crouched over in pain, I was stuck. It was a sight to behold."

Clea chuckles next to me. "I'm going to need permission to use this on my podcast."

"Permission granted, as long as no names are mentioned."

"You know me, girl, I don't ever mention names. I will say this: I appreciate your attempt to do something old school. I can't remember the last time I had a make-out session in the back of my car. I need to text Beast, let her know I'm coming for her."

"It was crowded and awkward, for a second," I say, "but also . . . really intimate and something I always thought about doing with him, back when I was sixteen."

"Totally fulfilled a fantasy," Lois says. "God, I can't imagine what that must feel like, being able to kiss your childhood crush." She leans in. "We all had mad feelings for Zac Efron, but I'd say your feelings toward Myles rivaled that. I could not comprehend the elation I would feel if Zac Efron in his glorious man form now came up to me and said he wanted to make out in the back of his car. I'm pretty sure I'd pass out before it even happened."

"Especially since he went from 'I'll have your daughter home by nine' to 'Your daughter calls me daddy.'" Clea shakes her head. "He is an excellent specimen of the human form. Even I would take a ride."

"Seriously, though, what a thrill for you," Lois says, and from the genuine happiness in her voice, I realize that this is what I was looking for, this sort of support, where my decisions about Myles aren't persecuted but celebrated. "I'd say the mood was killed then and there, but from what Roxane told us about this morning, the mood wasn't killed at all, right?"

"No." My smile spreads wide—I can't contain it. "He stayed the night . . ." I trail off.

"Did you have sex?" Clea asks.

"Not all the way, but we did enjoy each other's company."

Lois lowers her sunglasses. "Did you orgasm?" she asks very seriously.

"Several times," I answer.

Satisfied, she fixes her sunglasses back on her nose and grabs another strawberry. "That's a good man, then. I remember the first time I had an orgasm with Ed, it was life changing. I never experienced one before. I knew he was the one, immediately. If he could make me feel like that, then he was sticking around."

"Same with Beast," Clea says. "That girl is something else. Is that how it was with Myles?"

"Yes," I answer, and then because this has been in the back of my mind, I ask, "Do you think it's possible to feel like you belong to someone even though you've only truly known them for a week?"

"I know I married Ed because we got pregnant, but he also proposed to me after just five dates. He just knew. I knew too—we didn't need to spend months dating to find out if we were meant to be. So, yes, I think it's possible."

"I agree," Clea adds. "My parents were married after only a month of dating. They knew right away. Forty years later, they're still married."

"Why do you ask?" Lois says. "Are you worried about falling for a guy who lives in Greece?"

"Yes, but I also think I've already fallen a bit. He's just—"

"Well, would you look at this cozy little setup," Roxane says, breaking up our conversation. We all look over and find her on the pool deck, arms crossed in complete defense mode. "Looks like you gals are having some fun without me."

"There she is," Clea drawls and pats her chair. "Why don't you take a seat, relax with us."

"Well, I wouldn't want to intrude on your private conversation."

"We weren't having a private conversation," I say, my voice sounding tired because frankly, I am. I'm tired of this.

"Seemed like it. You know, seemed like you were all having fun without me, after I'm the one who suffered my sister's wrath this morning. It seems like you're all taking her side."

"Oh, for fuck's sake," Lois says, "we are not taking her side. We were giving you space so you could calm down."

"Calm down?" Roxane asks. "How am I supposed to calm down when my very own sister calls my soon-to-be marriage an absolute fraud."

"I did not say it was a fraud. I was just asking if you guys were okay or not."

"Of course we're okay!" she yells, her voice carrying throughout the pool area. "We're more than okay, actually. I just talked to him on the phone, and he can't wait to see me tomorrow. So, why don't you stop projecting your worries onto me."

"I'm not projecting. Lois and Clea were thinking the same thing as me." The moment the sentence slips from my lips, I know it was a bad choice.

"So, you three *were* talking about me." Roxane nods, anger burning in her eyes. "That's just great. Here I thought we were coming to Anissa's early to have some bonding time, but it seems like you're all just ganging up on me."

"'Ganging up' on you?" I ask, standing as my temper starts to rise. "If anyone has been ganging up on anyone, it's you three trying to hook me up with people I'm not interested in."

. "We were trying to make sure you didn't end up lonely, so sue us."

"I wasn't lonely!" I shout. "I was perfectly content."

"You were pining after that lifeguard."

"He has a name, it's Myles, and I was not. I actually was too scared to even approach him, but somehow, while I've been dealing with all of your insanity, I found solace in him. While you three were attempting to embarrass me, put me in situations I never wanted to be in, and hook me up with men I had zero interest in, he was comforting me, helping me when none of you would listen."

"He is not your type," Roxane says.

"How so?" I ask, taken aback.

"Because he runs at the first sign of any attention, he's aloof, and frankly he's had plenty of time to make a move, and he never did—not until you were vulnerable. That's what people call a predator, Tessa. But, of course, you're too naive to realize that. I'm just helping you."

"No, you're not," I yell at her, now really drawing the attention. "You're not helping at all. You're making it worse. And I don't know what's going on in your personal life that makes you think you can focus on mine, but I'm over it. I'm done. No more."

I think I've been pretty forgiving up until this point. I've dealt with everything Roxane has thrown my way. I've dealt with her teasing, her prodding, her picking on me, and I've taken it with chin raised and not a complaint. But there is only so much I can take, and the final straw is her trying to convince me that Myles is anything but the man that I know he is.

I won't tolerate it.

"Is that right? You're done?" she asks, shifting her stance.

"Yes, I'm done. With you," I say, unable to stop myself. Because I mean it. I'm done with this constant badgering, this know-it-all attitude of hers, her belief that she has all the answers for my life. *News flash, Roxane, you don't.*

"I see, so what does that mean? Are we no longer sisters? No longer friends? Are you just not going to show up to my wedding?"

"That's right, no longer friends," I say with finality in my voice. "I think the four of us are holding on to something that we had back when we were in high school, something that worked when we were younger, but now that we have our own lives, that contract we signed just doesn't work."

"You're just saying that because now, when it's time for you to live up to it, you don't want to."

"No, I'm saying that because that contract is binding us together when I don't think we share the same values, the same interests, the same consideration for each other anymore. Clea and Lois were right: we've all drifted apart, and I think it's about time we accept that and just go our separate ways." I move around the loungers and glance down at Lois and Clea, who are both sporting morose expressions. "I'm really sorry, you two. I know you tried, but I don't think this is working. None of this is working. I love you, but . . . I just can't mentally take the weight of all this right now. Not after what I've been through on this trip, not after Roxane's behavior. I'm done being the fixer—I'm going out on my own."

And with that, I turn on my heel and head straight to my room, where I plan on ordering room service and letting out a deep, deep breath—one that I think I've been holding on to for far too long.

CHAPTER SIXTEEN
MYLES

Tessa: No plans. Free whenever you are.

Myles: Perfect. I'll see you in a bit.

I pocket my phone and wipe down one of the three loungers on the beach I have left to clean before I need to leave.

After I left Tessa's room, I went back to my place, showered, changed, and then hustled over to the main resort to get started with work, only to be stopped briefly by my baba, who reminded me about the family dinner tomorrow night.

I didn't confirm or deny that I'd be there, but deep down, I know I will—I need to know what's going on. Given everything happening with Tessa, I've pushed the sale of Anissa's to the back of my mind, but it's still there, gnawing away, waiting for me to give it the attention it deserves.

"Are you headed out?" Toby asks, coming up to me.

"Yeah, just have to wipe down these chairs, and then I'm out."

"You going to go hang out with Tessa?"

I smirk. "What do you think?"

"I think you are." He picks up one of my rags and sprays down the chair next to the one I'm working on. "Word on the street is she was arguing with her sister and friends by the pool. Quite a few witnesses."

"Yeah, I heard," I say. Not from Tessa, but from every person who was working in the vicinity.

"Seems like the ship is sinking."

"It started to sink this morning. I don't know a ton about sibling relationships, but it wasn't pretty. There was a lot of blaming, a lot of cheap shots, a whole new level of anger."

"Well, hopefully they can figure it out." He swipes at the chair. "Saw your baba this morning. He was trimming a hedge. That was very uncharacteristic of him."

"He was?" I ask.

"Yeah. He was dressed up in coveralls and a baseball cap, but he removed the cap for a moment to swipe at his forehead. It was odd."

"Wait." I pause. "He was doing *lawn work*? Are you sure?"

"Yes. Can't forget that, your baba outside of his office, doing physical labor. I don't think I've seen that since your parents divorced, when he decided to just sequester himself to desk work."

"Yeah, you're right," I say as I stand straight and stare out at the sea, remembering the days before my parents were divorced. Instead of always hiding out in the office, Baba would walk around the property, offer help in any way he could. He was the one who taught me how to fix broken sinks, paint the walls, freshen up the property. He was hands on, and so was my mom. Together, they made Anissa's a family environment, a special place. And although Anissa's still has its charm, I can tell the difference between predivorce and postdivorce. It's . . . colder now, somehow.

"Why do you think he's doing it now?"

"I have no idea," I say.

Really . . . no fucking clue.

~~~
☀
~~~

Dressed and ready to meet up with Tessa, I take a seat on my bed and hold my phone in front of me, staring down at the contact name on my screen.

Mom's cell.

I've wavered between calling her and not calling her.

I know if Baba finds out that I asked her questions about Anissa's, he will have a goddamn cow, but I'm also wondering if she knows anything. Not that they talk—at least that I know of—but she's still partial owner of Anissa's, so if he's going to sell, she has to know, right?

They had to have talked about it.

I never thought about asking her until Toby brought up Baba earlier—something about the predivorce and postdivorce Anissa's struck me. Life was more fun when Mom was around, and now that she's not . . . it's different. Baba is different.

Everything is different.

But it's been years. Why sell now?

I need to find out, so on a deep breath, I hit send and put the phone on speaker, letting the ring cut through the empty silence in my apartment.

On the third ring, she answers, "Hey, my love."

"Hey, Mom," I reply. "How are you?"

"Good. Good. Just got done with my morning run. The park wasn't too crowded yet, so it was peaceful."

"Did you stretch on your favorite rock?"

"The rock of peace? Of course. I was missing you, though."

"I know. I miss our runs together in the morning."

"How's Greece? Feeling at home again?"

"Sort of," I answer. "Nothing has really changed. I'm just back where I left off."

"Any new responsibilities?"

"No," I answer honestly. "Doing the same old, same old. Sort of disappointed in that, but I think Baba is still bitter about me leaving."

"He's always been a stubborn man," Mom says. She doesn't say it in a nasty way, just in a knowing tone hard won from her experience with him. Ever since the divorce, Mom has never said anything mean about Baba. They parted peacefully. At least that's what it's felt like for me, besides the guilt my baba offers me about leaving for seven years, but we don't need to get into that again.

"I was actually wanting to talk to you about something Baba told me."

"Oh?"

"Well, he, uh, he told me that he plans on selling Anissa's, and I wasn't sure if you were aware of that?"

"I was not," she answers. "But then again, I sold him my shares almost a year ago."

"Wait, what?" I ask, sitting taller on my bed. "You sold? You never told me that."

"Because I didn't think it mattered. I wanted the money for my photography studio, and I had nothing left invested in Anissa's, so I approached him, and he sold, no questions."

"Did he pay you fairly?" I ask.

"Yes, of course. We worked out the price with the lawyers."

Huh, did he buy more than he could take on?

"From the distraught sound in your voice, I can tell him selling was not what you were expecting."

"It wasn't. I'm actually freaking out about it."

"Why?" she asks. "You wanted to buy that boutique hotel, right?"

"I wanted . . . well, I wanted both," I answer. "I wanted to do both with Baba. I wanted to expand Anissa's to the boutique but also keep the traditions alive."

"Have you spoken to him?"

"Yes, I've approached him, and he wants nothing to do with my help. He told me he was selling, it was a done deal, he had no choice because he was in the red, despite being sold out for the year. It just . . . Mom, it doesn't make sense. How can he be sold out for the rest of the year and be in the red? For a second, when you said he sold you the shares, I thought that maybe that was the reason, but you said it was done fairly."

"It was. And I saw the books—Anissa's is thriving."

Thriving? Then what the hell?

"So then . . . do you think he's lying? Toby hasn't mentioned anything about Anissa's falling apart or any discrepancies with employees being paid. Hell, the place looks just as nice as it did seven years ago. I don't get it."

"And he won't talk to you?"

"No," I answer. I push my hand through my curls, perplexed. "He's telling the family tomorrow. That's why I called, to see if you knew anything."

"Nothing strange has been happening?"

"The only thing that I know of is what Toby mentioned. He saw Baba today, trimming the hedges. He said he wouldn't have recognized him if he didn't take his hat off. Reminded me of how he used to do work around the property before you divorced."

"Hmm, well, I don't know what to tell you, other than you're going to have to figure out a way to talk to him."

"But is it weird, Mom? Like . . . he shouldn't be in debt, right?"

"From my knowledge, no. Anissa's has never had issues, nor has your father had issues with handling his own money. It's why he was able to buy me out. The only reason he didn't initially was because he wanted me to still be a part of Anissa's."

"How much say did you have in it, though? Were you just a silent partner?"

"No, he would call me every quarter, and we'd spend about two hours on the phone going over everything. He was very transparent. He never hid anything, and he was organized at every meeting, presented me with access to all of the documents, passwords, everything I needed to make sure he was running the business the way we used to."

"And everything looked good?"

"Everything went great."

I stuff my hand through my hair again, even more perplexed than before. "Then what the hell happened in the year since you sold? There's no way the company could have gone under that quickly. To go into the red fast enough to warrant a sell."

"Maybe it didn't."

"What do you mean?" I ask.

"I mean, what if it didn't go into the red? What if Anissa's is fine? You said it yourself: everything looks great around the property, employees are happy. Maybe . . . maybe he's lying."

"But why would he lie about that? He's a proud man, Mom. Saying that his company, the one thing he's poured his entire soul into, is failing—that's not something he'd do."

"No, it's not something he would do." She pauses. "I don't know, Myles, but it seems like you need to get to the bottom of this. I know your father and I are no longer a couple, but I do care about him deeply and only wish him the best. If he's not in a good mental state, that's something we need to figure out."

"But he's—fuck, Mom, he's so hard to talk to."

"Trust me, I know. It's his greatest downfall, communication. But that doesn't mean we give up on him."

"But you did, Mom," I say. "You gave up." I know it's a low blow, and it's not something that I'd normally ever say, but I'm feeling raw and exposed and confused—it just slipped out.

"I didn't give up, Myles," she says gently. "He pushed me away. I tried several times to fix things. You know this. He gave me no choice.

And even after the divorce, I never gave up on him. It's one of the main reasons I stuck around, because I wanted to make sure he was going to be okay. I didn't split ties with him until this past year because he was finally in a good headspace."

"You're right. I'm sorry, Mom."

"It's okay. I know the divorce was tough, and even though we all made it through, we probably didn't talk about it as much as we should have. We just wanted to make sure you had a normal childhood."

"I appreciate that. I really do." I let out a heavy sigh. "Okay, I'm sorry I bothered you with this. I have a date, and I know she's waiting, so I should probably get going."

"A date?" Mom asks. I knew she wasn't going to just leave it at that, and part of me wanted to say date on purpose—I'm that excited to go out with Tessa again. "With whom?"

"Uh . . . do you remember the Doukas family who came here every summer?"

"Is it with one of the twins?"

"Yes." I smile. She knows. Hell, *everyone* must know at this point.

"Wait, let me guess, is it the one who'd fly kites out on the beach? What was her name . . . Tina?"

"Tessa," I correct. "And yes, that would be her."

"Oh, Myles, you've carried a torch for this girl for how long?"

"Really long. And before you even ask, yes, she's amazing. I feel like I've known her forever. It's so weird. We just click."

"I like this a lot for you."

"You're not worried about the fact that she lives in New York?"

"Not in the slightest. If something is meant to be, then it's meant to be. You never know until you try, and if you don't try, you might regret it for life. And besides, it's not like you don't have a loving mother in New York already. So, I say, go for it. And please, take a picture and send it to me. I want to see you two together."

I chuckle. "Okay, I will."

"And if you need help with Baba, let me know."

"I will. Thanks, Mom. Love you."

"Love you too."

I hang up the phone and stand to my feet. Despite the fizz of anticipation over seeing Tessa again, I'm frustrated. I'm left more confused than ever and so ready for family dinner tomorrow, because I'm going in there with a mission: figure out if Baba is lying or not.

CHAPTER SEVENTEEN
MYLES

"Where are you taking me?" Tessa asks as she clutches my hand, blindfolded.

"Patience, Tessa."

"I have zero patience. I feel like we've been walking around the hotel for thirty minutes. Are you trying to confuse me?"

"It's been five minutes, and no, just trying to get you to the destination."

When I picked her up at her hotel room, I was greeted by her wide, gorgeous smile and her warm, welcoming arms. Without hesitation, she stepped right into my embrace and wrapped her arms around me before lifting her chin and offering me her lips, which I took full advantage of. And like I told my mom, it just felt like we've been doing this forever. It felt normal, but still new and fresh and exciting.

Once I kissed her deeply, she pulled away and did a small twirl for me. She said she'd gone to Oia by herself—I'm assuming after the pool fight; I didn't ask, didn't want to spoil the evening—and she picked out a dress she never would have picked out for herself. It's some kind of backless dress that reaches all the way down to her ankles. A beautiful light-blue color, it's different, but still very much her. She curled her hair into waves and pinned back the top half, showing off her blue eyes. Positively stunning.

I told her to pack an overnight bag, including her bathing suit, and she did, so with my bag and hers in hand, I lead her the rest of the way down the hall.

"Almost there?" she asks.

"Yes." I laugh. "Almost there, just a few more feet." When we reach the door, I pull the key card from my back pocket and slip it into the card reader. When it turns green, I push the door open and guide her in.

I set the bags down in the entry and then lead her to the center of the room.

I honestly couldn't have planned this better. The sun is setting through the open sliding glass doors, casting a brilliant glow of orange throughout the space. The wind is gently whipping at the curtains, lapping them up into the air and showing off the private dipping pool that is blocked off for total privacy, offering only one view—the setting sun.

Excited, I reach behind her and undo her blindfold.

"Okay, now you can look."

When her eyes open and settle on the sight in front of her, she lets out a low gasp as she walks toward the doors.

"Oh my God, Myles, this is . . . this is beautiful. Are we in one of the private suites?"

"Yes. I saw that there was a single-night break in booking, so the reservation ended today and starts tomorrow. It's open for tonight and tonight alone . . . making it ours."

"Really?"

I nod. "Yes. Just you and me, a pool, some room service, and whatever else you want to do."

"Wow, I can't believe how beautiful this is." She walks over to the dipping pool and tests her hand in the water. "Oooh, it's warm." She shakes her hand and then turns to me and smiles. "Oh, Myles, I think I'm going to make out with you a lot tonight."

That makes me throw my head back and laugh. "Well, then, I'm glad I booked this room. What do you want to do first? Order some food? Get comfortable? Swim? Talk?"

"Let's order some food, maybe some wine?"

"Not a problem." I pull my phone from my pocket and open up the Anissa's app to order directly from room service. I take a seat on the large king-size bed and pat the seat next to me for her. "What do you want?"

She perches next to me and presses her shoulder against mine as she looks at my phone. "Can we just do the tapas and a bottle of white?"

"Whatever you want, babe. Want some samsades?"

She shakes her head. "No, but some of those strawberries and chocolate would be good." She waggles her eyebrows, making me smile again.

"Not a problem." I put in the order and then turn to her. "Want to go sit out on the patio and talk until the food gets here?"

"That would be great." She takes my hand in hers, and together we walk out to the patio, to the outdoor wicker love seat in the shape of a half moon. These were new additions to the patios last year, according to Toby.

I sit down first, and she takes a seat. She drapes her legs over mine, and I place my hand on her thigh, keeping her close.

"I've been looking forward to this all day," she says.

"Me too. Oh, which reminds me." I switch my phone to the camera app and then hold it out in front of us. "I need a picture of us." She curls into my side, holding on to my arm, and leans her head against mine. I take a picture and then bring it close to take a look. Her smile is so genuinely beautiful and happy that it just reminds me that I'm in the right place at the right time with the right person.

"Oh my gosh, we look so cute. Can you send it to me?"

"Yeah. I have to send it to my mom too."

"Oh?" she asks with a chuckle. "Did you tell your mom about me?"

"I did. I was talking to her before I picked you up. She knew exactly who you were, and she asked for a picture." I send the pic to Tessa first, and then I send it to my mom before I pocket my phone.

"And what did you happen to say?" she asks.

"That I had a date, and when I told her it was with one of the Doukas girls, she guessed immediately that it was you. I told her that I really like you, but you know, kept things PG."

"Good God, I hope so."

"You don't want her knowing that you were caught, skirt up, by the Santorini police force in the back of my car?"

"*No*," she squeaks out.

"Did you tell your friends?"

"Well . . . yes, but that's different. They can handle that kind of information. Mothers, on the other hand, are not allowed to hear the intricacies of what happens in a relationship."

"Doesn't stop her from asking, though. And I'm sure she'll follow up tomorrow to see how everything went."

"I'm going to assume you're close with your mom."

"Yeah, one of my best friends. No matter the distance, she's always there for me. I remember when my very first girlfriend broke up with me. I was only in middle school, but I was devastated. She flew out here and stayed with me for a week. We did fun things like rent scooters and drive them all around the island, took boat rides to other islands, had picnics in the middle of nowhere, played cards down by the beach, anything to take my mind off the breakup."

"Did it work?"

"It did. And she never talked about it, not until her last day, when she was leaving for the airport. She held me by the shoulders and told me that girls would come and go in my life, but no matter what happened, she'd always be there for me, despite the distance."

"Wow, she sounds amazing."

"She is. I really cherished the time we had together the last seven years. Miss her already, but she has a fiancé now—he's a cool guy, and I like him, and she's starting a new chapter in her life. I'm happy for her."

"And you're trying to start a new one in your life, right? With the boutique hotel? You still haven't let me look over the numbers and how to make it all work with purchase of the property, renovations, and possible income."

"I know. I just feel weird asking you to do that, and with everything up in the air, I'm not sure it's worth your time."

"Don't you want to at least know if you can do it?"

"Sort of, but I'm also worried that if I find out the truth and I can move forward with the boutique idea on my own, I'd end up losing my baba and Anissa's at the same time . . . hell, I don't think I could stomach that."

"Ah, I see. Better not knowing, at least until everything is figured out."

"Exactly." I let out a deep breath. "I don't want to talk about it, though. This night is about you and me. Getting to know each other even more."

She snuggles in closer. "Okay . . . so, then let's get to know each other. I know your dreams. I know your family. I know your personality. Now I just need to know . . . you. What makes Myles tick?"

"A vanilla latte in the morning—I need a sweet in my coffee to make it bearable—some kind of hummus at some point in my day, and work. Something to keep my hands busy. I don't like being idle. I like to know that I can be helpful in some way."

"That makes sense since you grew up helping around the resort. But can we talk about the hummus comment?"

I laugh. "Of course. What do you need to know?"

"Do you eat hummus with a spoon? Or do you dip something into it?"

"I've eaten hummus with a spoon before, but normally I dip veggies into it, sometimes pita bread. But mainly veggies, or I have it in a salad, on my chicken . . . pretty much how Americans use ranch on everything, I use hummus on everything."

"Hummus on pizza?" she asks.

"I've had pizza where the sauce was replaced with hummus, and it was fucking good. So yes. If you want to know the way to my heart, it's hummus."

"Well, that's good to know. Taking notes . . . hummus it is. You know, since we're supposed to fall in love in a week and all. I can guarantee it with hummus."

"Smart woman." I kiss the side of her head. "What about you? What makes you tick?"

"Uh . . . well, I don't need coffee to survive like some people do, but if I were to drink it, I need, like, two percent coffee, ninety-eight percent sugar. But I do tend to live off a brisk walk in the morning with an audiobook. And before you ask, I'm really into fantasy. If I can get a walk in with my book for the day, then I know it's going to be a great day. Other than that, as long as I get some personal one-on-one time with my numbers and at least one salad during the day, then I'm good to go. Life feels great."

"Is there hummus on that salad?"

She laughs. "It seems like I'll be having more hummus on my salad from here on out."

"You won't regret it." I slowly stroke my thumb over her thigh. "Where do you walk in the morning? My mom is always running around Central Park, and I ran with her when I lived there—I wonder if we were ever near each other."

"I walk around in Central Park as well. There's no doubt in my mind that we probably passed each other at some point, which I think is crazy, not seeing you in all that time. And we lived *so* close. I guess I just wasn't looking for you."

"I was looking for you," I admit quietly, which causes her to pull away and meet my gaze. Every fucking day, I'd keep my eyes open for her, hoping that I'd run into her.

"You were?"

I nod. "I knew you were in New York, thanks to some snooping on my end, and when I was there, I'd look for you whenever I was out at a restaurant, running errands, jogging. I'd think, *How fucking cool would it be if I ran into her?*"

"I probably would have had a heart attack. I was absolutely convinced that you left Anissa's because I scared you away."

That makes me laugh. "Tessa, my baba owns the resort. Just because you called my lips luxurious doesn't mean I would throw that all away to avoid you."

"I didn't know your baba owned the resort, and I also thought that maybe you found out when we booked our vacations and you'd avoid being here for that time."

"Seems awfully inconvenient and like way too much work. Plus, I wasn't scared away. If I'd been in a better frame of mind at the time, I probably would've asked if I could buy you a drink."

"I would have stumbled with my words if you did, probably done something embarrassing like spit all over you while I spoke, and you would have regretted ever asking me to have a drink with you."

"Not true. I find stumbling over words and spitting rather endearing."

"No, you don't." She lightly pushes at me. "No one finds that endearing."

"Maybe not, but it would have been worth sticking around." I lift her chin and bring her mouth to mine, lightly kissing her lips. Her hand smooths up my neck to my cheek, where she holds me in place.

And we stay like that, making out, until our food arrives.

"So how often did you visit America when you were a kid? Because you don't have much of an accent at all," Tessa says. "Only a word here and there."

"I probably spent half my year in America. We'd go back and forth all the time, visiting my mom's family and spending the summers working at Anissa's. My teacher who homeschooled me—which I understand is usually a parent homeschooling, but my parents didn't feel comfortable being responsible for my education, so they hired a tutor—she was American as well and had a big influence on me and the way I'd speak and articulate."

Tessa slips her hand to the back of my neck, where she plays with the short strands of hair at my nape. It feels really fucking good. "That makes a lot of sense. Do you still speak with your tutor?"

"I do." I tilt my head to the side, encouraging her to keep tangling her fingers with my hair. "I visit her on her birthday every year. Mrs. Randall. She never let me get away with anything, but she'd also see when I needed a break and would be the first to sneak me out of the classroom and go do something fun. She'd always tell my parents it was a field trip, but I think they were all in on it."

"And what about friends? Did you feel like you needed kids around you? Like you missed out on the camaraderie?"

I smooth my hand over her thigh, dragging the long hem of her skirt up so her knees are exposed and I can press my palm to her skin. "Not really. I grew up with Toby—he has a similar Greek-and-American family—and there were other kids at the resort. I never felt like I was lacking in friendships. I think I enjoyed my childhood even more because I was able to learn in a different way. My mom and Mrs. Randall would take me to different historical spots all around the world to learn so I could see them in person. I'm fluent in English, Greek, and Spanish. I never felt like I struggled, and if I was struggling, I had one-on-one time to figure it all out."

"Gosh, I'm jealous," Tessa says as she dabs her mouth with her napkin. "My dad is Greek, of course, but Roxane and I can barely speak it beyond the basics. I even struggled when it came to writing papers for my English classes. I'm not someone who can look for the hidden meanings in things. I'm all about facts and formulas, and if you do something a certain way, there's a correct end result. If you leave things up to interpretation, for me, it doesn't make sense."

"And I was the one who'd spend hours talking about the meaning behind certain poems while lounging out by the cliffs. And this is going to sound very stereotypical, but I was very into Greek mythology. Still am."

"Really? Then who is your favorite Greek god?"

"Oh man, I have an idiotic response to this."

"Really? Do tell." She lifts her glass of wine to her lips and takes a generous sip.

"His name is Pan, ever heard of him?" She shakes her head. "Yeah, he's not popular, but he has the hind legs and horns of a goat, which, you know, is funny enough. But he also had a very voracious sexual appetite and would honestly have sex with anything that moved. Anything. Widely known as a sex pest, he was quite the whore, and there was something about his honesty that made me laugh. He was like, 'Yeah, I'm here for sex, what are you going to do about it?'"

"That is such a guy answer."

"I told you it was idiotic, but you asked, and I answered. Did you expect a more mature answer, like Apollo?"

"Sort of, but I like your answer. It's bizarre and original. I've never even heard of Pan."

"Not many have, probably for very good reasons. Being a sexual nymph doesn't really earn you a golden spot in history."

"No, but it leads to some good folklore."

"Very true." I pick an olive off our shared plate and offer it to her. She leans forward and opens her mouth. Gently, I slip my fingers past her lips and deposit the olive on her tongue. "I've never asked you. Why do you and your family come here every summer? You could go anywhere in the world, but you come here, like clockwork."

She chews for a moment. "My dad grew up in Fira. We'd come back to visit with family, but once his parents passed away, we came because Dad wanted to keep the tradition alive, and then it just became a habit. Now I couldn't imagine not coming here during the summer, although it's been a little sad the last seven years."

"Tell me about it. I remember when I saw you check in. I just finished up helping someone with their bags, I was returning a cart, and you spun around, asking Roxane something. I stopped dead in my tracks and did a double take. I wasn't sure if it was you at first, but when I realized it was, I told myself I was going to make sure I talked to you more this go-around."

"Is that why you came over while we were behind the boat?"

"Looking for the nonexistent earring? Yeah."

Her cheeks flush. "That was the first time I saw you, and I was freaking out."

"Yeah, I realized in that moment that it was going to be harder to talk to you than I expected. But then you came down to the bar in a robe without a worry or care, which really made it easier on me."

She presses her hand to her forehead. "God, please don't remind me."

I take her by the hand and pull her onto my lap. "But look at what that robe did. It brought us together. I'm pretty sure without that bold move, we wouldn't be where we are now."

"True, because I gave up on everything in that moment. My defenses were down, and I let the raw moment take over, leaving me ripe for the picking. You took advantage."

"Yeah, but I'd do it again."

With a laugh, she drags her finger over my lip. "Are you thinking what I'm thinking?"

"Strawberries?"

She chuckles. "No. I was thinking swimming."

"Oh yeah, me too."

She just rolls her eyes and then lifts off my lap. Tugging me by the hand, she leads me into the hotel room.

Swimming it is.

Tessa wet and in a bathing suit—yeah, not going to argue with that.

The water is fucking perfect. Not too warm, but just warm enough so it's not uncomfortable. The sun has completely set, casting the sky into a dark abyss, the stars like diamonds, a beautiful contrast. The evening is quiet, besides a few voices down below, but for the most part, it's peaceful. I decided to set the mood a bit and lit up the lights under the pool, leaving that as the only illumination on the back patio. I turned on some faint instrumentals for some background music, using my Bluetooth speaker that I brought for this specific occasion, and I of course brought the strawberries and the wine to the edge of the pool for easy access.

Now I just wait.

I got dressed first, taking two seconds in the bathroom to change into a pair of navy-blue trunks. For a brief second, and I mean brief, I thought about bringing out the Speedo, but then thought better of it. It might be too much all at once.

Wading in the pool, I'm gazing off toward the darkened sea as the back door opens. I turn around just in time to catch her step out into the patio wearing a red two-piece bathing suit. And excuse me as I pick my jaw up out of the water because out of all the years I've seen Tessa in a bathing suit, not once has she ever worn a two-piece.

Never.

Not that she needed to, but now that she is, holy shit. She's curvy, like an hourglass, her figure sloping in all the right places. The bottoms of her suit sit high on her hips and narrow thinly between her legs. The thin triangles over her breasts cover about 50 percent of them. The rest . . . well, that's exposed for my hungry eyes.

"Tessa," I whisper as she walks toward me, timidness in her step but confidence in her shoulders. "Wow, I, uh . . . I'm fucking speechless."

She doesn't say anything but instead slips into the water and walks straight up to me, putting her hands on my chest. When her wary eyes meet mine, she says, "I've never worn a two-piece before, and I'm pretty sure I'm about to shrivel up from mortification."

"Mortification? Why?" I give us some space and take her in. "Tessa, you look fucking amazing."

"I'm tempted to ask if you're just saying that, but I want to approach this with more confidence. So, thank you."

"You didn't have to wear a two-piece, you know." I rest my hands on her hips and pull her close.

"I wanted to. I wanted to try something different. I saw the bathing suit while I was shopping, and I had this wild thought in my head that I could pull it off. I'm still trying to decide if I can or not."

"Babe, you can. You really fucking can." I move her so she's up against the wall, which makes her smile. "There it is. Just what I was looking for, a smile."

Her hands land on my shoulders. "I wanted to come out here with all the confidence, step into this pool and right into your arms, but my insecurities roared louder than the confidence that bought this bathing suit."

"Can you talk to me about these insecurities? That's if you're comfortable."

Her finger circles my shoulder. "I've just always been the awkward twin. Roxane has this very vibrant, extroverted personality that rightfully garners all the attention—attention I truly never wanted, but still, she's always been able to light up every room she's walked into, even when we were young. And I just found it easier to shrink into her shadow instead of competing for the spotlight, and I think over time, that's made me more and more insecure."

"Being in your sister's shadow, I can't imagine that's easy."

"And it's not like she put me there. I just sort of . . . put myself there. And after this trip, I don't know, I just feel like I don't belong in her shadow anymore. I've found a sliver of confidence, and I want to keep moving forward with it. Hence the bathing suit. I've always wanted to try wearing one. I thought that maybe tonight would be the perfect night."

"You were right," I say as I move in even closer. Underwater, I take her legs and wrap them around my thighs.

Her hands loop around the back of my neck. "You're the main reason why I was able to step out here in this bikini."

"Oh yeah? How so?" I ask as I lower my mouth to her neck and pepper her skin with kisses.

Her head tilts to the side, giving me better access. "You make me feel special. Despite my awkwardness and my stumbling, you still look at me in this way that creates this ball of confidence deep in my bones."

"How do I look at you?" I ask as my mouth travels to her jaw, my hands now moving up to her ribs.

"Like I belong to you. Like there's no one else on this island that could garner your attention the way I can. Like you've been waiting for me for so long, and I've finally shown up."

"I have been waiting," I say as I lift my right hand to the back of her neck, where her bikini is tied. I pause at the strands, and when she doesn't protest, I lightly tug on them until they're completely loose. "I feel like I've been waiting for you my whole life." I let her bikini top fall between us, and then with my other hand, I tug the bottom strands until her top falls off. I gather the fabric and place it on the pool patio behind her.

Smiling, she says, "I've never been skinny-dipping before."

"No?" I ask. "I hate to waste this bathing suit, but I'm pretty sure it was begging me to take it off."

"Well, I can't be the only one skinny-dipping."

"Trust me, you won't," I say as I slip my hands under the fabric of her bottoms, pushing it down her legs while she assists me. I toss that on the pool patio as well and then reach for my own trunks, but she stops me and replaces my hands with hers.

"Allow me."

She dips her fingers past the waistband and pushes the fabric down until I'm completely free of the trunks. She flicks them behind us and then stands there, a little stunned but also looking slightly devious.

"You okay?" I ask her.

She nods, and then pulls me in close, her chest to mine, her pebbled nipples rubbing against my bare skin. With her legs wrapped around me, her ass bobbing against my erection, I pull her into the center of the pool, where we can see the sky better as we float under the stars.

"This is something else," she says as her fingers tangle through my hair. "If someone told me ten years ago that I'd be skinny-dipping with the guy I had a lifelong crush on, I never would have believed them."

"Same," I answer before I press my lips to hers.

She parts for me, allowing my mouth to take control, my lips to lead the way, my tongue to explore. There's hunger in the way she grips me, in the way her tongue matches my strokes, but there's also confidence. She wants me just as much as I want her—it's evident in every inch of her.

I float us around the pool, her mouth never leaving mine, her fingers digging deeper into my scalp, and when I bump up against the side of the pool, the water lapping around us, I realize just how goddamn hard I am.

How much I need her.

How much I've relied on this feeling with her, where nothing else matters around us. Just me and Tessa.

"You make me happy," I say quietly as my mouth drags across her jaw.

"You make me happy too, Myles," she answers as she lolls her head back, exposing her neck, which I take advantage of, running my tongue along the column and then back up her jaw and to that spot just beyond her ear. Her moan is soft, barely above a whisper, but it's loud enough to feel like a bolt of pleasure pulsing through me.

Sexy and free, she doesn't hold anything back. She lives in the moment, and even though she claims she has insecurities, they don't show with me, at least not on a deep level. I've watched her stumble through conversations and awkwardly bounce around, but when it comes to moments like this, when it's just us, she's natural, charismatic, addictive.

My hands glide up her sides, past her ribs, to her breasts. I grip both of them at the same time as my mouth falls down upon hers again.

"Myles," she says.

"Yes?" I ask as my lips descend upon her neck again. This time, I can feel her pulse quicken as I dip down closer to her breasts.

"I . . . I want to bring this inside?"

I pause and glance up at her. "Are you sure?"

When our eyes meet, she nods. "Yes."

"Okay."

I like being in the pool with her—it's hot, it's erotic, it's different—but I also want to make sure she's comfortable, so I take her hand in mine and we walk out of the pool together. I reach for a towel and wrap it around her before wrapping one around my waist. The terry cloth does nothing to hide my excitement, so I quickly wipe down.

Partially dried off, we both walk into the bedroom, where she drops her towel to the floor and then kneels on the bed. She snags my hand, pulling me in close and placing a gentle kiss on my chest, then my stomach. When she lowers down to my aching cock, she parts her beautiful lips and takes me into her mouth.

"Hell," I mutter as I gather her hair and bring it to the side so I can watch.

She's timid at first, gentle. Teasing almost because I think she doesn't want to hurt me, and given how big I am, I'm not sure she knows how to quite handle me just yet, but after a few swirls of her tongue around the head of my cock, she starts to grow more comfortable. Her hands grip the base, stroking at a fervent pace, and then she starts hollowing out her cheeks, sucking harder.

"Fuck," I groan. "Tessa, that feels too damn good."

My words of encouragement must spur her on because she moves her hand faster, gripping tighter while her tongue runs the length of my erection, dragging all the way up until she reaches the tip and flicks. She repeats this process several times until I feel a stir of an orgasm start to form in the pit of my stomach.

"Tessa." I swallow hard. "Babe, I need you to stop."

She pauses and smiles. "Getting close?"

I gulp. "Yeah, very close."

"Good." She starts to move back toward my dick, but I stop her and push her on the bed.

"No, not good. I don't want to come in your mouth."

"But I wanted you to."

"No, I want to come inside of you." I hope she's thinking the same thing, and when I notice the excitement in her eyes, I know we're on the same page. Relieved, I walk over to my overnight bag, pull out a condom, and slip it on before turning toward her. "On your back," I say before climbing up on the bed with her.

She settles on her back, her head on a pillow, and she spreads her legs, making room for me. I lower my body to the mattress and bring my mouth to her stomach, where I trail kisses.

Meghan Quinn

"What are you doing?" she asks.

"Checking if you're ready," I answer as I kiss all the way down to the spot between her legs.

"I am ready," she says, brushing my hair away from my forehead.

"Good, then that means you're ready for my tongue." I part her with my fingers and dip my mouth against her arousal, my tongue swiping in one long stroke, tasting just how ready she really is.

"Myles," she says, her back arching off the bed, her legs spreading even wider.

I don't respond. Instead I keep swiping at her, taking my time, performing languid strokes that I know will only heighten the experience but not give her the total relief that she needs.

She writhes beneath me, attempting to place my tongue where she wants me, but I don't give in. I keep at my pace while smoothing my hand up her body to her breast, where I pinch her nipple between my fingers.

"Oh God," she says, her body shifting beneath mine.

Loving her reaction, I keep playing with her nipple while pressing my mouth against her clit, lapping at her, giving her just enough to bring her to the edge, but not enough to push her over.

"Myles." She squirms again. "I need more."

Smirking, I lift my head and drag my tongue up her body. When our eyes meet up, I lean down and match my lips with hers, taking her mouth, claiming it as mine. I grip my cock, and I place it at her entrance. I feel a shudder of excitement rock through her right before I press an inch forward.

"Yes," she whispers, which gives me all I need to continue pushing forward, savoring every inch of her.

Slowly, inch by inch, I enter her until I bottom out. Her breath hitches as she stares up at me, eyes wide, a smile tugging at her lips.

"You okay?" I ask her.

304

"Perfect, Myles. You feel big, but perfect."

Smirking, I lower my head and kiss her again. "You feel fucking amazing, so good, Tessa. So good."

And with that, I start rocking slowly in and out of her, keeping the pace torturously mild so she can adjust around me. She feels tight, and what we're doing might feel really good to her, but I also don't want to hurt her. I focus on small, slow strokes while my mouth attempts to relax her even more with kisses up and down her neck, over her collarbone, along her jaw, against her lips, where I part her and find her tongue.

Smoldering heat beats up my spine with every swipe of her tongue, with every fingernail that digs into my skin, with the way her legs tangle around me, holding me in place, begging for so much more. It's her heels digging into my back that edge up my pace as my hips dip down and up, in and out, the friction growing ever headier.

"Yes, Myles," she calls out, her grip growing tighter, her moans louder.

"So fucking good," I say as my senses heighten, my need for this woman overwhelming.

Her hands glide down my back to my ass, where she grips me and pulls me in harder, telling me exactly what she needs . . . release.

I anchor one hand on the bed, next to her head, the other on her thigh to hold her tight as my hips start to jackhammer into her, pulsing hard, relentlessly, with a powerful force I didn't even think I had in me, but the need is too great, the friction is so hot, the pleasure is compounding, and I can't hold back anymore.

"Fuck, how close are you?" I ask her as I feel the distinct sensation of an impending orgasm ride up the base of my spine.

"Right . . . there," she says, so I drive harder.

Faster.

Building.

The heat between us soars. The sound of my body slapping against her echoes through the room as her moans grow longer, louder, to the point that they turn into one continuous moan.

"Yes, Myles. Right there. Please don't . . . stop . . . oh God!" she yells as I feel her constrict around me, gripping me so tightly that it takes me only two strokes before I'm coming right along with her, my hips stilling as we both convulse with pleasure.

"Fuck . . . me," I grind out as I seek every last ounce of ecstasy, finally collapsing when there's nothing left inside of me.

Her body is limp beneath mine, both of us spent as we catch our breath.

After a few moments, she sifts her hand through my hair. "I've never in my life come like that . . . ever."

I kiss her shoulder. Her chin. Her cheek. And then her lips. "Me neither, Tessa." I meet her gaze and connect our foreheads. "Fuck, that was so good."

She lightly chuckles, and her hand cups my cheek. "Really good. So good that I hope you're going to be able to go multiple rounds tonight."

"I'm yours for the night—you can have me as many times as you want."

"Well then." She pats my back. "Rest up, because I'm going to want you in multiple locations."

CHAPTER EIGHTEEN
TESSA

I've had sex before, many times, to be precise. Some good, some bad. Some average—nothing to write home about.

But what I experienced last night—now, that was a whole new level. That wasn't human; that was . . . that was what fantasies are made of.

After our first round, Myles held me close to his chest, we talked about anything and everything, and he peppered kisses all over my skin until I turned in toward him, mounted his body, and went for round two.

Round three consisted of using the strawberries and chocolate sauce.

Round four was in the shower to clean ourselves after the chocolate sauce.

And round five was slow, yet very hot morning sex.

I don't think I've ever felt more satisfied in my life.

Myles slips a light-blue T-shirt over his head and then fits it around his waist as I sit on the edge of the bed, watching him closely. "What's your day like?" I ask.

He takes a seat next to me on the bed as he slips his shoes on. "Family dinner is at three, so prepping for that. I think I have to help Toby restock the bar, but that's about it. What about you?"

"Family gets in early this morning. They took a red-eye last night. The chaos begins."

Which means my time with Myles will be cut down. The thought of possibly not seeing him every day actually makes me feel physically ill.

He wraps his arm around my shoulders and brings me into his side while pressing a kiss to my head. "Meet up with me tonight? We can hang out in your room, or you can come to my apartment, up to you."

"I don't care where. I know I'll just want to see you. Not sure what my schedule will allow moving forward, so I want as much time with you as I can get. I'm sure Roxane has informed my parents of my 'defiance,' and I'll be riddled with lectures about how my sister is stressed and I need to be kind to her."

"Have they heard your side of the story yet?"

"No, but I'm sure it will come up." I sigh and lean into him. "Last night was so special to me, Myles." I lift up and look him in the eyes. "You really made me feel like I matter."

"Because you do matter, Tessa." He lifts my chin and softly kisses me. "And last night was special to me too. It felt like the beginning of something."

"So, this isn't the end." I smile.

"Not even close. How about after my family dinner, I come to your room?"

"That works. After the day I'll probably have, I'm sure I'll really, really need to see you."

"Same." He kisses me one more time and then helps me to my feet. He picks up both our bags and walks me toward the door, holding it open for me, before walking me to my room, my arm linked through his.

"You know, we could just skip all festivities today and run away," I say as my stomach flips at what is awaiting me.

"Don't tempt me, Tessa. Because I would."

"Where would we go if we did?" I ask, curious.

"Hmm, would you want to escape or find a new normal?"

"Great question. Escapism is so appealing, but there's always an end, so a new normal seems like it would last longer."

We continue down the hall, our voices echoing softly. "So then, what would you want your new normal to be?" he asks.

"Well, I'd want to see you every day."

"Great answer. What else?"

"I'd want a place where I can be myself, without having to make accommodations for my sister, a place where she doesn't think she's better than me or needs to help me or pities me. I want to live freely, feel like I can do whatever I want without judgment."

"Give me an example," he says.

"Like last night. If I showed up to the pool wearing that two-piece, not only would Roxane have made a big deal about it, she would have also somehow picked it apart to the point that I felt like I chose the wrong one, and I'd have ended up changing."

"That's shitty."

"That's Roxane. I love her, but she's always been critical. Our entire life, the world has revolved around her and her opinion, and I've trailed behind."

"Well, not with our new normal," he says, kissing me on the side of the head just as we arrive at my door. He spins me toward him and then gently presses me against the door. Cupping my chin, he lifts my lips and kisses me. After a few minutes of sinking into his mouth, he pulls away and whispers, "Tonight, Tessa. Okay?"

"Okay," I whisper back, breathless.

With one final kiss, he hands me my bag and then takes off. Before I open the door, I watch Myles walk down the hallway, my eyes on his backside. And to my pleasure, he glances over his shoulder, offers me a wink, and then continues down the hallway.

Ugh, color me infatuated.

On cloud nine, I slip my key card through the scanner and open the door, only to stop dead, the air knocked out of me as I face my mom and dad, sitting on my bed.

"You . . . you arrived early."

"We told you we'd be here around ten," Mom says as I set my bag down. "We were expecting to find you in your room, not entering it."

"Uh yeah, I was just, uh, you know, going to get something."

"Is that right?" Dad asks as he walks up to me and offers me a hug. "Because it seems like you're returning after a long night. Hence the overnight bag."

"That is just some things I found in my travels."

"So, the phone call we received from your sister about you ditching her for a man has nothing to do with this?" Mom asks.

My heart sinks. Of course Roxane called them.

"Listen, she's been freaking awful ever since we got here. She's been trying to hook me up with all these different guys—"

"Philip didn't make his flight," Mom says.

"What?" I ask. "Like, he missed it and is delayed now?"

Mom shakes her head. "No, more like he decided not to get on."

"Wait, seriously?" I ask, heart sinking.

"Yes," Dad answers. "He called Roxane and told her he was having second thoughts and didn't think he was ready."

Oh God.

"Wh-when did he do that?"

"Last night," Mom answers. "We found out when we got here."

"Well, where is she? Why aren't you with her?"

"She's with Lois and Clea right now. Clea asked us to find you."

"Okay." I move toward the door. "Is she in her room?"

"I believe so," Dad says. "But Tess, I'm not sure she wants to see you right now. After everything she told us, she might not be in the right frame of mind."

"I can't just sit back and let her hurt," I say, determination settling over me. "She might have said some pretty mean things, but she's my sister, and I don't want her hurting alone. Why don't you guys get a little rest—I'm assuming your room isn't ready yet?"

"Not yet."

"Okay, well, take a shower, do what you need to do, and stay by the phone." I turn toward the door but look back at them. "He really said he's having second thoughts?" Both my parents nod as guilt consumes me. The things I said about Philip . . . I had an inkling that maybe things were rocky, but I didn't think it was true. Dammit, I should have talked to her instead of getting caught up in our stupid fight.

I make the short walk to Roxane's room and notice the security bar holding the door open. Gently, I push the handle and step into the quiet space. When I peek around the corner, I see Clea, Lois, and Roxane on the balcony, all staring out toward the sea.

I walk toward the sliding glass, heart in my throat, unsure of what their reactions will be. The anger of our fight rolls through my mind. I said some things I might not have meant. Well, sort of meant. Giving up on our friendship, on our sisterhood—I don't think I could ever do that. But sticking up for myself—I meant every word of that. Still, not sure the kind of welcome I'll receive this morning after the strong words I said.

"Hey," I say softly as I step out onto the balcony. Roxane's head whips up, and when her eyes narrow in on me, I can immediately sense this was a bad idea.

"What the hell are you doing here?" she asks, swiping at her dripping nose.

"Mom and Dad told me what happened—"

"Oh, so you're here to gloat, then."

"No, Roxane. I'm here to see if you're okay."

"I don't need you checking on me—you made your point very clear yesterday. You want nothing to do with us."

"Roxane, please. We can talk about this without getting into a fight, okay? Maybe we can call Philip, talk to him, see what's going on."

"No need to talk to him. The wedding is off," she says and swipes under her eye.

"Is that what he said?"

"It's what I said." Roxane stands from her chair and stalks past us, into her room. We follow, all quiet, unsure what to do in this moment. "You called it, didn't you, Tessa?" she says, venom dripping from her voice. "You said that something was wrong with Philip and me, so I guess you were right. You're always right about everything. You must be thrilled."

"I'm not," I say, my brow furrowing in concern. "Roxane, I know we've gotten into it the last few days, but I'd never be thrilled about something bad happening between you and Philip."

"Please, you were just begging for us to break up. From the beginning, you didn't like him. You were always jealous of the time he took away from you, and when we announced we were getting married here, you couldn't stand the thought that I was going to be the first one to get married at Anissa's when all along you fantasized about marrying the lifeguard here."

"His name is Myles," I say through clenched teeth. "And no, that's not how I feel. I thought you and Philip had differences, but you were so convinced he was the guy for you because you wore the stupid freaking perfume on your first date—you would have done anything to make it happen. Ever think about the fact that maybe you pushed too hard to have the perfect relationship, when really, it's not perfect at all?"

I know the moment the words slip out that I made a huge mistake, but I couldn't hold back. Something in me is driving this conversation forward, searching out the need to stand up for myself and the doubts that I've harbored, and fight for an honest relationship between my sister and me.

"*What?*" Roxane says, her face growing angry. "How would you even know anything about a relationship, Tessa?" I brace myself. I poked the bear, and now she's about to maul me. "You barely have any experience—hell, the longest relationship you've had was with a man who cheated on you. You have no idea what it takes to be with someone, to even find someone interested in you. So don't try telling me that I tried too hard. At least I put myself out there instead of hiding behind some stupid crush. And if anyone's trying too hard to be perfect for someone else, it's you with Myles."

"Don't, Roxane." I shake my head as I feel my own anger stirring. "Don't say something just to hurt me."

"Hurt you? I'm telling you the truth. I'm the only one who has ever told you the truth—"

"No, you minimize me," I shout back at her. "It's your mission in life to make sure I'm always and forever the secondary twin."

"Oh wow, fantasize much?" She rolls her eyes. "I have better things to do with my life than try to make you feel even worse about yourself."

"That's the problem," I say, taking a step forward. Lois and Clea stand off to the side, watching us volley insults back and forth—like always. Same rodeo, different day for them. "I don't feel less about myself, I actually feel great. I feel special. I feel like I matter. I've never let myself feel this way because I've always tried to make *you* feel good. I've spent my entire life tiptoeing around your feelings and trying to make sure you feel special."

"Oh please," Roxane says. "It's been the other way around. Do you know how sick and tired I am of carrying your insecurities around? It's been a burden, Tessa. *You* have been a burden."

I take a step back, letting her words sink in.

If that's how she really feels, then I'm going to make this easy on her.

Chin held high, I move past her and toward the door. "If I really have been a burden, Roxane, then I'm going to take it off your hands."

"Where are you going?" she says as I head toward the door.

"I'm leaving. The wedding is off, which means I'm relieved of my maid of honor duties. I'm going to go do what I want to do."

"You're just going to leave? My fiancé broke things off with me," Roxane shouts. "And you take this moment to find yourself? Don't you think that's narcissistic of you?"

"If anyone is being a narcissist in this room, it's you, Roxane. And I was here for you. I tried to calm you down, to offer support, but like every other situation in our life, instead of digging deep into your feelings, you have found some way to diminish me to make you feel better. Well, guess what, Roxane? I'm sick of being your punching bag. I'm sick of being the one who has to take the brunt of your unhappiness. I'm through."

And with that, I open her door and stalk through the hotel and down to the beach. If there's one thing I know, it's that I want to be as far away from Roxane as I can get.

CHAPTER NINETEEN
MYLES

"Oh, look at you," Aunt Velma coos as she pinches my cheeks and stares up at me from her five-foot-three stature. "*Agóri mou*, you've just gotten so tall, so handsome. Have you been eating?" She pinches my arm.

"Ouch," I say, rubbing the spot.

"You look thin. You need some food. Come to the kitchen, I'll feed you."

"I'm good, actually, Aunt Velma," I say. "I had some food before I came."

"Nonsense." She pulls me toward the kitchen, her frail arm looped through mine.

Aunt Velma is Baba's sister. He grew up with three siblings: Aunt Velma, Uncle Taki, and Aunt Cassia. They all married and bred . . . like bunnies. Meaning, I am currently being ushered through my aunt Velma's house dodging hordes of cousins who are talking, arguing, and even wrestling. All activities done very loudly, I might add. Baba was the only sibling to have one kid, and that's because my mom could only have one. So, while I might have been an only child, I had enough cousins to make up for it.

"Boris," Aunt Velma shouts to her husband. "Get Myles some meat."

"Aunt Velma, really, I'm okay."

"Sit." She pushes me down into a dining room chair. "Boris will bring you the meat."

I sigh as I lean back into the wooden chair and survey the household. To someone else, the raucous noise, countless family members, and loud Greek exclamations could be very overwhelming, but to me, it feels normal. It feels like I'm home—it was one of the things I missed whenever I was in New York.

Uncle Boris slides a plate in front of me and says, "Lamb," before walking away.

I stare down at the seasoned cooked meat, just a mound of it, and pick up my fork. There is no way I'm going to be eating all of it, but I need to get through at least some or I'll be insulting my aunt and uncle.

"Myles, *kamari mou*, I wasn't sure you were going to make it," Aunt Cassia says as she takes a seat next to me at the table.

Aunt Cassia is my favorite. She is chill, doesn't pressure me to eat like Aunt Velma, and she's always taken me under her wing, sneaked me away when things got crazy, and supported me when I wanted to move to New York City for the training program.

"Hey, Aunt Cassia," I say as I bring her into a hug.

"My oh my." She grips my shoulders. "Look who put on some muscles when he was gone."

I chuckle. "In my spare time I'd hit up the gym."

"It shows." She leans back in her chair and crosses one leg over the other. "So, how is my nephew? You look good, although"—she leans forward—"it seems like there is some worry in your eyes."

"Yeah, not sure how I'm supposed to eat this entire plate of meat."

She shakes her head. "No, the food is the least of your worries. What's going on?"

Did I mention Aunt Cassia has always been very perceptive? It's like she can read minds.

Sighing, I lean in closer to her. "Has Baba said anything to you about the resort?"

"Ahh." She nods in understanding. "He did mention something yesterday but swore me to secrecy."

"What did he say to you?"

She lowers her voice to a whisper. "That he was selling Anissa's and was telling the family today."

"Did he say why?"

"Claimed it wasn't making money." She folds her arms. "But I don't believe him."

"I don't either. I spoke to my mom yesterday about it, since she held shares, but she just recently sold them all to Baba. He's been very transparent about the numbers with her, and she said the resort has been thriving, so what could have happened where now he needs to sell?"

"Your mom sold?" she asks.

"Yes. I think she was moving on, you know?"

"I do." Aunt Cassia stares out the kitchen window. "You know, your baba took the divorce very hard."

"I know," I say.

"And he took you leaving very hard as well. During the first year you were gone, he actually spent many nights at my place. He'd cry almost every single time."

"Really?" I ask, surprised. "I wouldn't have guessed that, given the way he's treated me ever since I've been home. He can barely look at me, speak to me."

"He's hurt," Aunt Cassia says. "Well, no, that's not the right word. He's hurting and putting that hurt on you."

"What do you mean?"

"His biggest regret is not fighting harder for your mom, not setting aside his pride and fixing things with her. When I say she was the love of his life, she truly was. He had everything he wanted: the girl of his dreams, a son, the resort. You guys were a unit. And when the economy

317

collapsed, he let his stress and his emotions get the better of him and ended up losing everything that mattered to him. When you went to New York, he thought he was losing you too."

"I told him he wasn't losing me."

"Yes, but you were gone, and to him, that was losing you."

"He didn't make it easy," I say. "I tried talking to him. Calling him, writing him, but he wouldn't reply. If he needs to blame anyone, he needs to blame himself."

"I agree, but that doesn't mean he isn't hurt."

"Okay, but that doesn't explain why he's selling Anissa's."

"Yes, it does," Aunt Cassia says. "Don't you see it?"

"See what?" I ask. "All I see is that my baba is a stubborn man who doesn't know how to communicate."

"Let me ask you this: when did your mom announce that she was engaged?"

"Uh, like a year ago."

Aunt Cassia nods. "And when did she sell her shares to the resort?"

I pause and then slowly say, "Around the same time."

"Uh-huh. What was tying your baba to your mom this whole time?"

"The resort," I say, the dots starting to connect in my head.

"You know he hasn't dated since she left him. He hasn't even looked at another woman. Not once, because he was holding out hope that he'd be able to win her back one day. But now that she's engaged and she doesn't have a stake in Anissa's anymore, the place they built together, he's willing to give it up, because the memories are too painful."

Hold on . . . what is she really saying?

"So, you think there's actually nothing wrong with Anissa's, but he's just using that as an excuse to mask his broken heart?"

Aunt Cassia picks up a chunk of meat off my plate and nods. "Yes, I do. Anissa's is one of the premier resorts in Santorini, if not *the* premier resort. Your baba could get a pretty penny if he sold. And then he could be rid of the memories and start a new life, now that your mother has."

Holy shit, this makes so much sense.

"But . . . Anissa's is so much more than their relationship. It's where I grew up."

"Yes, it's where he was happiest, with his family . . . that he no longer has. He's a proud man, Myles, you know this, and he'll never openly admit to his reasons. He'd rather look like he failed at business than face the hardship of admitting he failed at love, at being a baba."

My heart sinks to the ground as everything comes into perspective. He hasn't been awful because he's been pushing me away; he's been awful because he already believes he's lost. He's lost it all.

"I need to talk to him, before he makes this announcement that I know will rock the whole family."

"That seems like a good idea." Aunt Cassia smiles and moves my plate in front of her. "Don't worry, I'll take care of this for you."

I stand from the table and then bend over and place a kiss on her forehead. "Thank you, Aunt Cassia."

"Of course, my beautiful, handsome boy."

I give her shoulder a squeeze and head out to the living room, where I know Baba is talking to Uncle Taki. I squeeze past Nikoli and Alexander, who are now wrestling each other to the ground, arms wrapped around each other's necks, going in for the kill. I dodge a few cousins who attempt to snatch me by the waist, and when I spot Aunt Velma, a disappointed look on her face—she has to know I didn't finish the meat—I head toward the corner of the living room where Baba and Uncle Taki are sitting, deep in conversation.

"Baba," I say, interrupting them. "I, uh . . . I need to talk to you."

"I'm speaking with your uncle," he says before turning back toward Uncle Taki.

"It's important," I say. "Really important. About Mom." I know I shouldn't entirely lie, but I know when I say something about Mom, he'll listen.

And just like I thought, he stands from his chair. "Where would you like to talk?"

"Front porch," I answer and lead the way. It takes a few seconds to weave through the crowd of people, but when we reach the front porch, we're thankfully met with silence as we take a seat on two blue chairs that rest just outside the door.

"What's going on with your mother?" he asks right away, concern on his face. "Is she okay?"

"Yes," I answer, making his brow crease. I know he's probably thinking I got him out here on false pretenses, but it's sort of about her, so I better start this conversation with her at the forefront. "I spoke with her on the phone yesterday."

"And she's okay?"

"Yes, Baba. She's fine. She actually told me that she sold the shares of Anissa to you. You bought her out."

He shifts in his seat. "Yes, she wanted a new space for her photography. I was happy to help her out."

"But you said Anissa's wasn't making any money."

"That's correct," he says, shifting. "Now, if that's all you have to say, I'd like to get back to my conversation with Taki."

"You're selling because you don't want to be reminded of the memories anymore, aren't you?"

He pauses, his body going rigid as he stares down at the ground, and for the first time in my life, I think I'm seeing vulnerability in my baba. He's always been tough, unmoving, very emotionless, but not here, not in this moment. I can see the deflation in his shoulders and the tension in his fingers as they grip into the armrest of the chair. This is a new man, a broken man.

"I'm right, aren't I?"

He clears his throat. "I'm selling because Anissa's is not making any money and I can't keep up with the cost."

"That's bullshit, and you and I both know that. And when I spoke to Mom about the numbers, about what you've told her, I learned that Anissa's has been nothing but thriving. Unless you lied to her?"

His tired eyes snap to mine. "I've never lied to your mom, ever," he says sternly.

"Okay, so then you're lying to me."

"I don't have time for this." He goes to stand, but I put my hand on his shoulder, holding him in place.

"You need to have time for this," I say. "Because this matters to me."

"It doesn't. You don't care—"

"I *do* care," I say with such conviction in my voice that he startles and finally meets my eyes. "I care more than you know. You don't think I miss being a family just as much as you?" I ask. "Because I do. I hate that Mom lives in New York City and you live here. I hate what happened to us and that I grew up in a broken home. But I was able to make it out all right because of Anissa's, because of the memories we have there, because of the traditions. I care, Baba, because Anissa's is my home. It's where I feel most comfortable, where my family had the best memories, and I know it might hurt you, but those good memories are important, despite the bad times we had to go through as well. And you're just going to give that away?"

He's silent as he sits there, still leaning forward like he's about to get up any second, but he never does. Instead, he stares down at the floor. "The moment I lost her," he quietly says, "I lost everything, Myles. You might not think this to be true, but when she left, a piece of you left as well. I could see it, everything slipping from my fingers. And then when you escaped to New York, I knew it was the beginning of the end. You moved on, your mother moved on . . . it was time for me to move on."

"But I didn't move on. That's what you can't seem to grasp. I went to New York because I wanted to learn, because I wanted to be able to come back here and grow with you. Grow Anissa's, grow the brand. I wanted to be a father-son duo, but you haven't allowed me to explain that to you."

He peeks his head up, but he doesn't say anything; he doesn't have to. His eyes no longer hold coldness, but curiosity—I can tell he's listening now.

So, I reach out and take his hand in mine, something he used to do to me when I was a kid. And I hold him tightly as I say, "I've always treated you and Mom the same. I've always loved you the same. Was it great that I got to spend time with Mom while I was in New York? Of course. I loved going on runs with her and having dinner, seeing shows together when I had time, but the plan was never to stay. We both knew that. The plan was to come back here and be here with you, because this is where my heart is. This is where I want to continue the legacy you created."

"You . . . you do?" he asks softly.

"Yes," I say, relief filling me now that I'm finally getting through to him. "Baba, when I say I want to run Anissa's with you, I mean it. And I don't want to just do this on my own—I want to do this together, you and me."

He finally sinks into his chair and brings his hand up to his eyes, body shaking while he sniffs softly.

Is he . . . is he crying?

"Baba?" I ask, now placing my hand on his shoulder.

He shakes his head, takes in a deep breath, and then wipes under his eyes, which are reddened and weathered. "I'm not doing well, Myles."

"What do you mean?" I ask, my thoughts immediately going to his health.

"With your mother moving on, with the engagement . . . I'm not handling it well. At all. I just love her so much."

A pain so deep buries in my heart as I pull him into a hug. "I know, Baba."

He wraps his arms around me, and then his body shakes against mine as he sobs in my arms. "I messed up, son. I messed up so much."

"It's okay," I say softly, rubbing his back, my mind reeling.

I've never seen my baba like this. He doesn't show emotions; he doesn't cry. And if anyone does cry to him, he's as stoic as they come. So the man who is currently turning into a puddle of emotions in my arms is a near stranger.

We stay like that for what I can only imagine is ten more minutes, until Aunt Cassia walks out of the house and finds us. The entire time, I'm wondering what is going to happen next. How can I help him? What can I do to make this all better? With a soft, sad smile, she helps Baba out of his chair and to my car, where we buckle him up. He rests against the side of the door, staring out the window.

I turn toward Aunt Cassia, desperation clawing up my throat. "I'm scared. I've never seen him like this before."

"He's a broken man, Myles. It will take a lot to fix him."

"How do I even start?"

"Giving him the love and attention he needs."

I bite on my lower lip. "Okay, yeah, I can do that."

"He needs you, Myles, all of you."

I nod. "Yeah, I can sense that."

She pulls me into a hug and then walks me to my side of the car, an easy silence settling between us. When we stop at my door, she cups my cheeks and offers me one more smile before taking off.

With a heavy heart and a new duty placed on my shoulders, I open the door and get in.

I know exactly what I need to do.

☀

Myles: Rough day. I don't think I can make it to your room tonight.

Tessa: Is everything okay?

Myles: Not really.

Tessa: Well, do you want me to come to you?

Myles: I'm with my baba right now.

Tessa: Oh, okay. I understand. Well, let me know if you can meet up, okay?

Myles: I will. I'm sorry, Tessa.

Tessa: Don't apologize. I'm sure you're going through a lot with your Baba. I get it.

Myles: Yeah, it's a lot heavier than I thought. What about you? Are you okay?

Tessa: Not really, but that's okay. I'm just going to hang out in my room and ignore everything.

Myles: Hell, okay, let me see if I can get my baba to sleep and then I'll come over.

Tessa: No Myles, really, it's okay. Focus on taking care of your Baba, I'll be fine.

Wall sconces shaped like seashells light up the long corridor, bringing warmth to the resort without flooding the guest rooms. I remember when Baba had the seashell sconces installed. It was right before my twentieth birthday. He thought the hallways needed an update, and that's what he chose. I thought they were corny at first, but they've grown on me over time—now I find them charming, a part of Anissa's that's original compared to the modernly designed resorts. The seashell sconces add character, something I need to remember moving forward.

I brought Baba back to his place, which is only a mile away from the resort, a small cottage right on the coast. It took me a second to get Baba to go to bed. He didn't want to talk; he didn't want to do anything, besides staring out at the sea beside me. So that's what I did, as I felt myself coming apart beside this new version of my father. But when he started nodding off, I convinced him to go to bed.

Now it's almost eleven, but I'm hoping Tessa isn't asleep yet. I feel bad I couldn't come over earlier, but there was no way I could leave Baba by himself, not after that breakdown.

When I reach her door, I send her a text instead of knocking.

Myles: I'm outside of your room. Open the door if you're awake.

Once I hit send, I wait by the door, but only a few seconds pass before it opens. Tessa is on the other side in a matching silk pajama set, her hair in braids, her face free of makeup, and her eyes full of concern.

"Myles, I told you, you didn't have to come."

"I wanted to," I murmur as I step into her hotel room and shut the door behind me. I slip my hand along her waist and pull her close before dropping a kiss on her lips. Her hand loops around the back of my neck, holding me in place, and in seconds, our kiss turns from sweet to desperate.

The worries and sadness of the past few hours melt away beneath her scorching touch.

Her other hand slips under my shirt, across my abs and over my pecs.

I move my hand down past the waistband of her shorts and over her bare ass, gripping it tightly.

She moans into my mouth.

I groan against her teasing hands.

Together, we move back into the room until we tumble onto the bed. I tear my shirt over my head as she does the same. I tug on her shorts, freeing her of all clothes. She unbuttons my jeans and pushes them down to my knees. I kick off my sandals, jeans, and briefs and climb on top of the bed, joining her, my mouth falling to her breasts.

I nibble on them.

Suck them.

Play with them until she's writhing beneath me, begging for more.

"I don't have a condom," I whisper.

"I'm on birth control," she mutters, giving me the green light.

Without another thought, I flip her to her stomach and prop her up on all fours. I position myself behind her but swipe my fingers along her arousal first. When I feel that she is more than ready, I position my erection at her entrance and then sink in.

Together, we let out a long, drawn-out moan.

"So good," I say as I grip her hips and move in and out of her.

There is an urgency in our movements, a powerful need to get as much of each other as we possibly can. She moves her hips against mine, I drive into her, and together we heighten the friction between us until we're both panting, straining, tightening together.

"Myles," she moans, her back arching.

I slip my hand down between her legs, finding her clit and massaging it while I continue to pound into her. The new sensation is enough to rock her to the edge. Her hands curl into the blankets beneath her while she cries out my name, her orgasm ripping through her just as mine crests.

My balls tighten, my cock swells, and I pull out right before I come and finish on her back, groaning the whole time as this everlasting sense of comfort wraps around me.

"Fuck, Tessa," I mumble as I slow my hand over my cock, and she collapses on the bed.

We both catch our breath, her on the bed, me hovering above her. Once I regain feeling in my legs, I give her a quick kiss and clean up in the bathroom before bringing a warm washcloth to her back, cleaning her up as well.

Once we're good, I crawl into bed next to her and curl around her heated body, my chest to her back. She clings onto my arms, and I bury my head in her hair, breathing in the scent of her.

"I'm sorry I couldn't have come earlier. I think it was a shit day for both of us."

"It was," she says softly. "And you didn't have to come at all, Myles. Seriously, I know you were dealing with your baba, and today was a big day."

"I know, but . . . I think I just needed to see you. I wanted to see you, and I know you wanted to see me. Or," I add, suddenly feeling vulnerable, "I *hope* you wanted to see me."

Turning in my arms and facing me, she cups my cheek. "Yes, I wanted to see you. Badly."

"Want to tell me what happened?"

"Philip called off the wedding, or Roxane did . . . honestly, I don't know who did. All I know is that it's not happening, and instead of dealing with it, letting herself actually feel her emotions, she attacked me again."

"Tessa, I'm so sorry."

"Thank you. I told her I didn't deserve to be treated that way, and I walked out. I was done."

"Good for you. How do you feel?"

"Empty," she answers. "But also sort of free. It's a bittersweet feeling. I don't like fighting with Roxane—it always makes me sick to my stomach—but I also don't want her to keep walking all over me. She always blames me for what happens or finds a way to make me feel bad so she feels better, and I'm over it. I haven't spoken to Clea or Lois either. It just . . . ugh, it all feels gross."

"I can imagine that's exactly how it feels. So, what are you going to do?"

She shrugs and draws her finger over the scruff on my cheek. "I don't know. I don't want to think about it too much, not right now. Maybe tomorrow, but today, I just want to focus on you."

Fuck, I feel so connected to her. Is that crazy? To feel like I've belonged here, tangled up with her, for so long? And now that it's finally happening, it just feels . . . right? Being here, in her arms, I feel so comforted. I feel like nothing can hurt me, that I can get through anything as long as I'm holding her hand.

"What happened with your baba today?" she asks, her hand falling to my chest, where she draws lazy circles. "Did he tell the family that he was going to sell?"

"Didn't get a chance," I say as I reach down and draw her leg up, lining her pelvis up with mine.

"What do you mean?"

"My aunt Cassia spoke with me before Baba's announcement. She connected the dots for me."

"What dots?" Tessa asks.

"The reason Baba was selling. It has nothing to do with finances or losing money. It's the exact opposite. He wants to move on because my mom no longer holds shares to Anissa's, the one thing that connected him to her."

"Oh God, that's so sad."

"It really is," I say as I drag my thumb over her skin, trying to commit the feeling to memory. "He was so in love with my mom. He hasn't dated anyone since they divorced, and now that she's engaged and free of Anissa's, he just couldn't bear to stick around. He says it's too painful."

"Oh, I could totally understand that. This place feels like a second home. Little facets and corners hold so much memory—I can't imagine what it would feel like for him."

"He's in rough shape. I'm not sure what I'm going to do about it all."

"I'm sure you'll figure it out. You have a great heart, Myles, the kind of heart that puts others first, that makes everyone happy."

"You think so?" I ask.

She nods. "I do."

With a sigh, I rest my forehead on hers. "I wish it was different."

"What do you mean?"

"I mean, I wish my parents were still together. I hate seeing my baba so upset, so distraught, so disappointed in himself, to the point that he's willing to give up the last thing that holds memories of his family. His life's work rests in this resort, and because he's so heartbroken, he wants to just get rid of it. That makes me sad."

"Did you ever think that maybe it's a good idea, that selling will help him move on?"

"Or is he just running away?" I ask.

"He could be," Tessa says as she presses a gentle kiss to my chest. "I think that's something you need to figure out."

"Yeah, I think you're right." I roll her to her back and lean on my elbow as I stare down at her. "I'm glad I came over tonight. Seeing you, holding you, it's made this sick feeling I had in my stomach all day go away."

"Same," she says as she spreads her legs, making room for me. "Now, how about we forget about our days and just focus on us?"

"I think that's the perfect plan," I say right before closing the space between us and getting lost in her mouth.

Myles: I'm sorry I left you in the middle of the night. I wanted to get back to my baba, just in case he needed me. But fuck do I wish I was waking up next to you this morning.

Tessa: It's okay, I totally understand. And I wish you were here too.

Myles: Not sure what today will bring, but I'll text if I have some free time.

Tessa: Same. I think my parents want to talk to Roxane and me together. Not looking forward to it.

Myles: That gave me anxiety just reading it. Good luck. I'll text you later, okay?

Tessa: Okay. XOXO

Myles: XOXO babe.

I knock on my baba's bedroom door before entering.

The room is dark, curtains drawn, not a single light on. There's no movement in the room, not even a soft snore. My heart sinks—Baba isn't even sleeping, just sitting in the dark. I set down the tray of food I brought him and make my way to the windows, drawing back the curtains, flooding the room into light. That's when I spot Baba sitting in his armchair in the corner.

"Hey," I say. "I brought you some food."

"Myles, you don't need to treat me like a child. I can take care of myself."

"But I want to help take care of you, Baba." His eyes flash to mine as I approach him with the tray. I set it down on his side table and then take a seat in the other armchair next to his. "How are you feeling?"

"Embarrassed," he says. "It was not my intention to break down in front of you like that."

"It might not have been your intention, but you needed it. How long have you been holding that in, Baba? Probably too long."

"Yes, but you're my son, and you're not supposed to see your father like that."

"That's bullshit. It's almost better I saw you like that."

"How is that better?" he asks. When he doesn't touch the food I brought, I decide to serve him myself, gathering meats, cheeses, and veggies onto a plate and handing it to him, encouraging him. I'm relieved when he takes a bite of salami.

"Because," I say, "now I know you're capable of emotions—that you care, and you're not some angry, bitter tyrant sitting in your office, despising me."

"I would never despise you, Myles."

"That's how it's felt ever since I returned. It felt like you wish I never came back, and I understand where your feelings are coming from now, but that's only because you expressed them." I look him in the eyes, and I feel myself crack open. "Baba, you don't have to put on this facade for me, this stoic appearance where nothing fazes you. I know it's not real, and I'd rather see when you're upset, when something is bothering you, because then we can talk about it. We can work it out together."

"You're not supposed to see me in a weak state, Myles." His brows sharpen in anger, but not at me, at himself.

"Says who?" I ask.

"It's how I was brought up. I'm your father, so I'm supposed to be strong for you."

"That's impossible to maintain. You're human, Baba. You're allowed to experience emotion. You're allowed to show it. And the fact that you're trying to hide it from me is only putting distance between us. Your frustrations and sadness come off as bitter and angry, and it's what's been pushing me away. Is that what you want?"

He shakes his head. "No. You're all I have left. I don't know what I would do if I lost you."

"Then let me help you. Let me be there for you. Instead of being embarrassed for feeling something, share those feelings with me."

He nods, and he suddenly looks very small. "Maybe if I shared my feelings with your mother, she never would have left me."

My heart breaks, because I can just see it in his eyes, the regret. It's so heavy.

"Baba." I grip his hand. "How about instead of thinking about the past, we consider moving forward toward the future."

He shakes his head. "I don't think I can."

So broken. It's what I keep thinking over and over in my head. My baba, the man I've looked up to my whole life, is human like the rest of us, full of flaws, living in regret, and unable to accept the fact that he needs to move on. It's devastating to witness, and I know that if I don't take care of him and help him through his pain, I very well might lose him.

And I can't have that.

I can't leave him.

So, I squeeze his hand. "You can move forward," I say. "With me by your side. You can."

CHAPTER TWENTY
TESSA

"Where's Roxane?" I ask as I take a seat in my mom and dad's hotel room.

"She's on her way," Dad says.

Both in their vacation garb—patterned shorts and polos with boat shoes—they sit across from me on their bed, looking less than thrilled. I'm sure this is the last thing they want to be doing on their vacation.

"Is the wedding really off?" I ask. A part of me thinks it's not true, that Roxane is just being dramatic.

"Yes," Mom says. "I spoke with Philip's mom last night. Seems as though he's been having cold feet for a while, and he thought he'd get over them . . . but he hasn't."

"Wow. I can't believe it," I say just as the hotel door opens and Roxane stumbles in looking just flat-out awful. Her hair is unbrushed. She's wearing joggers with one pant leg hiked up, the other down. She slinks forward in her slippers, her shirt inside out and mascara faintly plastered under her eyes.

This is not Roxane. Not the Roxane that I know. She's always so well put together. She'd never show her face like this in public. Even when I'm just coming over to her place, she still dresses up, wears some makeup. She always puts on a show of perfection.

But this . . . this is a whole new side.

When she spots me on the couch, she stops in her tracks.

She points an accusing finger. "What is *she* doing here?"

"We need to speak to both of you," Dad says. "And there will be no arguing about it. So, sit down."

Arms crossed, Roxane walks over to the couch and takes a seat, as far away from me as possible.

"Can you please tell me how on earth we came to Anissa's, and instead of seeing our two happy girls enjoying a week together, we walked into a hostile environment where you can't even look at each other?" Dad asks.

"That's what you're worried about?" Roxane asks. "Not the fact that I've been humiliated by my ex-fiancé?"

"We will get to that," Dad says. "But family first. Family is always first. So, tell us what's going on."

"Tessa believes I try to diminish her, when all I've ever done is try to pull her out of her shell and help her experience more in life."

"By humiliating me," I snap. "And I never asked you to do any of that."

"If I didn't, you'd probably still be in your khaki phase, where all you ever wore were shades of beige. What kind of life is that?"

"A life you shouldn't worry about," I say, anger piqued. "Just because it's not up to your standards doesn't make it wrong."

"Khaki on khaki is always wrong, even for zoologists."

"Girls, enough. What specifically happened on this trip?" Mom asks.

Knowing Roxane's not going to tell the truth, I jump in. "Roxane, Clea, and Lois brought the contract with them on vacation." My parents are fully aware of the contract, since we've referenced it so many times. "And because we're now thirty, one of the rules came up on this vacation. I forfeited my love life over to the girls."

"Oh *honestly*." Dad rolls his eyes.

"What? We signed on it," Roxane says. "And it was notarized. That's a legal document."

"You've been fighting over that?" Mom asks. "You girls are thirty years old."

"We have lived by that contract," Roxane defends. "Why would we just stop now?"

"So, you inserted yourself in your sister's love life?" Dad asks.

"Yes." Roxane holds her chin up high. "And we found some good prospects for her—"

"You call Jeremiah a good prospect?" I ask.

"Philip's cousin?" Mom asks. "Oh, honey, he's not a good prospect."

"See?" I seethe at Roxane.

"Uh, the only reason we had to consider Jeremiah is because she ruined a perfectly good prospect with Toby."

"The bartender?" Dad asks. "He doesn't seem like the kind of guy who'd settle down."

"Oh, shocking I'm validated again," I say with a roll of my eyes. "I told her I didn't want anything to do with these guys, or with being set up at all."

"Because you were just going to fall into your same patterns and follow the lifeguard around with your tail tucked between your legs," Roxane says. "And now you're getting your hopes up when you shouldn't."

I grind my teeth together, trying not to explode. "Myles and I are none of your concern."

"He is when I'm the one who's going to have to go back home and clean up the broken pieces of your heart. Just like I've done in the past, or have you forgotten how you are after breakups? You shut down, you hide, you crumble into a million pieces that take months to get back together."

"Who's to say he's going to break my heart?"

335

"He's not moving to New York," Roxane says. "His life is here. Your life is in New York. It's not going to work."

"Well, maybe . . . maybe I want my life to be here."

Roxane's expression falls.

My heart beats wildly at the thought.

Living here?

Not sure where that came from, maybe the depths of my subconscious, but the more I sit here and think about it, the more I start to realize how much I'd really love to live here.

But from the horrified look on Roxane's face, I'm going to assume the thought of me not returning to New York would just about push her over the edge.

"You can't leave New York. That's where we all live," Roxane says in disbelief.

"Well, maybe I'm due for a change."

"Tessa," Dad says, "are you serious?"

I have no idea. I haven't really considered life after this vacation, but my anger and annoyance have made me voice a mere glimmer of a plan, something I haven't even begun to think through, purely to garner a reaction. Well, it did its job. I'm even a bit shocked.

"I don't know, maybe."

"Wait, really?" Roxane asks. "But . . . you can't live here, the contract doesn't permit it. And . . . and you just can't." Her eyes well up. "Not with everything going on. Not with Philip leaving me. With Clea and Lois leaving."

"What do you mean, Clea and Lois left?" I ask.

"They left this morning," Mom says.

"Why?" This news hits me like a blow to the stomach.

"Because you two wouldn't stop fighting," Dad replies and pinches his brow. "What the hell has happened? This is not you two. This is not how you act."

Roxane and I sit on the couch, silent—I don't think either of us knows how to answer his question. He's right. This isn't us. We have our fights here and there, but to the point that we force our best friends to flee the country? Well, it's never been this bad. *We've* never been this bad.

Roxane sniffs, and when I glance over at her, I see she's crying.

What the hell? My stomach flips—I've never seen my strong, sassy sister like this.

"Roxane, sweetie, what's going on?" Mom asks.

She swipes at her eyes. "Can I have a moment with Tessa? Alone?"

Mom and Dad exchange glances before nodding. "We'll go grab some pastries from the corner bakery. Let us know if you need anything."

Together, they head out the door, leaving Tessa and me alone.

"What's going on?" I ask, handing her a box of tissues.

"Tessa . . ." Her eyes well up, and I start to get really nervous.

"What?"

"I did something really stupid."

Oh God.

"What did you do?" I ask, dread creeping up on me.

"I . . . I kissed Toby last night. Clea and Lois caught me, confronted me, and then we got into a big fight. We said some awful things to each other—it got so, so ugly. They said they didn't even understand why they were here and took off."

"Wait." I blink a few times. "You kissed Toby? When?"

"At the bar. I was drunk, upset, mad . . . feeling every emotion you could possibly feel, and he was being sweet and was making me feel better about my life. I grabbed him by the shirt and kissed him. He didn't kiss me back, he just kind of stood there, obviously scared that I was kissing him." She presses her hand to her forehead. "What was I thinking?"

"I . . . I don't know. What were you thinking?"

"I wasn't, I just . . . I just wanted someone to appreciate me. Someone to give me some sort of affection." Tears cascade down her cheeks. "Tessa, I'm so messed up."

"What do you mean?" I ask.

"You were right." She sucks in a sharp breath. "I was diminishing you to make myself feel better. I've done it our whole lives."

"Roxane, I didn't mean that."

She shakes her head. "No, you are completely right. I'm not happy. I haven't been happy for a while. I thought that maybe getting married would change things, that maybe if I started a family, I'd find that happiness I was searching for, but . . . I know that's not the case. And Philip picked up on my cues a few months ago. He felt me pulling away, and when he confronted me about it, I pulled away even more. This trip before the wedding . . . I know Lois and Clea wanted it to reconnect, but I wanted it to forget, to clear my head, to think about what I really wanted in life. But that's so scary to do, so I just focused on you. And sure, Philip might have called off the wedding, but I'm the reason he called it off, because I wasn't giving him what he needed. And I'm not entirely sure I can ever give him what he needs."

"Roxane, why didn't you say something?" I ask, feeling like I should have seen this. I should have noticed.

"Because I was embarrassed. I didn't want you to think less of me. I didn't want to be the one who broke the luck with the perfume."

"Oh my God, you can't seriously believe that is true, that it's real."

"I want to," she says while she plays with the wet tissue in her hand. "I want to believe there's this cosmic force holding us all together." She swipes at her tears. "Remember when Dylan Barber broke up with me?"

"Yes," I answer, confused as to where this was going.

"That was right before we found the perfume. I was absolutely devastated by the breakup. You remember, I thought we were going to get married. Granted, I was young, but still. I lost all hope when it came to love, but that perfume felt like a lifeline. Like all my fears of being unlovable were going to be solved."

"Roxane, you're not unlovable," I say, offering her another tissue. "You have to know that—guys were always coming after you."

"Yes, coming after me, but never *loving* me. They only wanted me for one thing, never for me. And then Philip came along—and sure, I had to change myself a bit, to morph into someone he could be with long term, but he liked me, he loved me, he proposed. It was everything I wanted. But all I've been able to think about these last few months is that he fell in love with a version of me that wasn't real. And how long was I going to have to pretend to be this person? And, of course, instead of talking to you about it, talking to the girls about it, I tried to hide it, place blame elsewhere, force you to find someone—and now I've lost everybody. You, Lois, Clea . . . Philip."

"You didn't lose us."

"Yes, I did," she sobs. "You're moving to Greece. Clea and Lois won't talk to me. The wedding is off, life is falling apart, and I only have myself to blame."

"I'm not moving to Greece," I say, even though it doesn't feel right making such a declaration without serious thought. "I—I honestly don't know what I'm doing. And Clea and Lois, we just have to talk to them. I think we all need to have a real conversation. Actually about our feelings and our ever-evolving friendship. We're older now. Lois has kids, Clea is getting more and more famous every day, and I'm starting to find a new part of myself that I really like. We're changing, and I think we need to set different expectations, so we don't fall apart like we did during this vacation."

She nods. "Yeah, probably." She pulls her legs in close to her and hugs them. "I'm sorry, Tessa. I'm sorry that I've been so awful to you. You don't deserve that."

"Thank you for apologizing," I say, knowing I deserved that apology. "But you have to know, even in our darkest moments, our most vicious fights, I will always be there for you—I will always love you."

Her teary eyes connect with mine. "I will always love you too, Tessa. I will always be proud of you, even if it doesn't seem like I am."

That hits me harder than I expected as a wave of emotion rolls through me. I haven't really been seeking Roxane's approval, not that I recall at least, but knowing she's proud of me really means something.

After a few moments of silence, she turns toward me. "Tessa?" Tears stream down her cheeks. "I'm . . . I'm scared."

And I can see that she is. In her eyes lurks a true fear I don't think I've ever seen before. So, I take her hand in mine, trying to pass on the new strength I've gained over the past few days. "Don't be scared. I'm here."

"Promise?" she asks shakily.

"Promise."

I pull her into a hug, and she clings onto me. "I don't know how to start over," she says through tears, "how to find myself, my true self. I feel like I've been faking it for so long." She lets go of me and blots at her eyes again. "I'm so lost, Tessa. And I know I have no right asking you for help, with how I've treated you, but I don't know what to do. I don't like myself, I don't think many people like me, and I have no direction. Like . . . what am I going to do? I was supposed to be married and living with Philip. I gave up my freaking apartment, and I don't have anywhere to live when I get back, and I don't have a job either, because I quit that—"

"What do you mean you quit your job?"

"I told you . . . I just ruined everything." She starts to panic, her breaths turning short. "And I kissed another man for no reason other than trying to prove to myself that I'm desirable. How pathetic is that? So freaking pathetic, and here I was calling you pathetic when you're not, you're so wonderful. So smart. You have it all together, and I just made you think you didn't to make myself feel better. Who does that? Who is so shitty that they do that to someone? God, you shouldn't even be sitting next to me. You should be laughing at me and walking away."

"Roxane, stop," I say, taking her hand. "You're starting to sound like me with this babbling." She lets out a sound that's halfway between a snort and a sob. "You're my sister," I continue, "my other half. No matter what you say, or the fights we get in, I'll always be there for you. Always."

"You shouldn't. I'm a shitty sister."

"You've had a rough patch, but we all have those." Her patch may be worse than others', but no need to mention that. She's turned a corner, she's confessed to messing up, and she's truly blown me away with her maturity in taking the blame. Rubbing it in won't do anything. Helping her . . . now, that is something I should be focusing on.

She shakes her head. "What do I do? I ruined everything."

"It's okay," I say, holding on to her tightly. "We'll figure it out, okay? We'll figure it out."

And as I hold on to Roxane and reassure her that everything is going to be okay, I realize that in order for everything to be okay, in order to help Roxane through this, I'm going to have to do damage control. We need our group more than ever now, and after our sorry display of friendship, I think that's the first thing that needs to be repaired, because we are nothing without our core four.

I can't do this alone, and I don't want to do this alone.

We all need each other, and it's about time I fix it all.

The phone rings.

And rings.

And rings.

"Hey, it's Clea, sorry I missed your call, but leave a message and I'll get back to you as soon as I can. Have a great day."

The phone beeps, and for the second time today, I leave a message on her voice mail.

"Hey, Clea, it's Tessa. I talked to Roxane, and . . . ugh, I don't know what to say other than I'm sorry. I don't want to apologize over the phone, so I hope that you can find it within you to meet up with me and Roxane when we get back to New York. I just wanted to leave a message to let you know I'm thinking of you, hoping you got home safe, and I'm sorry. Love you. Bye."

I hang up the phone and fall back on my bed as I stare up at the ceiling.

What a freaking disaster.

This is not how I envisioned this trip going. Not even close. It was supposed to be a fun girls' getaway, a celebration before the wedding. There wasn't supposed to be fighting; there weren't supposed to be hurt feelings.

But here we are.

And I have no idea what to do.

And the irony is that, for the first time in my life, I feel free, I feel good in my own skin, but at what cost? I'm only in this position because I fought with my sister and had a falling-out with my friends. Roxane and I created such a hostile environment that our friends couldn't even stand to be near us anymore. So this feeling of freedom, of confidence—is it really me? Or am I pretending to be someone else, just like Roxane has been pretending to be?

Myles: Sorry I couldn't make it over tonight.

Tessa: It's okay, I probably wouldn't have been the best company.

Myles: I'm guessing the meeting with your parents didn't go over well?

Tessa: The meeting was okay—it was the conversation I had with Roxane after that sort of rocked me. But I'm not in the mood to talk about it.

The phone rings in my hand, and when I see Myles's number on the screen, I answer immediately. "Hey," I say softly.

"Hey, so . . . I know it's late, but I don't like that you're not in a good mood. Would you be okay with me coming over? At least just for a minute? We don't have to talk about anything."

"Are you kidding? Myles, you don't even have to ask." I roll onto my side, feeling myself relaxing into the bed. Just the sound of his voice makes me feel better.

"Yeah, I didn't want you thinking it was a booty call or anything like that. I genuinely want to see you. I want to make you smile."

"I'd never think that," I say.

"Good, because I'm outside your door."

"Really?" A ray of relief courses through me as I stand from my bed, hang up my phone, and run over to the hotel room door. I open it and find a smirking Myles on the other side.

I pull him in, shut the door, and wrap my arms around him.

"Hey," he says as he kisses the top of my head. "That's quite the greeting."

"It's been a day." I look up at him and rest my chin on his chest. "I'm glad you're here, even though it's super late."

"Better late than never, right?" He leans forward, kisses me on the lips, and then kicks off his sandals before leading me over to the bed. Settling into the mattress, he rests his back against the headboard and then pulls me on top of his lap so I'm straddling him.

"Tell me something funny," I say, wanting to escape the events of today.

"Something funny, huh?" His hands fall to my hips, where he holds me tightly. "Um, I was helping a guest with her bag, an older lady, and in exchange for a tip, she gave me a kiss on the cheek. It was kind of sweet, but midkiss, she burped, laying a wet one right on my face."

"Stop." I laugh. "No, she didn't."

"She did, and I am one hundred percent positive that she had onions at some point today. But her lips were soft, some might say . . . luxurious." He smirks devilishly.

I give him a look, which only makes him laugh.

"What?" he asks. "They were luxurious."

I shake my head. "Never going to live that down, am I?"

"Nope. Never."

"Well, you've said some pretty dumb things too."

"Me?" He points to his chest. "Name one."

"We were eighteen. You were working the pool. I walked up to you and asked for a towel. You grabbed one, and when you handed it to me, you said, 'To dry yourself, my lady.'"

"I did not fucking say that." He cringes.

"Oh, you did. I remember thinking how weird it was."

"I've never said that in my entire life."

"Yeah, well, I've never called someone's lips luxurious before, so we all say stupid things when we're nervous."

"You never called anyone else's lips luxurious, because no one has lips as soft and plump as mine."

Enter hard eye roll.

"They're not *that* great."

His brows shoot up in question. "Oh, is that right? 'Not that great.' Okay, well, then maybe I'll just take my lips with me and head on back to my apartment."

I pin his shoulders to the headboard, stopping him. "You're not going anywhere."

"Oooh, bossy, tell me more." His smile makes me smile, and I realize just how much he makes me happy. Truly happy.

The kind of happy that only comes once in a lifetime.

The kind of happy I want to hang on to forever.

But . . .

But how? How can I hold on to it? With everything going on, with the inevitable distance between us, I'm not sure it's possible.

But I can't mask my emotions. Myles catches on to my mood shift and lifts my chin so I have nowhere else to look but at him.

"What's happening in that pretty head of yours?"

I could act like nothing is going on, that I just had a moment, or I can tell him the truth.

The first option will be a temporary fix, a haphazard Band-Aid at best, but if I talk to him, tell him how I'm feeling, then we very well might be able to find a solution.

I let out a deep breath. "You make me happy, Myles. I like being around you. I feel lighter, more free, more like myself with you."

"I like you a lot too, Tessa," he says. Tilting his head, he adds, "Like . . . a lot. But for some reason, I feel like there's a 'but' coming."

"I just . . . I just don't know how we're going to make this work."

His shoulders slump, and his grip on my hips grows tighter. "I was hoping you weren't going to bring that up."

"It's hard not to," I say. "When I feel so great around you, when I feel seen and adored, it's hard not to think about what's going to happen when I go back to New York."

He wets his lips and tilts his head down. "Maybe you don't go back," he whispers.

My heart flutters in my chest, my stomach doing all sorts of somersaults, because *oh my God*, he's asking me not to leave. What I wouldn't have done to hear those words a few hours ago, maybe even a day ago, but after the conversation I had with Roxane, I'm not sure . . . I'm not sure it's an option.

"I don't want to leave," I say.

"But . . ." His dark-brown eyes look up at me, pleading, and it nearly breaks me to say what I have to say next.

"But . . . Roxane is in a fragile place right now, and I know you don't have a sibling, so you might not quite understand what I'm about to say, but I have to be there for her. I have to help her."

"After everything she said to you?" he asks.

I nod. "Yes. She's family, she's my twin, and even though she's made this vacation a nightmare, she's also not mentally healthy right now, and I would never forgive myself if I just abandoned her when she needed me the most."

He nods. "I can completely understand that."

"I'm almost afraid to ask, because I'm pretty sure I know the answer, but if you wanted, you could come to New York."

He sighs and tilts his head back on the headboard. "You know I would, Tessa. You know I would jump on a plane so fast."

"But your baba . . ."

His lips thin as he nods. "Yeah, I can't leave him. Not right now. I don't think he'd survive it."

And just like that, silence falls between us. This connection we have, it's so strong, but the factors surrounding us are stronger.

We both know it.

We don't have to say it.

We just have to accept it.

My heart aches. My breath picks up. And my eyes well up with tears.

"Don't," he says, cupping my cheek. "Don't cry."

"I just . . . I don't know how—"

"Don't think about it right now, okay? Be here, with me." He pulls me closer and presses our lips together. Greedily, I kiss him back.

This man, I want him. All of him. I want to be able to see where this relationship takes us. I want to know what it feels like to have a relationship without a ticking countdown. I want to see what it feels like to wake up with him next to me every morning without thinking about how suddenly it could end.

But that privilege doesn't seem possible.

Not with all the external factors pulling us apart. So for now, knowing there is an end to this euphoria, I'm going to enjoy it.

I bring my hands to the hem of his shirt and pull it up and over his head.

"Tessa," he says quietly while moving his lips to my neck. "We don't have to do this."

"I want to," I say as my fingers thread through his hair. "I want to feel you inside of me, be as close to you as possible."

"Are you sure?"

"More than sure," I answer right before he twists us and lays me across the mattress.

Hovering above me, he says, "This isn't goodbye, Tessa. Do you hear me?"

I nod, even though . . . this feels more like goodbye than anything else.

CHAPTER TWENTY-ONE
MYLES

Groaning, I roll to the side, reaching for Tessa, but find only an empty bed and cold sheets. Confused, I sit up, rub at my eyes, and then search the room, only for my stomach to fall to the ground when I spot her sitting on her couch, packed suitcases next to her.

"Hey," she says softly.

"Tessa," I reply, rubbing my eyes still. "What are you doing?"

"Roxane stopped by this morning. You were passed out, but she asked if I could fly home with her today."

"Today?" I ask, feeling more alert than ever. "Why?"

"She's struggling, doesn't want to be here right now. Especially with wedding guests arriving, it's too much for her. My parents are staying to be with the family members who are flying in. They're going to make a reunion of it, but Roxane really wants to get home." Tessa swipes at her eyes. That's when I notice her tearstained cheeks.

"So, you're . . . you're leaving?" I ask, my body feeling like it was just hit by a fucking train, every muscle, every bone aching.

She nods. "I have to meet her in twenty minutes in the lobby."

"Twenty fucking minutes? Tessa, why didn't you wake me up?"

"I couldn't." She shakes her head. "This is . . . this is already hard enough. I didn't want to spend all morning dwelling on it. I just wanted to focus on packing."

"But . . ." I feel at a loss for words, unsure of how to handle this all. "Fuck, I'm not ready for you to leave."

Tears stream down her cheeks. "I'm not ready either, but I can't just let her go back to New York by herself, especially since Lois and Clea aren't even talking to us. She needs support, she needs me."

But I need you.

I need you here.

I need your strength.

Your mind.

Your heart.

I want you here, with me.

My confession, my plea, is on the tip of my tongue, but I know it won't do any good. I know it will only make it harder for her to leave, because she will leave despite my pleas; she will leave because that's the kind of heart she has. She will put her sister first, before herself. She always has, and she always will.

So instead of making this harder on her, I need to make sure this isn't the end. I need to establish that we aren't saying goodbye, that we are only saying "see you later."

I flip the covers off me and grab my briefs and jeans from the floor and slip them both on. Not bothering with my shirt, I take a seat next to her on the couch. Her tears are flowing down her cheeks, and unable to catch them all, I pull her onto my lap. She straddles me again as I lean back on the couch and let her tears fall to my stomach, wetting my skin.

"I don't want to go," she sniffles.

"I know." I smooth my hands over her thighs. "But this isn't goodbye."

"How could this not be goodbye? I live in New York, and you live in Greece. Correct me if I'm wrong, but that's a seven-hour time difference. That's over ten hours on a plane."

"That's just time," I say. "We're also a phone call away. A FaceTime away. A text away. We can keep this going—we just have to be creative."

She shakes her head. "It's going to be too hard."

"Harder than saying goodbye?" I ask, my heart in my throat.

She attempts to look away, but I don't let her—I gently cup her cheeks and keep her eyes locked on me.

"Are you saying I'm not worth trying?"

"What?" Her eyes widen. "No, not at all."

"Then why are you being reluctant?"

Her lip trembles, and she sucks in a shaky breath. "I don't want you to have to wait for me. I'm sure . . . I'm sure you could find someone else—"

"I don't want anyone else," I say, gripping her chin now. "I want *you*, Tessa. I want to make this work. It might be hard, but you're worth the hard. We are worth it."

She wets her lips and then quietly asks, "Why? Why are we worth it?"

"Why aren't we?" I ask. "We've spent almost our entire lives crossing paths, creating small moments in our timeline together, building up to this point where we finally collided. Are you telling me that this bump in the road is supposed to throw away all of that history? All of that longing? All of those moments of fantasizing and dreaming?" I shake my head. "No, Tessa. This is not where our story ends. This is just the beginning. So, I'm going to ask you again, would having a long-distance relationship be harder than saying goodbye to me, to us, to our history? Are you ready to just toss that all away?"

Her watery eyes blink, sending droplets of sorrow down her cheeks. Staring into her agonized gaze, I have the sickening feeling that she's going to end it, that she's not going to give us a chance. I feel sick to my stomach, and I'm truly considering telling her I'll go with her, even though I know it would bruise my baba, that it might actually break him—but that's how strongly I feel about her. I'm willing to leave my baba behind to be with her.

Finally, she presses her hand to my chest and shakes her head. "I can't let this go, Myles. I can't."

Relief washes through me, and I wrap my arms around her, pulling her into a large, unyielding hug. She returns the embrace, crying into my shoulder as I press my hand to the back of her head. "We're going to make this work, okay? I promise, we will work this out."

She just nods as she clutches me.

We are.

It might be hard.

It might be challenging at times.

But we're going to make this work.

☀

"Wow, dude, you look like absolute shit," Toby says as he sets a tray of freshly cleaned pint glasses on the bar. "What the hell happened to you?"

I push my hand through my untamed hair. "Tessa flew back home today."

"Wait, what?" he asks. "Why?"

"Roxane wanted to leave. She's going through some shit."

Toby looks away. "Yeah, I figured she was. She actually, uh . . . she actually kissed me the other night."

"What?" I ask, shocked. "She kissed you?"

"Yeah, then apologized after. Not sure about the details, but I know the wedding is off and she's dealing with some things, but I didn't think she'd leave. Anissa's is their sanctuary."

"I guess Roxane didn't want to deal with the wedding fallout." I lean against the side of the bar. "But fuck, I didn't expect her to take Tessa with her."

"So, you really said bye. Shit, how do you feel?"

"Fucking awful. Sick to my stomach. On the verge of a fucking mental breakdown." I press my palm to my eye. "Fuck, man, this . . . this is so much harder than I ever expected. I hate knowing that right now, in this very moment, she's flying away from me."

"You really feel that strongly about her?"

"Yeah, I really do," I answer. "And I'm not lying when I say I really thought about going with her. Throwing caution to the wind and following her, but . . ."

"Your baba," he says for me.

"Yeah. As much as I want to be with Tessa, I know it would break my baba, and I can't be responsible for that."

"So, what are you going to do?"

"I told her this wasn't goodbye, that we're not over, and that we're going to do long distance."

"From the deep V in your brow, I'm going to guess you're not entirely thrilled about that option."

"Would you be?" I ask.

He rubs the side of his jaw. "I've never felt strongly enough about someone to even consider it, so I'm not sure, but I can't imagine it's going to be easy."

"It won't be," I sigh. "But like you said, in this day and age, we have to at least give it a try, right?"

"Right." He pauses, eyeing me thoughtfully. "Think you could love this girl?"

I nod because yeah, I do think I could love her, as crazy as that sounds. I've never met anyone who's made me feel so accepted, so cherished, so wanted before. She creates this light air around me when she's near, she makes me smile even when I'm feeling dark inside, and I know

I make her feel the same exact way. The bond between us is so strong that it most definitely feels like it could be love. "Yeah, I think I could. A part of me thinks that maybe my soul already loves her; my heart and my brain just have to catch up. I truly think we are supposed to be together. Think about all the times we've crossed paths—that doesn't just happen for no reason. There's something between us, and if that means I have to figure it out over long distance, then I will."

He puts away the pint glasses, setting them carefully behind the bar. "If anyone is supposed to make something work, I believe it would be you two." He smiles. "And when you do finally marry her, because I feel like that's where this is all headed, what a hell of a story you're going to have to tell your grandkids one day."

That makes me smile too. "Yeah, I think you're right, Toby."

"If I'm right about one thing in my life, that's it. Guaranteed."

"Here you go, Baba," I say as I hand him a salad that I picked up from the kitchen before I headed to his place, then turn to the identical one I brought for myself.

After our conversation at Aunt Velma's house, I went back to my apartment and gathered some clothes, toiletries, and personal items and brought them over to Baba's house so I could stay with him.

"This looks good," he says softly but doesn't touch it—instead he looks out the dining room window toward the courtyard garden. The garden Mom used to take great pride in, and even after all these years, it still looks impeccable. There's no doubt in my mind Baba has kept it pristine as some symbol of the love he has for my mom.

"Are you going to eat it?" I ask.

"Yes." He clears his throat and picks up his fork. When his eyes meet mine, he pauses, and it feels like he's seeing me for the first time since I walked in. "Why do you look like you're in pain?"

Because I am.

Because Tessa texted me yesterday that she landed, making it official. She's back in New York. A stupid part of me thought that maybe she'd come running back into the resort, arms open, telling me she couldn't possibly leave me, but that was wishful thinking.

She's back in New York.

I'm here.

And so the journey of long distance begins.

"Just dealing with some things. Nothing to worry about," I say. "So, I was talking to Toby—"

"What things?"

"Huh?"

He sets his fork down. "What things are you dealing with?"

"Oh." I move my fork around my salad, particularly playing with a kalamata olive. "Nothing you need to worry about."

He crosses his arms over his chest and stares me down, his gaze unwavering. "You want to move forward, yes?" he asks. I nod. "Then I suggest we don't keep anything from each other, don't you think?"

"Yes, but I don't want you worried."

"I'm a grown-ass man, Myles. I don't need you sparing my feelings."

Okay, well, I guess we're moving forward, then.

"I, uh . . . I sort of started this thing with one of the Doukas girls, Tessa to be exact." I swallow.

"What do you mean, started a thing?"

"We sort of started dating. We've apparently both liked each other for a while, and this time, when she was visiting Anissa's, we finally got to talking. I asked her out on a date, and well, we started dating."

"And she went home, didn't she?"

I nod. "Yeah, she did. Not feeling too great about that, but we decided we'd try long distance."

Baba drags his hand over his jaw. "Is she important to you?"

"Yeah, she is. Very important. I think . . . I could love her, Baba."

He slowly nods and then picks up his fork. "Well, then tell me more about her."

His interest, that small gleam of curiosity, brings a smile to my face. So, I spend the next hour telling him all about Tessa. From when we first truly saw each other, to the sparse interactions we had growing up, to the way we used to look forward to summer because we knew we'd see each other from afar, to the kiss—you know, the "luxurious lips" kiss—to her in the bar, in a robe. Baba laughed; he smiled; he truly looked happier than I've seen him in a while. And when I told him about having to say goodbye, he reached over the table and squeezed my hand. It felt like . . . like he was actually trying. Like the grueling, angry man I've known for the last couple of years slowly melted away, and in his place, I found the compassionate man I grew up with. The man who'd spend Sundays with me, fishing off the coast. The man who'd patiently sit down with me and teach me the tools of the trade, like plumbing, gardening, and painting.

"Have you spoken to her?"

"Not much," I say. "I didn't want to bother her since she just got home."

"Bother her?" Baba's brow creases. "Myles, you can't give her space, not when you're so far away. You need to make sure she knows you're thinking about her, that she knows you're just a phone call away. You need to shower her with attention because if you're feeling this sick over her not being around, think about how she must feel. You can't let her think that you're drifting away. You can't put any sort of negative thought in her head—because the minute you do, she'll carry that negative thought around, she'll build on it, let it snowball, and that's when things start to fall apart." He lifts his water glass to his lips and quietly says, "Learn from my mistakes, Myles."

I know exactly what he's saying—he doesn't have to spell it out. *Don't fuck up like I fucked up.*

And if I've learned anything from my parents' divorce, it's that I don't want to go through the kind of pain they experienced.

So, I agree with my baba. "Okay, I won't. I promise."

"Good." He leans back in his chair. "So, why did you stay, then? When you could have gone back to New York with her?" When our eyes meet, he adds, "And tell me the truth."

This got real, very quickly.

And if we're starting anew, then I might as well be up front and honest.

"For you. For the legacy of Anissa's. For the opportunity to create something bigger, greater, that lasts longer than both of us. I stayed because you're important to me, and I want to prove that to you."

He clears his throat, his fingers drumming on the table. "You don't need to prove anything to me." He glances away. "What I said to you, pushing blame on you, it wasn't right. I should never have made you feel guilty for wanting to better yourself, for wanting to better Anissa's. I realize I've been quite selfish, and I've placed blame where it doesn't belong."

"You were hurting, Baba. When people hurt, they try to hurt others."

"That's no excuse. That's not even a reason. You are my son, and I never should have treated you the way that I did. I'm sorry." He looks me in the eyes. "Myles, I'm very sorry."

I don't know if it's because I'm missing Tessa, or the intensity in Baba's eyes, or the conversation in general, but my emotions get the best of me, and my throat tightens.

"Thank you, Baba. That . . . that means a lot to me."

"I owe you so much more than the man I've been. You deserve a father who doesn't make you feel less than you are, who lifts up you and your ideas. I realized that I haven't been that man for you, and that can't continue. I might have lost your mom, but I can't lose you too, and I'll be damned if I allow that to happen."

"You're not going to lose me. I'm here. I want to be here. I want to create so much more with you. I have ideas, Baba. I have plans."

"I believe it. You've always been a bright, intelligent man with aspirations and visions. You're very much your mother's son."

"I'm also your son, Baba. I'm a product of both of you."

He smiles tenderly. "That you are." Clearing his throat, he sits up. "Well, shall we get to work? I believe I have a lot of ideas to hear from you."

Smiling as well, I nod. "Yeah, let's get to work."

Chapter Twenty-Two

TESSA

"Thank you for meeting with me," I say as Clea and Lois both sit across from me at our favorite bakery on the Upper East Side.

I chose a booth in the far back, where we wouldn't be disturbed or distracted. The normally bustling bakery, famous for their pearl-sugar brioche, is usually brimming with summer tourists pawing at the chance to grab one of the famous baked goods. Thankfully, we beat the heavy traffic and are now perched in the back, in a dark-blue leather booth, a brioche to split between us and café au laits in each of our hands.

When we arrived back in New York, I'd barely unpacked before I begged Clea and Lois to meet up with me. I was grateful when they agreed—besides just wanting to see them, I needed a break from Roxane. She's been staying at my place, which is less than ideal, since I have a quaint one-bedroom apartment on the West Side near Columbus. It's the perfect place to live alone, but after two nights sharing a bed with Roxane, I'm regretting my decision to have a small apartment. Despite the lack of room, I've spent every free moment I have talking with her, working through some of our differences, reminiscing on the fun times we've had, and repairing what we so viciously broke in Greece.

"Well, you sounded desperate on the phone," Clea says, picking off a piece of the tortilla-size brioche.

"And although I love my kids, I already need a break," Lois says. "So, you lucked out."

"Well, either way, thank you. I know things got a little hairy back in Greece—"

"'A little hairy'?" Clea asks. "I'd call it a nightmare."

"Living nightmare," Lois adds.

"Yes, it could be called that. And I wanted to tell you that I'm sorry for how things got out of control. First and foremost, we're best friends, and I never should have treated you the way I did. Like you were dispensable, because you're not."

"Do you realize what it's like to be friends with you and Roxane?" Lois asks, growing serious. "It's hard."

"No cakewalk," Clea adds.

"Constantly listening to you two fighting about clothes, how to order a sandwich properly, the right way to wave down a taxi," Lois says.

"Or the importance of using the crosswalk, or what side to walk on when in the park, or countless, countless trivial arguments that truly mean nothing in the grand scheme of life—but because you seem to be competing all the time, you're always fighting. Always."

I swallow hard, taking it all in, because, yes, I realize they're not exaggerating. Just last night, Roxane and I fought for a moment about the better pizza place in my area. We paused, realized what we were doing, and apologized. So, what Clea and Lois are saying is completely valid.

I'm sure they're exhausted from it all.

"But," Lois says, cutting into my thoughts, "we love you two. That's why we've put up with the nagging, the arguing, the hurtful things you say to each other."

"I know," I say. "And I'm grateful."

"But it's gone too far," Clea says. "We've been drifting apart, and I think you were right in Greece, that we need to have our space and we can't hold each other accountable for rules and expectations we set when we were in high school."

"Hey." We all look to the side, where Roxane is standing in a pair of jean shorts and a simple *I Love NY* shirt, a drunken and ironic purchase during a wild night on Saint Marks. Hands in her pockets, she shyly asks, "Can I join you?"

I turn to Clea and Lois, who both nod, so I scoot over in the booth, making room for Roxane.

"We were just talking about our expectations for each other," I say.

Roxane places her hands on the table. "I'd like to say something first." She looks up, making eye contact with Clea, then Lois. "I'm so sorry about how I've been acting. There's no excuse for my behavior. I was too embarrassed to tell you the truth, so I attempted to focus on everything but my problems and ended up tearing us all down."

"You can't take all of the blame," I say. "I am very much to blame as well. I was pulling away when I should have been there."

"I think we all have been pulling away," Lois says. "With the kids and Ed, I've had a hard time keeping up with life in general."

"And between the popularity of the podcast and spending time with Beast, I think I've pulled away too," Clea adds.

We all look around the table, feeling the weight of our friendship, the danger of it all falling apart. We've spent over fifteen years sharing our lives, going through the ups and the downs, following these silly rules that we thought were going to keep us together forever. But in reality, they were slowly driving us apart.

I'm about to say maybe we should think about these rules again when Roxane places her hand on the table and leans forward.

"I think we need to promise each other, no matter what, nothing will come between us again," Roxane says.

Wait . . .

"Agreed," Clea says. "We've let too much fall between us."

Hold on . . .

"And we can't let that happen again, ever," Lois adds.

My mind goes straight to the one rule that I know is burning my very soul at the moment.

The distance rule.

Coming here, I was sort of hoping that we could readjust the rules to accommodate for these new chapters in our lives, but instead of adjusting, it seems like they're tightening up the contract, adhering to it more . . .

"From now on, no more secrets, no more avoiding each other, no more fights. We're sisters, and we need to keep it that way," Roxane replies as she reaches her hands out. I automatically connect my hands with Roxane's and Clea's, but while they chat about friends forever and how sorry they are, all I can feel is this heavy weight resting on my shoulders. We haven't really changed anything, the rules still exist, and my sister still needs me. Myles is still halfway around the world. It already feels like I'm drowning.

"Your phone is ringing," Roxane says from the living room, where she's doing her morning yoga.

"Is it?" I ask, jogging toward where I left it on the dining room table after breakfast. When I see it's Myles FaceTiming, I quickly bring it back to the bedroom, shut the door, and answer it.

"Hey," I say, intensely aware that my hair is half-curled, half-straight.

"Hey you," he answers, his face filling my screen. God, he's so handsome. It's been three days, and I already miss him more than I could imagine. "I like what you've done with your hair."

I fluff it a bit. "Think it will be a new trend?"

"If anyone can make it work, it's you."

"You flatter me too much."

"Not nearly enough," he says as he leans back on the couch in his apartment.

For the last three days, this is how it's been: he FaceTimes me when he knows I'm awake, and then we text all the way up until he goes to bed.

It's worked, but living without his touch, without being able to curl into his warm body, has already taken a toll on me.

"I miss you," I say as I sit on my bed.

"Miss you too. You look older. Have you aged in the last three days?"

"What?" I ask, the insult clear in my voice.

He just laughs. "I'm kidding. Just trying to joke about how it's felt like forever since I've seen you, but it's only been a few days."

"Very funny."

He chuckles. "So, tell me what you're up to today. Anything fun?"

"I have a meeting downtown. Getting ready for that, but it isn't for another couple of hours, so I have time. And then nothing else besides some work I need to catch up on. What about you?"

"Baba and I are going over those numbers you sent me, the initial ones about renovation costs and possible revenue. Thanks for doing that, by the way, babe. It means a lot."

"No thanks needed. It was fun working on a project that was different than what I normally do. I like numbers and all, but sometimes my job can become monotonous. I liked envisioning your idea and figuring out how it could happen financially. Are you nervous about showing him?"

"Sort of, but he's been pretty chill lately. Well, maybe not chill—that's probably not the right word. More like grateful. He told me last night that the reason he's been doing work around the resort like he used to do is because it reminded him of my mom."

"That's so sad. I almost wish she wasn't engaged and would give him a second chance, but I guess that's the romantic in me."

"I know. A part of me wishes that too, but then I see how happy my mom is. I know that moving on was good for her. I just hope I can help Baba move on as well."

"It will probably take some time."

"Probably. I told him about you, though."

"Oh yeah? Did he have any thoughts?" I bat my eyelashes at him, making him smile.

"Yes, he did. Told me not to fuck it up like he fucked things up with my mom. So, I took that to heart."

"You better have. Although I can't imagine you doing anything stupid."

"Trust me, it's bound to happen. I've done some stupid shit in the past."

"I think we all have." I sigh. "I spoke with the girls."

"Clea and Lois? How did that go?"

"We all got together and had a serious conversation about our lives, and basically said we're going to try harder." I gulp, knowing exactly what that means.

"That's good. Friendships are hard because they're ever changing. But you feel good about how it all went?"

"Yeah, everyone seems happy." Everyone but me. Instead of creating some leeway with the contract, we all just accepted that we need to try harder. And without that leeway, how am I supposed to have a healthy relationship with Myles? I can't. And that makes me want to crawl in a corner and not resurface.

It makes me want to . . . pull away.

Not let my heart get hurt again.

"So, things are good with the girls. What about Roxane?"

"Things are okay with the girls. I think it will take a bit of time for us to really heal, but we'll get there. As for Roxane, she's doing okay.

She's staying with me, which has been tough since I have a small place. But she hasn't been rude or mean. She's been subdued, not her normally vibrant self. Honestly, I'm kind of worried about her. She doesn't do much, other than yoga and work."

"She hasn't spoken to Philip?"

"No, but I believe I saw his name flash across her screen at one point, but she never said anything. So, I don't know. I'm not pushing her right now"

"Well, hang in there. I'm sure she'll talk when she's ready."

"I hope so." I heave a heavy sigh. "I should probably get back to my hair."

"Okay, yeah. Just wanted to see you and hear your voice."

"Thanks for calling. I'll text you later, okay?"

"Yup, talk to you later, Tessa."

"Bye, Myles."

I hang up and then set my phone next to me on my bed. I pause for a moment.

I feel . . . weird.

Sad.

Not like myself.

Seeing him, talking to him, it's like a brief moment of euphoria, but then it crashes down around me, spiraling me into a kind of sinking depression. My body aches, I have this need to cry, and I don't want to do anything other than curl into my bed and drift back to Greece.

I knew this was going to be hard.

But I didn't know it was going to be *this* hard.

I didn't think I was going to ache for him so much.

I didn't think I was going to feel this lousy.

Going into this, I thought that long distance would be hard, but also fun. That I'd get to know Myles on an even deeper level. And although I love talking to him, texting and FaceTiming, it just reminds me that there really doesn't seem to be an end goal to all of this.

It's hard not to be bitter, because if it wasn't for my need to help Roxane, maybe this would all be different. Maybe I would still be in Greece with Myles. Maybe I would be able to wake up to his smiling face rather than seeing it through a screen.

And it's been three days.

Three freaking days.

It has to get better than this, right?

Despair clouds my brain, pulling me away from the present.

At some point, will this feel like the new normal?

CHAPTER
TWENTY-THREE

Two weeks later

Myles: [Picture] Check out this sunset. I wish you were here enjoying it with me.

Tessa: Ugh. Gorgeous. Reminds me of our date at Fiora.

Myles: The same night we made out in the back of my car.

Tessa: I can still feel the breeze against my butt cheeks from my upturned dress.

Myles: I wish I could see your upturned dress right now.

Tessa: I wish you could see it too.

Myles: Ahhh, there's my girl. I knew you were in there somewhere hiding.

Tessa: What do you mean?

Myles: The last week or so it seems like you've been distant. I was getting worried.

Tessa: Oh, I probably was growing distant.

Myles: Why?

Tessa: This is just harder than I thought it would be. I think I was protecting myself by distancing.

Myles: I'm not going to hurt you Tessa, you have to know that.

Tessa: I know, but being so far apart is difficult.

Myles: We'll get used to it, I promise.

Tessa: I don't want to get used to it.

Myles: Neither do I, but it's either long distance or we don't try at all and I'm not ready for that. Are you?

Tessa: No, I'm not. But doesn't it feel like it could be easier?

Myles: Probably, but aren't the best things worth working for?

Tessa: Yes.

Myles: Then keep working at it with me, Tessa. We'll find a flow. Okay?

Tessa: Okay.

Myles: Good, and if you start doubting again, just call me, any time. I'll answer.

Tessa: I know you will.

One month later

Myles: Baba and I are going to see that boutique hotel today.

Tessa: Really? Oh my God! That's so exciting. How do you feel?

Myles: Nervous, excited . . . terrified.

Tessa: Terrified because you think he won't want to expand?

Myles: Yeah. We've come to a really peaceful place in our relationship. He's really taken me under his wing and he's brought me on the business side. It's felt so right, and I'm worried that when he sees the new hotel, when he hears all the plans I have, he's going to run scared.

Tessa: That's understandable. But you can't go in there thinking like that. You need to be positive. Show him your excitement. Your excitement will rub off on him. And if you get really nervous, just pretend you're showing it to me for the second time.

Myles: All good advice besides that last part. If I pretended I'm showing it to you, I might end up kissing my baba under a tree, and I'm not too sure how he would feel about that.

Tessa: LOL. Not sure how I'd feel about that either.

Myles: Ooooh, you claiming my lips as yours and yours alone?

Tessa: Yes.

Myles: Just a solid yes? No elaboration?

Tessa: No need to elaborate. I claimed them, they're mine, what's done is done.

Myles: I guess so and for the record, the same goes for you. Those lips, they're mine.

Tessa: Oh no, really? Hmm, so what happens if I accidentally kissed Harold the other day?

Myles: Who the hell is Harold?

Tessa: Sweet old man, some might say . . . furry.

Myles: Is Harold a pet?

Tessa: More like a mascot at the gym I go to. He was just so cute with his floppy ears.

Myles: Well, this Harold and I are going to have words. No one kisses my girl or gets kissed by my girl who's not me.

Tessa: Okay, but when he bares his teeth, they're vicious.

Myles: Just wait until he gets a glimpse of my canines.

One and a half months later

Tessa: Roxane has been acting really weird lately.

Myles: How so?

Tessa: Not toward me, we're pretty solid right now, but she's been sneaking around, wearing a big puffy jacket but it's still hot out.

Myles: Seems suspicious but I'm going to need more evidence.

Tessa: She baked cookies yesterday. She doesn't bake . . . ever. And they were not good.

Myles: Mm-hmm, okay, anything else?

Tessa: She's been taking phone calls outside of the apartment. Like her phone rings, she sees who's calling, and then she leaves.

Myles: Yes, that is quite suspicious.

Tessa: See! I don't know what to do about it.

Myles: Maybe you do nothing about it. Maybe you just let her figure this all out on her own.

Tessa: What if she's turned into a drug dealer or something? What if she baked drugs into the cookies she made? Maybe that's her way of transport?

Myles: Do you really think Roxane is capable of drug dealing?

Tessa: Possibly.

Myles: Maybe she's seeking out therapy. Baba has but he doesn't talk about it. Like . . . at all. He keeps it very close to him. Maybe Roxane is doing the same.

Tessa: Huh, I never thought about it that way.

Myles: That's why I'm here, babe.

Tessa: I really wish you were here. I miss you.

Myles: Miss you, too. We still on for our FaceTime date tomorrow night?

Tessa: Yes. I can't wait. I plan on wearing nothing.

Myles: So this is casual then?

Tessa: More like sexual!

Myles: Rawr!

Tessa: LOL! Please don't ever do that again.

Myles: Yeah, it didn't feel right.

One month later

Tessa: So, I got a package in the mail. It seems to be from you.

Myles: Jesus, that took a long time to get to you.

Tessa: But at least it's here.

Myles: Yes, now open it.

Tessa: I want to do it on FaceTime.

Myles: I'm driving with my Baba. It would not be appropriate.

Tessa: Oh yeah . . . well, I can wait.

Myles: I can't. Open it now.

Tessa: Okay. Opening.

Tessa: OH MY GOD! Myles, this is an entire box of Derby bars.

Tessa: You really do like me.

Myles: Ha ha. I do. There's something at the very bottom.

Tessa: Umm . . . what's this little lingerie number?

Myles: Hoping what you wear on our next FaceTime date.

Tessa: And what will you be wearing?

Myles: Same thing. Got myself a matching set.

Tessa: LOL! Now that is something I'm going to need to see.

Three months later

Myles: Sorry I couldn't text you this morning. Things have been crazy. How are you?

Tessa: Pretty good. I joined a book club here to keep busy. I got my book assignment today. Not so sure this book club is for me.

Myles: What's the book?

Tessa: A biography about Winston Churchill. Not really a history buff.

Myles: Yeah, that doesn't seem like you. Maybe you ghost the book club, just gradually step back.

Tessa: I think you might be right. I was excited about having something to do.

Myles: Roxane still being aloof?

Tessa: Yes. She's been more on her own lately despite still living with me. I've been alone a lot, too. I met up with Clea the other night and we had a good dinner, but she seemed distant and when I asked Lois to dinner tonight, she said she couldn't because she was making some soup that required all of her attention and she'd be damned if she didn't sit down and enjoy it. She invited me over, but I knew her mother-in-law would be there, and it just felt like I was imposing.

Myles: So, you're alone?

Tessa: Pretty much.

Myles: Hmm . . . seems like you should probably hop on a flight and come visit a certain someone.

Tessa: You know I can't, Myles.

Myles: I thought the reason you were staying in New York City was because of Roxane. If she's not requiring your services, then doesn't that mean you're free to go?

Tessa: No. She still needs me.

Myles: Does she?

Tessa: Yes.

Myles: Are you sure? Because from what you've told me, it doesn't seem like she does.

Tessa: You aren't here, Myles, you don't know.

Myles: True, but I just want to make sure you're not using her as an excuse.

Tessa: As an excuse to do what?

Myles: To not come out here.

Tessa: Do you really think I'd do that? If I wasn't interested in seeing you then I wouldn't be talking to you. I have my reasons for having to be here.

Myles: Yes, I know, but I'm just saying that it seems like the reasons don't matter anymore.

Tessa: I don't think you should be saying anything about it, actually.

Myles: Tessa, I'm not trying to get in a fight. I'm just trying to tell you that if you're free, come visit me.

Tessa: I don't need you to tell me when to visit you, Myles. Trust me, if I could, I would. So just . . . just stay out of it.

Myles: Okay . . . sorry.

Tessa: You know what, I should probably get going. I'll talk to you later.

Myles: Tessa, please don't leave mad.

Myles: Tessa, come on.

Myles: Tessa . . .

Two months later

Myles: Happy birthday, Tessa! I know it's not quite your birthday yet, but it's your birthday here and I wanted to make sure I was the first person to say it to you. Did you get my package?

Tessa: Thank you. And yes. I did.

Myles: Open it with me?

Tessa: I'm actually at Clea's place right now. We're drinking some strange cocktail concoction that Beast made up for us. In her spare time, she's decided to take up bartending.

Myles: Oh, okay, well, let me know when a good time to call is. Baba and I are just drawing up the boutique renovation plans with the architect all day, so I can step out whenever.

Tessa: Sure, I'll let you know.

Myles: Okay . . . hey is everything okay?

Tessa: Yes, but I really have to go. Talk to you later.

Four and a half months later

Myles: Remember that one summer when you and Roxane brought floats and tried to blow them up on the beach, only for them to be whisked away by the wind?

Tessa: Yes, mine was a watermelon. It got cut up on a bunch of rocks.

Myles: Some kids tried to do the same thing, and they succeeded. Although, they floated quite far and had to be rescued.

Tessa: Poor guys.

Myles: Baba had a sign made today that said "no floats in the sea."

Myles: Hey, you there?

Tessa: Yeah, sorry. Just getting work done.

Myles: Okay, well, if I'm bothering you just let me know.

Tessa: I just need to finish this excel sheet. I'll talk to you later.

Myles: Okay.

Five months later

Myles: Hey, are you still alive? I haven't heard from you in two days. Not trying to be a stalker here, but I miss you.

Myles: Tessa, you there?

Myles: Okay, I'm starting to get concerned.

Tessa: Sorry, was shopping with Lois. I'm all good. You good?

Myles: Not really.

Tessa: Why? What's going on?

Myles: You're pulling away, Tessa.

Tessa: I've just been busy, Myles.

Myles: Yeah, I've been busy too, but the difference between the two of us is that I'm making an effort.

Tessa: What is that supposed to mean?

Myles: It means that I've been putting in an effort to talk to you, and it seems like you couldn't care less about contacting me.

Tessa: That's not fair. Just because I don't text right away doesn't mean I'm not putting in an effort. I have a life too, Myles.

Myles: Wow, okay. Well, I thought I was a part of that life. Apparently not.

Tessa: Don't be passive aggressive. Just say what you want to say.

Myles: Say what I want to say? Okay, you've been absent, you've missed our last two phone call dates, you don't send me morning pictures like you used to even though I send mine. You are short and snippy with me, and I don't think I've done anything wrong.

Tessa: Okay, so what? Do you just want to end this?

Myles: What? No. Jesus Christ, Tessa.

Tessa: Well, clearly you're not happy, so maybe we just cut ties before things get too complicated.

Myles: Can you answer your phone, please?

Tessa: I'm not in a spot where I can answer right now.

Myles: Okay, well then let's talk about this when you are. I don't want to do this through text.

Tessa: Yeah, sure.

Two hours later

Myles: I've called you three times. Tessa, what the hell is going on?

Myles: Tessa, answer your phone!

Chapter

Twenty-Four

TESSA

"So . . . are you just going to sit there on the couch again, for the tenth night in a row?" Roxane asks as she slips her peacoat jacket over her cotton turtleneck dress.

"Yup." I pop a piece of popcorn in my mouth and search through the latest movies on Netflix.

"This isn't healthy, you realize that?"

"When you stop sneaking off into the hallway to take phone calls, you can lecture me on what's healthy and what's not healthy."

I can feel her blistering gaze. "I'm not going to get into it with you tonight. I have a party to get to, and I'd rather not show up in a bad mood."

"Sure, wouldn't want to be late." I shove a fistful of popcorn in my mouth.

"Okay, what's going on?" Roxane says. "You're acting like a bitch."

"Me?" I point to my chest. "How am I acting like a bitch?"

"You've been rude to me for the last week. Short tempered, flat-out rude. What's going on? Things not great with Myles?"

No.

Not even close.

And the fact that I know things aren't good, that he's angry with me, it makes me so sick to my stomach that I can't fathom putting regular clothes on and moving away from this couch. I just want to curl up and block out the world.

"Myles is . . . Myles. He's fine," I lie because the truth feels too brutal to talk about.

"Uh-huh. Whenever the word 'fine' is used for a sentence, it usually means the direct opposite."

"I just don't see the point of dating him," I say flippantly. "Clearly, it's going nowhere."

"What do you mean? I thought everything was fine?"

"Yeah, well, it's just the same thing over and over again. Call, text, call, text. There's nothing more, and you can only do that for so long. I'm starting to get—"

Knock, knock.

We both look toward the door, and since Roxane is the one standing, she goes to open it.

I glance down the hallway as I hear her open the door and then say, "Oh, hello. Wasn't expecting you."

"Who is it?" I call out from my cross-legged position on the couch.

Footsteps sound down the hallway and then, "Hey, babe."

My eyes widen.

My heart slams into my chest.

And I sit there, stunned, as I look up at a travel-weary Myles.

My mind flashes to Odysseus and Penelope again, the ten long years they waited for their romance to be rekindled. Sure, it's only been a year and a half, not ten years, but with the history between us and this long distance that's been sucking the soul out of me, it feels like ten years.

With only a backpack on his shoulders, he's dressed in black joggers and a dark-green hoodie. His hair is flattened by a black backward baseball cap, while his jawline is covered in a thick scruff.

Oh my God, he looks so freaking good.

So good that all the pain, all the emptiness, it just washes away with one look in his direction.

"My-Myles," I say, stunned. "What are you doing here?"

"Figured we needed to have a talk."

Roxane steps in. "Uh, I'll just be leaving. Probably going to stay at Clea's place. I'll see you in the morning. Myles, good seeing you." With that, she gives me a knowing look that says good luck, and then she takes off, shutting the door behind her, leaving me alone with Myles.

"Are you just going to sit there, or are you going to greet me properly?" he asks as he takes his backpack off and sets it on the ground.

"I . . . yes, sorry. Just surprised." I set my popcorn bowl on the coffee table, stand on my wobbly legs, and make my way toward Myles. Feeling like I've stepped into an alternate universe, I loop both arms around him and pull him into a much-needed hug. His warm, masculine scent pulls me down a rabbit hole of memories as I lean into his strong chest. All the time we spent in my hotel room, the night at Fiora, the night in the private suite, all his kisses, all our intimate moments. His arms encase me in a tight embrace, but he doesn't give me a second to rest my head, because he's moving my chin up toward him, and before I know it, his lips are on mine, and he's kissing me like he's never kissed me before.

Desperate.

Demanding.

Conquering.

As he kisses me senseless, one of his hands slides under the back of my shirt, where his palm presses against my lower back, pulling me in even closer, bringing me up on my toes. He takes mere seconds to heat up my entire body, to remind me exactly why I decided to be with him, because even in my darkest moments, he makes me feel light and bright again.

My desire for this man takes over, and I find myself pawing at his clothes, wanting him naked, but instead of obliging, he grips my wrists, pauses me, and forces me to look him in the eyes.

"What's wrong?" I ask.

"We need to talk, Tessa."

"What do you mean, talk? About what?" I ask, though I already know the answer.

"About us," he answers and brings me over to the couch, where we both take a seat. But I don't want to talk. I don't want to be brought back to reality, to the problems and awkwardness between us. I want to be caught up in this fantasy, this place where everything is right in the world.

So, I turn and straddle his lap, resting my hands on his chest.

"Tessa," he groans as I settle myself right on top of him. His hands fall to my waist while his head rests against the back of the couch.

"I can't believe you're here." I slide my hands under his shirt and against his skin. Warm, soft, delicious. I need him. I need to feel connected. I need to escape this prison I feel like I've been living in, the one in my head.

"Hey," he says softly as I try to move his shirt up. "Tessa, slow down."

I shake my head, my emotions taking over, the last few months crashing down around me. The pressure of taking care of Roxane, the intensity of a long-distance relationship, the withdrawal from Myles. It consumes me, it controls me, and I know the only way to escape it all is to get lost.

"Please, Myles," I say, tugging more on his shirt. "I need to . . . to forget."

"Forget what?" he asks.

Tears well up in my eyes. "Forget it all."

"Tessa, what's going on?"

I lean forward and press my lips to his before pulling back. "Just love me, Myles. Hold me. Take me back to before I left Greece."

He doesn't say anything. Doesn't kiss me back, just sits there. And that momentary pause is all it takes.

Shame and embarrassment wash over me as I lift up off him and back away. He doesn't want to take me; he doesn't want to love me. He came here to talk . . . Does that mean break up with me?

"I'm sorry." I shake my head, my tears dripping down my cheeks now. "I'm just . . . I don't know. I'm sorry." Unsure what to do, I turn away and walk to my bedroom, needing to take a moment to get my head on straight, but when I go to shut the door, a hand reaches out and stops it. Myles's hand.

And then he pushes through the door, puts his hands on my shoulders, and leads me to the bed, where he lays me down.

"Myles," I say, but then he tears his hoodie and shirt over his head and drops them to the floor. I drink in the sight of his chest, his rippling abs, his substantial biceps that look bigger than I remember. His hands find the waistband of my leggings, and he peels them off in one smooth tug before reaching for my thong and removing that as well.

"Shirt off. Now," he says, so I pull my shirt and my sports bra off and toss them to the ground just as he strips out of his pants and briefs, leaving us both naked.

Not wasting any time, he spreads my legs, moves over me, and then cradles the back of my head as his erection rests against my legs. Eyes intent on mine, he lowers his mouth and claims me all over again.

A whirlwind of emotions floods through me.

Heat.

Comfort.

Need.

Want.

It curls through my veins, pulses through my muscles, lights me up with the belief that this man . . . this is what's been missing. His touch. His presence. His mouth. This is what's been missing in my life, and it's so obvious in the difference between the way I was feeling only moments ago and the way I'm feeling now—like nothing, and I mean nothing, could hurt me.

While I move my leg around his waist, he brings his fingers to my center, sliding them along my clit, testing my readiness.

"Hell, Tessa," he whispers when he feels how wet I am.

"I want you, Myles," I whisper back.

Thankfully he doesn't make me wait. He positions the head of his erection at my entrance and then slowly sinks in. It's been months since I've felt him, since I've felt anything, and this moment feels like magic, like with every touch, every kiss, he's stealing me away from the sadness that's been consuming me, and he's bringing me back to the present.

Once he's fully inside me, he gently rocks his hips, setting a hypnotic pace that sets me on fire as his lips move down my neck, across my collarbone, and then pull at my nipples. He focuses on the right, rolling it between his lips, nibbling, sucking, creating an electrified force so strong in my body that I can't do anything but hold on to him tightly, wishing and hoping he never stops. And then he moves over to my left nipple, giving it the same treatment, driving me so wild that I start panting his name, begging for more.

He takes one of my legs and drapes it over his shoulder, and the new position sends him deeper, hitting a spot that immediately shoots a sharp blaze of white-hot pleasure up my spine. And from his relentless pulsing, the euphoric feeling builds and builds.

"Oh . . . God," I cry out, my orgasm hurtling toward me. "Myles, I . . . oh God!" He pulses one more time, and everything in my body seizes, stilling me as he continues to create the friction I'm desperate for.

I feel myself clutch around him, squeezing him tight.

His forehead connects with mine, and then quietly he says, "Fuck . . . me . . ."

His body stills.

He groans.

And he comes inside me, the sound of his orgasm easily the sexiest sound I've ever heard.

Together we both slowly rock back and forth until there is nothing left inside us, and he collapses next to me.

His hand links through mine, and he brings the connection to his lips, kissing the back of my hand.

"Fuck, Tessa, I've missed you."

Tears spring to my eyes as I turn toward him and curl into his chest, resting my head in the crook of his shoulder.

"I can't tell you how much I've missed you."

His arm loops around me, and he rubs my back. "Then why have you been pulling away?"

"It hurts too much," I say, my tears falling now as the past months wash over me. "Talking to you, it just reminds me that I can't have all of you, and it's painful."

"Why didn't you say anything?"

"I couldn't. Even thinking about it has been hard."

"Yes, but if you talk to me, I can help you."

"I didn't want you to think I was too weak, unable to handle the long distance."

"So instead, you distance yourself and make me think that you want to break up?"

"Break up?" I lift up to look him in the eyes. That would be the last thing I want, especially after having him here in person and feeling so . . . so light with him here again. "Is that what you've been thinking?"

"Yes," he says. "Why do you think I'm here? I flew out here to salvage our relationship. I don't want to give up on us."

"Myles." I caress his cheek. "I'm . . . sorry. I didn't mean to make you worry. I just . . . I haven't been handling this well."

"Pulling away from me is not the answer." His voice is sharp, but comforting at the same time.

"I know." I grip him tighter. "I'm sorry."

"I know, babe." He kisses the top of my head. "Hey, let's take a shower, and then we can grab some food and talk, okay?"

I nod against his chest. "Okay, but let me just hold you for a little while longer first."

Two days.

That's all I have with him. And it's not even two full days. When I asked him in the shower how long he was going to be here and he told me, I felt my heart sink in my chest. Two days isn't nearly enough time.

I want more.

I want a week. Two weeks. Hell, give me months.

Saying goodbye in two days is going to be so much more painful than the long distance we've been dealing with.

But I'm trying to put it in the back of my mind.

After we showered and he delivered one more orgasm before getting dressed, we ordered food and ate, and now we're curled up on the couch.

He slowly rubs my back while calming music plays in the background and candles flicker around the apartment, offering the only light in the space.

"So . . . what's been going on?" he asks. "Why are you pulling away?"

"I wasn't doing it intentionally," I say. "It just felt like it was easier because every time I saw you or I heard your voice, every time I saw your name on my phone, I remembered that I wasn't anywhere near feeling the joy I had when I was with you. That I wasn't happy."

"Tessa," he says as he lifts my chin to look at me, concern radiating from his gaze. "You have to tell me this. You have to tell me when you're not happy."

"But what's that going to do? Make you feel guilty? I don't want to put that burden on you."

"It's not a burden, Tessa. You are not a burden. You're my girl, and I want to know what you're feeling so I can make sure that you're okay, that you're happy."

"But I'm not happy." I shake my head. "I'm not even close to happy."

"Are you happy with me?" he asks.

"Yes, of course. I'm so happy with you, but I don't have the luxury of being with you. Being near you."

"That can change, Tessa."

"It can't." I shake my head. "There is no end in sight. We're just kidding ourselves."

He shifts so he can look me in the eyes. "I thought . . . I thought you were just out here because you were helping Roxane. That we would do long distance until that was all solved."

If only that were the case.

There's no end in sight because I'm trapped. I just rectified my relationships with my best friends and sister. They're still fragile at this point, so how could I possibly ruin everything again by considering moving to Greece? I feel so lost as it is. Losing them again would just destroy me.

So, I don't say anything. Instead I just let my tears fall.

"Tessa, tell me that was what the plan was."

"Myles, I . . . I don't know."

"What do you mean? What's holding you back?" The etch in his bothered brow, the downturn in his lips—it makes my heart ache even more, tearing me in two different directions. "Tessa." He tugs at my hand. "Talk to me."

"It's just . . . I can't leave here, okay?"

"You can't?" he asks. "Or you won't?"

"It's not that easy, Myles."

"Fine, then I'll fucking move here. If you can't, then I will."

"No." I shake my head. "No, you are not moving here. You have a life in Greece, a new hotel that you're working on. Your baba is there, and he needs you. You can't come here."

"Then what the fuck am I supposed to do?" he asks, standing now. "Just . . . just walk away?"

His words pierce me like a knife to the heart, burying deep. "'Walk away'?" I ask, gulping.

"Well, what else am I supposed to do, Tessa? Jesus Christ. If you won't let me move and if you won't move yourself, then what the hell are we doing?"

"I . . . I don't know," I say, my lip trembling.

"Me neither." He rests his hands on his hips and bends his head forward. "I just don't get it. Is Roxane really the reason you're going to stay here? You said it yourself, you're not happy, so why the hell would you continue to live in this purgatory?"

"She's my sister—"

"I'm well aware of who she is. But just because she's your sister doesn't mean you need to stay and bottle-feed her through life. She's a big girl."

"She needs me."

"Does she?" he asks. "Or do you need her?"

"I . . . I . . ." I don't have an answer. I don't think I need her. I need him. I want him. I don't want to live in a one-bedroom apartment and share a bed with my sister. I want to live in Greece, where I feel happiest. Where I have the best memories, where . . . where I fell in love.

Shaking his head, he walks back to the bedroom, grabs his shoes, and brings them into the living room.

"Where are you going?" I say, panic rearing up.

"I'm not going to sit around here and wait for you to talk to me. I came here to have a conversation with you, to understand why you decided to go long distance with me and are now changing your mind. But you can't give me any answers. You're just giving me the runaround. And you're clearly unhappy, it shows, but you won't take a chance at happiness either. So, I don't know what the fuck to do. I just know I can't stay here." Once his shoes are on, he picks up his backpack and heads for the front door.

"Myles, wait, don't go," I cry as I head toward the front door as well. "Please don't go."

But he doesn't listen.

He doesn't turn around.

Instead, he leaves, the door shutting behind him. Any ounce of happiness I had left inside me vanishes as I crumble to the floor.

I'm not sure how long I stay there, but by the time I pick myself up and make it to my phone, it's well past midnight. Doesn't matter. I send out a text.

Tessa: Myles. I'm sorry.

I clutch my phone as I make my way to my bed, the bed that still smells like him. And when my phone vibrates in my hand, my heart leaps.

Myles: Tessa, don't say things you don't mean.

Tessa: I do mean it. I'm truly sorry. Please come back.

Myles: Too late. I already switched my flight. I'm headed back early in the morning.

A harsh sob escapes me as I realize I truly fucked up. Without a doubt, I just hit rock bottom.

Chapter
Twenty-Five
TESSA

Roxane: Is it safe to come home? I'm outside, wondering if I can come up to the apartment or if you need more privacy.

Still in a ball on the bed, I text Roxane back.

Tessa: He's not here.

And then I rest my phone back down and curl into the pillow that smells like Myles, my thoughts replaying our conversation over and over again.

It doesn't take long for Roxane to make it up to the apartment, open the door, and find me. When she stands at the bedroom door and catches me curled up, she rushes over and sits down beside me. "What happened?" she asks, laying a comforting hand on my back.

"He went back to Greece."

"What? Already? Was it just a short trip?"

"He was supposed to be here for two days," I say, my voice hitching in my throat. "But . . . we ended things last night."

"Why?" she asks, pulling on my shoulder, turning me toward her.

"Because there's no point in staying together, not when we can't be together. He can't move. I can't move. So, what's the point?"

Roxane falls silent, and I know exactly what she's thinking about. The contract. The vow I made to her in Greece to help her—it towers between us like a giant elephant in the room.

"He . . . uh, he can't move?"

I shake my head. "No, he's opening up a new hotel with his baba, who needs him there—there's no chance he can move."

"Oh." She rolls her teeth over her bottom lip. "Well . . . then why don't you?"

"Roxane, don't." I start to turn away from her, but she holds my shoulder, preventing me from moving.

"Tessa, seriously."

"Seriously?" I ask, sitting up. "Seriously? Are you really saying that to me right now? Do you realize that when we were in Greece, even though you were making my life a living nightmare, I was actually enjoying myself? That for the first time since I was cheated on, I actually felt like myself? Myles and I . . . we have this bond, this weird history, and when we finally got together, it felt so right, so long awaited. Like we were supposed to be with each other. I was happy, Roxane. Really fucking happy. And you didn't see it, or you chose not to see it. And that was fine because I had him. But that all changed because I love you and I care about you, and you came to me asking for help. Begging for help. And I have always, and always will, put you before me, because you're my sister. My needs have never mattered. You . . . you've been the one that mattered in my life. So seriously? Yes. I am not moving there because you need me, because our friends need me, and because I will never . . . ever put myself first, no matter how much happiness rests on the other side of the world for me."

"Is that the truth, Tessa, or are you using me as a crutch because you're too scared to get your heart hurt again?"

"What little you know of me." I get up from the bed and head toward the entryway.

"Where are you going?" she calls.

"Anywhere but here," I say as I put on my snow boots and jacket. "I just need time."

"No, Tessa, wait."

I don't wait.

I don't wait one more second.

I walk out of the apartment door, down the stairs, and straight to the park, where I walk.

And walk.

And walk.

MYLES

I shut the front door of Baba's house and set my backpack down in the entryway before heading for the kitchen. Exhausted, heartbroken, and starving, I go straight to the fridge, hoping some of Baba's homemade hummus is waiting for me.

When I pop open the fridge, I hear a chair creak behind me.

"What are you doing here?" Baba says, his voice concerned.

I don't bother to look his way. Instead, I grab the container of hummus and some chopped veggies and bring them to the kitchen island, where he's sitting.

"Home early," I mutter as I take a seat and pop open the lids.

"Why?"

"We ended things," I answer. I pick up a carrot, scoop up a dollop of hummus, and plop it in my mouth.

"What do you mean, you 'ended things'?" Baba booms as he sets his book down and turns to face me.

"She didn't want to move, so then I offered to move, and she told me no, that I have to be here with you and the hotel. And that was that. There's no point in dating if we can't actually be with each other. I'm not going to have a long-distance relationship that doesn't go anywhere."

He smooths his fingers over his mustache. "Why did she not want to move here?"

"Great question, Baba," I answer sarcastically. "That's what everyone wants to know. Really strange, actually, because when I showed up, she was thrilled. She—hell, sorry to say it, but she was on top of me right away. She told me how unhappy she's been, and she said how glad she was to see me, so you'd think that would correlate to her wanting to make this happen, but it didn't. Instead, she just distanced herself even more."

"So . . . then go get her."

"No, Baba. She doesn't want me to go get her. She told me to stay here."

"But why?"

"Because of you and our work, and because even though she holds my heart, this is where I truly belong."

"Do you love her?" Baba asks.

"Yeah," I say without even having to think about it, as I've never been more certain of anything in my life. "I do, but it doesn't seem like that's enough. And I don't want to have to chase someone who's not willing to try. Hell, she started pulling away a while ago, and not from a lack of trying on my end. I've tried. I've done everything in my power, even flying there, to make sure that everything was going to be okay between us, but it can't be a one-way street, Baba."

"I know," he says quietly. "It was the same with your mother. She tried. And I didn't. I was the one who failed us." He lets out a deep breath. "It seems as though Tessa is the one who will fail you. There's no changing that, trust me, I'd know." He grips my shoulder tightly. "I'm sorry, Myles. I wish there was something I could do. Do you want me to talk to her?"

"Jesus, no," I say as I dip another carrot in the hummus. "I just . . . I just need to fucking forget about it."

"Do you think that's something you can do?"

"I think that's something I'm going to have to do," I answer. "Because if I don't, it's just going to eat me alive. If I think about it, it will consume me to the point that I won't be any help to you, Baba." I press my hand to my forehead. "If I think about her, I'm going to get caught up in all the ways that I can win her back, because fuck do I want her back. I love her so goddamn much, and it fucking kills me that there's nothing I can do about it. I feel so helpless, and that's a tough pill to swallow."

"There has to be something else we can do. I just want you to be happy, Myles."

"Thanks, Baba. But I'm not sure happiness is in the cards for me right now. Nor do I believe there's a solution."

Somberly, I take another bite of my carrot and lean back in my chair. I thought we had something special, a story that should be written in mythical books, about the two long-lost lovers who have been in each other's lives since they were young. I couldn't have been more wrong.

Our love story wasn't written in the stars; it was scratched out in the depths of torture, a fair warning to the lighthearted that love is not all it's cracked up to be.

And happiness? I'm not quite sure what that is.

Nope . . . my life is completely devoid of happiness.

TESSA

With tired legs, pounding head, and burning eyes, I open my apartment door after spending the entire morning and afternoon walking around a chilly Central Park.

"There she is," Roxane says, and I look up to find not only her standing in my living room, but Clea and Lois as well. "Why don't you take your boots and coat off and join us?"

"I'm good, thanks," I say as I remove my outerwear.

"Oh, cute that you thought it was an option. It's a demand." Roxane loops her arm through mine and brings me over to the dining room table, where a séance is set up. Well, not an actual séance, but resting on the round table is a legal pad, a folder, lit candles, a bowl of Chips Ahoy! cookies, and . . . the perfume.

"What's going on?" I say as Lois and Clea lead me to a seat, practically forcing me to sit down. "What is all this?" I glance around and spot Clea's mom sitting on the couch. Wearing a smart business suit, she flashes me a sweet smile. What on earth.

Roxane takes a seat as well and folds her hands on the table. "I need to speak to you three." She clears her throat. "I haven't been honest with you, and I think it's time that I confess something."

Okay . . . what the hell is going on?

"For the past three months, I've been secretly dating."

Clea and Lois seem unfazed as my mind feels like it's exploding. Dating? When? Is that why she's been so weird?

"What?" I ask. "Who?"

"Philip," she answers.

"Philip?" I shout. "As in your ex-fiancé?"

"That is correct." She nods. "After the wedding was canceled, I asked if I could pick up my things from his place. He said yes and that he wouldn't be there, but when I arrived, I realized he'd been lying. He wanted to talk to me about what happened. He said he didn't get on the plane because he was worried that I wasn't ready to get married, that I was having second thoughts, which caused him to have second thoughts. Anyway, we both said sorry and decided to go on with our lives."

"So where did the dating happen?" I ask.

"Funny, after I said bye, I started to think about how depressed I was. I kept thinking about how Philip loved to run and said that always made him feel better."

Lois clasps her chest and gasps. "Are you saying . . ."

Roxane nods. "Yup. I ran for fun. Well, the first run was more of a desperate attempt to run away from my feelings. The second time was because I wanted to torture myself. The third and fourth, well, those were because I started to get a runner's high."

"You did not. Don't say things like that," Clea says, shaking her head.

"It's true. Then, I joined a running club."

Lois slams her hand on the table. "Goddamn you."

"And Philip happened to be in that running club. He was much faster than me and was always ahead, but he started to slow down, and I started to speed up, and soon enough we were running together. Then we started talking, then . . . well, he asked me on a date, and I told him no, because I didn't think I was the woman he deserved in his life. And he told me to prove him wrong. So, I went on a date and told him everything that was wrong with me. I told him the truth about myself, and at the end of my spiel, he said he still loved me and wanted to take me on another date . . . and another . . . and another. So, we've been dating."

"Why . . . why didn't you tell me?" I ask, blinking a few times, too shocked to say anything else.

"Yeah, why didn't you tell us you've betrayed us in the worst way possible?" Lois asks.

"Because. I was embarrassed. I was worried it was too good to be true. And because I didn't want you, Tessa, to feel bad. I knew things were rocky with Myles, and I didn't want to shove it in your face."

"Yeah, well, communication is key, Roxane. I thought you needed me."

"I did. I do. You've helped me over the last couple of months, if anything, just by being here for me."

"What about the contract?" Clea asks, tapping on the folder in front of her. "And why did I have to drag my mother all the way from SoHo to be here?"

"Because it's time we make a change." Roxane reaches into the folder, pulls out the contract, and holds it up. "This is outdated. We have evolved. We have changed. Our interests are different, our desires are different, and our needs are different." Roxane looks around the table. "I like to run, and even though I love you three more than anything, I'm not going to change that. I will keep running. For me, for Philip, for my future, and I'm not going to stop."

"But . . ." Clea looks around.

I try to comprehend what the hell is happening, but I think my brain has stalled out.

And Lois twitches her bottom lip, looking guilty. "I was at Penn Station last week and heard these girls talking ill of Zac Efron, and I . . . I walked away."

"Oh my God!" Clea says, looking horrified. "How could you?"

"The same way you sprayed the perfume on yourself the other night to get Beast all riled up."

Another gasp from Clea. "I told you that in confidence."

"Well, well, well . . . looks like we're all betraying the rules, now, aren't we?" Roxane says. "And little innocent Tessa over there, guess what she's doing?" Trying to understand everything that's happening at the moment? "She's moving to Greece."

"What?" Clea and Lois turn toward me at the same time.

"Wait, what?" I ask, now more confused than ever.

"Yup. To be with Myles. So, looks like we need a new contract." And before any of us can stop her, she fans our old, sacred contract over one of the candles and sets it on fire.

"What the hell are you doing?" Lois asks, reaching for it, but Roxane merely dumps the cookies out of the metal bowl and sets the burning contract inside. Together, we all watch it go up in flames.

"That . . . that was our childhood," Clea says, sounding sad.

"Exactly. It was our *childhood*," Roxane says. "Now we're adults, and we need a new set of rules. We said it ourselves right after we got back from Greece—we all felt like we were drifting apart because life is pulling us all in different directions. It's impossible to keep up with these nonsensical rules when our lives are so different now. Which means, it's time to make some new ones." She uncaps a pen, grabs the notebook, and starts writing at the top.

"Can we, uh, can we just pause for a second," I say, pinching the bridge of my nose. "I'm having a hard time grasping everything here. So, you and Philip are back together?"

"Yes," Roxane says. "When I said I was with Clea last night, I was actually with him. He asked me to move in with him again. I told him I wanted to think about it, not rush into anything."

"Ah, you used me as a decoy." Clea clutches her chest. "That makes me feel special."

Ignoring Clea, I say, "And you didn't bother to tell me because you didn't want to hurt my feelings?"

"Because you were sad, Tessa."

"Because I couldn't be with Myles," I shout, startling Clea's mom on the couch. "I was staying here because of you three." I motion to all of them. "Because I thought I was needed. Because I thought we were strengthening our bonds. Because of that contract, because I'm a freaking idiot. But it's too late—we already broke up."

"Really?" Clea asks, looking sad. "But . . . you two were so cute together."

"No, you can't break up with the Bulge. You guys were destined for each other," Lois says.

"How the hell do you think it was going to work between us if one of the stupid rules is we have to live within ten miles of each other? Greece is really far away."

"I don't know," Clea says. "Maybe he was going to move here."

"It doesn't matter," Roxane chimes in. "Because that's no longer a rule. None of the rules exist anymore. The only rule that matters is this . . ." She writes a number one on the paper and circles it before writing and talking out loud. "From here on out, Clea, Lois, Roxane, and Tessa will no longer be tied down by the ancient rules that threatened friendship, but rather rely on the strong bond they now possess. The only rule that matters is that no matter what, we will all make an effort to speak to each other no less than once a week." She glances up at us as silence falls across the table.

Is this really happening?

Clea reaches out, takes the pen and paper, and adds, "Communication can be done through phone calls, texts, FaceTime, in person, and any form of telecommunication."

Lois reaches across the table and snags the pen and paper as well. "But no matter what or where they are in the world, they will always get together for each other's birthdays." She dots the pad and then she pushes it toward me.

I look between everyone. "What do you want me to do?"

"Sign it," Roxane says.

"But . . . this can't be real."

"Oh, one more thing." Clea takes the pen and paper from me. "And from here on out, we all agree that the perfume belongs to Clea and Clea alone." When she looks up, she flashes a mischievous smile. "Beast really, really loves it." Then she signs it and passes it around the table as her mom watches closely from the side with her notary bag in her lap.

Roxane signs.

Lois signs.

And when the notebook is placed in front of me, Roxane says, "Go ahead, Tessa."

"But . . . what about the dating rule and . . . and the distance thing?"

"Nonexistent." Roxane waves her hand. But I'm still stunned. I still don't know what to do, so Roxane reaches across the table and takes my hand. "Tessa, there is nothing holding you back, and there is nothing that should hold you back, from your happiness. Myles clearly makes you happy, and it's about time you put yourself first for a change."

"But . . . we broke up."

"Nothing like a good makeup to get the waterworks flowing, am I right, ladies?" Roxane asks, seeming so light and free, and I realize . . . maybe I've been so caught up in my emotions, in convincing myself that I'm the victim, that I haven't noticed the change in her. Has she really been so happy that my own unhappiness has been blocking her from telling me the truth?

"What about you guys?" I say to Clea and Lois. "Are you upset?"

Lois shakes her head. "I honestly think Roxane is right. We've been holding on to something that isn't necessary. It's not the contract that holds us together . . . it's us."

"And now that we are aware of what can happen if we don't pay attention to our friendships, we won't let it happen again," Clea says. "Also, I hate seeing you this upset, Tessa. I think we all saw you blossom when we were in Greece. You belong there. You're happy there. You're happy with him. Stop wasting your time in New York when you can start a new life in Greece."

"And be with the man you love." Roxane smiles at me and nudges the notepad. "Go ahead, sign."

Still unsure because it feels so sudden, so out of the blue, I pause, trying to truly read their eyes. And I'm seeing nothing but genuine support, camaraderie, and agreement.

They're serious. This is really happening.

Roxane doesn't need me.

They don't need me.

The only person who needs me is . . . well, me. And for the first time in forever, I'm going to put myself first.

I'm still skeptical, but love for these three women swells within me as I sign the document. A moment later, Clea's mom is at my side, stamping and notarizing.

"Well, ladies," Roxane says, a smirk on her face, "it looks like we need to buy a plane ticket."

☀

MYLES

"Baba, I'm not trying to be insulting, but that tile is outdated."

"It's the same tile that's in my bathroom."

I wince. "Yes, and that tile is outdated."

His brow pinches together as he studies the other options. We've been sitting out by the pool with booklet upon booklet of tile samples, trying to find the right one for the boutique hotel. With renovations underway, we're attempting to design the entire place together, equally, but I'm finding that to be a challenge. Baba has—*ahem*—vintage sensibilities, but I'm trying to find a more modern feel.

He scratches the top of his head. "Let me see that inspiration picture of yours again."

Christ.

I flip open to the page in my inspiration notebook and show him the white Montauk Gin ceramic subway tiles.

403

"I'm going to go grab us another drink while you look at those," I say as I stand, needing a second to breathe.

We've been pretty consistent on picking the same thing—for the most part—but tiles will be the death of me. I feel it. Baba wants an old-school, hand-painted tile that has pops of yellow in it, while I want to keep things very neutral, bright, and white. I spent thirty minutes trying to explain to Baba that the tourist appeal of Santorini comes from the whitewashed buildings and blue-domed roofs against the beautiful Aegean Sea.

He didn't understand why that should prevent us from having pops of yellow.

We went around and around, and now I just need a second.

I move past our shared table and head toward the restaurant. Luckily for me, I can just walk back to the kitchen, grab a drink, and then bring it out to the table. I fill up two glasses with our freshly brewed iced tea, add a lemon in each, and then head back out to the table, where I stop midway, heart pounding.

Glasses in hand, condensation collecting around my fingers, my eyes zero in on the woman speaking to my baba. From a distance, she looks a lot like Tessa, but I know that can't be . . . right?

Baba gestures.

The woman adjusts her straw hat.

And then she glances in my direction, and my breath is knocked from my lungs. I feel like I'm falling through empty space, with nothing to grab onto.

It's Tessa.

It's actually her, standing beside my baba in a long black strapless dress and a straw hat. What is she doing here? Did he call her?

I don't have much time to think about it because she heads in my direction. Unsure of what to do with the drinks in my hands, I turn to the table right next to me, set them down in front of two unsuspecting people, and face Tessa just as she reaches me.

"Tessa . . . hi," I say awkwardly.

"Hey." She twists her hands in front of her. "Do you think we could talk? In our nook?"

"Uh, yeah," I answer, and without another word, I follow her to the little nook, grateful it's unoccupied. She takes a seat on a couch, and unsure of what to do, how to act, or why she's here, I take a seat beside her.

"I won't keep you too long," she says. "I know you're picking out tiles with your baba. But I, uh, I just thought I'd tell you that I booked a room here."

"At Anissa's?" I ask, not sure I'm hearing her right.

"Yes. Luckily there was a cancellation. It's just me. No one else. And I'll be staying for a bit."

My breath catches in my throat, making my words come out tight. "How long is a bit?"

"A while." She tucks a strand of hair behind her ear. "Your baba gave me a discount, so I was thinking a couple of months. He was able to pull together some rooms. I might have to rotate around, but he can make it work."

"Months?" I ask, my brows shooting up to the sky while hope builds in my chest.

"Yeah, you see, I kind of fell for this guy while I was here on vacation with my demanding, annoying, but also loving sister. I didn't realize how happy he made me until I couldn't be with him anymore. And instead of telling him about these silly rules and promises I made to my friends or how I assumed I had to protect my sister, I made him feel like he didn't matter, that he wasn't worth fighting for." She scoots closer and takes my hand in hers. "But he is. He's so worth it because he makes me feel so much joy with just one smile. He makes me feel protected, wanted, needed. He makes the colors around me feel brighter when he's near. He makes me laugh when I'm sad. And throughout my entire life, when I felt like a nobody, he made me feel like I was a somebody." Her thumb rubs over my knuckle. "I found you . . . and you found me, in spite of the obstacles in our way and the long-awaited time we've spent to actually be together. You're . . . you're my Odysseus, and I'm your Penelope." My smile grows wider. "I love you, Myles. Very much. And it was awful of me to let you walk out that door in New York. I never should have let you get away, and if you let me, I will spend the rest of my life proving to you how much you mean to me."

I swallow hard while my heart pounds so rapidly that I feel like I can't breathe.

"You love me?" I ask.

She nods. "Very much, and I'm sorry if I made you feel any different. You are my man, the one I want, the one I need."

I smirk because I know, in this moment, when I thought things were at an end for me and Tessa, it was only the beginning. She not only loves me but moved here to be with me. In a matter of seconds, I went from going through the motions of picking out tiles to learning that my girl is here for me.

Cupping her cheeks, I pull her in close and press my forehead to hers. "I love you too," I whisper. "Please tell me you're serious about staying here."

"Dead serious. I'm all yours, Myles. You won't have to wait until next summer to see me."

"Jesus fuck, I hope not," I say right before I capture her lips with mine.

Her mouth parts, our tongues collide, and everything feels right.

Everything feels in place.

Like the stars are aligned again because my girl, the girl who's been in my life since I was six, is back in my arms, ready to give this a try. I don't think I could ask for anything more perfect than having her here, in Greece, with love in her heart and her soul tangling with mine.

EPILOGUE
MYLES

"You may kiss the bride."

Fuck yes.

I pull Tessa close and press my lips to hers while our families and friends cheer around us.

Four months. That's all it took. Four months, and we were engaged and planning a wedding for the summer. I'll be honest: after a week of having her back in Greece, I knew she was it, that I was going to propose. I got the ring after a week because I was dead set on marrying her—nothing was going to stop me.

I told my baba about the ring a week later, and he told me to give her time to adjust. It was one thing to vacation in Santorini; it was a whole other thing to live here, especially coming from New York. And he was right—Tessa had some adjusting to do—but I was there every step of the way.

When I pull away, I gently press a kiss to the tip of her nose and smile. Fuck, is she beautiful. In a white Grecian one-shoulder wedding dress, she walked down the aisle just now looking like a goddess, wearing a flower crown and holding a matching bouquet.

Lois, Roxane, and Clea stand to the side, all wearing similar dresses in a pale blue. Myself, Toby, and Philip—yes, I've grown to know the guy, and he's really fucking cool—are all wearing khaki linen pants, white button-ups, and boat shoes. Tessa wanted us to be casual and comfortable.

When choosing a wedding venue, the initial thought was to have it at Anissa's, but after talking it through, we decided to break in the boutique hotel because it holds so much meaning. If it weren't for Tessa and her encouragement, I don't think I'd have ever pursued expanding into a new location.

And with Tessa's help—she's put her financial consulting on hold for now to work full time with Baba and me—we were able to not only make the boutique hotel happen but also save money during renovations. She also was a good tiebreaker when it came to decision-making. Guess whose side she almost always took?

"I would like to introduce you to Mr. and Mrs. Cirillo."

Our family and friends all stand, still cheering, while I take Tessa's hand in mine and walk her down the aisle. I smile at my mom, who is now married. I smile at Rita, Baba's girlfriend, who has really brought him out of his funk. Tessa and I have been on a few double dates with them, and Rita is just what the love doctor ordered for Baba. She's fun, pushes Baba out of his comfort zone, and, most importantly, cares about him deeply.

When we reach the end of the aisle and turn toward the bridal suite, which is to the right of the olive tree, the central point in the boutique hotel, I dip down and scoop her up into my arms.

"What are you doing?" she asks with a laugh.

"Giving us some alone time—the photos and reception can wait."

And it's much-needed alone time. Our families came in a week ago, and we haven't had peace since. Roxane and Philip are still dating, but from what I've been told, Philip is planning on proposing at the end of the trip. They've spent a lot of time in Greece the last couple of months, really exploring all the islands and—according to Roxane—exploring each other. Even though we've had a rocky start, Roxane has grown into a friend, the kind of sister-in-law I'll always cherish. She loves Tessa more than words, and she's finally finding better ways of expressing it.

Lois and Ed brought their kids this time, which of course eased Lois's worries and stressed her out at the same time. She doesn't want them talking to her while she's at the pool, but she also wants to hear about every little thing they're thinking. I'd say she's the pure definition of motherhood. And Ed, he's actually a really nice guy.

Then there's Clea and the Beast—also known as Sylvia. Unable to call her by her nickname, I went with her real name, and it's starting to catch on. They're living their best life—as they say—child-free, debt-free, and work-free. They have jobs—Clea is still doing her podcast, and Sylvia is a personal trainer—but they don't consider it work because they love it so much. They've spent most of the past week in their hotel room.

I push through the bridal suite door and set Tessa on her feet before looping my arm around her.

She beams up at me. "I can't believe we're married."

"I can't believe it took this long." I smirk. "With how much our lives have mingled, you'd have thought we would have been married a half a decade ago."

"I wouldn't have been ready for you—I was too shy back then."

"Nah, I think you were perfect then, just like you're perfect now." I pull her in closer, looking for those lips.

"Knock, knock," Roxane says from the doorway.

I should have shut it.

"What's up?" I ask.

Clea and Lois appear as well. "We just wanted to tell you something," Roxane says, a mischievous grin lighting up her face.

"What?" Tessa asks, brow furrowed.

"The perfume, it worked."

What are they talking about?

"Huh?" Tessa asks. *Right there with you, babe.*

409

"You know the night we sprayed it on you to entice Toby?" Lois says.

"Yes," Tessa draws out.

"Well, do you remember who you saw when you turned around? Who made eye contact with you?" Clea asks.

"Uh . . . no," Tessa answers.

"It wasn't Toby," Roxane says. "It was *Myles*. He was carrying glasses, and you two both exchanged a look. The perfume never even touched Toby. It was always Myles. Just like Philip was always mine."

"And Ed was mine," Lois adds.

"And Sylvia is mine," Clea says.

"See?" Roxane shrugs. "It worked all along." With a smile, she puts her arms around Clea and Lois, and together, they all walk out of the suite, shutting the door behind them.

"What the hell was that about?" I ask, more confused than ever.

Tessa chuckles and wraps her arms around my neck. "Don't even freaking ask."

READ ON FOR AN EXCERPT OF *ROYALLY NOT READY*, BY MEGHAN QUINN

Prologue
KELLER

"Come in."

I adjust my tie and then push through the ornate, wood-carved door to the king's bedroom. The curtains are drawn despite the time. Just the smallest of cracks in the velvet fabric let the morning rays filter through, lighting up the room so I can see King Theodore resting in his four-poster bed, covered in heavy burgundy fabric.

His attending doctor, Armann, buckles up his bag, adjusts the spectacles on his nose, and then heads toward the door.

"See you tomorrow," King Theodore calls out.

"Yes, tomorrow." Armann glances in my direction, offering an annoyed glare, before he heads out of the bedroom, leaving me alone with the last-remaining royal.

"Keller, my boy—" He turns his mouth into his crooked elbow and heaves a horrendous cough that has plagued him for the last few weeks. After two bouts of pneumonia, Dr. Armann has now placed him on bed rest in order to get him back to his fully functioning self. "Excuse me." He takes a deep breath, but it falls short from the lack of lung capacity. "Thank you for meeting with me."

As the private secretary to the king, I'm his right-hand man, his most trusted advisor. Unfortunately for me, it's been an uphill battle with this job. My predecessor had forty-five years on me before he passed away, and when I was hired, few believed a thirty-two-year-old belonged in this position. The only person who'd trusted me was King Theodore, or Theo, as I call him only when we're alone.

By the side of his bed, there's a burgundy wingback chair that I take a seat in. Pen and notebook in hand, I cross one leg over the other and say, "It sounded urgent when you called me."

"Yes, well, this is an urgent matter," he says right before coughing again. His light blue eyes squeeze shut, and the sparse pieces of hair on the top of his head hitch with every violent hack. He rests his head on his pillow and presses his large, meaty hand to his chest. "I need you to find her."

Confused, I shift in my seat and ask, "Find who?"

He's silent, catching his breath before he opens his eyes and says, "The only heir left."

This is where things get tricky.

Let me give you a quick rundown.

Theo is an only child and the sovereign of our country. He married Katla and had four children.

They more than covered the old verbiage, "we need an heir and a spare." They doubled down.

Pala was born first. The picture-perfect princess who always wore lavender, delighted the people with her flower crowns, and was well-known to try to sneak her cat, Norbit, into every state dinner. When she was at university, she met Prince Clinton of Marsedale, fell madly in love, and married him. But, because Clinton would one day become king of Marsedale, that trumped Pala's throne, and she abdicated to live with him. It's a sore subject.

Second born is Rolant, the troublemaker. Always pressing his luck, never following the rules, and single-handedly created the Fire Task Force—also known as *Rolant fucked up, and now we need to put out the fire.* His demise was inevitable. One drunk night led to him rolling around on one-thousand-year-old sacred moss, and the next day, he was exiled from the country.

Third born, the most promising of the four, despite being the third in line for the throne, is Sveinn. The listener, the do-gooder, the humanitarian. Known as the earth lover, Sveinn was good at everything. He married Kristin. After five years of marriage and no offspring, they were brought into the king's quarters where Kristin admitted to having an affair with her lady's maid. A brilliant lesbian love affair. They ran off together. Sveinn, on the other hand, found the nearest boat, set sail, and is still yet to be found—despite the king's men's best seafaring efforts—six months later.

So that brings us to Margret, the youngest. Fascinated with travel, she was bound and determined to flee from the chilling temperatures of her homeland and explore the humid climate of Miami, where she met the love of her life, Cameron Campbell, a larger-than-life food tour guide. And together, they had one child.

"You want me to find your American granddaughter?" I ask.

Theo slowly nods his head. "You must. Without her, we jeopardize losing our country."

"What do you mean?" I ask, now leaning forward.

"As you are aware, we are a constituent of Arkham, and according to our bylaws, if there is no heir to the throne, then the monarchy dies with me."

Which would be detrimental to the country.

"And with the battles we've fought over the years with Arkham, there is no doubt they will not only destroy our culture, but they'll take over our people." A cough bubbles up and he sputters a few moments before regaining himself. "I can't have that." With his tired eyes fixated on me, he says, "If it were my choice, you, my son, would take my place, but it must be blood."

"I know," I say, my throat choking up.

I failed to mention the fifth child because the fifth doesn't matter. The fifth grew up in the palace just like the other four, but lost his servant parents at twelve, was orphaned, and then one fateful Christmas Eve was taken in by the king and queen.

He has no right to the crown.

Instead, he . . . or I . . . have dedicated myself to protecting what is mine. This palace, and this man resting on the bed in front of me, practically lifeless with a gray complexion, are mine to protect.

"I need you to find her, Keller, and I need you—" He coughs again. I wait patiently for him to finish before picking up a glass of water from his night table and offering it to him. He nods as a *thank you* and takes a sip. "I need you to train her."

My concerned brow pinches together. "Train her?"

He nods slowly before resting his head on the pillow. "Yes, she will not know of our country, our traditions, or our culture. If she is to take the crown, she must be prepared. The country will not take kindly to an outsider." His tired eyes flash to mine. "And if anyone can prepare the next sovereign, it's you."

Want more? ROYALLY NOT READY is now available, pick it up in Kindle Unlimited.

About the Author

Photo © 2019 Milana Schaffer

USA Today bestselling author of romantic comedies and contemporary romance, wife, adoptive mother, and peanut butter lover, Meghan Quinn brings readers the perfect combination of heart, humor, and heat in every book.

TEXT "READ" to 474747 to never miss another one of Meghan Quinn's releases. Message and data rates may apply.